Sign up for our newsletter to hear
about new and upcoming releases.

www.ylva-publishing.com

Other books by Lee Winter

Shattered
Requiem for Immortals
The Red Files

the brutal truth

Be careful what you wish for

lee winter

Dedication

To Charlotte, the most enthusiastic ice queen fan I've ever met. Long may our aloof goddesses reign.

Acknowledgements

My book could not sing without my wonderful betas adding their voices to the choir. Thanks to Char, for her all-round ice queen expertise, Anne for lashing my terrible French into submission, and Sam, for raising the bar and always telling me what I needed to hear. At Ylva, I have much gratitude to Sandra for the superb editing and Astrid for her reassuring belief in this book and in me.

CHAPTER 1

The Apocalypse

The apocalypse arrived when Maddie Grey had shampoo in her eyes, was half awake, and attempting to block out the whine of prehistoric plumbing from her ears.

"Mads! It's the Armageddon!" Her flatmate, Simon Itani, thumped on the bathroom door, scaring the life out of her.

"What the hell?" Maddie shouted back. Her childhood friend had his good points, but he couldn't exactly be considered trustworthy when it came to reporting end times.

"Your boss is texting you. Looks official. So I'm making the leap."

Her boss never texted her. Maybe Simon was on to something. Maddie shut off the shower, quickly dried off, and pulled on battered shorts and a T-shirt. As she towel-dried her hair, she stared blearily in the mirror at the rings under her eyes. No sleep again. Not surprising. She was having more nightmares about getting lost and trying to find her way home. Her subconscious wasn't exactly subtle. It was usually that nightmare or awkward sex dreams about the ex-girlfriend she hadn't seen in three years. She'd always wake up anxious, aroused, and annoyed. Craving Rachel only because her ex was back home in Sydney was kind of pathetic.

The door thumped again, louder this time. "Are you decent?"

Maddie glanced at herself one last time and pulled a face. "Hard to say."

The door flung open, resulting in way too much daylight.

Ugh. "You better be on fire." Maddie glared at Simon. No singed hair.

"Even more exciting." He ran his fingers through the trimmed two-day growth on his jaw.

"Wait, more exciting than a fire?" She reached for her tracksuit pants, rammed one leg in, and pulled them over her shorts. Sounded like a crisis worthy of properly getting dressed.

"Yep!" Simon tossed Maddie her phone. "It's big. Which you'd know if you hadn't slept the morning away. It's eleven, and it sounds like your boss can't wait."

Maddie snatched up her phone. "Give me a break," she grumbled. "I work night shift. I do need to sleep sometime." She read the text message, her stomach twisting with anxiety. "They're calling everyone in for a noon meeting. I guess the rumours were true. That company that bought us out last year? The owner's finally noticed us and is probably coming in to gut us today."

Simon nodded, a sage expression on his face.

She narrowed her eyes. "You sneak. You read his message?"

Simon lifted his hands in innocence. "Only cos your boss's name flashed up. I wanted to see if it was important enough to rouse you from The Showering Dead." He scratched his slightly rounded stomach. "So, she's really on her way? *The* Elena Bartell? She who monsters itty-bitty papers to feed to her empire? And looks shit hot while doing it?"

"Looks like." Maddie gave the message a final, morose glare. "Trust you to care more about her looks than her tactics."

"Au contraire, Mads, I can care about both. That woman's a bloody media genius. They did a case study on her at business school. Let me tell you how she racked up her first hundred mill—"

"Can't wait for that story. Meanwhile, I'm not sure if I'll even have a job by tonight. And with you moving back to Sydney soon, this is a total disaster. How am I going to afford rent on this shoe box on my own with no job?"

"Could be worse. You could actually *like* that shitty job you're about to lose. I've seen you steel yourself to go into work. But now..." He gave her a grin.

Maddie huffed out a breath. "First, you could *try* to sound sorry for me. Second, I'm not going back to waitressing."

"Hours would be better. And you might actually talk to people again. That has to be a bonus."

"Okay, working for *Hudson Metro News* might not be perfect, but it's a reporting job—finally. It's what I'm good at. When I waitress, people get hurt." Maddie's mind drifted back to several regrettable incidents. At least the chef's hair had grown back. Well, except his eyebrows.

"Come on, Mads, didn't you come to New York to live the dream? Not tolerate the dream?"

A muscle in her jaw twitched. She hated it when people talked about the Dream. New York had never been her dream, although admitting that was social suicide. The truth was that every day she woke with a sinking feeling. The brightness, the buzz, and the constant rush left her feeling like a dead pixel on a Times Square billboard. Her friends back home wanted to live vicariously through her, so what could she say? *It's great. So great. Yeah. Just. Wow.* Each day she cringed a little more at not living up to everyone else's dream. Why didn't she fit into a city that *everyone* fit into?

Simon was still talking. "You've been stuck doing the crapola shift, spending all your days sleeping and barely seeing the sights. So my point is, hoo-fucking-ray! You'll be fired from a job you hate. We'll celebrate tonight with the Fun Factory. Okay?" He paused and raked his gaze over her clothes. "And don't change a thing. That outfit totally says 'fire my ass'."

Maddie glanced down at herself. He had a point. She must be more tired than she thought. That drug bust she'd been working on overnight had taken it out of her. "I'm not even working today." She yawned. "I don't have to get glammed up if it's my day off. It's the Aussie way."

"Famous last words. Seriously, you want my advice?"

"Hell no. You can't dress to save yourself, and my day's disastrous enough as it is. So rack off and let me get my ass into gear."

His laughter drifted through the door, as she toed it shut behind him. But Simon raised a good point: What *did* one wear to their apocalypse?

Maddie hauled herself into work with dark glasses affixed to stave off the beginnings of a tiredness headache and an all-black ensemble more befitting a gothic rock group than professional attire.

On the L train commute, she studied the Elena Bartell bio page she'd downloaded before she'd hit the subway. The chief operating officer and publisher for dozens of newspaper and magazine mastheads had sculpted, short, jet-black hair, pale features, and form-fitting designer clothes. There was a sleekness to her, like a lean, sci-fi action hero, and a dangerous look to her cool eyes.

She was listed as forty, although she could pass as years younger. The woman was notoriously media shy—ironic, given her profession and how much the camera loved her. Bartell had risen as a fashion writer on *CQ* magazine and, at one point, was being tipped as its future editor. Instead, Bartell had disappeared.

A year later, she'd turned up as the new owner of a small group of failing regional papers. Within a year, she'd turned them into profit; within two, she'd made her first million. She'd scored her first $500 million by age thirty-five.

There was only one publication the media mogul had created from nothing herself—*Style International*, a fashion magazine which had five editions worldwide—*Style NY, Sydney, Tokyo, London* and *Paris*. That personal investment told Maddie that fashion mattered to Bartell, and her job at *CQ* hadn't just been a stepping stone. She'd been passionate about it—at least at one point.

Maddie looked down and considered her outfit. She winced. Her bold choice born of exhaustion and a faintly rebellious streak was not looking so smart right now.

She scrolled down her phone and found a brief mention of a husband in 1999, a reporter turned author who was gone by 2001. There was a second husband now. Richard Barclay. Lawyer. She glanced at his photo and suppressed a shudder. He might be toothpaste-commercial handsome, but he had a smug-bastard face.

So, two sharks had fallen for their own kind? That figured. From everything she'd read, Bartell seemed to love nothing better than to strip a business to its rafters, if she could squeeze some money out of it. They'd even given her a nickname to go with her corporate cleansing. Tiger Shark. Maddie put away her phone and stared out the window at the underground blackness. Was the *Hudson Metro News* about to be another victim of the media mogul's rapier-sharp teeth?

As Union St station neared, she considered the prospect of being fired. Simon was right, although she'd never admit it. Eight months of working there, and she hated her job. Except for one thing—she was finally doing what she had told all her friends and family she would do. Be a reporter in New York.

The train pulled up. Maddie stepped onto the subway platform, nose wrinkling at the familiar stench of urine and rotting garbage. Time to face the apocalypse.

For a harbinger of doom, Elena Bartell was beautifully turned out in steampunk chic. A wide silver buckle adorned ebony ankle boots, standing out beneath black, tailored pants. They were a dark contrast against her crisp, white linen shirt, set behind a silky, black-and-silver embroidered vest with a fob-watch-style chain running from a button into its pocket. Maddie was transfixed. How unexpected.

Bartell's compact body radiated power and control and drew every eye to her. Even standing with the paper's editor, general manager, and news chief, three men who each had six inches on her, she was easily the most authoritative person in the room.

Scanning the gathering, Bartell's eyes were clear-blue and sharp. She smiled faintly through the introduction droning on in the background.

"...a delight to meet our new owner, Elena Bartell." Maddie's editor, a bespectacled, harried-looking man whom she had never had cause to meet—so lowly was her status—stepped back, clapping.

Bartell stood in front of the eighty *Hudson Metro News* staff members and waited for the polite applause to die. She held the ensuing silence until the only sounds were someone's phone in the distance and the clatter of a printer spitting out pages nearby. Her voice was measured and pitched low, yet it carried to the back of the room where Maddie stood, half hidden by a pillar.

"I'm sure my reputation precedes me," Bartell said, voice dry. "I'm sure you've been told all sorts of terrible tales about who I am. I know the names I've been called, some more creative than others. And I'm sure you've been told all sorts of ruthless things about what I'm going to do to your paper." She stopped and slid her gaze over the room. "And it's all true."

A panicked murmur spread through the crowd.

She eyed them coolly. "It's time *Hudson Metro News* grew a pair or got out of the game. The facts don't lie. You're an underperforming commuter rag with only one news breaker on your entire reporting staff and only one ad rep who meets the sales targets. Your publication's online presence is a joke. An occasional updated weather report, front pages from two days ago, and only two lines on where to buy advertising. Not to mention, with a balance sheet like yours, you deserve to be scrapped. It would be a mercy killing."

Maddie winced. Okay, so it wasn't the world's greatest paper, but it wasn't that bad, surely?

"Of course," Bartell continued, "I could inject capital, grow your online presence with a cutting-edge website, and find you a team of star marketers to boost brand awareness. But this is a saturated market, and you have no point of difference. I'd be just throwing good money after bad."

Maddie's heart began racing, and she glanced at the ashen faces around her.

"However," Bartell said, "funny things happen when backs are to the wall. Occasionally, in their death throes, people have the ability to surprise me. So the bottom line is this—you're on notice. I'm giving you six weeks to impress me."

Relieved and shocked gasps filled the room.

The media mogul held up her hand. "I will base myself here for the duration. It will give me an opportunity to assess who has talent, whether you deserve a financial investment, or whether being shut down would be a better option. If you have been holding back, then dazzle me in the coming six weeks. Be warned—my reputation for firing incompetent people on the spot is no lie. So, in six weeks' time, on March 15, I'll know whether any of you have what it takes. For your own sakes, do not disappoint me."

March 15? The Ides of March? Maddie blinked.

Bartell's gaze roamed, then paused on Maddie, sliding up and down her outfit. A frown creased her brow. "That's it. We're done." She exited the room without another word.

The general manager adjusted his crimson silk tie, mumbled something vague and conciliatory about impressing their new boss, and the meeting broke up.

Maddie stared at Bartell's departing figure. *We're done?* What kind of interpersonal skills were those?

"Holy shit," Terry, the court reporter beside her, said to no one in particular. "I need to call my wife. That shark's gonna gut us. I could see it in her beady eyes." He flicked a glance at Maddie's outfit. "She sure didn't like what you're wearing, huh? Didn't you get the memo she was coming in?"

"It's my day off," Maddie protested. "It's not like I'm wearing a coat of freshly killed baby seals."

Terry gave a sour laugh. "She'd probably want one if you did."

"Yeah." Maddie sighed. She was going to be out of work within six weeks for sure. One thing she knew about newspapers was that no one ever noticed the person on the graveyard shift. They weren't seen or heard, and their jobs were never saved. With that depressing thought, she sidestepped the milling groups picking over Bartell's speech and headed for the elevator. She had a bed to crawl back into.

When she reached the hallway, the elevator doors were closing, so she called out for the shadow she glimpsed inside to hold them. The doors kept closing. Maddie sprinted and threw her arm into the gap. The doors paused, then slowly reopened. She skidded inside, finding herself face to face with Elena Bartell, who looked irritated at having an interloper. So—travelling with minions was obviously against Bartell's religion.

Maddie could smell her perfume, a soft, faintly spicy caress that made her want to sway forward for more. She stabbed the already lit up *Ground* button in annoyance at that random thought and leaned into the side wall as far away from Bartell as she could manage. She swung her gaze upward to the numbers ticking down.

"Bold choice," Bartell abruptly said, shattering any hopes for escaping this elevator ride unscathed. "Does your garage band have practice now?"

"It's my day off." Maddie was startled to have been addressed. "I didn't expect to be called in for your special Ides of March speech. The day Caesar got knifed? Interesting choice of dates."

"A millennial who knows history? Well, well."

Maddie shrugged.

"I suppose stranger things have happened." Bartell examined Maddie's clothing as though it offended her on a cellular level. "So you...voluntarily...wear this?"

Maddie frowned at the glint in those cool eyes. "Yeah," she said in her most neutral tone. "I do. It's comfy."

"Even knowing I'd be here today to evaluate you all."

"Are you planning on firing me based on my outfit?" Maddie asked politely, turning to look at her properly.

"What if I did?" Bartell's eyes were challenging. "One's wardrobe choices speak to their professionalism and whether they wish to be taken seriously. As opposed to the appearance of having crawled out of a nightclub at 4:00 a.m. for example."

"That's..." Maddie shook her head in disbelief. "So..."

"Go on." Bartell's expression dared her.

"If you fire people because of what they wear, you could lose someone brilliant. What if someone had this incredible talent but couldn't dress to save themselves? How's that good business?"

Bartell gave her a sharp look. "And is *that* what you are? An incredible talent? Dressed up in a gothic sack, just waiting for me to bother unravelling?"

Maddie's mouth fell open. She clanged it firmly shut. "I didn't say that," she mumbled.

"What do you do here?"

"The graveyard shift. I write briefs on the news events happening in the middle of the night. Sometimes they get followed up by the day shift and expanded on. Sometimes not." *Shit. I'm rambling.* Maddie hastily jumped to the point. "Crime. I write crime. Mostly. And, um, obits."

The edges of Bartell's mouth twitched at that, which spiked Maddie's irritation.

"And you're not from New York. Not with that accent."

"Sydney."

"Living the dream, then? Country mouse here to dazzle us city folk with your incredible talent and woeful dress sense?"

"Hey, Sydney is no country backwater. I came here for a change of scene. And I'm making the most of things." She aimed for nonchalance, but winced internally at how stiff it came out, like privileged apathy.

Bartell gave her an assessing look. "You sound like you'd rather be back home. Perhaps I should do you a favour and fire you now." Her voice dropped to a soft, loaded tone. "You can scuttle back to Sydney in relief it's all over."

"No! I can't!"

"No? Well then, Graveyard-Shift Girl, *are* you a good journalist?"

"I…" The elevator began slowing. Maddie scrabbled for an answer. Her university professors all said she had talent. On the other hand, she had nothing spectacular to point to that she'd done in the past eight months at the *Hudson Metro News*. Nothing beyond short police briefs and occasionally touching obituaries that probably no one read.

"If you can't answer a simple question," Bartell said, giving her a look so direct that it felt like an X-ray, "then perhaps your secret little fears are right: you *don't* belong here. We're done."

Maddie stared at her as the doors dinged and opened. Was "drowning in New York" written all over her face?

"Oh, and improve your wardrobe. I don't want to be looking at a deconstructed beat poet for the next six weeks."

Bartell swept out of the elevator, leaving Maddie to grind her teeth. "Well, we can't all afford yesterday's steampunk, can we?" she said under her breath. She pushed off from the back wall and took two steps out of the elevator before freezing.

Bartell was standing just around the corner, staring back at her, hand inside her bag.

She'd heard?

Bartell's expression was hard, as she plucked out her phone. She spun on her heel and pulled her shoulders back, with an insanely expensive-looking, Hermes-stamped handbag wrenched tight on her shoulder. She stalked through the foyer, pressing a button on her phone, and began barking instructions.

A blonde woman, all clopping heels and bony elbows, rushed forward to meet Bartell outside the building's giant glass doors and pointed her to a chauffeured black BMW.

Way to go, Maddie thought. *In a single elevator ride, you actually guaranteed you'd never get a job at another Bartell Corp masthead. Anywhere. Worldwide.*

And that was a *lot* of newspapers.

She definitely should have stayed in bed.

That night, Maddie experienced Simon's idea of a Fun Factory. It involved alcohol and lots of it. Specifically, bottles of strange colours, which her housemate mixed and matched and turned into exotic-looking homemade cocktails.

After drinking Simon's third concoction—dubbed Car Seat Cover— Maddie confessed what had happened in the elevator.

Instead of being sympathetic, he laughed his head off. "Wha-did-I-tell-ya!" he said with a snort. "Stick a fork in yourself, you're done. You're cactus! I mean you did look like a death worshipper." He slugged back something obnoxiously green.

"No, it's she just has stupidly high fashion standards. I mean, I looked a tiny bit goth but not *bad* bad. I...it's streetwear. I looked normal!"

"You looked like a death-cult member. But that's okay, Mads. Look, let's recap your day—Elena Bartell, world-famous media mogul, told you off for looking unprofessional, and then you sounded your usual underwhelmed self about your job, New York, and life in general. After that, you couldn't tell her you were a good journalist when she asked, and finally...for the perfect cherry on top...you insulted her by telling her she was decked out in yesterday's fashion."

"Yesterday's steampunk can look hot. Not my fault she took it the wrong way. It was kinda H.G. Wells if you want to know. Like, from that show, *Warehouse 13*?" Maddie slurped her drink.

He lifted his hands. "Her again—you and your posh British actresses."

"Except Bartell isn't posh, just cold."

"So cold that instead of firing you on the spot, she just jumped in her car and drove away?"

"Uh. Yeah."

"So stop fretting then. If she was as thin-skinned as you think, you'd already have your marching orders."

"There's still time. I'll probably find them on my desk when I clock on tomorrow evening." She peered at him and stuck out her glass for a refill. "The yellow thing this time."

As Simon obliged with her cocktail, he asked, "Don't you think a global media mogul has more things to worry about than the midnight-shift girl on a second-rate paper she's thinking of gutting?"

"I guess." She drained her drink in one hit.

"You guess? I bet Madame Slash-and-Burn has forgotten all about you by now."

"Good point." Maddie brightened. "Actually, great point! I'm, like, an amoeba in the scheme of Elena Bartell's world. Right?" She felt a burst of hope and thrust her glass out again. "Some green with the yellow this time. The blue one makes my tongue look like some weird Outback lizard."

"You may even be lower than an amoeba," Simon agreed amiably as he poured. "Single-celled organisms probably get more thought than you. Fear not. Cheers."

"Cheers." She clinked her glass against his. "Wait, aren't amoebas single-celled organisms already?"

"You're asking the business studies major?" Simon squinted at her before slugging back his drink.

She laughed and, for the first time in hours, felt kind of positive.

BlogSpot: Aliens of New York

By Maddie as Hell

Today there was an old woman sitting on a garbage can outside my Williamsburg apartment building, next to the auto repair shop. She sang softly to her bags of junk, a chaotic pile of blankets, clothes, newspapers, and food wrappings. Off-key and missing some teeth, she swayed gently to the rhythm. A scraggly white dandelion dancing in the wind, hairless in a few places but undaunted nonetheless. The upturned hat in front of her gleamed inside with a few coins. As I passed her, I realised one of the bags was actually a small child. The girl, maybe aged ten or so, had old, old eyes. She didn't smile at me or the woman beside her. She stared into the distance.

I swayed along with the song for a few moments, before dropping a few notes into the hat. That earned a wide, toothless grin.

Look after her, I thought.

As I walked away, I wasn't sure which of them I'd meant.

CHAPTER 2

Tales from the Dark Side

Elena Bartell's lips curled as she listened on her phone to the witless prattling of her allegedly top editor-in-chief of her Australian fashion magazine. It might be just after four in the morning in Sydney, but she had questions that needed answers. She was being whisked away in her car from the commuter rag to which she'd given a stay of execution. Although if that disastrously dressed reporter in the elevator was the standard of staff they employed, Elena probably shouldn't have bothered.

Her gaze slid out the window, as she reviewed the odd meeting. The reporter had an expressive face beneath her pixie-cut titian hair. Elena had recognised the intelligence behind her intense, green eyes. They were also the only eyes that had lit with recognition at her choice of date on which she would announce the fate of the paper.

Still, it seemed the woman's appreciation of history might be her only redeeming feature. In fact, Graveyard-Shift Girl was lucky to still be in her employ, but Elena had been too astonished at being insulted to do anything more than walk away. Not that it mattered. The insolent Australian would be unlikely to survive the axe any more than her underperforming colleagues would.

Speaking of cursed Australians... Elena pursed her lips and moved the phone away from her ear a little. Jana Macy was still jabbering away, trying to cover her ass.

"Enough!" she spat down her phone. "Your excuses are inane. There is no sound reason *Style Sydney*'s circulation should be in a death spiral. Turn the circulation figures around and quickly. Try to remember you're supposed to be part of the world's premier fashion magazine imprint. Run some actual in-depth fashion stories. I wouldn't paper the staff bathroom with the features you've been commissioning. And make some hard budgetary decisions, or I'll come down there and make them for you, starting with your contract. We're done." She ended the call with a vicious punch of her thumbnail.

"Felicity," she said, not glancing at her chief of staff, who was on the other side of the spacious rear seat. "I believe I told you I wanted a new PA by the time I reached the *Hudson Metro News*. And yet all I see in this vehicle is you. Was I not clear enough? Did you feel keeping me fully staffed was somehow optional?"

"No, Elena. It's just, she got lost." Felicity began tapping on her phone. "Or something. I told her when," her voice rose to a desperate height, "I told her where. I told her not to be late. And she keeps texting me with updates on her attempts to get here. And she's miles away—still."

"Fire her. Get me a new assistant who is not geographically challenged. We're a global company, so one would think grasping how a map works would be a prerequisite."

She flicked a glance at Felicity, who showed no reaction to the order. Why would she? PAs were changed like heels when they failed to meet her standards.

The record for the longest-lasting assistant was still sitting at a year, nine months, and two weeks, or so she often heard Felicity tell the new PAs. The title holder was Colleen, a sweet-faced, plump Scottish girl with an impenetrable accent, blinding red hair, and an eidetic memory. Elena had personally written the girl a reference when she'd moved on. The event was so rare that the astonished woman had cried great, gulping, alarming sobs that made Elena regret her largess instantly.

Elena scrolled through her text messages and stopped on one. Her husband wished for her presence at yet another party. The health insurance company Richard worked for had more parties than lawsuits against it. She sighed as she studied the invitation. It all became clear.

She typed out her reply.

*I'd rather see flares make another comeback. Besides, I thought
you had a convention on then? Miami? What changed?*

She already knew the answer. He was busy sucking up to the new
vice-president, a man who had yet to forge alliances, so they'd all be
sniffing around to toady up to him. Richard was singular in his hunt
for status and power. There was no way he'd miss the opportunity.
Ironic that people thought *he* was the charming, less ambitious one of
their coupling.

Elena hadn't felt the need to share that she knew the VP's wife,
Annalise, because Richard would insist she make use of the connection.
She and Richard saw power differently. For her husband, it was about
boosting his ego, getting attention, and having people admire him. For
Elena, power was finding a company on its knees that everyone said
was worthless or a lost cause, and resurrecting it. Breathing life into
a corpse? Creating a heartbeat from absolute death? *That* was power.
Her ability was in seeing the possibilities and talents buried in a forest
of media deadwood. But most people only focused on the destruction,
the dying products she pulped, not the ones she pruned to allow fresh
growth. What she did was a skill that few could understand.

Elena dropped her phone in her handbag. Her mind wandered to
the usual place it did when she recalled her underappreciated abilities
in times long past. Times best not raked over.

"I will temporarily base myself at *Hudson Metro News*," she told
Felicity. "I've informed them I'm giving them six weeks to prove
themselves. You will work from there, too."

There was no disguising the confusion on the woman's face.
"Seriously? Oh right, sorry, I mean of course you're serious. When are
you not?"

Her chief of staff gave Elena a pained look. Little was hidden on
the woman's face—and right now it bore dismay, shock, and a hint of
revulsion.

"Problem?" Elena asked in a warning tone. She did not have to
explain herself to anyone, although Felicity had been with her long
enough to raise the occasional question. But not today.

"No," Felicity said quickly. "It's nothing."

"Are you quite certain? I'd hate for you to withhold your insightful thoughts," Elena said in her softest tone. Only a fool would take her words at face value. And Felicity was no fool.

The other woman's eyes widened. "N-no. I would be honoured to work with you out of a building the size of a fish tank with an equivalent aroma," she said politely, her voice clipped.

Surprise jolted Elena. "You've been inside?"

Felicity nodded. "It smells like the Hudson it's named after. I mean just the lower floors—the advertising and finance departments. Our accounts team members were green at the gills when I had to visit them there last year. It was right around when you first bought them out. There were some due diligence papers I needed to collect."

"Maintenance costs..." Elena said under her breath. "Add it to my list of pending issues for that little rag."

"Yes, Elena." Felicity's head bobbed up and down. "May I ask...you say you've *informed them* you'll assess them for six weeks. What are you really going to be doing there?"

Elena regarded her, impressed at how nimble her chief of staff's mind could be at times.

"Why do you ask?" she said.

"On most new acquisitions you know in days or a week what their future is. Usually just from going over the books. I mean, I know you got the *Hudson* in a bundle of other commuter papers, so maybe you don't know enough about them, but still...*six weeks*?" She petered out under Elena's intense scrutiny. "It's just, um, interesting..."

"Yes, it is interesting, isn't it? Any further questions?" She injected steel into her voice, and Felicity shrank back at the tone, shaking her head.

"Good. I need you to get one of our lawyers in London to lean on my useless ex-husband and get him to grasp the importance of not mentioning my name to talk himself up in interviews." Her voice dropped to chilly. "Remind dear Spencer that the confidentiality clause he signed upon our divorce has teeth. Expensive ones. Oh, and if he takes credit for my career one more time, I *will* have him blacklisted. He'll have to get his next book reviewed by a non-Bartell Corporation publication. And how many of those are left on either side of the Atlantic these days?"

"Yes, Elena." Felicity scribbled a note. "And I'm not sure. Not many."

"Mm. Contact the Australian executive team, as well as their national accountant, lawyers, and Don McKay on the board, and tell them all to examine the spreadsheet I'm emailing them. Something's going wrong at *Style Sydney,* and the rot needs to be stopped before it gets worse. I need explanations. I want Don in the loop in case I have to do something drastic...and expensive.

"Then book my Lexus in for a service. I want to do a run to Martha's Vineyard to convince Stan to sell. Maybe he'll be more open to compromise on home ground. And tell Perry no, I will not wear pink to the Publishers' ball; I'm not a sixteen-year-old prom queen or a tea-cosy. I don't care how 'exquisite the cut' or 'brilliant the new designer' that he wishes to promote. He's an art director for a global fashion magazine empire—tell him to think like it. I want daring not dreary, and I'm perfectly capable of finding my own dress if he doesn't grasp that..."

She paused, as she was reminded of her bizarre ride down in the elevator with that green-eyed fashion tragic. Elena still couldn't believe she'd been trolled by the graveyard-shift reporter. How...disappointing. She would have to find out who she was. It had been a very long time since she'd had someone directly spit insults at her. And never an underling still in her employ.

"We're done," she ground out.

BlogSpot: Aliens of New York

By Maddie as Hell

They promised to visit. They haven't. The reasons pile up like unpaid bills. I get it. They're busy. Life gets crazy. But I long for the wash of home, and wish I could afford a ticket back.

I want to hear, hidden in their broad accents, the hum of cicadas in summer and the gentle tik-tik-tik of backyard sprinklers.

I want the smell of them to be a reminder of the salty air of Bondi Beach, mixed with the tang of vinegar from fish and chips spread on butcher's paper across the sand. I want the whiff of cut grass and eucalyptus trees and the faint disinfectant on the train to Bondi Junction, which always signalled the start of the weekend.

I want the taste of them. In the hello-again kiss, brushing tanned cheeks, I want to find the unique, almost dusty, taste of the air back home.

When they promised to visit, was it a lie told knowingly? Do they think having my best friend here means I don't need them? Even if we didn't work the wrong shifts, my housemate has absorbed New York into his skin. He's become the city I recoil from.

I miss them.

CHAPTER 3

New Yorking Badly

Maddie flopped onto her sofa, considering her options. It was mid-morning, and she was officially awake. Dressed even. Ready to seize the day. She'd slept off the Fun Factory hangover, but Simon had still looked as if he wished he could end it all when he'd schlepped off to his business internship. Such a wuss, she thought fondly. She yawned. Then again.

She never felt fully awake anymore. At first, she assumed it was the night shift messing her up. She'd get home around 1:45 a.m., pace her apartment, or cook up some treats until she felt tired or until a rumpled Simon crawled out of bed and threw something at her. Then she'd fall into bed and sleep until noon.

But it had been getting worse. Maybe it was the bad dreams. She was sleeping later and later. Maddie sighed and wished she could just hit the beach and let the sun poke her back into life for a few months. But they were at the pointy end of winter in New York. She definitely missed watching Simon half drown himself at surfing. He'd been at it for years and still couldn't survive a half pipe. He was pure shark biscuit. She yawned again.

She should probably do some housework or attempt a half-hearted floor workout to a DVD. Maddie stared at the silent TV. Then at the floor.

Or not.

She rose and headed for the kitchen cupboards to take stock. A trudge to the grocery store for more baking supplies would do her some good. That almost counted as embracing New York, didn't it? If you squinted?

Losing interest, she considered her final option. She could update her page. Maddie's secret blog about her experiences here filled the hours between waking, feeling guilty about not "New Yorking" properly, and going to work. Not even Simon knew she did this. It was hard to make friends at work, given the hours she worked. Her blog made her feel less lonely, not so much of an alien, and it felt nice to be followed by so many others who also felt as out of place as she did.

Maddie resolved not to dwell on how bad she was at the New York experience. She had bigger things to worry about. Like staying employed. And tonight, she had her first shift back at work since the unfortunate run-in with Elena Bartell.

Maybe she should just take another nap and not think about any of it right now. She headed back to the couch, flopped down, and pulled the blanket up to her neck. No harm in that.

Maddie got to her desk at five minutes to five and combed her fingers through her cropped red hair. After dumping her canvas backpack on her desk, she rooted through it for her lunchbox that she'd prepped for dinner. She took it to the office fridge and returned with a steaming mug of coffee.

The graveyard shift was not as exciting as she'd first thought it would be when she'd won her job. That had been such a shock—a call out of the blue. Someone had seen the résumé she'd passed around everywhere when she'd first landed in New York. She'd been so thrilled. It was her chance to prove herself at last.

Her friends meant well with all the Facebook good wishes and emails, declaring she'd be doing Pulitzer-winning stories in no time. But it was all just pressure. She'd done her best and flung herself into stories, trying to get the notice of the paper's bosses.

Instead, anything good she dug up overnight, the day-shift crime reporters would take and develop. They had the luxury of having people around they could interview at length. They even got to do their jobs embedded within the New York Police Department, which had set up an office for all the media outlets.

As for Maddie? Well, who was awake at midnight and wanted to talk break-in statistics with her or bat around a few crime trends?

Maddie pulled up the wire feeds on her computer. They were summaries of breaking news from the press agencies—such as AP, Reuters, and AFP—that the paper subscribed to. These slid across her screen in reams of type. As words filled her screen, she scanned them with a dispassionate eye, looking for stories she could expand on. They had to fit her beat. Crime. If the subject wasn't dead, about to be, or in the process of getting its ass arrested, she moved on.

Seeing nothing that would interest the readers of the *Hudson Metro News*, she picked up her phone. She had a laminated list of seventy-seven police precincts across the five boroughs stuck to her desk divider. Technically, she wasn't supposed to call any of them directly. So, her first call of the night always went to the deputy commissioner, public information—or DCPI as the job was known. Bruce Radley was usually on duty now.

"Hi, it's Maddie at the *Hudson Metro News*," she said, after Radley answered. "Anything happening?"

"The usual, Miss Grey. I've already emailed you the day's media releases along with everyone else."

Radley always sounded so long-suffering, as if she'd bothered him, even though it was his job to be called up by the media all night. He made a point of calling her by her surname and drawing out the title Miss, because it was never Ms. Some passive aggressive shit, probably.

"Yes, I see that," Maddie said politely, tapping on one small briefing note that had caught her eye. "The serial jewel thief on Longley Ave— what are we talking, crown jewels, society women's baubles or...?"

"A break-in at a couple of old pensioners' apartments. I don't think the stolen goods were worth much."

She doodled on her page. "Okay. Hope you catch them. Hey, the drug bust two nights back was pretty impressive," she said in her most casual voice. "Fourteen arrested."

The key to drawing out an officious little roadblock like Radley was to slip in something you really wanted to know about as an afterthought to something you had no interest in. Sometimes the man had his guard down and didn't notice and things slipped out. But not often.

"Mmm, yes, I did enjoy your little story, Miss Grey," the deputy commissioner said, but Maddie picked up the wariness. *Damn.* "What's your interest in rehashing it?"

"Oh, just wondering why thirteen of them have had their charges dropped. There was such a big show of it all over the news. Fourteen arrested! Major drug breakthrough! And now, nope. All of them free, bar one."

"It's all in the media release. It went out yesterday—your day off I gather."

"It's not in the media release, though." Maddie frowned and called up the briefing email in question. "It just says charges are proceeding for one person. I've looked and..."

"What can I say, Miss Grey? It's old news. Charges stuck on one of them; can't speak to the others."

"But..."

"Anything else? Anything that's not yesterday's news?" Extra snippy now.

Maddie wondered what she'd trodden in. Had the arrests been all bullshit to start with just to make the nightly news, and they knew it? And then, when everyone's backs were turned, they'd dropped the crap charges and followed through with the only guilty person? Or was the remaining accused even guilty? This smelled fishy as hell. Maddie knew she'd have to follow it up, or the curiosity would kill her.

"Which precinct handles the area that the bust was done in?" She flipped back through her notes from two days ago. "101st?"

"Miss Grey, it is highly advisable for the media to direct all their calls to my office and not bother individual precincts, which will simply direct your inquiries back to me. As you well know."

"I hear you." She underlined 101 in her notes. "So you'll send me a statement on why thirteen arrests were dropped? Otherwise I'll just ring 101st and ask direct."

"You can't. It is *strongly* advised..."

He could advise her all he liked, but he couldn't actually stop her from picking up the phone and calling them. She wondered whether his bluster worked on the rest of the media. Were the other journalists all compliant and went along with this arbitrary rule? That's not how she'd been taught. Maddie tapped her pen on her notepad, interrupting his speech on NYPD regs. She'd heard it dozens of times.

"Okay, so when can I expect your statement?" She doodled a circle around the 101 and wrote "Queens" beside it.

"I'll get back to you later, Miss Grey," he finished, dismissing her, and hung up.

Maddie rolled her eyes. Sure. She wouldn't be getting a statement from him tonight or any other night on this. Or, if she did, it would be one paragraph long, say a fat load of nothing new, and be emailed within the next thirty seconds. A straight-up copy and paste. She could set her watch to it. Maddie looked up the 101st Precinct and dialled.

"Hi, this is Maddie Grey from the *Hudson Metro News*, could I speak to the deputy inspector, please?"

"She's left for the day."

"What about whoever's supervising there now?"

Maddie hit refresh on her email. Nothing.

"He's busy. And besides, shouldn't you be calling the DCPI?"

"Yes, but I need a small clarification that the DCPI can't help me with. It's just background about the drug bust at Redfern Houses two days ago. Could you get the desk officer to call me when he's free? Won't take a minute."

"I'll tell him you called. Name?"

"Maddie Grey at the *Hudson Metro News* crime desk. My number's—"

Click.

She sighed at the unsubtle message that they wouldn't be calling her back. Just then, an email from Radley landed.

Forty seconds. He was getting slack.

The NYPD has no further comment on the drug operations on Sunday at 00:40. Charges are proceeding in the case of one Ramel Aiden Brooks, 18, on multiple counts of possession of a controlled substance, namely, quantities of Vicodin, ecstasy, marijuana, and oxycodone. The arrest was carried out at an apartment in New York City Housing Authority's Redfern Houses, Far Rockaway.

So—nothing new; no further comment. And if anyone at 101st Precinct rang her back, she'd buy a lottery ticket. Such was life. That's why the day shift was where the action was. Deputy inspectors, for instance, worked regular hours and tended to return calls.

God, this job could be boring.

Maddie worked her way through the rest of the NYPD media releases in her inbox. A flasher was doing the rounds of kids' parks. The description was laughable—trench coat and combat boots. Nothing else. There was a shooting in the Bronx, but no fatalities beyond someone's hotted-up, black muscle car. Break-in stats made her pause. She wrote that one up, highlighting the safest and most risky areas in New York. No shocks. It was pretty much a standard evening's haul.

Maddie checked her watch. That late already? She headed for the office kitchen and grabbed her lunchbox. It contained a basic ham sandwich, a sad little Tim Tam (the last of her chocolate treats from Australia until her mother sent more), and a can of diet cola. High living. Not the most appetising selection, but the staff canteen had shut hours ago, and she couldn't face how many people would still be bustling around on the streets outside, even at this time of night.

Back at her desk, Maddie leaned back in her chair and contemplated her existence. She did that a lot lately. *Why am I so bad at cracking New York—personally or professionally? What made me think I could ever do this?* She was out of her depth and drowning.

Giving her soda a morose glare, she cracked the can and had a sip.

It wasn't as if she hadn't been here long enough. She couldn't use that as an excuse. Hell, Simon had been in New York half the time she had. He'd been born with a gregarious soul and seemed to know half of everyone in no time. Everyone loved Simon.

Her phone rang, so she dropped the can back on the desk and flipped the phone to her ear. "Maddie Grey, *Hudson Metro News*."

"Sergeant Malloy, desk officer for 101st Precinct. You had questions about the Redfern Houses drug bust two nights ago?"

Maddie scrabbled for a pen, in a state of shock. The fact he'd called back meant he'd actively had to track down her number, which his office hadn't taken. Malloy had to *really* want to talk to her. "Yes," she said, heart thudding.

"That one was *all* Queens Narcotics Squad's baby. This ain't nuttin' to do with us. Don't call again. 'Night."

The phone went dead. Maddie stared at it. *Or he really wanted it on the record that his office was not involved in something stinky.*

"Hey, chickee."

She started.

The editor's secretary and office gossip-hound, Lisa Martinez, was shoving her cell phone in her bag and smiling at her. "Forgot my phone again. Had to come back for it."

Lisa wasn't a friend, but they were cordial enough, and she often passed along the day-shift gossip that Maddie missed as the lone night-shift girl.

"Did you see the new thing? In the lobby?" She leaned over the desk, giving Maddie an unexpected view of her ample assets.

"What thing?" Maddie slid her gaze higher.

"Oh, a li'l thing called Jake. Squeezed into a security uniform. Muscles up to his nostrils!" Her eyes glazed over. "Tell me you wouldn't want a prime piece of that."

So wouldn't.

Lisa gave her hair a toss and told her in a fascinated tone, "I think he's from Texas. He's got that way of speaking. You know—all drawled-out words, like he can't bear to say them fast. He can pat me down any day. Am I right?"

She looked to Maddie for backup, as though she had an ogling comrade-in-arms.

In the eight months Maddie had worked at the *Hudson Metro*, Lisa hadn't yet picked up on her complete indifference to girly bonding. Especially on topics she had zero interest in. Like swooning over men with muscles. Or men at all.

"I met him on the way in. He only seems to know five words," Maddie pointed out with a grin. "None of which are longer than three letters. What would you two even talk about?"

Lisa exploded into a fit of giggles, forcing her mammoth bosom to rise and fall under her blouse. She gave her long, dark hair another flick. "Ha, *chica*, you seem to think I like my men for their conversation."

Maddie forced a smile. "Ah. So, anything happening? I wasn't here yesterday. What did I miss?"

"Oh, honey, it's all on!" Lisa's voice dropped to a conspiratorial whisper, even though they were the only two people in this part of the building. "So Jake's been brought over from Bartell Corp, because the tiger shark thought our night security sucked."

"It does," Maddie said. "I mean Garry's a nice guy, but a seventy-year-old with a bad heart and two hip replacements shouldn't be our first line of defence at midnight."

"Well, the boss lady obviously agrees cos *zzzt...*" She ran a finger across her throat. "No more Garry. Hello, Jakey." Her eyes lit up.

"Lisa, you're married," Maddie said, half amused.

"True, but I'm not dead yet. Anyway," Lisa continued shooting her an unrepentant look, "the other huge bomb is that our big *jefe* is gone." She pointed behind Maddie.

Maddie swivelled around to check out the general manager's glass, corner office. She sat so close to him that she could often hear snatches of his phone conversations. The reverse was also true. Colleagues always gave her sympathetic looks whenever they found out where her desk was. No one wanted to sit under Barry Bourke's all-seeing gaze.

The only person who sat closer to Bourke than Maddie was his secretary. Melissa had a double-length desk immediately behind Maddie and right outside her boss's office. His now *completely bare* office.

Maddie frowned. She suddenly realised Melissa hadn't talked her ear off tonight, as she usually did between five and six when the secretary was winding up her day. Maddie's gaze dropped to Melissa's desk. It looked as bare as the general manager's. How the hell could she have missed that? Well, she had been kind of preoccupied with her own employment issues.

"So Bartell fired him? And Melissa, too?"

"Yup. Just like that. Guess Elena wanted his office." Lisa cackled. "And Melissa went with him. Her choice. Guess the rumours about those two were true."

"So much for Bartell's fancy speech about us all getting six weeks to prove ourselves."

"Yeah, but what did Bourke expect? His expenses are...were... *insane*. I know—I put through some of the invoices to Accounts."

"I doubt Bartell's expenses will be any less, though. Come on, the woman owns a private jet for God's sake."

"But that won't be billed back to us. You know, from an accounting point of view, she's already saving the paper a ton of money by ditching Bourke's greedy ass."

"Still seems kind of arbitrary to me." Maddie shook her head. "How does she know Bourke wasn't a genius? She barely knows him." She was still rankled by their elevator conversation, when Bartell had taunted her about possibly firing her on the spot.

"Well, you'll know sooner than the rest of us what she's like," Lisa said with a naughty gleam in her eye. "Hell, now she's sitting behind you, you'll be able to hear pretty much everything she's up to. So, don't forget to pass on any good gossip."

Sitting behind me. Maddie glanced back at the glass office with a sinking feeling. She was damn sure she didn't want to be this close to the woman. Maddie realised Lisa was waiting for an answer. "Um, nope. For some reason I think low-level espionage would get my ass toasted in no time. I need this job to pay rent, especially seeing my housemate's leaving soon."

"Oh," Lisa said with a pout. "Okay, I suppose. Well, enjoy virtually sitting in her lap, though. You two are gonna see an awful lot of each other for the next six weeks. She'll be peering out at you from her desk every day like *el demonio*!" Lisa laughed heartily and waved good night.

Maddie recalled Bartell's snide dig at her—"I don't want to be looking at a deconstructed beat poet for the next six weeks." It was going to be awkward as hell if Bartell really didn't like looking at her. Although Maddie didn't work normal hours, so the problem of Bartell being unimpressed by her wardrobe wasn't going to be an issue.

It wasn't as if some highly successful, world-famous media mogul would want to be sitting in her poky, borrowed office for hours on end. The fact she was here for six long weeks was weird enough. But being here after hours too?

Maddie was pretty safe. She exhaled in relief.

BlogSpot: Aliens of New York

By Maddie as Hell

Expectations are one of life's most powerful, invisible forces. They crush our throats tighter than any necktie. We chafe at them, deny they exist, pretend we don't care about them, yet we can't get enough of them. Expectations alter our world. They can win or cost us a job, a lover, a lawsuit, a life.

We are addicted to expectations. Me, I'm the expectations junkie. Check me out, living the life I'm expected to. I could be failing happily back home. Instead, I'm succeeding miserably here.

I know focusing on expectations is a pointless waste of mental resources. They aren't real. They're entirely in our own minds.

And yet, I'm always going back for another hit.

Why?

CHAPTER 4

Habits of Highly Successful Media Moguls

As it happened, Maddie didn't know anything about the habits of highly successful media moguls. It turned out that Elena Bartell liked to spend most of her day outside the office, or so Lisa informed her, and only turned up at *Hudson Metro* at about three each day with an uptight blonde woman in her slipstream. She was the same woman Maddie had seen with her the first day. She now sat in Melissa's old desk, right outside Bartell's office, and Maddie was exactly a single 180-degree chair swivel away from her.

The blonde's name was Felicity Simmons. Uptight wasn't even the start of it. She was sniffy and huffy and all sorts of snobby, as though she'd been pumped full of private-school elocution lessons, but loyal to a fault about her boss. Every now and then, though, her accent slipped and there was the faintest Midwestern twang. Maddie grinned. She was such a fraud.

"What are you looking at?" Felicity demanded when she caught her staring.

Where to start? The tight, hair-sprayed bun and severe, angular body that made her look like an Eastern European ballet dancer? The preternaturally wide eyes, pronounced cheekbones, or thin lips with a slash of purple lipstick that gave her an emo-librarian look?

"Is there anything you don't do? Where are you going to get tickets to that show by tomorrow morning?" Maddie asked. "Doesn't your boss know it's sold out?"

She'd overheard Bartell's clipped demand when she'd started work. No one had been able to get tickets to *Song of Eternity* for months.

"She knows," Felicity said in a curt tone. "She also knows that I have contacts with the law firm that covers the show." She huffed.

"And ordinarily, this would not be my job at all. But Elena is without a personal assistant at present."

She looked frazzled, appalled, and every kind of exhausted. Not that Bartell seemed to appreciate the woman. From what Maddie had seen, her boss was both demanding and dismissive of Felicity.

"Why not quit?" Maddie asked. "If she's that much hard work."

"Quit!" Felicity looked askance. "Are you insane? Do you know what my job even is?"

Maddie shrugged. "Shit kicker to a media overlord."

"I am no such thing. And she's...complicated."

"She is mean to you. Like, King Kong-sized bitch mean."

Felicity rolled her eyes. "Yes, well, it's not personal. No one understands her." The *like I do* was unspoken, but Maddie heard it all the same.

"And if you knew half the things she had to endure on a day-to-day basis, all the balls she has in the air that she juggles, you'd be astonished," Felicity continued. "But no, you're like the gutter press. All you want to focus on is how she does things, not what she does. But what do you know anyway? Aren't you the obituaries girl?"

"And crime." Maddie shot her a grin. "It's the bread and butter of a commuter paper."

"Fascinating, I'm sure."

"Come on, it's a skill to get a large-scale drug bust told in 150 words," Maddie said, ignoring the sarcasm. "But you're right, it's kind of boring after a while."

Felicity's expression was incredulous. "And you're sharing all this, why?"

Maddie grinned. "I mistook you for a human, and I thought we were making small talk."

"Wrong on both counts. And I have an actual career to attend to. That means keeping Elena organised and on schedule, her contracts up to date, and having everything she needs, including tickets for two to *Song of Eternity*. Not hearing prattle from the office junior who could be unemployed within weeks."

"Wow. Low blow." Maddie was kind of impressed by how little Felicity seemed to care about whether she was liked. She and her boss were made for each other.

Felicity shot her an indifferent look, so Maddie took the hint and returned to work.

The hours bled together, and before she knew it, it was almost midnight. She glanced around to find the usual empty office. Sofía, the cleaner, was vacuuming somewhere, but Maddie couldn't see her. The light was still on in Bartell's office, although the woman wasn't anywhere in sight. With a sigh and a grumble about environmentally unaware media executives contributing to greenhouse gasses, she pushed off from her chair and headed into the office. She stuck her head in, reached around the corner, and flicked the switch.

"Who did that?" an outraged voice said from somewhere in the darkened room.

Maddie started, snapped the light on again, and looked around.

A dark head bobbed up from floor level behind the desk, and Maddie stared into the furious glare of Elena Bartell. Craning her neck, she could see a yoga mat on the floor under Elena. Oops. Shit.

"I was stretching!"

"Sorry," Maddie said. "Really. I thought you were gone. And—"

"And you thought you'd save a tree in the Amazon or something?" Bartell rose to full height, stretching her arms above her head and swaying, left and right. Her arms were toned and clearly used to exercise. Her new position had the effect of thrusting her chest forward, encased in a tight, white T-shirt.

Maddie's cheeks heated up. "I...uh..."

Bartell swivelled her neck, as though shifting the kinks, not taking her eyes off Maddie. "Oh very enlightening. Thank goodness you're a journalist where words are your skill."

Maddie pulled a face. "Yeah. Um, I didn't know you were here. Think how much money I could have saved you, turning out the lights and all?"

"Mm." Bartell shook out her arms. "Since you're in here, ruining my brief window of relaxation, you can make yourself useful. Chai latte with non-fat milk, extra hot."

"Um, you know I'm not a PA, right? And if our kitchen stocks chai latte, I'll sell my house."

"Who said anything about you getting it from our kitchen? And you don't have a house to sell; I'd be surprised if you're not renting a broom closet. As for not being a PA, you don't seem to be much of a journalist either, so this is a step up."

Maddie bit down her annoyance at the jab. Not much of a journalist? How the hell would she know?

"I'm sorry I wasn't more direct. I'm not your PA. I'm your junior crime and obits writer." She said it politely, but this had to be a suicidal approach. Still, there was no way she was going to do a midnight run to the 24/7 Times Square Starbucks from now until Bartell gutted the *Hudson Metro News* and moved on. She did not want to become a Felicity, who took fawning to new heights.

Bartell eyed her, fingers on her hips, drumming ferociously, and Maddie thought she was about three seconds from being fired. Deciding retreat was the best option, she hastily added, "But I should get back to work, and I'm sorry I ruined your yoga thingy."

She returned to her desk, feeling those eyes on her the entire time. Her shoulders slumped. Seriously, what had she done to earn the wrath of Bartell? How could anyone be that pissed off about having a light turned off on them? Or was it something else? She wasn't still mad over yesterday's steampunk reference? God, was that it? Either way, it looked as if Bartell hated her guts, and Maddie wasn't helping matters much.

So what was she going to do about it? Sit and mope for the rest of the six weeks? She twiddled with the Sydney Harbour snow dome on her desk, gave it a shake, and watched the improbable snowflakes wafting down. It was done now, right? She'd already pissed off her new boss, and she couldn't take it back. So she should just...be herself. Stop fretting. Do whatever she'd normally do.

She slapped Sydney Harbour back in its place and opened her computer feed to check the wire services and media releases. Later, she would put through yet another call to the Queens Narcotics Squad. A formal request for an interview through DCPI had gone nowhere. So maybe the drugs squad would get tired of being badgered by the crazy Aussie and actually return her call? Or not.

When Maddie arrived at work the next day, there was a new PA sitting next to Felicity—a fearful young woman with legs up to her chin and the balance of a day-old kitten. If she wasn't trying to pick her way around on platform shoes, she might have a hope at doing her job. Maddie watched out of the corner of her eye, as the skittish assistant leapt up and down with every request from Bartell, her face becoming more and more panicked.

Maddie spun her chair around when she disappeared on yet another errand, and her gaze connected with Felicity's. "I give her three days. She's a human meltdown."

"Generous. I'm expecting her to resign by day's end. I found her in the bathroom with tears streaming down her face. Said her work situation was 'not what she'd expected'." Felicity's fingers swished to form derisive air quotes. "Did she truly think working for a global media legend would be a breeze?"

Maddie shrugged, and her gaze darted back to the awkward woman, heading back with paperwork under her arm, her legs wobbling. "Uh-oh." The woman face-planted in front of Elena in a tangle of limbs and a squeal loud enough to draw every eye on the floor. She clutched her ankle.

"Hell, she's sprained it." Felicity picked up the phone. "I'll book a temp, then start the hunt for yet another new PA. She won't be walking on that ankle anytime soon."

"I'll get some ice."

"Don't bother. I'll call her a cab as well. She can deal with it at home."

Maddie shook her head at Felicity's callousness and went to the office kitchen anyway. After finding ice at the back of the freezer, she wrapped it in a kitchen towel. Maddie headed back, ignoring Bartell's cool gaze from within her office, and handed over the cold package to the PA, who was now in her seat. Huge, tear-stained eyes greeted Maddie.

"Thanks," the assistant whispered, placing it on her ankle. "It hurts like hell. And Elena just fired me."

"Oh," Maddie said. "Well, she does that. A lot. Or so I'm told."

The wet eyes in front of her went wide, her focus lifting to behind Maddie's shoulder.

She turned and found Bartell a foot behind her, regarding them.

"I believe you have work to do," she said to Maddie. "I understand nursemaid is no closer to the duties of a journalist than personal assistant is. Or have I misunderstood your job description as you explained it to me?"

Maddie patted the younger woman's leg gently and rose. "She was in pain."

"As was I who had to listen to her wailing."

Maddie gave her a dark look and returned to her desk. *Of all the rude, insufferable, unfeeling bitches.* She shot a mutinous glare over her shoulder.

The security guard with muscles up to his nostrils had arrived to help the wounded woman out of the building. Bartell was ignoring the entire scene, back at her computer, a look of indifference on her face.

Christ. Elena Bartell was not just a cold fish, but snap-frozen sushi.

Maddie shifted her attention back to work. She was due to write an obituary. Some teacher had died after fifty years in service. Maddie had to choose people who would resonate with their audience—such as business leaders, celebrities, sporting stars—but they did leave it up to her when no one famous had died. Mrs Mavis Swenson looked as if she'd lived a life of mundane, until Maddie read what her children had listed as her hobbies. Mountain climbing? Abseiling? She put Maddie to shame.

Maddie was twenty-six, and her career misstep had cost her so much time. She'd lost two and a half years doing a level-four certificate in hospitality and catering management so she could step into her family's business. Instead, she'd switched to a journalism degree six months before she was due to get the diploma. Her parents had been appalled, begging her to at least finish the course. She hadn't seen the point. Six more months doing something she hated? No thanks. The downside of changing careers was that she now felt like the oldest junior reporter in history, and she was still treading water.

A few hours later, a flash of blonde in her vicinity caught her eye. Felicity was trying to explain to a temp what her duties would be. Not that she was doing a particularly thorough job.

"That's Elena's office. She is God. Do what God says, whatever she says, and we won't have a problem. Understood? Good. Now get the chai latte order I wrote out for you. Go!"

When the woman disappeared, Felicity flopped down at her desk with an aggrieved sigh.

"How do you even get any work done if all you do is induct new PAs and temps?" Maddie asked, swivelling her chair to face Felicity.

"I'd get a lot more done if the dead-people writer would stop bothering me."

Maddie ignored the dig. She was realising by now that this passed as Felicity almost being friendly. "Hey, what do you *actually* do for your boss? You're not a PA, because you keep hiring them for her. I've narrowed it down to somewhere between 'whatever Elena wants' and 'something to do with law'. So which is it?"

"Both. I'm her personal chief of staff. I have an MBA and a Harvard law degree. I could have set up my own practice."

Maddie stared at her. She seemed too young for all that. "Then why didn't you?"

Felicity gaped at her. "Be serious. Look at who I'm working for! I'm witness to some of the most crucial media moves made this century. I'm the woman that almost a hundred attorneys from all over the world call when they have business with Elena. I keep the Titanic headed away from the icebergs, thank you very much."

"Oh? A hundred attorneys? I mean…is that supposed to be good?"

"Oh my God, can you really be this…this…*Australian*? Elena is a business legend. And I'm her right-hand woman. She relies on me. I'm at the cutting edge of everything. I prep contracts for signing, and I advise on risk assessments of business acquisitions. Like this one." She waved at the newsroom.

"So *you're* why she's here? You told her to buy this place?"

"Don't be ridiculous, I did no such thing. If I had my way, this pitiful paper would be at the bottom of the Hudson. It was in a bundle of mastheads she picked up for a song. Some of the other publications in the bundle had merit."

"So if this place is such a hole, why is she even debating keeping it? And spending six weeks thinking about it—which seems a long time for someone like her."

A mystified look crossed Felicity's face. "Elena is a brilliant businesswoman. I'm certain her strategy will reveal itself. Even if someone can't see it, she *always* has it. She thinks ten steps ahead of the rest. I'm learning a lot here. It's an incredible opportunity."

"Yeah?" Maddie studied her for a moment. "Then why do you always look so miserable?"

There was a soft snicker of laughter from the glass office behind Felicity, and both women froze. Panic filled Felicity's eyes, as she silently implored Maddie to tell her whether Bartell had overheard their conversation. Maddie's eyes lifted and locked on directly with Bartell's. *Oh shit.* She'd heard all right.

Maddie lowered her gaze back to Felicity's and gave the faintest nod. The woman lost all colour from her cheeks. Maddie wanted to give her a shake. She took her job way too seriously. Of course, at least Felicity *had* a job. And she had a great career path and future prospects, all working for someone she worshipped. Because make no bones about it, the woman was head over heels for her boss. Or at least madly in love with the idea of her.

Sucks to be her, Maddie thought sympathetically, and reached back for Mrs Swenson's file. *Oh great. Mount Kilimanjaro by the time she was thirty.*

Nope, Maddie had no right to be judging Felicity Simmons. Or anyone else.

A flood of tears greeted Maddie when she arrived at work the next day. She discovered the woman from Finance, Josie something, being patted on her back by colleagues.

"What's your boss done now?" Maddie dumped her bag on her desk and turned to Felicity, who had an expression of pure irritation on her face.

The chief of staff shot Maddie a frosty glare. "Of course you'd blame her. Actually, that Josie woman's child got sent home from school with some disease involving large quantities of vomit. The father's home with the boy, but I gather your news boss is insisting Josie stay and file her copy on the New York City executive budget, not go home to her son. I dread to think what sort of copy she'll file anyway. But, frankly, this is all on her. She should have thought of all this before she had kids."

Maddie choked on the absurdity of the statement. She wondered if Felicity's ballet-dancer bun was too tight. "Uh, what? Josie should have worked out *before* she had kids that one day her son would get sick and that would conflict with a big news story? Does that make sense in your head?"

"*Please.* Parents play the parent card far too often. They get all the holidays off, are always going home early or to the school for some play or concert or whatever. You don't see me wailing because someone in my family has a sniffle. If you're serious about your career, it's simple: don't procreate."

"Felicity." Bartell's voice was even chillier than her glare, as she leaned out of her office. "Where are the London contracts? And why is my latest temp missing? I need her. Now."

Felicity flew off her chair as though it was scalding. "Elen... I-I'll just go and track her down. I think she was trying to work out the photocopier." She scampered off.

"What is that *noise*?" Bartell frowned. She took a few steps out of her office, and her gaze drifted to the inconsolable woman, who was now attempting two-fingered typing between wiping streams of tears away.

"The finance writer," Maddie said. "Josie. Doing the budget story."

"Must be a terrible budget."

Maddie bit back a snort of laughter, unsure whether she was serious.

"She's making a scene. Unacceptable." Bartell stalked towards the distraught woman.

All eyes in the office swung to watch, as Bartell Corp's imposing boss rapped on the hard drive tower on Josie's desk to get her attention. "What is this?" Bartell said, voice tight. "You are at work and have a diseased child?"

"W-what?" Josie sniffed.

"I will not have a human incubator putting this office at risk of contamination."

"But it's not…not catching. I mean…you can't catch gastroesophageal reflux, it's—"

"Go home," Bartell said, drawing herself up to full height. "At once. I don't want to see you back here until you are at nil risk of spreading any vile germs to the rest of the staff, and especially me."

"B-but the budget…"

"Home," she said. "*Now.*"

"Ms Bartell, can I speak to you please?" Dave Douglas, the news chief, had a pinched look as he inserted himself into the scene, his gaze flicking to his finance reporter and back.

"No! I do *not* have a minute. I am supposed to be doing a conference call with Hong Kong. Instead, I'm wasting my time within disease-catching distance of this loud, infected…person." Bartell glanced back at Josie, who was frozen in her seat. "What did I say? *Leave!* And do not come back until you are safe to be around."

Bartell turned on her heel and strode back to her office.

A flicker of anger crossed Dave's face, and he clamped down on his jaw. He pointed to a man sitting not far from the finance reporter. "Take over, Robert. Deadline's an hour. I think most of it's done. Right?" He glanced at Josie for confirmation.

Josie nodded between sniffles. She pushed a folder Robert's way, mumbling a few instructions.

As Bartell passed Maddie's desk, the media mogul paused at her open curiosity. "You have an opinion?"

"Nope," Maddie said. "But Josie's not a disease risk any more than you are." She lowered her voice and took a gamble. "And I think... maybe you know it too."

Bartell's eyes flashed a warning. "I'm sure there are more Kilimanjaro-climbing teachers who need eulogising far more than I need your medical opinion."

Surprise flooded Maddie. "You read my obit?"

"Someone had to," Bartell said. "I doubt our readers did, given where it was run. Now, why aren't you working? We're done."

Maddie turned to face her computer and watched as Josie virtually sprinted from the building, a look of profound relief on her face. Maddie wondered if anyone else understood the favour Bartell Corp's president had done for her. She could see the incredulous faces of the rest of the staff, exchanging furtive looks. They'd probably be tweeting about their draconian, germaphobic overlord in two minutes under smart-ass aliases.

But Maddie knew the truth. What germaphobe did yoga on a mat on some run-down office floor?

How...unexpected.

BlogSpot: Aliens of New York

By Maddie as Hell

Someone once said: "Be yourself; everyone else is taken." Surely this is the hardest advice ever offered.

We all wear masks. We're all practiced liars, neatly curating ourselves for the benefit of others. It's only natural, isn't it? We don't want strangers to know we're secretly nervous or shy or intimidated or cowardly. That we're not brave enough or smart enough or well-off enough or that we're barely coping. So we fake the ease and perfection of our lives. I'm the first one to admit I've posted a grinning selfie of me at Times Square with #lifegoals in the caption. I'm a fraud. But writing #drowningslowly or #lostandembarrassed doesn't have the catchiest ring.

You never truly know what's under anyone's mask until you take one corner and start to peel. It awes me that anyone would allow another human to do this to them. To willingly say, hey, this is me. Do you still like me?

The advice might be right—but by God, it's asking a lot of us.

CHAPTER 5

Exotic Balls and Exorcisms

Maddie arrived home just before 2:00 a.m., feeling twitchy as hell, and the need to bake hit her. Hard. It did sometimes, and fortunately, Simon never complained too much at being woken to the sound of a cake beater or oven timer going off at all hours. Of all the addictions to have, at least baking meant a payoff for Simon, too, given he always got to sample the spoils in the morning. Still, she really did owe him big time for all the ways she ruined his sleep patterns.

Maddie hummed as she stirred the ingredients in her mixing bowl. Quinoa flakes, vanilla protein powder, almonds, chai spice, medjool dates, and coconut. She thought of Bartell...*Elena,* she corrected herself...and her late-night cravings for chai tea. The flavour of Maddie's exotic protein balls would likely please any fan of that tea variety.

As she worked, she contemplated Josie, so desperate to get home, and Dave, who had been wearing his "this is nuts, we're on fucking deadline" face. Maddie frowned and sprinkled in a little more coconut.

Elena had descended like a thunderstorm, doing Josie a favour dressed up as a bitchy reprimand. It had been quite brilliant, now she thought about it. Elena couldn't have directly overruled the news chief about a story without shredding his authority, and she needed him to retain the respect of his staff to be effective. So she made it look like some strange, personal issue that allowed her department head to save face, Josie to go home, and Elena... Well, she came off looking petty, weird, and void of any empathy. She'd put her tiger shark mask to good use.

No one else might have understood what she'd done, but Maddie did. She wondered what was really under the mask. Elena might have allowed this one crack to show, but her mask seemed welded on like armour the rest of the time. Did she even take it off at home? Surely she did. As Maddie stirred, her wooden spoon turning into a blur, she decided it didn't matter. Either way, the woman deserved a little reward for her dark-arts gallantry.

Sixteen hours later, Maddie was back at work. She checked the clock. It was almost four, so she was an hour early. She glanced at the empty corner office.

Elena was absent from her desk, and Felicity and the temp were also nowhere to be seen. The trademark black, glossy handbag perched on the media boss's desk told Maddie that she couldn't be too far away.

She plucked a small container from her backpack and emptied six little balls onto a paper plate that she'd nabbed from the kitchen. Maddie slid the plate onto Elena's desk and adjusted the presentation three times until she was satisfied. Then she backed away.

As Maddie returned to her desk, her heart was thumping, and she felt as if she'd achieved something special. Which was ridiculous, really. All she'd done was put food on her boss's desk anonymously. Food she might not even eat. Because, come to think of it, how silly would it be eating strange food when you're the boss that people love to hate? Or just hate to hate?

Okay, so she hadn't thought this through. It was a dumb thing to do. Really dumb. Hell. Maddie pushed her chair back to go and retrieve the plate, only to find a blue-eyed gaze fixed on her as Elena plucked, studied for a moment, and then bit neatly into a chai tea ball.

Maddie swallowed at the same time Elena did. A look of surprise flitted across Elena's face, and the hint of a smile. Then nothing. Elena turned back to her computer.

Facing her own computer, Maddie listened for the sound of spitting. She waited, ears straining, for five minutes. When nothing happened, she tried to go back to work. Her heart only slowed its pounding after she reminded herself it wasn't as if Elena knew the treats were from her. There were plenty of people still in the building at four. The offering could have been from any of them.

She peeked eight or nine more times throughout the night, and the little pile of balls had almost disappeared by the end of it. Not that she'd been stressing about it or anything.

Nope, not at all.

The tenth time, Elena looked straight at her and gave a faint smile as she popped the final ball into her mouth.

Not for the first time, Maddie wondered what on earth Elena was thinking.

Elena chewed slowly and pondered Madeleine Grey. Her little food balls were a most unexpected offering. The way the junior crime reporter had watched so fearfully as she tried the first one instantly told her the identity of the chef. As offerings went, they were sublime. Not that she would share that with her. It was a fool's errand to get too friendly with the staff, especially those likely to be fired in a few weeks. Her mood darkened at the reminder. The figures on the *Hudson Metro* were worse than she'd expected. Her plans were now a certainty. She would have to get Felicity to make the appropriate calls.

Her thoughts returned to Madeleine. What did Elena know about her? She was from Sydney. She was a reporter. She was homesick, most likely, if their elevator conversation was any indication. She seemed... unhappy. Madeleine probably wasn't even aware of how frequently she glanced at the global time-zones display on the far wall. Her head tilted left, where the Sydney clock was, then her shoulders would slump. She also often picked up her Sydney Harbour snow globe as she talked on the phone, caressing it, giving it a shake, before returning it to its spot with a tiny pat. This was not someone embracing a new city.

Elena stared at the coconut flakes that had fallen on the plate.

Madeleine. Also known as Maddie. How many Australian reporters in New York had that name anyway? She stopped cold as the realisation hit her.

After turning to her computer, she typed in an address she knew by heart. Elena never missed *Aliens of New York*. When she'd first discovered the blog about eighteen months ago, she'd gone back and read all the previous entries. They were pretty much the same— observant, nuanced, sometimes beautiful, and always sad. The author could convey the ache of loneliness better than anyone she'd ever seen.

Elena related to that a little too well. Juggling her media empire, she didn't have a lot of time for close friendships, but it didn't mean she was immune to the emptiness of that choice at times. Even her husband, some days, felt more like a partner in conquest rather than someone interested in knowing the woman behind her success.

Maddie as Hell captured the subtlety of human flaws, hopes, and frailties. Her perceptiveness was addictive, like a secret shared to a select few. Elena had always imagined the blogger to be someone much older, wise, with ancient eyes and a stillness to her.

It was unnerving to work out *Maddie as Hell* was not ancient, still, or steeped in wisdom. She was just a lost, homesick, young reporter. Someone hapless, chaotic, and unfathomable, not to mention a fashion tragic...and yet she wrote words that stirred Elena.

She shook her head, closed the blog window, and turned to better observe the paradox that was her junior crime reporter. Elena chewed slowly and watched.

Now that Maddie had seen a crack in Elena's mask, she found herself curious to find more evidence. She was just bored, she told herself. It had nothing whatsoever to do with the odd way she felt when that intense gaze settled on her and studied her like something of interest. Something to be puzzled out.

Elena did that sometimes. Maddie knew not to read anything into it. In the scheme of the woman's global empire, Maddie was still a single-cell organism of no consequence.

Lisa had been right about one thing. Maddie was well situated to hear Elena's conversations. She often caught snatches of phone calls.

Sometimes Elena spoke to her husband, and there was a tone to her voice that Maddie found hard to pin down. It was neither cool nor warm. The pitch never seemed much beyond professional or, occasionally, pleased. It was all so one note and... She paused, surprised when she finally identified it. Almost bored. Yes, that was it.

Elena's husband bored her? Hell. Maddie felt sad for her.

The only warmth and softness Maddie heard was reserved for discussing someone called Oscar. Suspicions of an illicit affair abruptly ended, however, when Elena requested her housekeeper get him neutered and his toenails clipped.

Maddie also was well positioned to see who came for meetings. Occasionally, men with cheap suits and document tubes under their arms would arrive, not making eye contact with any *Hudson Metro* staff. Sometimes the suits would be expensive, the men's gazes not shifty but smug, and they would shake Elena's hand with authority and be pointed to visitors' chairs, the door closing.

"Board members," Felicity said once, when she caught Maddie's curious stare. "A necessary evil."

"I thought Bartell Corp was her company? Isn't she like the queen of all she surveys? Why does she have to put up with anyone she doesn't want to?"

"Yes, of course it's hers. But it's a publicly listed company. She's president and chief operating officer. She still has the board, the chairman, and CEO to be nice to. And the CFO, as well, if she's outlaying some large expenditures."

"Right," Maddie said, becoming curious. "Do they say no often?"

Felicity's eyes narrowed. "Even once is too often. They think she just comes up with her business decisions on a whim. But she always has a plan, even if they're not smart enough to see it."

Maddie studied the men in suits. Only one of them touched Elena's arm, and she allowed the familiarity. His photo was in a framed picture on the wall behind Elena's desk. "Who's the tall one with silver hair?"

Felicity's face became the perfect impression of someone sucking on a lemon. "Frank Harkness. They go a long way back. He mentored her when she first started out in corporate media. He's the one board member she actually likes."

Maddie's gaze drifted over the rest of the men. "They all look like funeral directors."

Felicity's purple lips contorted once and then let out a strange, sharp burble.

Maddie looked at her in confusion before realising she was laughing.

"Yes," Felicity said, head bobbing. "They do."

Felicity straightened as though she had suddenly remembered laughing on the job was unprofessional. "Enough show and tell. Get back to poking the dead. I have a big speech to write."

Maddie took the hint and turned to face her computer.

Ten seconds later, Felicity threw down her pen and coughed.

Maddie spun back around. The chief of staff looked bursting to say something. "Yes?"

"It's Elena," Felicity said, practically vibrating with pent-up excitement. "I'm writing a speech, because she's New York's Businessperson of the Year." She beamed. "Of course, it's only right. I mean, who else has done what she has? Taken a little publishing company into a global concern?"

Who else, indeed? Maddie sat back. Well. This news deserved some sort of recognition.

Elena walked into work the next day, head reeling from some of the absurd budget cuts Jana Macy had suggested for *Style Sydney*. Macy truly thought removing the free magazines on the coffee tables in her building's foyer was one of the "serious cuts" Elena had demanded of her? The woman was delusional. She sighed. She would have to fire her. Incompetence surrounded her.

Elena dropped her Hermes handbag on her desk and paused. A strange plant had been placed two feet away. She sat cautiously and studied it. The plant was a bright, glossy green with a thick stem that looked related to the parsley family.

"Felicity," she said with a low growl, "why is there parsley on my desk?"

Felicity scampered into her office. "I...oh...have no idea at all. I thought you'd put it... I mean... Is that...? I don't think it is parsley. My sister works at some herbology place; I could ask her what it is. I mean if you'd like?"

"A herbology place?" Elena peered at her, astonished at the thought anyone in Felicity's family was less than a type-A career climber.

"She's the black sheep in the family. I mean...hippie, greenie, crystals, the whole bit," Felicity said as though it were a grim confession. She took out her iPhone, took a snap of the plant, and tapped a few buttons in the phone.

Elena's gaze shifted past her, outside her office. The crime desk was empty, but since it wasn't even close to five yet, Grey was not likely to be the culprit. This time. She cast her eye about for other suspects.

"It's an *Angelica archangelica*." Her chief of staff smiled at her sister having identified the weed for her. As she kept reading her phone, her smile fell away.

"What is it?" Elena asked.

"Oh, um, never mind, it's...probably, I mean..."

"*Felicity.*" She levelled a cool glare at her until the woman wilted.

"It goes by a lot of names, holy ghost root, um, archangel, masterwort. Popular in..." Felicity gulped in a breath. "Ah, witchcraft and..." Her face screwed up, and she winced.

Witchcraft? Elena felt her irritation stir. "And?" She waited, drumming her fingers on the desk.

"Exorcisms."

She gave Felicity a long, cold stare. Well, it had been a while since some underling had decided on a full-frontal attack. At least this one was original. In years gone by, she had been left shark teeth, sex toys, voodoo dolls, and devil tridents. "I see. We're done."

"I don't think whoever did this... I mean maybe it was just a j-joke."

"We're *done*." With that Elena swept the plant into her waste bin, clamped down on her jaw, and focused on work.

Maddie was in a pretty awesome mood by the time she returned to work after sneaking in her green offering that morning. Her latest blog post had been well received. And one of her followers, Jason, had been really complimentary about it. He was a single dad who really felt the isolation of his city more than most. It felt nice to have helped him feel more connected to others.

She settled into her chair and—as had become her habit these days—immediately pivoted to look into the office behind her. There was just something about Elena that drew Maddie to her. She couldn't explain it if she'd tried. Elena was like a curious knot to unpick.

The media mogul's expression made Maddie freeze. She was bent over her desk, typing furiously. Her mouth was pulled down. Was she angry? She might just be focused, so that didn't mean anything. Maddie strained to see, but couldn't spot the plant she'd placed there this morning. *Huh.*

She wasn't entirely sure she'd gotten the exact variety of *Angelica* right, but her internet search last night said it meant "inspiration". As Felicity had said, Elena had taken a little publishing company into a global concern. That was something inspiring.

Maddie worked steadily until a sharp noise made her turn. Elena had slammed the phone down in its receiver and was glaring at it. Maddie spun around and whispered to Felicity, "What's crawled up her ass today?"

"Some lowlife left her a deranged gift." Felicity glowered, as though she wished to find the culprit and flay them alive. And then flay them dead, too.

Maddie's stomach dropped into freefall. "W-what?"

"A witchcraft plant. Can you believe it? They use it in exorcisms and the like. Elena tossed it, of course. People are disgusting."

Maddie's gaze fell to floor level. A mangled green leaf was poking out of the trash can.

Oh. She took in the deep lines on Elena's face. Her gift had backfired. Spectacularly.

"You didn't happen to see anyone put that on her desk?" Felicity asked her. "She's on a witch hunt for who did it. No pun intended."

"No, I didn't see anyone." Well, it was the truth. Her stomach sank even further.

"What's *your* problem? You look like someone shot your puppy. With a bazooka."

"Nothing." She swivelled back to her desk. "I have a few obits to catch up on. No rest for the dead."

Felicity sniffed. "Whatever. Not like I care."

Maddie called up the website she'd found when half exhausted last night. The one that said *Angelica* was inspirational. With the benefit of sleep and hindsight, she could see it was just an almanac a farmer had thrown together. She dug further and discovered that there were actually more than sixty varieties of the plant. Trust her to have bought the exorcism kind.

Maddie had to make this right. She called Simon. Last night's can't-sleep-baking frenzy would come in handy. She just needed a delivery boy.

Later that evening, when Elena stepped out of her office, Maddie snuck in with her peace offering and a printout of the original page that claimed the plant was inspirational. She also scribbled out a note.

To fix any misunderstandings, I give you more angel, less devil.

And then her signature velvet-angel-food cupcake was left beside it. Thank God, Simon hadn't already eaten them all.

Hoping it was enough, Maddie went back to work. She was vaguely aware of Felicity packing up her things and leaving for the night and the office emptying out around her. She kept working hard until a shadow fell over her desk.

"What's the meaning of this?" Elena asked, voice low, holding up the cupcake in a pincer grip. "Are you mocking me?" She dropped the baked good on Maddie's desk.

"N-no!" Maddie's eyes went wide, her stomach lurching. "Never. I meant what I wrote."

"Then what *are* you doing? Leaving me offerings like spoor around the office?"

Maddie flushed. Spoor? *That's* how she saw it?

"I just wanted to say well done." Maddie felt miserable under that burning gaze. "But I'm sorry if you see it as some sort of an attack. It was an accident. I didn't mean to offend you. Don't worry. I won't do it again."

Elena peered at her for a long time, so long that Maddie began to shift in her seat.

"You truly never meant that ridiculous plant to be a witch reference?"

Maddie gave her head an adamant shake. "I had no idea there was more than one meaning."

"So what are you congratulating me for?"

"Businessperson of the Year. That's amazing!"

"Is it? Third year in a row. I suspect they are simply lazy. I could fill a room with all the trinkets and titles various organisations feel the need to foist upon me. They just want the publicity that would come from my attendance."

Maddie blinked at her. "So you don't think it's an honour?"

"I don't do any of this for honours. If people throw awards at me for just doing my job, I can't very well stop them. I will appear on cue, read Felicity's speech—a variation, no doubt, on her previous two—smile, wave, leave. It's good for publicity and share prices, but that's all."

"Um." Maddie tried to hide her shock. Because it all sounded so ungrateful, not to mention kind of...empty. "You don't want to even hear you've done well? That's kind of sad, don't you think?"

Elena glared at her. "You don't get to judge me. I employ thousands of people worldwide, and they rely on me to get things right, not swan about at various award nights. I make one mistake, and papers and magazines close. You have no idea what it's like to be me or have the focus I require just to do my job as well as I do. You don't know me at all."

"No, I don't know you." Maddie took a deep breath and said the most insane thing she ever had. "So tell me. I'd like to know you. I really would."

"Excuse me?" Elena rocked back on her heels. "Is this some Australian thing, just blurting out statements like that?"

"You know, I get asked that a fair bit." Maddie gave her a rueful smile. "Like, whether I always just say what I think or whether there's any thought behind it. I'm not too sure of the answer myself. I know I can be blunt, but is that so bad? And you didn't answer my question— would you like to talk to me anyway? There's no one here but us. I'm like a vault, I promise."

Elena stared at her as if unsure what to say or do with that unlikely suggestion. "I..." she faded out. "No."

"Oh." Maddie swallowed. *Yeah, of course. What was I thinking anyway?* She felt her face flush and the tips of her ears burn. "I... It's okay. I really do need to shut up sometimes and not—"

"I have a contract to go over. And a report to submit." Elena glanced at the far wall, with the time-zones display. She frowned. "By ten."

"Oh!" Maddie couldn't hold back her smile. Elena hadn't turned down her offer as a bad joke. She'd just said she was busy. "I mean, so, another night, then? I admit I'm even more impertinent after a coffee in me. But I can be pretty amusing too. Half the time I have no clue where my mouth is going. I'm told it can be gobsmacking to listen to at times."

Elena's lips quirked. "I'll bet. But no. I do have work." She started to leave, then stopped, turned, and picked up the cupcake she'd dumped on Maddie's desk minutes ago. "A shame for it to go to waste."

"Yep." Maddie tried to sound neutral. *Hot damn.* As Elena turned to go, Maddie grinned so wide her cheeks hurt.

"And stop smiling," Elena said on her way to her desk, not looking back.

How did she do that?

"It's blinding," she added.

Maddie laughed.

Okay, so that was not the worst thing to ever happen.

BlogSpot: Aliens of New York

By Maddie as Hell

I remember the time I learned to ride a bike. I pushed off from the curb at my old house on Mitchell St, South Penrith. I was wobbling like crazy. My older brother was holding his sides from laughing and calling out names, and my mother was telling him to be quiet and offering me encouragement.

I fell off. It hurt. I got back on. I fell off. It hurt some more. I got back on.

When people say something's like riding a bike, I think maybe they mean it will hurt sometimes, but it will get better.

Today, I remembered how to smile.

I wonder whether it will hurt later.

CHAPTER 6

An Exercise in Tolerance

It became a...thing between them. Oh how Elena hated the imprecision of that word. Late at night, when no one was around, Madeleine increasingly shared things with her. As if Elena was anyone else and didn't run a multimillion-dollar global organisation and could fire her with the twitch of a finger.

At first, she'd tried to dissuade the woman. Distance was required. "I'm sure you'd rather be writing about dead people," Elena had suggested one night. "I know *I'd* prefer you were."

Madeleine had merely laughed.

Tonight, the woman was wearing some ode-to-grunge T-shirt for a band that probably shouldn't have gotten out of a Seattle basement. Her dark blue jeans curved snugly around her ass. And the boots, black and shiny...well, the boots Elena approved of. She owned a few of that style herself, although hers weren't knock-offs. But the shirt was an abomination. Grey, bland, and formless, it did nothing to flatter Madeleine's appealing shape.

"Why do you wear that?" she asked. "Ugly rock bands as workwear?"

"You don't like Alice in Chains?" Maddie seemed intrigued. "You know, being on the midnight shift, the only perk of the job is getting to dress how I like. It's not like I see anyone."

"You see me." Elena gave her a pointed look.

Madeleine stopped. "Oh. Yeah. I guess, well, yeah, I do. So you want me to dress for you?" Her eyes flew wide open. "Oh hell. That came out wrong."

Elena withheld a snort of laughter. Really, squirming Madeleine was her favourite kind. She wondered when that had happened. Having a favourite kind of anything regarding this woman. "Why wear rock bands at all?"

"They're not just rock, though. They're grunge. They're a protest to the boring sameness of '90s music, a primal scream that music should be more than mass-produced, predictable pulp."

"Until all the grunge bands were ripped out of Seattle, signed to record labels, and became mass-produced, predictable pulp." Elena smirked. "Sorry, but your protest music sold out."

"Oh, it's not my music."

"What?"

"I don't really like grunge music." She gave Elena a bright smile. "I just really like the shirts."

Elena felt a headache coming on. The woman was utterly impossible. Figuring her out was akin to doing her corporate taxes in braille. While stoned.

"You don't like grunge," Elena repeated.

"Nope."

"I'm probably going to regret this, but where are your musical tastes inclined? Loud Australian pub thrash?" Even as she said it, she couldn't actually picture it. Not someone who wrote blogs the way Madeleine did.

Madeleine shot her a mysterious smile. "Too hard to explain. I'll have to show you."

Elena frowned. "How?"

"Tomorrow."

Elena found a USB stick on her desk the next evening when she came back from a dinner meeting. It had the label: *Music 4 E.* She glanced at the crime reporter's desk. Madeleine was on the phone, her fingers playing restlessly with the snow dome. Elena could hear conversation snatches. Something to do with following up a drug bust of some sort.

Well. It was a relief not to be drawn into another riddle of a conversation. She really did have a lot of work to do. Such as a Skype call with a Chicago publisher contemplating selling. He was so close to signing, she could taste it. And Elena still had to review the budget notes for *Style Sydney* that her accountant had sent over. So, she had absolutely no time or interest in putting that USB drive into her computer.

It was damned impertinent anyway. Leaving things for her.

She wasn't even remotely curious.

The USB stick stared at her. Elena glared at it.

She would put it out of her mind. Maybe tomorrow, when she was less busy. Or the next day.

Fifteen minutes later, Elena flung down her pen and shoved the stick into a USB slot. She dug out her earbuds, plugged them in, and stole a glance back to Madeleine's desk.

Still on the phone. Excellent.

She hit *Play*.

Four minutes later, she closed the music video and stared at her screen. Removing the USB drive, she considered throwing it across the room in frustration. Why did Madeleine persist in being without category?

It was like that *Aliens of New York* blog of hers. She flicked to the tab she had opened earlier in the day. The wonders of smiling now? Elena was well aware of what had prompted the blog. This was her fault. She was somehow encouraging Madeleine. She didn't mean to. Forming a friendship with an employee was a terrible idea. She knew that. But some part of her was unwilling to play hardball and enforce the divide. And now she really needed to know—how could one person be so curious, so contradictory? How did she defy every box and label?

"Well?"

Elena's head snapped up to find Madeleine only a few feet from her. She stabbed her browser window closed. "Well what?" She gave her a steely look, hoping her shock at almost being caught wasn't showing.

"What'd you think of Veruca and Trinix?"

Elena slid the USB stick across the desk towards Madeleine with some haste. "Those can't be real names."

"Probably not." She ignored the flash drive.

"So. Latvian folk singers," Elena said evenly. "In the middle of a forest, with dancing nymphs."

"Yup."

"Dancing lesbian nymphs."

"That'd be my guess. Although it was a bit hard to tell with all the rising mist."

"It sounded like Kate Bush on LSD."

Madeleine tilted her head. "Fair. I'll pay that. And I like Kate Bush too."

"As do I." Elena studied her. "How on earth did you find them?"

Plopping into the visitor's chair, Madeleine gave a shrug. "A friend recced it in a comment on a blog I...um, follow. So does this mean you liked them?"

"I wouldn't go that far." A blooping noise sounded, and Elena turned. Her Skype call. Damn. She wasn't ready for the man.

"We're done," she muttered to Madeleine, disturbed at how easily she'd allowed herself to be distracted. It was unprofessional. She did not do unprofessional.

There was no movement, and she glanced back. Madeleine was eyeing her with a guarded look.

"We're done," Elena repeated, wondering why she hadn't heard her the first time.

Madeleine flinched. She left, movements jerky, closing the door behind her with a sharp clunk. Since Elena rarely closed her office door, it was a pointed act.

She frowned at the response. Elena was still frowning when she activated her incoming video call. "Nathaniel, good evening."

He offered the usual pleasantries, but Elena's gaze slid back to the crime desk. Its reporter was hunched over, shoulders tight. Surely she wasn't offended? It was hardly the first time Elena had dismissed someone in such a manner. It meant nothing.

Or was it the dismissal itself, not the manner which bothered the woman?

Elena's frown deepened. Yet another reason why this…friendship was a foolish idea. She was Madeleine's boss. Madeleine must surely grasp that now.

So why do I feel so unsettled?

A throat cleared.

Elena forced her focus back to where it belonged. "Nathaniel, where were we on our deal?"

Three nights passed, and neither of them spoke to each other. Which suited Elena fine. She accomplished much more work without Madeleine's chatter about things that held no importance. And the distance helped reinforce that they were never meant to have been friendly in the first place.

On the fourth night, Elena wore one of her favoured outfits to work, which involved a vest, pants, boots, crisp white shirt, and a fob watch. And that night she noticed Madeleine's reaction to it.

Actually, it would be a miracle if Madeleine got any work done, because she'd spent most of the evening watching Elena. Her gaze virtually clung to her, yet she seemed unaware she was doing this. Belatedly, Elena recalled this was the outfit she'd been wearing when Madeleine had derided her the day they'd first met. It occurred to her the intense scrutiny might therefore not be the flattering kind.

As she exited her office, she felt the woman's eyes fixed on her again.

"What?" she asked, irritation rising. She stopped dead in front of Madeleine. "Does my wardrobe really offend you so much that you have to bore holes in it all evening?"

"Huh? God, no!" Madeleine started. A blush spread up her cheeks. "Is that what you think? That I don't like it?"

"I *know* you don't. I recall your verdict well. I heard you dismiss it as 'yesterday's steampunk'." Her lip curled in disdain.

Madeleine shook her head. "Hey, you got it all wrong. I think retro steampunk is the hottest look ever created. Hell, I've got all the *Warehouse 13* episodes H.G. Wells was in to prove it."

Elena blinked at her. "You feel I dress like some old, dead, male writer?" This was mystifying. Had she offended Madeleine so much that she was now openly insulting her again?

"Oh wow. No! Far from it. Okay." Madeleine scribbled a note to herself. "Tomorrow. Wait till tomorrow, then you'll see."

Elena sighed and kept walking. Possibly, flying Ukranian cows doing mist dances were in her future.

Tomorrow brought with it Felicity in a snit over the new PA, a widening, budget black hole in Sydney, and a disc sitting on her desk. She squinted at the image on it. The TV show, *Warehouse 13*, appeared to be science fiction. Definitely not for her. And she definitely didn't have time for this. Not after those Sydney numbers.

She ignored the disc for most of the night. She also ignored the furtive looks Madeleine kept shooting her way, assessing whether the disc had moved position on her desk, no doubt. It made her more adamant not to watch the damned thing at all. She didn't have time for distracting nonsense.

At ten, she called Amir to bring the car around to take her home. She picked up the disc, intending to drop it on Madeleine's desk with a stern warning of "no more".

Instead, she saw the hopefulness in the woman's green eyes, her gaze fixed on Elena's fingers clutching the disc. Pressing her lips together, she bit back her first response, slid the disc in her handbag, and said nothing as she left for the evening.

And if there was a small, relieved sigh behind her, she chose not to notice it.

The next day, an eager gaze met hers. Elena ignored it, went into her office, and dropped her handbag on the desk. She didn't want to start a long conversation about the magnificence of a smart, entrancing, nineteenth-century woman in gorgeous steampunk vests.

She particularly didn't want to hear an I-told-you-so. It was bad enough having to admit that Madeleine's enraging fashion insult the day they'd met had actually been a compliment.

She reached into her bag, pulled out the disc, and headed over to Madeleine's desk, where she slapped it down. "Acceptable," she said, in a tone that brooked no further discussion. After pivoting swiftly on heel, Elena returned to her office, relieved at putting an end to the conversation before it even started. She really was much too busy. As she settled into her seat, she glanced back at Madeleine and paused in her tracks.

The young woman's expression was pure delight.

Elena's heart did an embarrassing, pleased little flip at having put that look on Madeleine's face. She clenched her jaw. This was absurd. She shouldn't care what Madeleine Grey thought of anything. She was just an occasionally interesting employee.

Her brain blew her a raspberry.

Several nights later, Madeleine slid a plate of crisp, golden pastries on her desk. "Try them," she said, sounding cheerful. "They're my homemade apple tarts. You'll thank me."

Did her persistence know no bounds?

"I don't think I'd thank the extra three-hour workout required if I do," Elena replied, although in truth they smelled delicious.

"Workout, huh? Go on, just one. I'll give the rest to Sofia. She deserves some perks cleaning up after the slobs in this office."

"That is true." Elena contemplated the tempting little bundles.

Madeleine reached over and snagged a pastry herself and took a large bite. Her eyes rolled back in her head. "Mmm." Her eyes held a wicked gleam.

"You know, it's customary not to eat one's gifts for someone."

"Just proving they aren't poisoned. Come on. Just a bite."

In spite of all her internal protestations, Elena succumbed. *Oh.* Her taste buds did an ecstatic tap dance at the divine sensations.

Apple, raisins, and cinnamon flavours burst across her mouth, and she forced herself not to make the obscene sounds of appreciation she was dying to. This clinched it. Madeleine's cooking was better than sex—which wasn't saying much given how overrated she'd found the bedroom activity to be. These bundles of bliss were like embracing heaven. Or, as she finally told Madeleine when she could talk again, "they have a certain appeal". If by appeal she meant kissed by the gods.

That unfortunate admission had proved a mistake. The woman clearly felt the need to gloat.

"Knew it." Madeleine beamed at her. "You're a hardcore, secret carbs fan. I make spicy cheese sticks you'd love. Tomorrow night?"

Elena almost quivered at the thought. However she offered her firmest head shake. "Absolutely not."

Madeleine's joy dipped a little.

"I won't be here," Elena said, baffled at her sudden need to explain. "I have meetings. It's time to pull the *Style International* teams into line. They're not sharing their copy as much as they should. It's blowing out the costs. What's the point of having sister publications if you don't content share? I mean really."

"Ah, I see. These are the things that keep you up at night?" Madeleine munched on her pastry.

"No. These are things easily fixed. What keeps me up at night…" She paused and realised she'd been seconds away from revealing something personal to a woman she barely knew. "What keeps me up is how to get the obits writer to actually write her obits instead of playing chef."

A flicker of disappointment flared across Madeleine's face, but she still nodded. "I hear you. Let me find Sofia and then get back to work." She picked up the plate of treats and turned to go.

"Actually…" Elena reached forward and snagged another. "I'm sure Richard would appreciate one as well."

Madeleine eyed her for a moment and then smiled. "Right. For *Richard.*" She winked.

Elena gave her a withering glare, sighed, and waved her away. Great, now she *would* have to give it to her husband in order to prove Madeleine wrong. Damn she was maddening.

Nonetheless, a part of her, the part that was sometimes tired of feeling so isolated, was charmed at the young woman's attentions and attempts at conversation. With a sinking feeling, she realised it was getting more difficult to keep her at arm's length.

If she was being honest—and when wasn't she?—Elena allowed these talks because there were no witnesses. Because it was novel having someone not dislocate their spine in a craven need for her professional approval. It was rare being occasionally teased. It was especially different being talked to like a real person by someone who seemed to have no agenda beyond boredom.

If Madeleine was doing this in some misguided attempt to keep her job, she had to know by now that all Elena cared about was hard work and clear-cut results, not cooking and chit-chat. In fact, she was fairly sure Madeleine was not only well aware of that, but she didn't particularly care for her job in any event.

She also tolerated Madeleine's friendly overtures because the woman was honest about herself. It was irresistible, like a breath of fresh air after decades of enduring every acquaintance she'd ever had lying to suit their agendas. What agenda did this curious Australian have? Or was she, as her blog often suggested, merely lonely and lost? Did Madeleine actually even know why she did half of what she did?

"Why do you waste your time trying to know me? I won't be here in two weeks," Elena asked. "Shouldn't you be looking for a new roommate or some such thing?" She'd heard the entire Simon-returning-to-Sydney story by now.

"Sofia's heard all my stories. And she's stopped laughing at my jokes."

"So I'm...fresh meat?"

"I wouldn't put it quite like that."

"Oh, how would you put it?"

"Like...you're here and I'm here, and it's nice to have company sometimes. Don't you think?"

"I see."

Elena should really stop encouraging Madeleine by engaging with her. It wasn't fair. This rapport thing they shared was transient. She had to keep reminding herself it would be over soon. They'd each move on, and that would be that. No point forming attachments that would make the process messier.

Madeleine crossed the news room and offered her tray of treats to the fifty-something cleaner bustling past with a trolley full of dusters, cloths, and buckets. Even from her desk on the opposite side of floor, Elena could see how much the woman's face lit up. She gave Madeleine an engulfing, happy hug, exclaiming with delight.

Elena certainly understood the woman's reaction. Madeleine created food that could make the gods go weak at the knees. She sighed and slid her gaze back to her folders. Distractions were something she did not need this close to deadline on two critical deals.

Two nights later, a chai latte appeared, steaming, on Elena's desk. She didn't even bother to lift her head. "I am fairly sure I recall you telling me you weren't my PA."

"I'm not." Madeleine dropped into the visitor's chair opposite.

Elena frowned faintly at the presumption, which only made the other woman laugh.

"If I just do it randomly, not an order or obligation, wouldn't that make it taste better?" Madeleine asked. "Well, it's a working theory."

Elena reached for the cup and sipped. It tasted the same. "I'd keep working on that theory, Madeleine. Now if you don't mind..." She gestured at her work.

"Hey, call me Maddie. I won't tell. I mean, while I like that French way you say Madeleine, it's not really a name I answer to." She grinned.

What is she grinning about now? She did that a lot, now that Elena thought about it. Was Elena's company truly so amusing? Unlikely.

The woman remained in the seat, which was not the one at her desk, where she should be working. Elena contemplated ordering her back there. Instead she cleared her throat and dropped her pen. "Tell me, why are you even here?"

The reporter frowned a little and folded her arms. "How do you mean? I work the late shift. Or do you mean the paper? It was the first reporter job I could find here."

"I meant New York. You told me the day we met that you were 'making the most of things' here. It was a somewhat underwhelming endorsement of your life, if I recall."

"I...guess it was." Madeleine twiddled her fingers against her knee. "I really miss home. The beach, all my friends, the endless summer, double-chocolate Tim Tams, backyard cricket. It's opposite world here, lifestyle wise. But the truth is, I can't leave." She looked up and gave a tiny scowl.

"Why?"

"I feel too guilty not to be here."

A cautiousness entered her features, which Elena had not seen in a month. She found she missed the open face of the woman she usually conversed with. "Guilty?"

"Yes. I was originally studying to be a catering manager. I almost finished the course, before I admitted to myself I hated everything about it."

"Then why were you doing it?"

"My parents have their own catering business in South Penrith, Party to Go. I was supposed to take it over one day. And I tried. But I just... It was pointless. I can cook, sure, but I can't manage. I hate managing. Writing's my passion. My parents were devastated when I dropped out and switched to a journalism degree instead."

"So, how did you get from there to New York?" Elena asked.

"A year into my journalism studies, my uni friends were having a party, and we all got the genius idea while half sloshed to apply online for a green card in the lottery. The odds are so low that I went along with it." She gave a shrug. "I'd forgotten all about it until almost two years later. My mates were at my place and moaning about the fact they'd just found out that they missed out. I admitted I hadn't even looked on the visa site where they post the names. They demanded I check right then and there, so..." She shook her head. "I mean it was crazy. Only fifty-thousand people are chosen from all over the world and yet... I logged in and there it was. My name. Marked as eligible."

"Oh dear," Elena drawled.

"Yeah." Maddie gave her a wry look. "My friends were screaming with excitement. Even my girlfriend at the time was so jealous, despite the fact she hates to travel. And my parents were all, 'Well, I suppose if you're going to turn your back on the family business, we understand at least if you go to New York. That's a once-in-a-lifetime opportunity'. So I felt..." She bit her lip.

"Obligated?" Elena asked. Her brain circled back to *girlfriend*. Did she mean...? Yes, she was fairly sure she did mean it that way. That might also explain those Latvian lesbian music nymphs. Or not.

"Yes." Madeleine slid deeper into her chair. "How could I tell them I didn't want that dream? Who comes to New York and isn't thrilled? Every day I felt like a fraud."

"Do you still?" Elena asked, already aware of the answer.

A cloud crossed Madeleine's face. She didn't answer; merely shrugged. The helpless look said it all.

"I see," Elena said. "You're doing a job in a city the whole world wishes to live in, and you're miserable?"

Madeleine didn't disagree. Her eyes met Elena's. "Not entirely. At least not...recently." The words were so soft, weighted with such meaning that every warning klaxon in Elena's body went off. She fidgeted with the papers in front of her, then fiddled with her pen, as she wondered what to say to that.

A jangling phone broke the tension, and Madeleine's brow puckered. "That's mine. Gotta get it. Enjoy your tea."

She bolted for her desk, her tight jeans and pale-green shirt a blur.

Elena sipped her tea, watching as Madeleine became all business, hunched over the phone at her desk, her pen busy. She was disconcerted by this woman she barely knew, who shared so much of herself. It was unthinkable. She couldn't imagine ever lowering her guard so much with anyone, even her husband, to share her real self. Madeleine really was like no one she'd ever met. Mystifying and full of contradictions. And what did she mean by saying she'd been miserable except for recently? It sounded very much like she meant their time together. Time that would soon be up.

Tilting her head, Elena could see the side of Madeleine's face and hear her conversation surprisingly well. The acoustics in her office were excellent, and it had allowed her to pick up a considerable amount of information about office politics.

Madeleine slammed down her phone, grabbed her jacket, and rammed her notebook into a shoulder bag. "I got a lead in Queens. Been chasing it for ages, and it's finally paid off. Gotta go," she called to her. "Catchya later."

Queens? "At *this* hour?"

"The only time he says he can do it. His mother's just left for her second job."

Mother? How old was he?

Elena bit back the words she most wanted to say. *Stay safe.* She was a media mogul, and Madeleine was her crime reporter. This was all part of what the woman did for a living. She didn't need coddling. Elena turned back to her work and resolved to think about it no more.

It was hardly her fault that her brain chose to ignore her.

BlogSpot: Aliens of New York

By Maddie as Hell

Bruno, the mechanic who runs a car repair shop next to my apartment building, once told me "when the world gets too overwhelming and things feel too big for us to fix, just change your little corner of it".

I tried to do that. I held a tearful young man's hand at one in the morning and made him a life-changing promise. I went home and wrote his story. In another day, it will belong to the world. What will the world make of it? Will it fix what's wrong or make a liar of me?

Bruno also says we should change our engine oil more often. Make of that what you will.

To change a corner of the world, click here: <u>Ramel Brooks Campaign</u>

CHAPTER 7

Inner Sanctum

Maddie hung up from Simon, who was packing in readiness to go home and realising he didn't have enough space for half the tourist junk he'd been buying for the past ten months. No, she didn't want to keep his Statue of Liberty flashlight or the freaking huge, yellow cushion in the shape of a New York cab. After fifteen minutes of haggling, she managed to convince him to pack almost all of his crap and haul it back home.

At the thought of home, she gave her snow dome a fond jiggle. She was dying to hit the beach and shake out her cobwebs. Shame it was all raincoat and boot weather here, or she'd have tried Orchard Beach in the Bronx. She'd have to wait a few months. Her phone rang again, and she glanced at her computer clock. Just past six.

"Hell, Maddie, it's *hell*!" Felicity said without a greeting. "I have to be in two places at once. And you're the only one in that cursed office whom I'm speaking to, aside from the obvious."

Maddie tried to pick that apart. "You need a favour."

"Yes, I need a favour, and I can't..." There was a pause, and Felicity called out to someone, "Can't you drive any faster? I have to be at the airport five minutes ago. Do you understand that? *Comprendes*? Christ..." Her sputtering breath returned closer to Maddie's ear.

Maddie rubbed her forehead. "Just tell me what you need."

"Right, yes! My desk, in the third drawer, there is a green USB drive. Do not touch anything else. You'll need to deliver it to her office."

Maddie frowned. She flicked her gaze to the empty, glass cubicle behind her. "Her office? But—"

"Yes! God, are you mentally impaired? Not that flea pit at your building, I mean Bartell Towers, obviously. Top floor. Do not give that

USB drive to anyone else, not security, not someone who claims to be an assistant, no one but *her*. Do you understand? I will throttle you if you give it to anyone but Elena. This is vital."

Maddie rolled her eyes. "Why me? I'm supposed to be writing the crime briefs right now. Can't you get one of her staff to do it? Like her driver or..." *Anyone but me.*

The thought of facing Elena again after having shared half her life story the previous night was unnerving. She didn't know why she'd revealed all that. Maddie had overshared like hell, then spent a sleepless night second guessing herself at how she must have sounded. How embarrassing. At least, this time, she'd been spared the painful "we're done" dismissal to remind her of her single-cell organism status in Elena's world. Regardless, it was probably best to give it a long as possible before seeing each other again.

"No!" Felicity said. " No one else can do this! I need someone who knows where my desk is so they won't spend half the night rummaging through everyone else's drawers. And I need someone with half a brain cell. You qualify, just *barely*. Okay? God, why are we debating this? I'd do it myself, but I have *Style Tokyo*'s editor-in-chief flying in, and I'm supposed to be there already to meet the flight. Mihoko Morita does not tolerate lateness! And Elena will skin me alive if she doesn't have that data in her hand in twenty minutes! She has half her empire on standby waiting for those figures to drop. Now—her driver will be downstairs waiting for you. So go! Hurry!"

Maddie's phone went dead. "You're welcome," she told thin air as she stared at the phone. Well, okay. She glanced at her outfit—black jeans, scuffed boots, an old Doors T-shirt, and a black leather jacket. If she'd known she'd be entering the Bartell Corp's inner sanctum today, she might have dressed up. Okay, maybe not, but she might have worn her nice boots at least.

She jumped to her feet and raced to Felicity's desk, wondering why her heart was thundering so hard. Was it adrenaline? Or just nervousness at seeing Elena on her home turf?

Once she located the USB stick, she rammed it into her jeans pocket, then grabbed her security pass and bolted down the stairs rather than waiting for an elevator. A sleek town car with a smartly dressed man beside the passenger door waited in front of the building.

"Ms Grey?" the man asked. "I am Ms Bartell's driver, Amir."

"Yes. We have to go to—" she began as she scrambled into the back seat.

"I know." He strode to the driver's side. "I'll have you at Bartell Towers in no time." He pulled out into the traffic. "Are you going to *Style New York's* office?"

"No. Why do you ask?"

"It's in the building. I drive a lot of models and designers there at all sorts of hours. Sometimes their photographers like to shoot at night."

"Oh? No. I'm not a model or a designer." Maddie laughed at the ridiculous suggestion. "I'm just dropping something off for Elena."

"You're meeting Ms Bartell?" He sounded intrigued.

"Yes," Maddie said, uncertain as to why that was unusual.

"*In* Ms Bartell's office?"

"Why?"

"How long have you been working with Ms Bartell?"

"Um, it'll be a month tomorrow. Why?"

He met her eye in the rear-view mirror and looked impressed. "I have driven her for a long time. It is not often people visit her there. Only her inner circle, or so I gather. So it's a bit unusual. That's all."

"Oh, well, it's an emergency. It was supposed to be Felicity."

"Ah, I see."

They lapsed into silence, as Amir picked up the pace through New York's well-lit streets.

Maddie became more and more anxious as the drive continued. Eventually, they pulled up before a gleaming round tower. "Is this..." The big *B* on the side of the building answered her question. "...it?"

"Yes, Ms Grey," Amir said. "I am instructed to wait for you. But feel free to take your time."

"Thanks." Maddie jumped out and headed through large rotating glass doors. A set of seven-foot-tall, glass security doors loomed in front of her.

The security guard beside it rose, eying her suspiciously.

"Maddie Grey to see Elena Bartell." She slid her fingers into her pocket to retrieve her security ID.

"Yes, Ms Grey, I was told you were on your way. Sign here." He examined her ID, as Maddie signed the visitor's book. He pushed a button. As the doors opened, the guard passed a silver card to her. "Insert this into the elevator next to the *EP* button."

"EP?"

"Express to penthouse. It's just below the *H* button." Before she could ask, he added, "For helipad."

Maddie nodded and tried to look cool about the fact she was visiting someone who owned a building with a helipad on it. She headed for the elevators he indicated and glanced around while she waited. No expense had been spared. The floors were polished marble. A series of sofas were black leather. The landscape art on the walls was sublime, probably the real deal.

The gleaming doors opened, and Maddie stepped inside. Soft, classical music was playing. Reflective, black glass surrounded her. She slid the card into the *EP* slot, and the whoosh was instant. The numbers flew by... 20, 25, 30, 35... Maddie's stomach dropped, and the soothing music failed to do its job. Finally, the elevator shuddered to a stop, and the doors slid open.

Maddie pulled the card out, pocketed it, and stepped forward.

Springy, luxurious carpet cushioned her boots. The elevator sat in the centre of the room, like a doughnut hole, ringed by a curving walkway. All around stretched a 360-degree view of New York. Frosted glass walls, coming out at right angles from the windows, divided the space into wedges.

Directly in front of her was one wedge containing a low, white leather sofa—a Mies van der Rohe reproduction. She recognised the iconic design from the one in Simon's dad's office. A pair of garment bags was slung over the back of the sofa. Two matching designer chairs faced it, and a low, glass coffee table, scattered with *Style NY* copies, sat in between.

An elegant, dark-skinned man in a stunning suit eyed her from the sofa, as she turned left and began her slow circle around the elevator. She shot him a smile, but he didn't return it, watching her progress with interest.

On her circuit, she walked past a kitchen. The next "wedge" had blacked-out glass walls and a door and was marked as a bathroom. Beyond that, she passed a twelve-seat boardroom table, with an enormous monitor on one wall, presumably for video meetings.

And finally... She came to Elena's office. Against the dividing glass wall to the right was a sleek, long bookcase bursting with books and magazines. In front of that sat a desk and a stylish, leather, designer chair in which Elena sat, angled towards the window. She had yet to notice Maddie's stealthy approach.

On the other side of the desk was a coffee table and, around that, three straight chairs, their backs to the window. Two of these were presently filled by a pair of men in expensive suits, holding large notepads and wearing anxious looks.

Maddie examined the rest of the office. The glass wall facing Elena had several framed newspaper front pages and iconic *Style* magazine covers affixed to it. Nestled in the far left corner, against the window, was a beautiful, Japanese silk partition—possibly a changing area of some sort. Maddie supposed Elena had to do many a quick wardrobe change at work before going to various events.

The executive chair swung around, and Elena met her eyes. Maddie was about to slide the USB stick onto the desk and say what is was, but Elena shook her head and pointed to beyond the opposite wall to the area to where she'd started her circuit. Where the elegant man in the fine suit sat.

A disembodied voice rang out from the phone on Elena's desk, alerting Maddie to the fact she was in the middle of a conference call. The man spoke French too fast for Maddie's high-school lessons to translate every word.

Elena frowned and jotted down some notes.

"C'est impossible! Votre date limite est ridicule!" she replied. Elena's gaze shifted to her underlings, who gave a vigorous pair of nods.

Maddie edged away, trying to get the gist of it. Something about an impossible deadline? She headed onwards to the next "wedge", and lowered herself into a chair opposite the man. His deep-green suit, mustard tie, and polished shoes were expensive, probably bespoke. He was billiard-ball bald, in his late-thirties or early forties, and manscaped to within an inch of his life. *Fashion designer maybe?* His eyes were intelligent and assessing, and he had high cheekbones that would put a supermodel to shame.

"I'm Maddie Grey," she said, after a moment.

"We meet at last. Perry Marks." His wide lips curled up in greeting.

"At last?"

"Felicity seems to think your outfits worthy of many entertaining monologues. But she's never said who you were. So you're important enough for her to rant about, but not important enough to give me details." He slid a critical gaze across her outfit and tapped his lip. "Hmm. So you're not a designer, not an executive..." His gaze trailed across her thighs, which were normal sized. "Definitely not a model."

"Hey!"

He smiled, and his white, perfect teeth, dazzling against his dark skin, almost blinded her. "It's rare for me to meet a regular woman in this building," he said with a cheeky grin. He patted his chest above his heart. "So I apologise if I'm in a state of shock. Anyway, I give up. What do you do?"

"I'm a junior crime reporter at *Hudson Metro News*."

"Ah, the little rag that's sucking all our fearless leader's attention. Getting an audience with Elena these days is like visiting the queen. Even for me. So...why are you here, Junior Crime Reporter?"

"Just doing a favour for Felicity. I have something to drop off." She held up the USB drive.

"So leave it here. I'll give it to her."

"Felicity vowed to flay me alive if I didn't deliver it to Elena personally."

"Ah. That does sound like the indomitable Ms Simmons."

Maddie laughed at that. "So, what do you do?"

He gave a rueful chuckle. "Ouch, my poor, poor ego. In my industry, everyone knows me. I'm *Style International*'s global art director. If it's trendy and fashionable, then I was the one who helped make it so."

"Seriously?"

"Scout's honour."

"Votre attitude est décevante. Je ne suis pas ouverte au compromis." The burst of French from Elena was loud enough to travel to where they sat. Something about a bad attitude and no compromise? Maybe?

"She shouldn't be too much longer," Perry said in a hushed voice, leaning forward. "She's insulting the man's professionalism. When she gets to threatening to reduce his budget, too, she'll be done. Or she'll just fire him." He lifted his broad shoulders as if unsure which and not caring either way. Then he tugged at his cuff to straighten his jacket back to perfection.

"Oh," Maddie said back in a whisper. "Who is she threatening?"

"*Style Paris* has just signed an insanely overpaid, rising-star model, which has blown their annual budget by twenty percent. To make matters worse, the girl boasted about the size of the deal all over social media, so there is no face-saving way to cancel it and pretend it never happened. Even if there were, *Style Paris*'s new hot-head editor won't replace her and thinks suggestions he do so are 'interference by *Américains imbéciles*'. It will end badly if he doesn't get it through his thick skull who he's dealing with. Elena could blacklist him and make it so he'd only ever be able to work in retail in Iceland. Which would be a shame, because I rather like Iceland."

"She cares a lot about her fashion magazines, doesn't she?" Maddie says. "I mean, *Style* is not just another masthead to her, is it? It's what she loves, right?"

Perry studied her curiously. "You really don't know her, do you?"

"I'd like to," Maddie said earnestly. She paused as she wondered why that was. Why had she been trying so hard to get to know her boss? So much so, she'd probably made an idiot of herself by oversharing yesterday. She bit her lip. *Because Elena is fascinating*, her brain whispered to her. *And beautiful. And a mystery. And I love to unpick a mystery. I want to know who she is and how she thinks about anything and everything. I want to know her.*

Perry hadn't replied, as if sensing there was more.

"But no, I don't really know her," Maddie continued. "I mean, I haven't known her long. I just want to know who she is when she's not playing a god. You know?"

"What if I said she's not playing? Would you believe it?" Perry leaned forward.

Maddie couldn't work out if he was joking. "I'd say she's good but not that good."

Perry laughed and leaned back again. "True. Or perhaps it's a matter of perspective." He studied her for a moment. "Do you know that everyone asks me about her because we're good friends? They all try to find out about the businesswoman. What makes her tick? Who does she favour politically? Their reasons are clear. But in twenty years, you're the first person who actually sounds sincere when asking me about the woman behind the power. No ulterior motive."

"Really?" That was both startling and depressing. Who wouldn't want to know the real Elena?

"Yes, really. So I will tell you her secret." Perry gave her a tiny smile. "Well, it's not such a secret if you watch her for as long as I have. Anyway, the thing about Elena is fashion always comes first."

"Fashion." Maddie gave him a sceptical look. "Seriously?"

"Absolutely. Oh, she might deny it and talk about her media vision, but it's not what drives her." He waved his hand towards Elena's office. "She is a woman in love with beauty in all its forms. Those who propose a project that offends her sensibilities because it is ugly get cut loose. Because Elena sees herself as a curator of beauty, first and foremost. People who don't understand that, don't understand her."

Astonished, Maddie stared at him. She ordered her thoughts. "That's just... It makes no... Okay, well let me tell you something. There's an eighteen-year-old kid I'm doing a story on. Ramel Brooks. He was hanging out at his friends' place when the drug squad raided. Ramel, unlike his druggie mates, is a straight-A student, with a college scholarship lined up. But after everyone got arrested, his loser friends all claimed they were innocent and that Ramel was a big-time drug dealer. Now they got cut loose and he's carrying the can for all of them."

Perry frowned. "I don't see what your story has to do with Elena."

"I had to look into this kid's eyes while he told me, voice shaking, that every day he sees his mother's doubts in him. She wonders if Ramel did it, and that's what's breaking him—more than the betrayal of his friends, the dodgy charges, or the threat of years in jail. Stuff like this is what I see in my job. Life is so bleak for some people. And my working day is sharing that bleakness. Truth is, news is mostly just slickly packaged pain. It's ugly and depressing. When my story runs tomorrow, people aren't going to say, 'Oh, how beautiful'. They'll say 'Sucks to be Ramel'. So how can Elena see beauty in the news? I don't get it. If what you say is true, how can she even be in this line of work?"

Perry's gaze turned thoughtful. "Look, when you see a newspaper, you see its content. The good, the bad, whatever. Elena doesn't see that. She sees the basic beauty in what she has built. Your sad little story is just a cog in a news machine that she has remade so efficiently that to her it all becomes art."

"Art?" Maddie gaped at him. "Come on, that's crazy."

"No, that's *business.* At its core, it doesn't matter what you produce— if it's made well and effective, to the person who designed it, it will be beautiful."

"Tu es viré!" came a bark from the next room. A phone slammed down.

Funny how she hadn't even raised her voice, but her lethal tone sent a chill down Maddie's spine.

Perry's head tilted. "Hmm. Well, I suppose that was inevitable."

"She just fired him," Maddie said, slowly deciphering the words. "The French editor."

"Mm. She will do worse to him than that."

The executives were now filing out, and the rat-a-tat of Elena's demands drifted over. "See that Marcel never works for any of my publications again. Meanwhile, find out if Stan has shifted his stance on selling those six titles. I saw him at Martha's Vineyard recently, and it's in his eyes. He wants to retire and play golf. So, send him a membership for whatever the closest five-star course is. It'll eat him up that he can't play because business is interfering. All right. We're done." There was a pause. "Perry!"

"My cue." He rose, picked up the two garment bags resting on the sofa, and strolled towards the office.

At the opening to her office, he greeted Elena warmly and then unzipped the top bag. Their murmurings reached Maddie's straining ears. Something about an upcoming ball and several famous designers. She leaned forward, craning her neck to see around the frosted glass wall that separated them. Luckily they were still only barely inside Elena's office. A flash of glitter caught Maddie's eye, as Perry lifted a dazzling blue dress from the first bag.

"Absolutely not," Elena said. "I'll look like a mirror ball. Show me the other one."

Perry shifted out of sight, and when he reappeared, he was now holding a deep red dress. He waved it about with a flourish.

Maddie craned to see it better and was leaning almost horizontal to the seat now. *Oh. Oh wow.* That would look incredible on Elena.

"Mm. Acceptable. And I like this shade of scarlet. Well, more garnet, really, isn't it? Give me a moment. Let me try it on."

Elena stepped farther into her office, now out of Maddie's line of sight. Probably to change behind the Japanese screen in the corner that Maddie had seen earlier. Perry was still by the door, sliding the blue dress back into its garment bag.

A few minutes later, Elena spoke, her voice too low for Maddie to hear, and Perry spun around. She could see only a slice of his back and nothing of her boss. Damn it.

"Gorgeous." He sounded impressed. He took a step backwards, back into Maddie's line of sight. "Better lighting by the door," he said. "Can you step forward? Oh yes. Turn? I need to see the cut at the back."

A flash of red swirled into view and then was gone.

Maddie wanted to groan in frustration. And now her straining neck was hurting.

"Yes. Perfect," Perry said.

"Heels?"

"In the bag. A besotted offering from Stuart Quinz. Personalised. You'll see."

A rustle sounded, and then came a low, feminine purr of approval that made Maddie swallow hard.

"Oh my. Please thank Stuart. Now the dress...whose is it? Duchamp? Or someone else? If I'm to be catapulting some new designer into the stratosphere by wearing it, tell me it's someone worthy at least."

"You were right the first time. Véronique Duchamp."

"Ah," Elena said. "Perfection as always. All right. Good choice, not that she needs more publicity. But her dress will do nicely."

"Excellent." Perry took another step backwards and was now outside of the office. He reached forward, fingers wiggling. "I have to say, the flow from the bust is sublime."

Maddie leaned far off her chair, desperate for a peek at the "sublime" bust in question. She lost her war on gravity, and, after a comical three seconds trying to stop herself from falling, her thud was both loud and humiliating. She scrambled to her knees.

"What on earth...?" Elena stepped out of her office, hands on hips, and pinned Maddie with a cool stare.

Maddie gazed up at the vision before her. The dress was...*oh*. Perry wasn't wrong. It clung to every curve. It was gorgeous. Stunning. And the bust? *Oh God. Wow.* The garment's cleavage went all the way down to Elena's stomach, showing a tantalising triangle of smooth, flawless skin. Maddie could see the swell of bare breast from either side of the dress, and her mouth went dry. She slid her gaze higher and caught an incredulous look on Elena's face.

"Um, hi?" Maddie pulled herself to her feet.

"Am I to take it from this dramatic display that you approve, too?" Elena asked.

Maddie blushed, lost for words. She nodded.

Perry laughed. "It must be good, she's robbed of speech." His eyes twinkled, and he turned back to Elena. "No adjustments needed. I'll leave it with you and make my escape. You can have fun repairing Ms Grey's stunted vocabulary." He gave Maddie a wink, gathered the "mirror ball" blue dress, now stuffed back in its garment bag, and headed for the elevator.

"It's so stunning," Maddie said, still transfixed. "Who is Véronique Duchamp?"

"Perhaps the world's greatest designer," Elena replied, "which you'd know if you had even the slightest interest in fashion." She spun around and went back to her office.

Maddie followed. She rounded the corner and found the media boss standing at the window, staring out.

"How can anyone get to be as old as you are...what, mid-twenties?... and fail to grasp even the basics of fashion?" Elena asked the glass in front of her.

Maddie thought about what Perry had said, that people who didn't acknowledge the part of Elena that loved fashion failed in her eyes. She wondered how to answer the question truthfully.

"Fashion speaks to everyone differently. I mean, while it never really interested me—"

"I'm shocked." Elena's tone was mocking but contained amusement too.

Maddie shoved her hands in her jeans pockets, her gaze sliding over the beautiful back before her. The scoop in the back of her dress ended just above the curve of her ass. It was exquisite. The dress, not her ass. Actually, no. Both were. "But it doesn't mean I can't appreciate the beauty of fashion. Especially when it's right in front of me."

There was a silence, and Maddie lifted her eyes, finding Elena had been watching her in the window's reflection. Their gazes locked.

"And how do you know what beauty is if you don't understand the most basic thing about style?"

"I have eyes." It came out more as an exhale, and Maddie saw surprise in Elena's reflection.

Maddie glanced down, unsure what she was doing, because she sure as hell couldn't be flirting with Elena Bartell. That would be insane. She noticed a silver frame on Elena's desk. Between pictures of powerful billionaires and elite fashion designers was a photograph of Elena with her husband. She stared at it. At him. His expression was so predatory. Why did the smug bastard always look so hungry? In every online photo she'd ever seen, he always looked the same.

Out of her periphery, she saw Elena turn from the window and notice what Maddie was looking at.

Elena's face shifted from intrigued to cool. "So...you don't look Japanese." Her voice was now all business.

"Uh...no?"

"The next visitor I expected in here was Mihoko Morita. Unless *Style Tokyo*'s editor-in-chief has become an Australian with a cult-band fetish, you are not her."

"Oh, well, I think Felicity's picking her up right now. That's why I'm here, not her. She asked me to drop this off." Maddie put the USB stick on Elena's desk.

"Playing courier? But I thought you were a reporter. Isn't that what you keep telling me?" She gave Maddie a dissecting look.

"It sounded like an emergency," Maddie said. "Soooo...uh...you're welcome."

She fidgeted. It was weird being in here, in the inner sanctum, seeing how powerful Elena really was. The way the executives had bowed and scraped on their way out. Elena had her own driver and a fancy luxury car and a *helipad*, for God's sake, probably with an actual helicopter parked on it. And that dress she was wearing? If it wasn't worth five figures, she'd be shocked.

Elena studied her for a few moments. "Ah," she said, eyes glinting. "And now you see."

"See what?"

"It's unsettled you seeing me here." Her tone was wry. "Well, you don't have to remain, since it makes you uncomfortable." She gave her fingers a flick in Maddie's direction, her lips drawing down. She fiddled with some paperwork on her desk. It was incongruous since she was still wearing her killer red dress. Garnet dress. Whatever.

"You're wrong."

"What?" Elena lifted her head.

"I mean yes, sure, this place is...well, it's..."

"*Pretentious*, you can say it." Elena's eyes sparkled.

"I mean, yes, this office is all business. But that's not you."

"Oh? And who am I? You think you now know?"

"No, not yet. But I do know this—this place might be your life, but it's not you. This is just where you rule the world from. Nothing else."

"*Nothing else*? Surely ruling the world is more than that?" Elena scrutinised her. "Do you think so little of what I do?"

"No! Yes. I mean... I didn't intend it that way, and you know it."

"Do I?" Elena's gaze was intense. "You know what they call me, don't you? All the names? Not to mention all the ruthless things I'm supposed to have done? The rumours are not without foundation."

"Of course I know what they say. Even if it's all true, that's not my point. They've left out stuff, haven't they? You're not your image. Like, I know you sent Josie home to be with her kid. You didn't do it because you thought she was infectious."

Elena gave her a cool look. "Betting on my humanity is not a safe bet, Madeleine."

"I'll take that bet anyway." Maddie lifted her chin. She was met with disbelief, and smiled. Without waiting for a reply, she spun on her heel and headed for the elevator.

The doors opened, and a handsome man stepped out, passing her.

Maddie's step briefly faltered, as she recognised Elena's husband. Her neck craned up. The man was impossibly tall.

"Oh, hello." An assessing gaze drifted over Maddie. It lingered. "I didn't know Elly had company."

Elly? Ugh. Maddie turned her attention back to the media boss. Elena's jaw tightened. Maybe she didn't like the nickname, either. Or the way he was fixated on Maddie's chest.

"Richard?" Elena asked. "Why are you here?"

"I was in the neighbourhood." He finally stopped staring at Maddie's curves and turned. "Thought I'd see if you're free. But, honey, what a perfect dress." He gave a low, dirty chuckle. "Lemme have some of that."

He strode over to her, slid his arms around her, pivoted her around, and gave her a sudden, thorough kiss. As he did so, he kept his gaze firmly fixed on Maddie, who was frozen to the spot.

Whatever he saw on her face seemed to amuse him. He pointedly slid his hand to his wife's ass and gave it a possessive squeeze.

Maddie shot into the elevator, sparing herself the vision of whichever of Elena's body parts Richard was going to brand next with his wandering hands.

Clearly, Elena's taste in dresses did not extend to husbands.

CHAPTER 8

Miss Bartlewski

Elena leaned back in her Philippe Starke designer chair, having changed into her original outfit, the garnet dress now back in its bag. Gazing out the window, she contemplated plaguing Felicity for an ETA on Mihoko. Perhaps she should spare her chief of staff a meltdown; Felicity was highly strung enough.

She couldn't focus, thanks to Richard's over-the-top PDA. Why he still felt the need to fawn all over her in public mystified her. It made her uncomfortable.

Elena assumed it was because he liked to show off his prize catch. She was well aware that her wealth and status made certain men, like Richard, prone to crass preening—but she thought the novelty would have worn off by now, four years on. Tonight, she'd ordered him home only to look over his shoulder and discover the *Hudson Metro News's* junior crime reporter had also disappeared.

The memory of Madeleine's guileless defence of Elena's humanity also plagued her. The girl was wrong, of course. Elena was ruthless when needed, and that was necessary. Without her tiger shark alter ego, she'd have been eaten alive in business years ago. These days, she slipped into the persona without thought. That Madeleine insisted on trying to find something more was...unsettling.

She hated this feeling. Elena had no time for wide, trusting eyes that seemed to beg friendship from her. No time for cute, clever wordplays that blurred the lines between admiration and something else.

Did Madeleine Grey truly not understand? Didn't she grasp what she was in Elena's world? An employee. A disposable one at that, who—just like all the others who didn't meet expectations—could be discarded at any time, if business required it.

Clearly, this was her own fault. Elena had been too lax, allowing the young woman to see more of her than she should. She should have snapped Madeleine back into line weeks ago. Why hadn't she? Why had she allowed a rapport to develop between them, knowing the fate that awaited?

Because she was interesting company, the little voice at the back of her brain whispered. Because she treated Elena like a woman worth getting to know, not a powerful contact to cultivate. Because the curious Australian was one of the few people on earth who seemed to genuinely like being around Elena. And, deny it as she might, because it made no sense at all, the feeling was mutual.

Even so, for all Madeleine's earnest speeches, she had no clue at all who Elena really was. But to be fair, who did? Not even her oldest friend, Perry, or her past or current husbands knew the whole truth.

She closed her eyes and remembered back to a time she preferred to forget. She'd been born Elena Zofia Bartlewski, into a life no one would want. Poverty had its own smell, she'd often thought. It was rising damp, rotting waste, and urine, mixed in with shattered booze bottles, cigarette butts, and human despair.

Her grandparents, who had fled Poland during the rise of the Nazis, had made a new life in New York, where Elena was born. She'd grown up with her parents, grandmother, and three brothers, above her uncle's run-down tailor shop in Greenpoint, Brooklyn. She'd hated her life and the stifling expectation she would one day work in a local garment factory.

As she entered her teenage years, she knew she would be nothing like the worn-out, sallow-cheeked neighbours she passed each day. Elena had places to go and ambitions to accomplish. She would be a *someone* one day. She'd show all those stupid, cruel children at school, who mocked her name, her faint Polish accent acquired from years spent at the knee of her live-in grandmother, or her too-big, hand-me-down shoes.

Her mother had taught her to sew at an early age, and she enjoyed it, but her design eye truly flourished the day she stumbled upon some discarded, glamorous fashion magazines. She'd scoured them for every detail, her eye darting from the unique cuts of the bold styles to their stitching and fabric flow.

Her heart pounded furiously. Faster even than that day Jenny Copeland had kissed her on the cheek and called her pretty before sliding her hand to Elena's waist and squeezing.

Oh yes, Elena Bartlewski, gaze locked on fashions the likes she'd never seen before, at that moment knew exactly where her life would lie. She would run a magazine like this one day. She would leave behind this grinding, grey life and her mother's and grandmother's depressing existence spent taking in their neighbours' washing. The world was bigger than dirty old buildings, peeling paint, and graffitied walls. Bigger than mouldy rented apartments cursed with leaking pipes and cracked walls.

So, she planned. Elena continued at school, ignoring countless offers to date the neighbourhood boys, their hair slicked back and eyes gleaming as they stared at her suddenly developing chest.

At age seventeen, an advertisement in one of the big papers caught her eye, and she could barely dare to hope. She dressed in her best outfit—she'd made it herself from design ideas sourced from an impressive, new American magazine called *CQ. Catwalk Queen.* The glossy publication needed an assistant to the deputy features editor. Elena didn't have any of the qualifications they listed, and she was too young, but she desperately wanted the job.

The interview had been curious. On the one hand, the lady with the expensive perfume and designer suit had taken one look at Elena's threadbare résumé and almost thrown her out of the office. But as her manicured fingers hovered her application over what appeared to be a towering reject pile, she suddenly asked Elena: "Why fashion? Why us?"

Elena's entire being felt lit up as she explained. She began with the dreamhow fashion crossed countries, divides, ideologies. How even poor Jewish girls could see the same wonder of an exquisitely cut ensemble as a rich socialite in Manhattan. How, at the end of the day, fashion was transcendent...like music or great art. It needed to be celebrated. She added how it had changed her life by giving her a dream of her own. And, for good measure, she mentioned, in passing, that she'd run the fashion publishing world one day.

The interviewer, a poised woman in her forties with a shock of white-blonde hair, promptly dropped Elena's résumé back on her desk, staring at her, open-mouthed. "Where *did* you come from?" Then she peered at Elena's dress. "And where, pray tell, did you get *that*? I do not recognise the label. And I pride myself on knowing them all."

Elena launched into enthusiastic detail, explaining how she quite liked the cut of Pierre Cardin's new women's suits and had incorporated that flair across the shoulder and bust, but felt the style of Hubert de Givenchy was more interesting and classic, so she'd based most of her outfit on his latest design on page 124 of *CQ*'s March issue.

"Although," she continued after inhaling quickly, "the Givenchy in *Vogue,* on page 76, was probably more engaging to the masses, with the longer cut and clever use of contrasting tones, but the one in the *CQ* issue was *definitely* more classic. There was no comparison in the end."

Elena had stopped and sat back uncertainly when the other woman ceased breathing, and she'd wondered if it was somehow wrong to take inspiration from famous designers. She had blushed then. Maybe she'd made a dreadful faux pas, because who was she? A poor seventeen-year-old girl who hemmed rich people's clothes after school for petty cash. And, oh God, maybe it was tacky that she'd taken elements from more than one designer and fused them to create a whole new look. Was that not done?

She swallowed and contemplated crawling out then and there, before things got any more humiliating.

The other woman seemed to read her mind. "Stop fidgeting. You will not go anywhere. Now, you are completely unqualified for the job you applied for..."

Devastation washed over Elena. It was so overwhelming that she gasped.

The interviewer lifted her hand and continued, "…but so help me, I will not let you leave these doors without being on my staff somewhere. Let me talk to Human Resources. Don't move an inch."

And that was the day Elena Bartlewski entered the world of publishing. Initially, she was a personal assistant to Clarice Montague, the woman who had just interviewed her. A woman she later learned was a brilliant editor. Clarice would drill into Elena the need for excellence in all things.

By her twentieth birthday, Elena Bartlewski was no more. Elena Bartell was born, and that byline appeared on her well-researched and increasingly prolific fashion features. She became features editor at twenty-two, under Clarice's guiding hand and much to the shock of many more seasoned staff.

By twenty-four, she'd acquired the appropriate accessory for every ambitious young woman in the late nineties—a husband. It went with the shoulder pads, charcoal business suits, and pastel blouses. Clarice told her it would stop any whispers about where her interests might lie. The suggestion there might even be rumours had shocked her, because she'd had no time to date anyone. Still, business was business. So she'd proposed to Spencer Fielding, the up-and-coming *CQ* books editor, during her lunch break one day. He'd looked at her, startled, over his glasses, and blurted out, "Yes, of course."

Spencer had a few rumours of his own he'd wanted put to rest, she found out later.

It was a perfectly bland pairing, not lit by excitement in or out of bed, but, well, that was marriage, wasn't it? After the first month, they didn't even bother with the marital bed. She'd never understood what the fuss was about on that score. And if she ever felt the tendril of desire for someone else or noticed the sensuous curve of a model's neck or a well-shaped female backside, that was something else she pushed aside. Business came first. Ruling the world meant sacrifices. It meant you did not get distracted. You certainly did not explore *certain things*, no matter how tempting.

By twenty-five, she was being groomed to take over for her retiring mentor as editor-in-chief of *CQ*, destined to become the world's youngest fashion editor. She would be the toast of the town. Adoring, doting, and ambitious designers would arrive from all corners of the world to kiss her feet. She would win it all.

Except that never happened.

Clarice died, suddenly, as her blackened lungs gave out after all those classic long-handled cigarettes, and Elena's anointing instead turned into a power struggle.

Emmanuelle Lecoq. Even her name filled Elena with loathing to this day. Elena had resigned a month after the job she was meant to have was stolen from under her nose.

The day Clarice died with her beautiful LV heels firmly on, everything changed. No one else knew, but she'd left Elena a collectible, black Hermes bag along with a note, *It's all yours now.* Inside were all the documents pertaining to the *CQ* shares Clarice had acquired over the years in bonuses and stock options. She had bequeathed them to Elena.

So Elena found Tom Withers, a brilliant accountant and business manager, and through him cashed the shares in slowly over twelve months, to ensure *CQ*'s stock didn't plummet. She began a small company she called Bartell Corporation. And because he was no longer needed, she dispensed with the husband.

Spencer had merely shrugged, packed a suitcase, and banked her divorce settlement cheque. She hadn't seen him since, except when he bobbed up to promote his latest novel in her newsfeeds. Elena didn't miss him in the slightest. She had no doubt the sentiment was mutual.

Bartell Corp was just the start. It was her ambition to go global. One of her earliest investors told her she operated just like a tiger shark. The tiger shark, the man explained, was the garbage disposal unit of the ocean, which could eat anything and not only survive it, but thrive.

It was true; many of the papers she acquired were junk, which was why she could buy them so cheaply. But more often than not, they all had something that was unique or worth salvaging. Elena became adept at sifting through the newspaper entrails, extracting the treasure, and tossing the rest aside. And as the years passed, Tiger Shark stuck. Not to mention a few other, less savoury, nicknames.

By twenty-seven, she had made her first million by flipping some bargain-basement newspapers into something worthier. By twenty-eight, she had enough cash flow to start a global fashion magazine to rival *CQ*. *Style International*. And by thirty-five, she'd conquered New York and half the rest of the print media in the US. That was when they named her *Time*'s Person of the Year.

When she called her mother, wondering if maybe her family had not heard the news, the older woman seemed more interested in telling Elena about Wit's new fiancée. As though her younger brother's banal love life was somehow the equivalent of Elena dominating the US publishing world in just one decade.

Her mother compounded the awfulness of the moment by adding—with an even more wistful tone—that it was high time Elena started dating again. Even Jenny Copeland was now "dating that nice boy, Billy Day, the baker's son, around the corner".

A cold prickle shot down Elena's spine. Her mother, despite her good points, had all the perceptiveness of a wet sock. So why had she mentioned Jenny?

By the time she hung up, Elena was in no mood to celebrate anything. She opened a bottle of Château Lafite Rothschild Pauillac 2010 in her latest penthouse apartment—this one overlooked the Hudson—and sat alone, in the dark, watching the boat lights go by, as she drank it all.

Elena had married Richard the following year. Not for her mother. No, it was just that he was so, well, suitable. He wasn't terrible company. A lawyer and a healthcare executive. He travelled the world. He had prospects. He could network like no one she'd ever seen. All that charm and all those connections? Watching him in full flight, she had come to see how it was done.

She'd learned a lot. Like how Emmanuelle Lecoq had beaten her so well. No one would beat her that way ever again. So when Richard, a man of the few skills she did not possess, asked her to marry him, his eyes aglow as though Elena was a delectable merger proposition, she'd immediately said yes.

He was, she supposed, adequate in the bedroom. Better than Spencer, at least, in that he had some interest in her. She felt no fireworks, though, not that she had expected any. But Richard was constant and clever, sharp, and bitingly funny. She had come to appreciate him. He understood ambition. He didn't sneer at the excitement she felt at her newest acquisition. No, he would help her celebrate with that same look in his eye he'd had when he married her. Power was his ultimate turn-on.

BlogSpot: Aliens of New York

By Maddie as Hell

The loneliest place on earth, I think, is the New York subway after midnight. Not just for people like me, finishing their late shifts, who stare with tired, empty eyes out the window, drawing into themselves, tighter and tighter. It's the others. The people who have nowhere else to be. They are there for the warmth or the escape. See, once you get off a train, you have to have a purpose. A destination. But on a train, you can just sit and contemplate with no pressure to do anything.

Sometimes I think I've spent too long just sitting, watching the shadows flash by at speed, not excited to get off and be wherever I'm supposed to be. It's easy to be a passenger. Life is about purpose, not sitting still. It's a shock to realise I allowed my whole existence to become something to be watched from a worn-out train seat.

I started really noticing the colours outside last week. When had they become brighter?

And today, I woke up and couldn't wait to get on with my day. I had a story I was proud of in print, an idea for a follow-up that could make a difference, and someone fascinating who I'm looking forward to seeing again.

I examined myself in the bathroom mirror and didn't recognise who looked back. I think I've been too long riding the rails, watching the world through windows. High time to get off the train.

What are you doing to me, New York? Playing with my affections like this? I may even start liking you if you keep this up.

CHAPTER 9

Collateral Damage

As Maddie dropped her bag at her desk the next day, Lisa bustled up. She nudged her in the ribs and plopped her curvy ass on Maddie's desk.

"Hey," the secretary said, "that was a great story this morning. The kid on the drugs charges? It really impressed Dave, and *nothing* impresses our boss."

"Cool," Maddie said with a grin. "I'm glad."

"I really liked that you started and ended it with the same line—*'Tell Momma I didn't do it'.* It was...artistic."

Maddie shook her head in disbelief. "Last night someone tried to tell me that the news machine could be beautiful, and today you say my story was artistic." She laughed. "You're all mad."

"Oh, hon, it was classy. I liked it. Take the compliment, okay? Cos you won't get too many around here."

"I didn't do it for the kudos, though. The kid has a college scholarship riding on this. He just needs good lawyer money now."

"The FundMeNow campaign you mentioned in your article should help." Lisa nodded. "I chipped in ten bucks this morning."

"That's great. He's a good kid. He's scared and feels so alone. It took courage for him to speak to me."

"Dave says the day shift is following it up. There's talk of an internal investigation into the charges. They look fishy."

"That's what I was saying! Way I see it is the drug squad sees Ramel as collateral damage. Like, they're not stupid, they probably know he didn't do any of it, but they're just letting his buddies go free so they relax and they can follow them to the drug suppliers or something. In the meantime, though, Ramel loses his scholarship."

Lisa nodded. Silence fell, but still she stayed, fiddling with her wedding ring and looking pensive. That was weird because this was now the longest conversation Maddie had ever had with the woman.

"I...actually...*we* need a favour," Lisa said.

"Oh?"

"I know you said you wouldn't help before, but this is serious. We need you to get us the latest gossip on Bartell. Something's going down. She's had wall-to-wall suits in with her all morning, and it looks serious. I've tried talking to that stuck-up pit bull of hers, the blonde with the fangs and bun hair, but all I got was that we'd find out in 'due course'."

"Felicity is an acquired taste." Maddie wondered why she was defending a woman who said horrendous things but always acted as if she'd said something perfectly reasonable. Maybe she was growing on her.

"So you'll find out for us what all the fuss is, okay?" Lisa pressed. "We're counting on you. And Stan and I need to know if I should be looking for a new job real soon."

Fear was clear on her face, as was a hint of desperation, willing Maddie to agree. It felt wrong to use her personal connection like this. Besides, Elena would probably ignore any business questions she put to her. Rightly so. It was presumptuous to even ask. So Maddie should just say n—

"Please? I've seen the way Bartell watches you. She does it a lot. I think she hates you the least of any of us. You're our best hope."

She watches me? Madeleine bit her lip and then sighed. "I'll try." Hope leaked from Lisa's expressive brown eyes, and Maddie's heart sank. "Lisa, I can't promise anything."

"I know. Just ask. That's all we want. Into the dragon's *boca* you go. You can do it! You went into Queens in the middle of the night for your interview, right? If anyone can get the dirt, it's you." With that, she sashayed back to her desk, shooting several milling reporters the thumbs up.

Maddie sighed and logged on, splitting her screen to see the newsfeeds coming in from the wire services. She also grabbed her obits folder to see who needed a write-up.

A low voice called from the office behind her. "Madeleine."

Glancing over her shoulder, Maddie saw blue eyes watching her. She rose, headed for the glass office, and slid into the visitor's chair. Elena was writing something in front of her. For two minutes, Maddie was left staring at the woman's immaculate black hair, fine cheekbones, and aloof expression while she continued scratching her pen across her paperwork.

"Do you understand that most people who become journalists have ambition?" Elena suddenly asked, without looking up. "I know I did. They write with the hope of a breakthrough of a national story, in the hopes it will propel them ever higher. Not you, though. Do you know why that is?"

Maddie fought the urge to deny it. She waited.

"Because you aren't a journalist."

"What?... No!"

"Oh yes." Elena stopped writing and fixed her with sharp eyes. "You have no ambition, no drive, no understanding of what it takes to be in this profession. You hate your job. You hate this city. You hate your life. So tell me why? Why, Madeleine Grey, are you even here? In New York? Still?"

No words came to Maddie, and she felt herself withering under her scrutiny.

"I'll give you a hint," Elena said. "Because, deep down, you're as beige as your name. You have no killer instinct. You don't like who you are, and you don't even *know* who you are. But we both know what you're not—a journalist."

Maddie gasped, her hands forming tight balls. "I can write," she protested.

"Yes, you can write. It may surprise you, but that is not the issue. You write well when it suits you. Your story today was exceptional. I believe I actually saw your hardened news chief tear up for half a second. You have a skill to evoke a response through words. I've been studying you, and you excel when you have an emotional connection to the subject you're writing about. The obituary on the train guard who gave his life to save that passenger on the tracks, for example. An emotional piece which obviously touched you."

Maddie nodded numbly.

"And did you reach out to the family, too? Offer them support? Maybe send flowers to the funeral? Or, knowing you, baked goods?"

Maddie looked at her hands. *It was just some brownies. Practically baked them in my sleep.*

"And we come back to your story on Ramel Brooks." Elena eyed her closely. "It was you who set up that charity page to crowdfund a decent lawyer. Correct?"

"Um." Maddie started. "Okay, yes. I sent all the passwords to his mother with instructions on how to get the money. She just needed a hand in getting started. The internet isn't her thing."

"Mm. How predictable of you. And then there was your story on the former property developer who carried out an armed hold-up. That was about as flat a story as I've ever read. And it's because you didn't care about him."

Maddie shot her an indignant look. *Who would care about some entitled ass terrifying everyone because his business had gone belly up?*

"That's what I thought. Madeleine, that's not a journalist. A journalist needs to be able to find a way to do their job, regardless of whether the story's *speaking* to them. So my conclusion stands—you might know how to write, but you are no journalist."

Maddie's heart sank, and she felt anger and humiliation warring. "I..." She stopped. "What's wrong with always wanting to care about what you write? What's wrong with having an emotional investment in the subject? No reporter has complete objectivity. That's a myth. So what's wrong with acting like a human *and* a reporter?"

"What's wrong with it?" Elena's eyes took on a flinty quality. "It's an impossible standard. Most of what a journalist writes has no emotional resonance. You will burn yourself out trying to find one. You will suffer and flame out in very little time."

"You can't know that. Why are you writing me off?"

"Madeleine, you can't actually believe this career is a good fit for you."

Silence fell between them. Maddie's hands balled into fists. Did Elena understand her so little—even after all their late-night chats— that she didn't grasp how much Maddie loved to write? How was it Elena didn't get that she could be a great reporter? No one could tell her otherwise. This was bullshit. She opened her mouth to say as much when Elena's hand came up to stop her.

"Don't bother. The rest of the office will find out at the end of the day. I am aware it's only been a month, but some things have moved faster than I anticipated. I'm closing down the paper." She pinned Maddie with a pointed look. "And I'm going to do you a favour. A big one—you're fired."

Maddie felt her stomach drop through the floor. How could she? Maddie realised she'd actually begun to put some trust in this woman. Elena's betrayal stung, more than if she'd actually leaned over the desk and slapped her. "How is that a favour?" she ground out.

"I'm sparing you clinging to a failed experiment out of some misplaced sense of obligation. You don't want to be in New York. And you don't belong in journalism."

"So that's it, then? You're just throwing me...all of us, to the wolves?"

Elena tilted her head. "No, not all of you. I have identified two staff members as worthy of redeployment within Bartell Corp. But I do not need a journalist with a talent as unpredictable as yours—a talent so pinned to whether she's *feeling* her story."

All Maddie's rationalisations died on her tongue, as she stared into Elena's eyes and saw only ice staring back. Cold. Empty. "I don't know you." Maddie glared at her and stood to leave.

Elena's jaw twitched, and a small frown appeared. "I already told you who I was last night. I told you not to bet on my humanity. It's just you didn't believe me." She nudged an open manila folder to one side.

Maddie's attention fell to it, and she read upside down. It was a press release. The title said *"Hudson Shard Announced"*. What the hell was a Hudson Shard? A Post-it note was stuck to it.

Received from publicist, Feb 6. Pls approve.

Just under a month ago. Realisation slammed into Maddie. "You never intended to save anyone's jobs or this paper, did you? You've always been planning on turning this building into a skyscraper."

"This building *is* ideally sited." Elena leaned back in her chair. "Close to the heart of New York City, easy transport access. The air above it is worth many more times that of the newspaper below. It will become an office space that will be highly sought after. Possibly a New York landmark by the time I'm done. It will be iconic. Beautiful."

"So all this time, you've been pretending to check out the talent on staff, but, what, you've been running surveyors and engineers through? Keeping it on the quiet?"

"Staff tend to do intemperate things when they know they're about to lose their jobs," Elena said with a nod. "It's smart not to reveal your hand to anyone. I told you before, I let nothing get in my way. I play the game well, because I play it smart."

"Except it's not a game for us; it's our lives. And you told us...you said..." She swallowed back the lump in her throat. "You let us believe there was hope."

"It's *business*." Elena regarded her. "Besides, I can talent spot people at the same time as I talent spot a building's bones. My development plans were submitted this morning. You were the one who hand-delivered them to me last night. But you can read all about it in the *Wall Street Journal* tomorrow, along with everyone else."

Maddie stared at her. "Why would you do this? Get into office space? You're in the media business!"

"I'm in the *profit* business. And when I see an opportunity, I seize it. Wherever it might be; whatever it might be." She gave Maddie an appraising stare. "As I tried to warn you last night—nothing and no one gets in the way of that. You *really* should have listened." She slapped the folder shut and gave Maddie a look of finality, tilting her head towards the door. "We're done."

A coldness shot through Maddie's bones. Holding Elena's hard gaze, she realised she could see nothing at all of the woman she thought she'd known before. She stood. "You really are what they call you," Maddie said with rising fury. "A calculating, icy, money-hungry bitch of a shark."

Three days later, Maddie found herself semi-comatose on the sofa, staring at the debris of several chocolate and Fun Factory benders, and a wall of Simon's packing boxes. Her head hurt. Stomach too. Not moving ever again seemed like a sound plan.

Her phone rang. With an indignant grumble, Maddie scrabbled around for it and answered.

"She's going to Australia next," Felicity's clipped voice announced without so much as a hello.

"Screw you and your asshole boss." Maddie slurped the remnants of her bright blue Car Seat Cover concoction.

"Whatever. Look, *Style Sydney* is in a tailspin, and she wants to fix it before it hurts the whole *Style International* brand. She'll need a PA. The one here now is useless. Plus, she wears green eye shadow. *Green!* God, she makes you look fashionable."

"Huh?" Maddie peered at her phone. "And you're sharing this why?"

"Are you interested?"

"In working for Elena? She just fired me!"

"Yes, I am quite aware of that. She fired everyone. Moving on—"

"I'm not the PA type. I don't do PA-ing. I. Am. A. Journalist."

"Not. According. To. Elena."

Maddie was beside herself with frustration now. "Do you not get that she just fired me? I may have also called her a shark."

"Well."

"A calculating, icy, money-hungry *bitch* of a shark."

"Is that a yes or a no?"

Maddie frowned. "Look, I don't know what Elena wants from me, but—"

"Elena wants someone fluent in kangaroo speak or whatever cultural mangling your people do down there, and she'd prefer someone she knows. And she told me to tell you the position gives you your fondest wish."

Maddie shook her head. "I'm going to regret asking this, aren't I?" She rubbed her bleary eyes. "And what is this fondest wish?"

There was a smug snicker. "A face-saving way to return home."

"Face-saving? I'd be going back as a PA, not a journalist! An assistant!" Maddie couldn't believe her ears. "Oh, I get it…" So this was Elena's revenge for not having the last word and for Maddie calling her a few choice names? Hiring her as her lackey. "She thinks I'm going to give up my career as a journalist to get down on my knees and kiss her a—"

"Ugh! You would be her personal assistant, you idiot. That is hardly giving up anything. That's a job with *status*. Surely even your feral, dingo-bred clan from Outer Bog Swamp have heard of Elena Bartell?"

Maddie groaned at the pointlessness of arguing with Felicity Simmons. "Just give me a simple answer to this: why would she want to hire *me?*"

"She said you'd ask that."

"And?"

"It's business."

Maddie ground her teeth. "Not for me it's not."

"Suit yourself. You know I could find a truckload of PAs who would jump at this opportunity. But if you'd rather cling to the delusion you're cut out for New York when you're so miserable that even I can see it, and I have no interest in your life whatsoever, then I can't stop you."

"Then why not get one of those truckload of PAs to do it?" Maddie said with a snarl. "Tell you what—if Elena Tiger Bitch Bartell wants me to be her personal assistant, she can damn well ask me herself." She ended the call with a vicious stab of her finger. *There.*

An hour later, Maddie mustered the energy to go grocery shopping. She'd just made her way gingerly down the stairs of her apartment building, head thumping, when she spotted a shiny, black BMW slowly creeping up Humboldt Street towards her. Maddie watched it, wondering if the luxury vehicle was lost. Unless it was stopping by Bruno's next door for a service?

It pulled up, and a familiar driver stepped out.

"Ms Grey?" Amir said.

She looked at him. Then at the car. Then at him again. Her not entirely sober brain struggled to process what she was seeing.

Finally, the back passenger window rolled down. Elena peered at her through dark sunglasses. "I'm a busy woman. Can we move this along?"

"Move what along?"

"I refuse to conduct business shouted across the street. Get in."

Amir walked to the opposite rear door and opened it, looking at her.

Maddie hesitated, then sauntered around the car and slid inside.

Amir closed the door and walked away.

Maddie took in the smell of Elena's familiar perfume, mingled with leather from the fancy seats. She looked down at herself, in torn jeans, an old T-shirt, and denim jacket. She folded her arms. "Yes?"

"I understand you wished to discuss the terms of your new employment?"

"No, I wanted to hear it from your lips—a personal invitation to be your assistant."

Elena regarded her. "You wish to go home. I'm paying. Isn't that good enough?"

"No. Come on, you fired me. And then I called you a bunch of insulting names, and now you're offering me a job."

"Apparently. So?"

"But why?"

"Do you not want to go home?"

Maddie blinked. Wasn't that the million-dollar question? She did. More than anything. "Yes," she admitted.

"Then what is there left to discuss?"

"I'll be your PA, for God's sake. Not a journalist."

"I am aware."

"Is this a screw you? Offering me a debasing job that has me satisfying your every whim?"

Elena's expression became withering. "Really? Is that what you think of me?"

"Who knows how your mind works?" Maddie flicked invisible lint off her jeans. "You're mystifying."

Eyes narrowing, Elena said, "Well, you appear to suffer from the same malady."

Maddie side eyed her. "So how long have you been circling the block, debating whether to get out and knock?"

Elena gave a long-suffering sigh. "The job is yours. Take it or not. It's up to you."

"Did you regret it? The things you said?"

"They were all true." Elena's face hardened. "Every word."

Maddie regarded her, anger rising. "You booted me out the door like trash."

"I did no such thing." Elena removed her sunglasses and leaned closer, examining her intently. "Honesty is essential to personal growth. I prefer the truth in all dealings, even if it's the brutal truth, and you should too. Besides, I really did do you a favour."

"You actually believe that, don't you?"

"Of course I do."

Maddie licked her lips, anxious about asking her next question, but she couldn't not. She had to know. "And what about us?"

"Us?" Elena looked at her oddly. "You would be my assistant, Madeleine. I would be your boss. What 'us' could you possibly mean?"

"So it'd be like New York never happened?" Maddie clarified. She fidgeted. "All the things between us...like, your firing me? Not to mention...um...everything else?" *Our talks*, she wanted to say. *Our almost friendship. You always looking at me like you wanted to know more. All the times I watched you and couldn't stop. The intriguing conversations, the intense moments, late at night with no one around. Missing you when you weren't there. It couldn't be so one sided. Could it? Could she just erase it like it never happened?*

Elena opened her mouth, lips pulling down as though about to say something cruel and dismissive. She closed it again. Her nostrils flared. "That would be for the best."

"Why choose me? I mean, you've made it clear you don't even like me."

Elena glowered at her. She gripped Maddie's hand, hard. "That was business. I could not have been clearer. You really must learn to separate the two."

Maddie studied her face, watching the small clenching of her jaw at odds with her impassive eyes, and wondered about all the things she wasn't saying. Then she dropped her gaze to their connected fingers.

Elena snapped her hand back as though startled to find she'd even touched her.

Maddie considered her for a moment longer, then turned to stare out the window. "Simon's leaving in three days," she said quietly. "His visa's expiring."

"Ah. The roommate."

"You know, he only got his internship here to hang out with me. Funny thing is, he loves it here more than me. Isn't that ironic? I'm on a green card and could stay here indefinitely, but the guy who would kill to stay has to go. Anyway, it'll be weird being in New York without him."

"He sounds like a good friend—one who might miss you a great deal if you didn't return home with him."

"We've been inseparable since we met as kids." Maddie murmured. She stared at the trees lining the street and the red brick of her apartment building. Elena was eerily accurate as always, although she doubted the woman cared much about the argument she'd just made. To Elena, invoking loyalty would probably be just a clever argument, a face-saving way for Maddie to say yes. So why did Elena even want Maddie to be her PA? It made no sense.

This was all too hard, especially since Maddie wasn't even remotely clear headed. She tried to sift through all the competing arguments in her fuzzy brain. She had come to appreciate Elena and enjoy her company, come to love the glimpses behind her mask, and the woman had suddenly squashed her like a bug. Hell, she'd even just admitted she had no regrets about doing it. On the other hand, Maddie wanted to go home. Desperately. It would be depressing being alone and jobless in New York. She remembered how isolated she had felt before Simon joined her. Maddie suppressed a shudder and turned to face Elena.

"I'll take your offer. For Simon," she said. To hell she would confirm to Elena how pathetic she was, that she couldn't cope with being alone in New York. Maddie shot her a steely look. "And you can call me your PA all you like, and I'll do that job as best I can, but I'll always be a journalist. And I *will* prove that to you. Just so you know that. Okay?"

Elena regarded her evenly. She sniffed. "I'll have Felicity process your paperwork."

BlogSpot: Aliens of New York

By Maddie as Hell

Goodbye, New York. Sorry I never understood you, as hard as I tried. We had our moments, didn't we?

Remember that laughing old woman outside Saks Fifth Avenue, who tried to hug everyone she passed and called them Sally? I've often wondered who Sally was. A lost daughter? An absent lover? It doesn't matter; we all got to be Sally and have a hug that smelled of wet wool cardigan and nutmeg. I think that old woman's life must be a delight, because everywhere she turns she finds exactly what she's looking for.

I wish that had been the case for me. I came to New York hoping for the Dream. I leave now, having lost a little of myself, found a little of myself, and learned some harsh truths about the mistake in assuming that everyone sees the world…and friendship…as I do.

But no tears, New York. It's not you; it's me. I'll pretend we were the best of friends, if anyone ever asks.

And they will.

CHAPTER 10

Living the Dream (Take Two)

Maddie brushed the sand off her knees, adjusted her beach towel, and leaned back on one arm. The stop-start, low rumble of traffic on Campbell Parade at Bondi faded away behind her, as she took in the curling sweep of blue water and about a hundred tanning sunbathers. Seagulls swooped overhead and skidded along the sand, eager for discarded bread crusts or chips.

"They only had Coke Zero," Simon said, appearing behind her and plopping the soda can into her lap. "I couldn't be buggered going next door, so you'll have to live."

"Thanks." She cracked the tab, enjoying the satisfying hiss, and scrunched its bottom firmly in the soft white sand.

Simon placed a fat parcel between them and dropped beside her. His long legs stretched out in front of him, toes sticking out from the brown leather of what Maddie liked to call his "Dad" sandals. He unwrapped the paper to expose a glorious tangle of fish and chips.

Maddie swooned at the fish smell mingled with sea salt. "Oh yum! God, I've missed this. All of it." She waved at the scene in front of her. "You know, I had no idea I was such a beach bunny until I was deprived of it."

"Really?" Simon plucked out a fat chip. "So is Bondi how you remember it? Or Sydney?" He squirted some tomato sauce onto the edge of the paper in a loud blurp.

"Yep." She dunked her chip in the sauce puddle. "I feel at peace here. Which is dumb when you think about how loud and busy Sydney is. I mean, temperature aside, it's not *that* different from New York. But it feels like home."

"Mm." Simon chewed slowly. "I loved New York. Something's always happening. But you're not a something-always-happening kinda girl, so I get it."

"Nope. But that's not why. It's just that it was like everything in New York was about ten degrees off kilter to what I'm used to. It felt just enough like here to fool me. I mean a city's a city, right? But I was tense the whole time. I think my subconscious knew I was out of place, and it never let me forget it."

"I figured you were in a funk. You slept too much. No one can like being unconscious that much."

"Oh." Maddie reached for another chip. "Well, I sleep fine now. So do you miss it?"

"Of course I miss it. But I've got a new reason to stay here now."

"Ah yes, the infamous Caroline. A workplace romance." Maddie elbowed him in the ribs. "You move fast. Is it serious?"

"Not a clue. Playing it by ear. Although, I can't wait for Mondays now. Seeing her again. It's like reverse Mondayitis." He broke off a chunk of fish and tossed it in his mouth. He chewed for a moment, then regarded her. "What about you? You going to get back with Rachel? She's been sniffing around, you know, trying to find out when you're going to be hanging with our old group again."

Maddie sighed. "Rachel and I had nothing in common but being gay and our journalism course. She also plans to be in the closet until the day every last member of her family is dead. And her family is huge. I'm not sure why we stuck it out as long as we did. She didn't even write me over there."

"Huh." Simon shrugged. "Okay, scratch the Rach. But we need to hook you up. You've been in the dumps for too long. Who do you like? What about your boss?"

"My...what? Elena?"

"Yeah, speaking of hot office romances, you and the tiger shark. Why not?"

"She is a married woman! And straight!"

"I notice you didn't deny liking her. So, what's the deal? Have I hit a nerve? You're drooling over her now?"

Maddie dug her next chip viciously into the sauce. "I do not drool over her." She glared. "She fired my sorry ass, remember? There is *no* drooling."

He laughed. "You have the hottest boss in the history of bosses, but there is no drooling. Got it. Oh hey, let's do the patented Simon Itani test." He waggled a chip at her. "So, when you think about going into work next week and starting your new job, what's it feel like not having seen her since New York? First reaction—go!"

Maddie studied the crispy crumbs of the fish and prodded them with her finger. *How does it feel? Like a soft fire. Like churning. Nerves and excitement. Like missing out on something close enough to taste. Honey and spices and temptation and...* She frowned.

"I feel pissed off," Maddie lied. She didn't meet his gaze. Simon was far too good at reading her. "It's a reminder of how overqualified I am. Like my uni degree is withering away, turning to dust, while I'll be fetching coffees and page proofs. I'm looking for another job, of course, but journo jobs are hard to come by. Fairfax and News Corp are both having another round of redundancies."

"Yeah?" He squinted at her. "Well, that sucks. Sorry, Mads. Geez, this topic's a downer. Hey, wanna hear about my footy training? We've got a new player with the Penrith Roos. He's a total joker. He took a bottle of Gatorade, a box of rubber bands, a pair of stockings, and..."

Maddie let his voice fade out. Her mind drifted back to his question. Excitement rose up again. It was like a sick, thrilling tension. She'd always assumed it was nerves. New workplace and all. At the thought of Elena, her stomach clenched again, as if a nest of butterflies were partying in it. How long until they were in the same room again?

She glanced at her watch and caught herself. *Oh God. I really am counting down the hours until I see her again.*

Day one of her new job as personal assistant, and Maddie was a mess. She'd tried on half a dozen outfits, not entirely sure what was required of her or how much she should change her look to accommodate the role. She was half tempted to rock up in her graveyard-shift outfit of jeans and a grunge T-shirt, but she was fairly sure Elena's scathing rebuke wouldn't be worth it.

It was a little unsettling to realise how much Elena's opinion mattered.

She finally settled on wearing the uptight emo-librarian look Felicity favoured. That seemed like a safe bet.

Induction from HR had been painless, and before long she'd settled into a desk side-on to and outside a glass office that bore Elena's name.

After getting her bearings, introducing herself to people, and trying not to wonder where Elena was, she'd made a mental list. Three simple, achievable goals.

First, she would become the perfect, professional assistant, one for whom New York had never happened and who did not engage in banter or share personal stories with a woman who had no heart. A woman whose opinion, Maddie decided, she should not care about one way or another.

Second, she would prove to Elena that she was a journalist.

And third, she would convince herself that seeing hints of Elena with her guard down no longer excited her. Because it would be Maddie's undoing, seeing these glimpses. Signs Elena might be human after all.

No, she absolutely wasn't going to think about their almost friendship ever again. Because, as per point one, perfect, professional PAs did not do that.

How hard could it really be to stick to that? Her destiny was in her own hands, after all. She could do this.

Her best-laid plans were sorely tested the moment she glanced over at Elena's open office door. She could smell her. Her perfume, mixed with the sharp scent of ink from proofs and a hint of chai tea. Elena wasn't even in her office, but it felt as if she was just there. Watching her. Like always.

Maddie frowned and distracted herself by sorting out her own desk, sliding pens into drawers, rattling a tray of paperclips.

"What *is* this?"

Maddie looked up to be met by Elena's long, hard stare.

"Who are you supposed to be?" Elena came around Maddie's desk for a better look before pointing at the mid-thigh, grey skirt.

"Your personal assistant." Maddie hated the words the moment she said them. "It's what Felicity wears."

"I see." Elena's lips pursed. "Well, if you must be a clone, try to at least emulate a professional whose look you actually like."

She stalked off. That became the sum total of all she'd said to Maddie all day. Any assignments for her arrived via email. The pings of the incoming messages were constant.

Elena, ensconced in her office, looking as regal as a queen, never glanced up, never made eye contact, never said her name in that beautiful French way she used to, with the last e of Madeleine turned into an a.

It was ridiculous, this no-talking thing, because her boss was sitting *right there*. Within easy earshot. Instead, Elena gave Maddie a wall of silence.

Her wardrobe critique, both mocking and cool, remained in Maddie's ears for the rest of the day.

Emulate a professional whose look you actually like? *Fine.*

The following day Maddie sauntered into work wearing her own version of an H.G. Wells vest. Plus chunky boots. She'd given the fob watch a miss, because she wasn't *that* derivative, but her message was clear.

All morning she waited for a reaction. No new work decrees pinged from Elena, who had been in and out of the office without a word or look, so Maddie was bored. She adjusted the photo of her family on the desk, along with one of her goofing around with Simon. She spun around on her chair a few times when no one was looking. Rummaged around her desk. Dug up something called *The PA's Unofficial Handbook* with a note on the front to *read this VERY carefully*. A few folded papers were wedged inside. They contained a list of names of some sort. *Weird.* And where did she know the name Frank Harkness from, anyway? She noticed some notes in the margin. She started in dismay when she realised what the list meant. Just then, the outer door banged open.

Elena came striding in, so Maddie thrust the handbook and its hidden list back in her drawer to study later. She sat up straighter, hoping she wasn't looking too eager, as she waited for a comment on her outfit. How would Elena take her clear imitation? She waited. And waited.

Elena passed her, glanced at her, and didn't say a word.

Three hours later, Elena stopped at her desk and studied her new look properly. Finally, she nodded. "Where are my budget reports from the Kensington Group? I should have had them on my desk an hour ago."

And that was that.

Over the next few months, little changed. Maddie fetched cups of tea, made calls, took notes at meetings, picked up samples, memorised the unofficial handbook and its sobering details, and traded witticisms with Perry. She even picked up a little about how fashion worked. It was entirely unintentional, but she couldn't unknow it now.

Maddie had tried to work on her second vow, but she spent so much effort being the consummate PA that she'd had no time to write anything beyond scribbled memos and food orders. Some nights, she sat at home, staring at the wall, trying to write but too exhausted to tap out anything beyond her name. She told herself she was looking for a new job, a real job, even though she had made no effort to do so.

She didn't even have the creative outlet of her *Aliens of New York* blog anymore. Jason, the single dad who'd loved it, had taken over for her. That seemed fair, since he was actually in New York. But it meant Maddie often stared at the walls, robbed of words, wondering what had happened to her writing dreams.

Her thoughts drifted to where they usually did. She tried very hard to forget the woman she'd once known. It helped in some ways that Elena was direct, cool, boss-like, and shared nothing. Well, almost nothing. Because no one was an empty void. And Maddie always noticed the small, subtle things most people missed. As hard as she tried not to see, she saw them. It made keeping her last vow more taxing than ever. Maddie didn't like to dwell on what it meant. It shouldn't be this hard to ignore a boss who had gutted her old paper and fired everyone. It shouldn't be this hard to pretend she wasn't human.

But the struggle was getting worse. For instance, she tried hard not to notice whenever she heard a low, deep laugh from a certain corner office.

She also knew she definitely shouldn't notice whenever Elena wore her H.G. outfit. Maddie shouldn't be mesmerised by the way the black pants stretched across the woman's tight, shapely ass, the pull of the vest at her waist and breasts, the crisp, white shirt that was always opened three buttons, revealing a hint of cleavage, not to mention the jaunty boots and the swing in her hips as she moved.

Noticing things like this wasn't an isolated incident. But it didn't mean a thing. How could it? Because Maddie was the consummate professional, and her boss barely even acknowledged her existence.

Simon dropped by on the weekend, looking about as smitten as a man could get. Caroline had seemingly moved from "playing it by ear" to "can't take my eyes off her".

"I wonder when it changed?" He looked puzzled. "How did Caro go from regular girl to most fascinating girl in human history in five minutes? How does that even work?"

Maddie didn't have an answer but spent the next two hours patiently feeding him pizza and beer while he listed the woman's many virtues, some considerably more shallow than others. His puzzled comment stuck with her, though. When had it changed for her?

After three sleepless nights in a row, Maddie decided she blamed the red dress. Garnet dress. The one that had stopped time when Elena tried it on for Perry in her New York office. That had been the moment. Ground zero. Ever since then, she had been hyperaware of everything about Elena. The way she ran her fingers through her hair when she was tired, the way she tapped a pen against her lips. Maddie had dismissed it as a simple attraction at the time. Chemistry. Her boss was stunning; Maddie had eyes. So what? It meant nothing.

But now she was aware of her and aware of her own awareness. Elena was all she could think about. She worked close to the woman, all day, every day. With the barest movement of her head, she could look right at her. So, she took advantage of this, often. Far too often. Maddie had finally come to an unfortunate conclusion—she wanted her boss.

The worst part was that it wasn't just chemistry. Try as she might, she couldn't crush the kernel inside her that cared for Elena. She wanted her to be happy. She wanted to connect with her again the way they used to. Wanted to see her throw back her head in laughter. Or in ecstasy. That thought thrilled her. It was a fantasy that sent shivers through Maddie. God, how she wanted her in every way imaginable.

It was insane, feeling this way, even knowing what Elena really was like. Driven and focused, she only cared about her business. And, at the moment, business meant her baby, *Style Sydney*. A fashion magazine that careless executives had somehow allowed to dive in circulation.

The first meeting with *Style Sydney*'s management team after Elena touched down was seared in Maddie's brain. Elena had laid down the law with a pointed, furious speech about how the glossy mag had drifted from its passionate, core base of fashion readers into more mainstream topics that the now fired editor-in-chief had more interest in. But as pretty as luxury cars and Sydney Harbour real estate could be, and despite the expensive, $50,000, full-page ads they brought in, the topics had led their audience to abandon them for a more fashion-focused magazine.

This, apparently, was the reason for most of Elena's wrath. Because the nearest rival the readers were bailing to was *CQ*, the same magazine Elena had left under a mysterious cloud.

So far, all Maddie had found out about that, while getting to know Perry, was that Elena had been groomed to be editor of *CQ*. Instead, Emmanuelle Lecoq had won the top role and become the most famous name in fashion-editing circles.

And now, in Sydney at least, the magazine that Elena had set up to crush *CQ* was losing readers to it by the thousands. The war drums were being pounded. Elena was in battle mode. And in spite of every feeble, internal protest, Maddie found it a thrilling sight. Her boss could stride in and own a room like no one else.

Australian Fashion Week was coming up, and Elena had demanded a splash so big that the world, not just Sydney, would notice that her pet publication was a premium *fashion* magazine.

"Madeleine," Elena called softly.

"Yes, Elena?" She dashed into the office, with a notebook and pen poised.

"She's coming. It's confirmed." Elena's eyes were bright, and she was almost vibrating with energy.

"Oh-kay."

"Véronique Duchamp," Elena said, sounding impatient, "has confirmed as the headline designer, opening for Australian Fashion Week. So this is it." She rapped a fingernail on her desk. "We need her. This is the answer to our sales slide. *Style Sydney* needs an exclusive interview with her."

"Okay." That didn't sound so hard. She could call Lucy in Editorial and tell her to...

"Madeleine!"

She stopped scribbling and looked up.

Elena shook her head as though she were dim-witted. "Véronique is a prickly designer who has granted no one an interview in thirty years. Thirty. Years. And yet her fashion has been world leading for almost all that time."

Maddie frowned. This was far more than a little problem to solve.

"Such an interview would be a game changer for us." Elena tapped her chin with her index finger. "We need to get her attention. We need to stand out from the rivals. *CQ* will also be trying every trick in the book to get their own exclusive. They've been desperate for an interview for decades. That must not happen." She grimaced. "Lecoq will be coming for Australian Fashion Week this year, now that Véronique's confirmed she'll be here."

"Oh." Maddie wrote furiously, a little surprised Elena had even said the woman's name. She usually avoided it. "How do you propose we...?"

"Flowers. She loves them. Send so many that even Véronique can't ignore them. Something expensive—send them to her home in Paris. Martine will know the address." She waved her hand. "Make it happen."

Maddie scurried off, musing over the odd look in Elena's eyes. Funnily enough, it constituted the happiest she had ever seen her boss. Her killer instinct was being stoked. It was...irritatingly attractive.

After returning to her desk, Maddie emailed Martine for Véronique's address and then called up the site of the French floral boutique that Bartell Corp had an account with. A soft ping announced Martine's reply. Maddie opened the incoming email and copied out the address. She flicked back to her online cart and pasted in the address, as she remembered how thrilled Elena looked. Post-orgasmic even. The thought made her swallow.

She caught herself. This was so bad. Maddie was crushing on her boss. A boss who treated her like every other PA she'd ever had. To Elena, Maddie was clearly just a pair of arms for fetching tea or proofs. Sighing, she stabbed, over and over, the *nine* button on the *Nombre nécessaire* box on her flower order.

Despite how pathetic she felt about her secret desires, Maddie hadn't been able to tear her eyes off her boss. Since Elena had fired *Style Sydney*'s editor-in-chief, Jana Macy, she was now filling in, doing Macy's job herself on top of everything else. It was fascinating to watch her shift in focus to fashion—as well as trying to save something, rather than shutting it down. Perry was right. Elena was born for fashion. The corporate raiding and empire building was just a numbers game she liked to win. But here, in the cut and thrust of a style magazine, actually running it, hands on, Elena Bartell came alive.

There seemed to be nothing Elena didn't know about the process. From the designers to the layouts, she was across all of it, and the staff at *Style Sydney* knew it. They snapped to attention when she lifted the bar with her incisive demands. There was no faking her expertise. Among her *Style* staff she was a goddess.

When they gushed about her, her ideas, her genius, Maddie would say nothing. What did she know about fashion? She spent a lot of time nodding. Every now and then, Elena would enter the room and catch her glazed expression while the staff was discussing "peplum inspiration" or "material viscosity". Elena's look always contained equal parts of amusement and mockery.

It was hard to let go of that nagging voice telling Maddie that maybe all of this was Elena toying with her, and she was playing a long game Maddie hadn't yet figured out. And yet, just when her distrust had reached its peak of paranoia, she found two emails while cleaning out and sorting Elena's secondary email account.

Dear Ms/Mr E.B., Your donation of $10,000 is making a difference. Campaign: Ramel Brooks Lawyer Fund. Thank you.

The next email, issued less than two minutes later, announced that the Ramel Brooks Lawyer Fund had reached, and exceeded, its target amount. It was dated the day Elena had fired Maddie. She stared at the email for a good five minutes. Gratitude washed over her. Her boss had transformed the young man's life. Any quality lawyer could crush the prosecution's feeble case, so Ramel would be off to college as planned. He'd even have plenty of money left over for textbooks.

Yet no one would ever know who did this.

That donation wasn't a unique event, either. Maddie had so far stumbled across paperwork for anonymous donations to a women's shelter, a Polish inner-city community centre and its youth basketball team, and a receipt for bail money to free a group of transgender activists in North Carolina who'd been arrested protesting prohibitive bathroom laws.

If that wasn't unexpected enough, there was the incident last week. On Maddie's birthday, a cupcake was sitting on her desk when she arrived at work. Red velvet. No card. No note. Just that. It looked eerily familiar. She sniffed it. *Oh. No wonder.* She smiled and made a call.

"Hi, Mum, I just wanted to thank—"

"Darling! Happy birthday! I was just going to call to check you're still coming over tonight. Simon will be here and your brother, too. I'll be cooking that Moroccan dish you love. And my famous sponge for your cake. Yes?"

"Definitely." Maddie was drooling all over her desk. "I mean if I get out of work on time."

"Pssh, don't worry about that. You will."

Maddie stared at her phone in confusion. Then she remembered her reason for calling. "Thanks for the cupcake. Red velvet—my fave! Looks as delicious as ever."

"Don't thank me, I just took the order."

"What?"

"Of course we don't normally take orders for a single cupcake, but when she said who it was for, well, you're a special case. Your brother dropped it off on the way through. Chris had to go into the city anyway."

"Um, she who?" Maddie felt baffled by the entire conversation. "Who ordered it?"

"Your boss, of course. Didn't she say? She rang to find out your preferred cake and order it for your birthday."

Maddie was definitely hearing things. "Elena? Elena Bartell ordered this? For me, personally? And she knows it's my birthday? I never told her."

"Oh yes. And she knew—wouldn't it be in your file or something? Anyway, she obviously appreciates you, and she sounded lovely. We talked a little bit. Bonded over dogs, of all things. You know how I love rare breeds. She has a Cirneco dell'Etna, did you know that? I'd love to see it one day."

"Dogs."

"Anyway, I explained tonight's plans for you, and she promised not to keep you. She said she'd make sure you'd be free. So, seven?"

"Free."

"Maddie, focus, darling. Seven? I hate to rush, but I have the Fredericks luncheon to prep for."

"Sure." She'd felt light-headed. "Seven."

"All right, then. Until tonight. Bye, honey." *Click.*

Maddie looked at her phone, the cupcake, and then over at Elena. She scrambled shakily to her feet and walked to Elena's desk until she was staring at the impassive face of her boss.

Elena didn't look up. "Problem?"

"No. I just... I wanted to say...for the cupcake. Thanks!"

"Mm. Consider it payback."

"Payback?"

"I did appreciate many of your evening offerings." Elena glanced up, her gaze half-lidded. She nudged a pile of folders across her desk. "These need filing."

Maddie returned to her desk, arms overflowing, trying to understand what had just happened. Had Elena actually made mention of their time together in New York? That was a first. She hadn't been any closer to figuring out what it all meant when, at six on the dot, Elena called her in.

"Go home," she said, sounding annoyed. "You're chewing the lid of your pen too loudly, and it's ruining my concentration. So go. Now."

Maddie hadn't been using her pen.

Which was in her drawer.

And had no lid.

Such discoveries were both endearing and maddening. One moment Elena was a shark who shredded whole companies; the next she was the wry, smart, occasionally thoughtful woman Maddie had caught glimpses of in New York. Elena Bartell defied definition. She was impossible to pin down.

A blush warmed Maddie's cheeks, as she imagined pinning the woman down in a very different way. She shook her head in annoyance and forced herself to focus on the work at hand. This, this...crush... would soon pass, and she could get on with life.

She hit *Enter* on her order for flowers and then winced at how high the total cost was. Oh well, Elena had wanted that Duchamp woman's attention. She'd certainly get it for that price.

CHAPTER 11

The Truth Bet

Elena Bartell was not a woman who liked to be denied. Which was why when Véronique Duchamp not only rejected Elena's floral tributes but denied her an interview on the grounds that journalists were all lowly *cafards*, Maddie slammed on her metaphoric hard hat.

"*Cafards*!" Elena hissed as she spun her chair away from the window and raked Maddie with a cold glare that lowered the temperature at least ten degrees. "She calls *me* a cockroach!"

"Well, to be fair, uh, Elena, she calls everyone that," Maddie said in her most reasonable tone. "All of us. All journalists."

"Us?" Elena eyed Maddie with deliberate care, voice silky.

Uh-oh. She was in a worse mood than Maddie had thought. "Yes." She lifted her chin.

"Mm." Elena spun her chair back to the window. "I tried to get an interview with that woman when I was a junior writer at *CQ,* and then off and on over the years since. This year, I thought, *maybe*, because there are succession talks. Her daughter may be taking over. Véronique will want to explain the changes and how they affect her dynasty. I sent a roomful of flowers on that ungrateful creature's sixtieth birthday. Now this! *Cafards*!"

No kidding. Maddie had been there for God's sake. Véronique hadn't even sent an acknowledgement. Maddie thought she knew why. Flowers were the only thing everyone knew that the mysterious designer liked. So, Elena had joined a queue of every other hopeful wellwisher, from *Vogue* and *Elle* to *CQ,* using floral tributes to vie for favour with her.

Elena glanced back, catching Maddie mid-thought. Her shapely eyebrow lifted. "Something to add? You have some contrary thought in that fevered brain of yours?"

"What?" Maddie said, startled. Her boss's mood had degenerated from irritated to full-on bitch mode.

"Your face." Elena waved her hand. "It speaks volumes. What is it?"

"I...Nothing."

"*Nothing,*" Elena parroted back at her and gave her a sharp look. She'd been doing that a lot lately. "Could you actually be less honest? Is truthfulness too hard? Am I asking the universe?"

Truthfulness? People didn't want the truth. She told Elena as much.

Elena gave her a contemplative look. "The world would run much more smoothly if people were able to give and receive the brutal truth. Without omission. Without guile or bright, fake smiles."

Maddie gave her boss a sceptical look. *Yeah, sure.* Where had the brutal truth been at the Lancôme gala two nights ago when Elena had patted Richard's arm and suggested they should "give the drinks a miss tonight" because Elena wanted to cut down? Maddie had known what Elena really meant the moment she'd overheard the whispered words. She wanted *him* to cut down.

"So quiet." Elena's look was challenging. "I remember a time when you were more than keen to share your passing thoughts with me. There was a time you'd feed me homemade goods and tell me your secrets without a lick of self-censorship."

There was an edge to her voice—both speculative and dangerous. She had not mentioned New York since Maddie's birthday. This was new. Maddie eyed her. Had the goal posts just shifted?

"You told me those days were over." Maddie's tone was cautious. "Back when I took this job."

Elena said nothing and tapped her fingers on her desk. She gave her a cool look. "Out with it. Véronique? You had a contrary viewpoint. So share."

So they weren't touching that topic. Maddie sighed. "The flowers. They were a bad idea. We just became one of the rest, clamouring for her attention. We didn't stand out. We needed to not be one of the other 'cockroaches' begging to be seen."

"And you, of course, would have known how to stand out? I suppose when one wears garage-band club gear, it is hard not to be noticed."

Maddie resisted the urge to roll her eyes. Elena brought up her old look so often that Maddie wondered if she missed it. "I didn't say that I would have known, but yes, I think I could have gotten her attention way better than five thousand euros worth of flowers did." *There.*

"Is that so?"

Maddie ignored the mocking tone and nodded.

"You are aware, no one in the world has yet won an interview with her?" Elena's voice dropped to a challenge.

Maddie hesitated for a second. "Yes."

"Yet you, my personal assistant, with limited journalism experience and zero fashion sense, believes she could get Véronique Duchamp's attention better than *Style Sydney*'s team of experts? Better than *CQ* or *Vogue*? Better even than me, who has tried for two decades?"

"Yes. I could get Véronique's attention." Squelching her brain's plea for sanity, she added, "I'd bet on it."

Elena eyed her with keen interest. "You'd *bet* on it?"

Maddie gulped. The intrigued, predatory gleam in Elena's eye was doing funny things to her insides. She licked her lips nervously. Well she'd committed to insanity already, might as well go all in. "Okay. Yes. Sure."

"You. Would. Lose," Elena said with absolute certainty.

Maddie's eyes widened, as she realised her boss might actually be considering this.

"If I win," Elena began, "and *I will*, I want something from you that you seem incapable of doing anymore."

"What?" Maddie was mystified as to what she could possibly have that Elena would want.

"Honesty. An entire day of complete honesty. Every question asked, you answer truthfully. None of your perfectly safe answers that tell me nothing. None of your boring, Stepford-wife blandness I've endured of late." Elena's eyes were sharp and bright now. "The whole truth to me. On everything. Well? You may surrender now." Her gaze flicked back to her layouts, and without looking up, she added, "I will not be shocked."

Maddie stared at her. What sort of a crazy-assed bet was this? Elena wanted to hear all the times in a day that she was pissing her off? All the times Maddie admired her ass and wanted to push her against her desk and... *Oh.* She coloured as she realised the full horror of what Elena's terms would entail.

Elena's cool eyes flicked back up and seemed to be dancing with mischief.

Did she know? How could she? Maddie's brain was in freefall.

"Still here?" Elena said with a lazy drawl. "Please capitulate, then exit. Some of us have work to do."

The mockery set Maddie's teeth on edge. It was just so...Elena. This presumption of victory. Of thinking she knew people so well. Like when she told Maddie she wasn't a journalist.

"I'll do it," Maddie said. "And if I win, you have to do the same. The brutal truth to everyone for a day."

Elena leaned back in her chair. "I do that anyway. Not much of a prize. But suit yourself." She gave a tiny shrug.

Seriously? Elena thought she didn't lie? Everyone lied. "Fine. A whole week if you lose, given you seem to think it's so easy."

"Since there is no chance of you winning, you have a bet." Elena's expression was smug. "You have from the time Véronique arrives here ahead of Australian Fashion Week, till the end of the month, when she leaves. Would that be sufficient for you to pull off the impossible? Or should I say, the delusional?"

Maddie glanced at the desk calendar beside Elena. Three weeks? She was insane to agree. This was complete madness.

In spite of herself, she found herself nodding. She stuck out her hand.

Elena took it, her warm, soft skin sending a pleasant shock through Maddie's fingers. She shook it and oh so slowly released Maddie's hand as she smiled. It was a smile that established who was the shark and who was the foolish piece of plankton.

"Good. We're done."

CHAPTER 12

The Game is Afoot

Maddie hit newspapers, the internet, magazines, and gossip columns. The secret to reaching Véronique had nothing to do with the designer. Elena had said it herself. Succession plans. The daughter would be the key. She'd have her mother's ear at the very least. And, by the sound of things, she'd also been overlooked by a media pushing past her to get to her mother.

So, Natalii Duchamp (two i's, she assiduously noted) became Maddie's sole focus for the next week, as she read everything about her she could get her hands on. Thanks to Natalii's small but public, social media presence, Maddie discovered her interests (abstract art, rap, photography), education (a tiny French school, then an elite design college), and goals (to have her own fashion line)—if Maddie's basic French was accurate.

It was interesting, that last point. How would having a world-famous mother cramp Natalii's fashion design dreams? Was she resentful? Driven to better her? Or did she just ignore it?

She called up Sydney gossip site *Glam Slam*. The Duchamps' arrival at Sydney Airport, four days ago, had caused a mini sensation. A tall, thin man pushed a trolley piled high with luxury suitcases. Véronique was beside him, impeccably dressed, barking instructions in French at the stoic-faced man, while lighting a cigarette. Natalii hung back, looking bored. She was about thirty, pale, and with slicked-back, midnight-black hair. Her clothes comprised a distressed indigo denim and T-shirt ensemble that was definitely not part of her mother's range.

So. Rebellious, then. Maddie made some notes and hit *Play* on the now infamous scene of an airport security guard ordering Véronique to put out her cigarette. Véronique did so—on the man's polished boot.

Only the excited throng of photographers had prevented that from escalating into something much worse. While all eyes in the video were on the indignant Frenchwoman and the enraged guard, Maddie studied Natalii.

The woman had taken a step back and had turned away from the scene, her face tight and closed. Her body language screamed, *I'm not with them.* Her arms were folded across her chest, revealing biceps that were extremely well toned. Maddie added another note—gym junkie.

She switched to the series of *Sydney Confidential* photos taken the previous day of Véronique. Thick sunglasses and a stylish, floral dress with an outlandish silver cape. The designer was stepping out of The Pierre at Double Bay, using her closed umbrella to jab at the paparazzi, shooing the *cafards* away. Maddie noted the hotel's name, did a quick Paris-to-Sydney time conversion, factored in a day for jet lag, and grinned. She set the alarm on her phone.

At six the next morning, Maddie stopped in at work, fired off a few emails, and grabbed the gym bag she'd brought with her. Just as she turned to leave, Elena strode into the office. What on earth was she doing in at this time?

"Going somewhere?" Elena asked, expression curious.

Grip tightening on her gym bag, Maddie said, "I have a lead on Véronique. I thought I should jump on it now if you want me to have a chance at getting that interview."

Bet or no bet, Maddie knew her boss would give her entire impressive wardrobe for an exclusive with Véronique.

Elena studied her, incredulity clearly warring with interest. "Go," she said, "but make your abject humiliation swift. I need you back at noon for the department heads' meeting."

"Yes, Elena. On the staff meeting, I mean. My abject humiliation is yet to be seen," she added, shooting her a grin.

At her boss's sceptical look, Maddie laughed and hurried out of the office.

Maddie glanced at her watch. Half past six. Good. She'd bet Natalii was still on Paris time, making it eight-thirty at night in her world and a pretty ideal workout time, given the Duchamps had a ball they were expected to attend in the evening.

Praying her hunch was right, Maddie adjusted her gym bag on her shoulder and headed to The Pierre's elevator. As luck would have it, several residents were heading to the amenities floor, too, and swiped their access cards. She followed, slipping in behind them.

The small but elegant gym was nearly empty. There were no French design heiresses in sight. She slid onto an exercise bike with a good view of the door and began to pedal.

Twenty minutes later, the room had completely emptied out, and all Maddie had accomplished was a sweat.

Suddenly, irritable French spoken in rapid fire shattered the quiet whirring of her exercise bike. Maddie snapped her head around to see Natalii Duchamp stomping through the door, loudly berating someone on her phone. She looked wrung out, wearing the sort of bone-weary tiredness of someone who wasn't on local time yet. Their eyes met, and the Frenchwoman immediately muttered *"au revoir"* and hung up.

"Désolée," she murmured and dumped her towel beside a bike two along from Maddie's.

Maddie rifled through her rudimentary French and plucked out the definition. *Sorry.* She shot her a smile. *"Ce n'est rien,"* she replied, hoping it meant "that's fine".

Natalii paused and cocked her head. "Your French is awful."

Maddie reddened. *Oh crap.*

"But finding even one person in your insular little country making any effort at the second language is rare." Natalii studied her and sniffed. "So, *mademoiselle*, I appreciate you for the effort you make."

"Thanks. Um. *Merci.*" This time she mangled it on purpose and grinned.

Natalii winced but then laughed and waggled her finger. "Ha. Terrible. I am Natalii."

"Maddie."

"Mad-dee?"

"It's short for Madeleine. My mother used to love the French books as a girl. I mean, different spelling but still. She was a huge fan."

"Ah, *Madeleine.*"

Maddie stared. She'd pronounced her name exactly the same way as Elena did.

Natalii moved closer and slid onto the exercise bike beside Maddie's. The LCD screen lit up as she punched up the incline. "So," Natalii continued, "you are visiting Sydney, too?"

"No. Visiting this gym, though, yes."

Natalii nodded and began to pick up her speed. She was fast, *really* fast. Maddie began to lift her own pace.

"What about you?" Maddie asked. "Staying here long?"

"My *mère* is here for the fashion week. I am here for her."

"But not for you? You don't like fashion?"

"I like it well enough. I like *my* fashion. I like young people's fashion. *Maman* designs for, how do you say? The power-suit femmes."

"Ah," Maddie said. It was true. Everyone who was anyone wore a Véronique. But it wasn't anyone aged under twenty-five.

"What is your job, Madeleine? Do you like fashion also?"

"Not exactly." She started to puff now that she was reaching for the speeds Natalii was at. "I work as an assistant to someone working in the industry at the moment. My boss is good with fashion, like freakishly good, but I can take it or leave it."

Natalii's expression was intrigued. "So you have a boring job in fashion? How is this possible?"

"I guess it's not for everyone."

"Then why is it that you stay?" She tilted her head. "Is it your boss? Your eyes, Madeleine, when you talk of her, they take on a look."

"A look?" Maddie panicked. *Was she that transparent?* "N-no! That's crazy. I don't! There's no look. I'm totally look free! What are you talking about?"

Natalii blinked at her. "I merely meant you perhaps admire her. What did you think I meant? Why do you react this way?"

Maddie wobbled on her bike at her mistake, causing Natalii to smirk. "Ah," the Frenchwoman said. She tapped her nose. "*Oui.* Now I see."

"You see nothing! I mean my boss is a *woman* for one thing!" Maddie said, desperate for her secret not to be so damned obvious. "So whatever you're thinking is wrong."

Natalii ceased to laugh...and pedal. "*Wrong?*" She glared. "What is bad with this? I see nothing wrong with embracing the love of a beautiful woman." Her expression dared Maddie to disagree.

She almost fell off her bike a second time, realising what Natalii had just revealed.

"I'm... I mean... No... That is... I'm not opposed. There's nothing wrong with... Of course not. I mean I'm very...but obviously not with... I mean with her *never*. She's straight. And *married*. And did I mention straight? So it's impossible. And she doesn't like me even a little. Not like that. Not even in any other way, either. Well, actually I'm not sure...because there was this one birthday cupcake." Maddie blew out a breath, beyond embarrassed. Really, what *did* Elena think of her? She wished the question didn't torture her as often as it did.

"Ahhh." Natalii resumed pedalling. "The forbidden love?" She looked thoughtful. "Well. This is a problem."

"Not love!" Did she have to completely ignore Maddie's protests? "I never said that. It's not *that*, okay?"

"What is her name? Your love that you cannot have?"

Maddie scowled. Was she being deliberately obtuse? "I can't say. You'll recognise it. She's famous."

"So?"

"So, I don't want any part of this conversation ever getting back to her. It's embarrassing, okay?"

"Ah. You feel I, some anonymous stranger, could somehow risk your heart? This is it?"

There was no way to answer any part of that question without lying. Natalii was not some stranger. And maybe it was true Maddie's heart *was* involved, at least a little—whether she wanted to admit it or not. She debated how to answer. Maddie really didn't lie well, and Natalii was far too astute.

"You're not an anonymous stranger," she admitted. "I recognised you when you came in. I know who your mother is too. And she doesn't like my boss much at all. She called her a *cafard*."

Natalii gaped at her. "*Merde*! You work for the insane flower lady? The Bartell woman? There were blooms all over *Maman*'s house. The smell! I cannot believe this. Your boss is the infamous cockroach!" She gave a wheezing sound that could have been a laugh or something much worse.

"God, I'm *so* sorry! I really didn't think."

"Wait, *you* didn't think? You did this?"

"Yes, I'm her assistant, like I said. I'm really sorry. Don't blame Elena. She left all the flower ordering to me."

"You must feel very much for her to take the blame for this. Your *amour*—it is this powerful?"

Maddie shook her head in frustration. "I never said anything about love."

"You wish to have her, though, yes?" Natalii's tone was teasing. "I've seen this Bartell's picture. She is very beautiful. I would wish to have her, too, if I worked with her."

Maddie scowled.

Natalii laughed heartily.

"I apologise to you, poor Madeleine. I was seeing how green with jealousy you are. I have no interest in your insane flower lady. I have my own Adèle back home, and she keeps me well satisfied. But now that we are bonded over our mutual lady loves, we will go out tonight. You will take me to the club for the gays, *oui*? Girls with the girls? I wish to see the, how is it called? The Sydney scene. Then, if you do this, I will forgive you making *Maman*'s house smell of blooms."

"But...I mean...I..."

"No, no." Natalii waggled her finger. "It is fine. We will look at the beauties but not touch. We must be virtuous for our ladies who have our hearts. *Oui?* Meet me out the front of this hotel tonight at nine." She climbed off her bike. "I have some things to do now I should not put off if I am to be so engaged tonight."

"I...um...okay." Maddie gave up. Great. Of fucking course, she'd have to hit her first gay bar ever with the lesbianish daughter of the most reclusive designer in fashion history. A daughter who was supposed to be going to some high-profile ball tonight but was planning to blow it off. With Maddie. At a gay bar.

She wished she hadn't been such a quiet, book nerd in her uni days and had gone and done the whole gay nightclub thing at least once. She forced a smile, which turned into a nervous gulp. How the hell could she be anyone's guide to something she'd never done?

"That sounds like fun," she mumbled.

"Oh it will be! And bring all your gay *amis*!"

Right. *All* her gay friends. "Uh, yeah. See you tonight."

CHAPTER 13

Skyfire

The only gay *amis,* well *ami,* Maddie could find on short notice was Simon. Who wasn't even gay but metrosexual enough that he could at least pass as one for a night if she begged him. He wouldn't care—he'd probably find it a good excuse to swap cocktail recipes with the bartender. The worst part was having to ask him because...well...it led to certain sticky questions. About who she drooled over, or didn't, for instance.

Simon knew all about Maddie's girlfriends over the years. It's just there weren't that many. There'd been a secret thing with the closeted Rachel, a crazy month with crazier Monica. In New York there was a regrettable one-night stand with a fellow waitress after their staff Christmas party. After that, there'd been no one else.

Then she'd met Elena. And Maddie sure as hell didn't need Simon knowing about how her hormones sat up and purred around Elena. It was embarrassing enough admitting to herself how gone she was on her boss.

Simon was looking at her funny. "Wait, so let me get this straight." He tugged on his best eggplant jacket. "This gym chick, what's her name, Natalii, that you just met has, out of nowhere, insisted you get all your gay mates together for a night out trawling the gay scene around Sydney?"

"Pretty much."

"So why'd she ask you of all people?" he asked. "Oh wait, you fancy this woman? You told her you're gay? Shit, awesome! Say no more, Mads. Of course I'll help. Haven't I been saying for months you need to get back on the bike?"

Maddie reddened. "No, I don't fancy her! And I didn't tell her I'm gay. She just assumed a local girl would know all the hottest spots and asked me to show her."

Simon gave her a long, doubtful look. "All the hottest *gay* spots. Can you join the dots for me, cos I'm lost. You don't want to date her, but you do want to show a total stranger around gay Sydney. Since when does Ms Introvert Maddie Grey do things like that?"

"Don't look at me like that. Okay, it's simple. I'm just trying to win a bet, and to do that, I have to get an interview with Natalii's mother. That's it."

"A bet?" His eyes lit up. "Who with?"

Maddie sighed. "Elena."

"Colour me shocked." Simon grinned. "Now it all makes perfect sense. The boss you're fixated on."

"I'm not—"

"Mads, not sure if you're aware, but you talk about her all the time. *Elena thinks this. Elena's won that.* Well, I think she's really hot—as in a swallow-your-own-tongue, super-villain kinda way. So I get it. So the bet's about impressing her. That's cool."

God. This was the reason she hadn't wanted to ask Simon for help. He knew her way too well. She gave him an aggrieved look. "You talk about Elena a lot too. It's not just me."

"Of course I do. I studied her business model at uni, along with those of Rupert Murdoch, Bill Gates, and Steve Jobs. And now my best friend is her PA—come on, that's amazing. But, Mads, you don't talk about her the way I do."

Maddie gritted her teeth. This conversation was going nowhere safe. "Can we just focus? Look, the bottom line is, Natalii doesn't know I want an interview with her mother. I'm being friendly and helpful, like showing her around wherever she wants to go tonight, and hoping to get in her good books and meet the mother later."

"Intrigue! Gotcha. I can do that." He gave her a kind smile. "But you do look extra freaked out. Is this your first gay club or something?"

She gave him a pained look.

"Figured. Hey, it's cool. I've been to a gay club before. Remember Mitch? From footy? He asked me to be his wingman one time, so no worries, okay? Been there, done that. I've got your back—unless of course some gorgeous chick makes eyes at me and then, bam, under the official wingman rules, all bets are off."

Maddie rolled her eyes. The odds of him being hit on by any woman at a gay bar were at sub-basement level. "Okay. Deal."

It took Simon all of six minutes to be hit on by some cute woman and disappear from her side at Manscape on Oxford Street. How the hell did that even happen? Like, seriously. And how had that awful pick-up line even worked?—"Hey, I'm not gay or bi, but I am Lebanese!" followed by snorts of laughter.

Clinging to her overpriced espresso martini and watching Simon's retreating back in dismay, Maddie turned to find Natalii staring at her.

"Why would you take us to a club for the *hommes*?" the Frenchwoman demanded. Natalii looked super hot tonight, in tight, black leggings, white T-shirt, and a slinky jacket of faux snake skin. At least Maddie hoped it was faux. "Do I look like I want to oogle-oogle at the boys?"

Maddie gave her a feeble smile. "I'm really sorry. Simon said the place is usually mixed. Tonight's some special thing."

"Oh *oui*, Simon! Your obviously not-gay *ami*. He flirted with me the moment we met."

"Um... Yeah, he does that. He's incorrigible around pretty women. Sorry."

"Mm," Natalii said, but she appeared mollified at having been called pretty. "And so where are the rest? Your other friends? The *lesbiennes*?"

Maddie reddened and stared at her drink, hoping a nice sink hole would open up and swallow her. "Does a Lebanese friend count?" She gave a pained chuckle.

"Terrible joke." Natalii glared at her and folded her arms.

"I don't have any." Maddie's admission made her feel like the worst loser. "No gay *amis*."

"How is that possible? This is Sydney! Mardi Gras, Oxford Street! You work in fashion!"

"I lost touch with my exes. And I worked a lot of night shifts."

Natalii studied her for a few moments before apparently deciding she was sincere in her loser status. "Okay." She whipped out her phone. "I shall be the one to find us some fun." She tapped a few buttons and made some swipes across her screen. "First, we go to Butch and Femmes." A tap. "Then Lady Luck. Then Pinkheart." Tap, tap. "Then Grrl Fantasy. *Oui*? They are all within walking distance. Your Oxford Street has much convenience."

It was past three in the morning by the time Maddie crawled out of the last nightclub. Natalii and her exotic accent had been popular with the clientele, and even Maddie, to her embarrassment, had to dodge phone numbers waved her way. She hated being the centre of attention, but with Natalii next to her, it was hard to avoid.

"Tsk, *non*," Natalii had declared sternly at one woman who tried to practically hump Maddie's leg on the dance floor. "*Mon ami* is off the table. She loves a scary woman who would drown you in masses of dead blooms. She is not for you. Go!"

"I don't lovvve her, Nat," Maddie said, slurring and feeling more than a little merry for all the free drinks that had come their way. "I mean, I don't think so. But thanks anyway."

"So you keep telling me. But there is too much of the protesting. Not just on your lips but in your eyes. And now it is time we go home. But first, I have something I must do." She pulled out her cell phone and made a call, speaking in rapid French. "It is done." She gave a taunting smile and eyed Maddie. "Outside now. We must wait for the ride and then…skyfire."

Skyfire? Maddie's pleasantly buzzed brain turned that one upside down and all around, unable to fathom what it meant. She followed Natalii outside and shivered against the cold. Her jeans, long-sleeved

T-shirt, and leather jacket were no defence against Sydney's frigid, early morning air.

Within fifteen minutes, a limousine turned up and, hot on its trail, a clutch of paparazzi on motorbikes and in cars.

Véronique Duchamp slid out of the back seat and tottered over on skewer-thin stilettos, screeching at her daughter in French with a sprinkling of English. Maddie worked out only about two words in every ten. The gist was something about her daughter ditching the ball and asking if this was where she'd been all night. And then, in sharp English, who the gutter wench was beside her.

Gutter wench?

"And so it goes, *ma chérie*," Natalii muttered to Maddie with an expression that was both amused and rueful. "*Maman* disapproves of me. And you. Of course she would hate you much worse if she knew your boss's name. Worse still if she knew what it was you were really up to tonight, *oui?*"

"Up to?" Maddie swallowed. "What do you mean?"

Natalii whispered in her ear. "You think you are the first to try and get to my *mère* through me? Tsk, Madeleine, I thought you realised I was smarter than that. No one can use my hotel's gym without actually staying there. So your motives? Already I knew. But you were also honest about knowing me. I could see you were so confused about your lady. Your eyes? They are so...what is the word...wistful when you speak of her. So I got a fun evening, and I think you got an education on what else there is out there. And now, I give you a gift of the skyfire."

With that, Natalii took her in her arms, dipped her, and kissed her thoroughly as the frenzied paparazzi snapped pictures. Flashes lit up the street. Out of the corner of her eye, Maddie was dimly aware of Véronique stabbing her finger towards Maddie as she shrieked at them.

Natalii let her up and winked.

Maddie stared back in a daze, at last understanding what skyfire meant. *Fireworks.*

"To make your lady of the many flowers *green*." Natalii grinned against her ear. "Something to make her think about what she is missing, yes? You are very welcome." She cupped her cheek. "*Au revoir.*"

And with that, she was gone, sliding inside the limousine after her mother, who was still berating her and being thoroughly ignored.

"Hey, love. Dave Stevens, *Daily Tele*," a masculine voice said near her ear. "Can we get your name? How long have you been on with Véronique's kid? What's she like in bed?"

SYDNEY CONFIDENTIAL

French Connections

It turns out the eccentric and elusive French designer Véronique Duchamp, in town for Australian Fashion Week, may not be one to party, but her daughter certainly is. Natalii Duchamp, 31, hotly tipped to be taking over her mother's global design empire this year, was spotted romancing a mystery woman outside Grrl Fantasy. The Oxford Street nightclub, famous for plenty of celeb lesbian hook-ups, saw Ms Duchamp pucker up with the redhead, pictured above, while her mother offered a shrill, French and English running commentary that dented all eardrums and didn't sound in the least bit flattering. (Unless "gutter wench" has a new meaning.) So who is this lucky lady being wooed by Ms Duchamp? Let us know. We're all ears, dears!

"You are SO unbelievably dead!"

Maddie groaned, pulling the phone away from her ear to better manage the chai latte, garment bag, and bulging folder of "highly urgent" proof sheets she was juggling, as she rushed down Elizabeth Street.

"I mean it," Felicity continued. "She's on the war path. She fired two models at the Whale Beach shoot before seven—one for being too tall and one for being too *too*, whatever the hell that means—and I think Aleisha is about three seconds away from a nervous breakdown, because how's she supposed to manage a shoot showcasing different swimwear body shapes with only *one* model? Perry's trying to calm Elena down. So where the hell are you? Where's her damn calming tea? And, oh yes—what on God's green earth were you thinking!"

"Hey," Maddie said in protest, "Natalii kissed *me*! And I'm almost there."

"Do you think I care who braided whose hair? It was unprofessional! You let that French devil spawn try to swallow your tonsils in front of cameras, and Elena threw the *Tele* so hard across the room I think the headline is now imprinted on the glass."

"She *what!*"

"Oh God! No! She's just threatened to fire Perry. We're all doomed. No one's safe. Get your pathetic ass up those stairs in two minutes or so help me, I'll kill you myself. Oh, and for the record, I'm not helping you clean out your desk. Because you brought this on yourself. You and your stupid wandering lips."

Maddie sighed. "But I didn't..." She waved her pass at the security guard. Her call ended just as the elevator opened.

She scurried into the steel box, pushed the button, and waited impatiently as it counted up the floors. Okay, so she might be about to be unemployed. Again. She needed a strategy. Something not involving catering. With her parents. She wouldn't ever be that desperate.

Her mind went blank.

Crap.

When the elevator opened, she raced out. The editorial staff milling around their desks stopped mid-conversation and averted their eyes. Great. So no chance they hadn't spotted the twenty-seven news stories and forty-one blog references that had circled the globe about the Sapphic-smooching daughter of fashion's most elusive family.

Not that she was counting.

That wasn't even the half of it. Simon had been sending her text after text. "I left you alone for five minutes!" he'd bleated at her in the first message that seemed to gasp all on its own thanks to all his shocked emoticons. It was followed by, "Okay, five hours, give or take. But not the point! Mads, call me!"

She had not. Nor had she returned the calls from her parents, her brother, or Lisa, the gossipy former *Hudson Metro News* secretary in New York. That one read:

OH! So THATS why u didnt like Jake? ☺ Whatevs floats ur boat. Call me!

"Finally!" Felicity said in a hiss, as Maddie rounded the corner. The chief of staff snatched the tea out of her fingers. "She's only asked for it, like, ten times." Felicity scrambled into Elena's office like a highly strung poodle, teetering on her nose-bleed-high Manolo Blahniks.

Maddie put down the folder of proof sheets and hung the garment bag she'd picked up for her boss in the small closet outside Elena's office. She plopped in her seat and turned on her computer.

"Ms Grey..." a voice floated from the other room.

Maddie's head snapped up at the use of her surname. *Uh-oh.*

Felicity exited Elena's glass office with an I-told-you-so look.

Maddie grabbed a notebook and headed inside.

She saw Perry first, looking dashing in a lilac shirt, his hands tucked into the pockets of his dark grey Armani jacket. His thumbs tapped the outside of them in a nervous beat. He turned fully to watch her enter, a curious look on his face.

Relief coursed through her. He still seemed employed, so that was a start.

"Yes, Elena?" She focused on her boss's narrowed eyes, Maddie's pen poised for notes.

"Well, well, look what the gossip columnists dragged in." She raked her gaze over Maddie. "You know, *Ms Grey*, when I predicted your abject humiliation, I had no idea you'd take me so literally." Her voice dripped with ridicule.

"I can explain!"

Perry began to edge past them towards the door.

Smart man.

"Explain?" Elena plucked a worse-for-wear newspaper off her desk and held it up. It showed Véronique jabbing a finger towards Maddie while screaming in her face. A face that was covered in the soft lips of a certain sexy, young Frenchwoman. "While I did not expect you to win our bet, I never expected you to do the polar opposite. I don't recall asking you to antagonise the world's leading fashion designer into an aneurysm."

Perry froze, and his head whipped around, intrigue lighting his eyes. "Bet? What bet?"

"Our bet," Elena said, teeth gritted, ignoring him, "was to acquire the attentions of the mother, not the daughter. And I wanted an interview, not a blood feud!"

Perry looked from face to face and back to the article. "Wait...your bet was about whether Maddie could get Véronique Duchamp's attention? *The* Véronique Duchamp? Who loathes and detests all media?" He gave a low whistle. "Okay." He turned to his boss. "So what does she get now that she's won?"

Elena snapped her head around to glare at him at the same moment Maddie's jaw fell open.

"Won? Does *this* look like she's won?" Elena pushed the paper right in front of his nose.

Perry edged a finger to the top of it and pushed it down and out of his face. "Actually, yes, it does. If attention was the goal agreed upon, I'd say Véronique looks fixated on Maddie. No attention lapse there at all."

"I meant *positive* attention!" Elena said. "Madeleine knew exactly what I meant!" She turned to Maddie, who promptly nodded. "See!"

"But that wasn't the bet. Was it?" A naughty smirk spread across his face.

Good God, does the man have a death wish?

Elena's expression looked like thunder.

Perry smiled back, apparently unmoved. "Well, you both win, then. Or lose, if you prefer. Maddie *did* technically get attention from the designer. But not the attention you wanted. So what do you both get?"

Maddie stared at Elena, who was sending daggers at her art director in a way which would make most men cup their gonads and mutter "mercy".

"Uh, honesty," Maddie said, still in shock. "We each have to tell the whole truth. Me for a whole day. Elena for a week."

Perry rocked on his polished heels and looked incredibly impressed. "Bold move, Maddie." He turned to Elena. "But how will that be any different for you?"

Elena smiled and seemed to regain some of her equilibrium. "My point exactly."

"Mmm." Perry ran a hand over his bald head and then glanced at the clock. It was nearing eight in the morning. "So, time starts now?"

Maddie bit her lip. "Why not, ah, call it a draw, and we both walk away?"

Studying her for a moment, Elena shook her head. "I knew it." Her eyes were taunting. "No backbone whatsoever."

"Ooh." Perry's eyes widened. "I believe, Maddie Grey, you just got called a coward."

Maddie glared at them both, unable to believe what she was about to do. "Fine! Time starts now."

"And my day just got a whole lot more interesting." Perry beamed. "Yours too, I imagine," he told his boss.

"We shall see." Elena studied Maddie again, her expression now far too pleased to be safe.

"Uh, I should get back to my desk," Maddie croaked, sliding her pen onto her notebook.

"Why?" Elena asked, tone silky. "And remember, honesty *is* the best policy."

"So you don't ask me anything I don't want to answer." Maddie reddened. "And so I can't see you looking at me like a steak you're about to rip to shreds and feed to piranhas."

Perry gave a snort of laughter.

"Perry," Elena said, her voice dropping to a low tone, "leave. I believe my brutally honest assistant and I have some things to discuss."

Maddie gulped.

CHAPTER 14

The Brutal Truth

Perry left, shooting Maddie a tell-me-everything-later look that she would have laughed at if things weren't so serious. At that thought, she glanced back to her boss, who was watching her with a dangerous expression. All other thoughts fled.

"Sit." Elena leaned her elbows on her desk, steepling her fingers. "Any confessions before we start?"

"Confessions?" Maddie hesitated. "If this is about last night..." She faded out, not exactly sure what she could add to an already catastrophic catastrophe.

"Did anything useful come out of it?" Elena asked, eyes sharp. "Aside from assorted hickeys?"

Maddie ignored the jibe. "I learned Natalii is really smart. Not easily fooled. And she and her mother clash a lot."

"Such as about whom her daughter kisses at three in the morning outside an infamous lesbian bar?" Elena's tone dropped to cool.

"How did you know it was four? That wasn't in the news article."

Elena shifted a layout proof to the left. "I don't see how that's relevant." She shifted it back to the right.

"It is to me." Maddie licked her lips. "How did you know?"

Elena gave her a sour look. "Felicity found out."

"Why?"

Maddie wondered if she'd pushed too hard when Elena's expression darkened. There was a long silence.

"I asked her for more information," Elena said, voice tight. "Felicity contacted that odious photographer and asked for further details of the events from last night. Nothing more." She waved her hand as though it was of little consequence.

"But why?" Maddie asked again before she could stop herself. She bit her lip.

Elena gave her the same acidic look she usually reserved for Emmanuelle Lecoq. "Why you kissed that Duchamp woman is a far better question."

"Not from my perspective," Maddie whispered.

"I can see you plan to take liberties with this bet. You know where the door is."

"What? That's cheating! You..." She petered out under a glare so frosty it would have re-iced the polar caps.

"Be very careful what you say to me next, Madeleine. I may have indulged this silly bet of yours, but I am still your employer. You are easily replaced. There are always others desperate to take your job. Never forget that."

Shock rocked through Maddie at the callous words. *Easily replaced.* How could she say that? Maddie had put up with a lot from her demanding boss since she'd become her PA, and she'd taken it because she remembered the other side of her, the things they never talked about. Shared moments, laughing or challenging each other in New York in the middle of the night, when they were alone. And while those moments were never far from her mind, much as she wished they were, she'd been the perfect assistant in Sydney. Maddie had made sure nothing of her real thoughts had ever glimmered through the cracks.

Until now.

As her anger rose, she allowed it to show at Elena's heartless words. Telling Maddie she was nothing. That's really what she'd said, wasn't it? She'd just admitted Maddie didn't matter. *You are easily replaced. There are always others desperate to take your job.* Did Elena even believe that? Maybe she did. She shook her head at Elena's closed face and felt her teeth bare. "They wouldn't be so desperate for it if they knew exactly what it entails."

Elena went still and stared at her. Every part of her expression radiated danger. "Oh?" *So soft.* "And what is it you think is so terribly onerous that an assistant of mine has to endure?"

Common sense and self-preservation caught up with Maddie, who squelched down her anger. "No. You really don't want to know."

"As it turns out, I do," Elena said. "And leave no whimper of injustice or tragic complaint unaired. I'm sure this will be most enlightening." She leaned back in her executive chair, studying her.

"You don't want to know the answer," Maddie tried again. "Trust me." She scrambled out of her chair and edged to the door. "I have some filing to do, calls to make..."

"Stop. Sit. Proceed." Elena pointed at the chair Maddie had just vacated. "You did agree to be honest with me."

Maddie froze. She just had to open her big mouth. Her anger had leaked and now, here she was, about to shatter Elena's world. She swallowed. Then sat. And began.

"Your PAs have to do the impossible," she said, wondering if she could distract her with the smaller stuff. "That's okay if we could actually also get five minutes for food. Trying to dodge city traffic with low blood sugar is...not fun."

She tried to smile, but Elena stared back at her stony-faced.

"That's it? How very terrible for you. Pack snacks. Harden up."

"We also get paid a crappy wage," Maddie said, "and work hours that are so long it's hard to remember what sunlight is some days."

"But you get invaluable experience," Elena said with a curt tone. "You are seeing the world of publishing from the very highest levels and gaining insights that many at your age would never hope to. Your objections are ridiculous. When I started out, I worked seventy-hour weeks and never once complained. I stepped up and took advantage of the opportunity."

Maddie folded her arms. "Well, fine. But then there's the harassment."

She had vowed never to share this secret, but Elena's challenging, mocking look pressed all of her buttons. The shock on Elena's face was almost worth it. At her stunned silence, a new, sinking feeling warred with Maddie's anger.

"What?" Elena's tone was incredulous.

Maddie forced herself to continue, her throat tightening at the thought of what was to come. "Some of your executives, associates, and friends act inappropriately around your PAs. They do it because they think we're disposable. They're right."

"Who?" Elena's voice was barely audible.

"Some big names try it on. We have been propositioned..."

Elena snorted, and her shoulders relaxed. "Propositioned? Is that all? You can't work out how to say no, so it's all my fault? If you knew what it was like when I was starting out... My God, the things that—"

"I haven't finished!" When Elena's jaw clamped shut, Maddie continued. "If it was just the endless come-ons, it'd be something your assistants could handle, but hands wander. A few do much worse. These men think they can grope your assistants, shove hands up our skirts, say disgusting things. The ones who are the worst of the worst and a serious threat to safety make the list."

"List?"

"The assistants' blacklist. It's a list that all the previous assistants leave in the bottom of the drawer in a handbook, to warn the next PA. It's a safety list. Any name on that list—we should never be alone with them, and never get cornered. Ever."

"I want the names on your little list." Elena's lips pressed firmly together as though she was trying not to say something else. Her eyes flashed and fixed on Maddie with a scary intensity.

"Why? Would you really cut off world-famous photographers who helped put your magazine on the map to see justice done for your lowly assistants—some of whom weren't with you for longer than a week? What about the sleazy board member? How could our feelings matter next to his importance to your company?"

Elena hissed in a breath. "You...all of you thought that I wouldn't care?" Hurt seared her face. "All of you involved in this conspiracy of silence thought I would have forgotten what it's like to be a young woman in business? I dealt with misogyny every single day!" Her glare was furious.

"Frankly, Elena, your assistants thought you wouldn't want to be put in the position to have to choose. Based on the comments on the list, I get the impression most didn't actually want to know which side you'd have picked if you'd been told. Others thought you knew and had turned a blind eye. More than a few feared being fired. Either way, they thought silence the safest option—they all know that, for you, Bartell Corp always comes first."

Elena's gaze drilled into her. She looked about ready to fire an entire department, and Maddie hunched over. And she hadn't revealed the worst of it. Not by any means.

"Their names." She stabbed her desk with her manicured index finger. "And there will be repercussions. I don't care who these harassers are."

"But it's not just names of people who work with you. A few others outside of Bartell Corp also see your assistants as easy targets, because everyone knows they don't last long."

"I'm not going to ask again."

Maddie's heart began to hammer. She wished she could say anything else but what she was about to utter.

"The list." Maddie exhaled. She could name them in her sleep as she was so hyperaware of them whenever they were in her orbit. "Jonathan Polden and David Pettigrew." Two of Elena's two most talented fashion photographers. Both men had won international awards. "Stanley Links." One of her well-regarded, successful newspaper managers. She swallowed at the next name. "Frank Harkness." Elena's business mentor, who sat on the board. They often travelled together. His picture was on her desk, for God's sake.

She took in the paling face opposite her and balled her fingers into tight fists. There was no easy way to say this final name. "And... Richard Barclay."

The strangled cry at the mention of Elena's husband made Maddie feel like the shittiest creature on earth. That feeling lasted all of two seconds.

"How dare you!" Elena looked ready to slap Maddie. "Is this some sort of a sick joke?"

"Elena?" Maddie gaped at her.

"Get out!"

"I'm only being honest," she said, her tone beseeching. "When he drinks too much, when we have to drop something off at your place or at events, sometimes he tries to pin an assistant against the nearest wall and get his hands inside our..."

"Disgusting lies!" The shout was so loud, the glass walls seemed to shudder. And Elena had never, in Maddie's entire existence working for her, raised her voice like this. Not once.

Felicity threw herself through the door from the outer room, her eyes blown wide, heaving breaths puffing out her cheeks.

Maddie didn't blame her. An earth-shattering cataclysm had to be afoot. Maddie shrank even farther against her chair.

"Elena?" Felicity's gaze darted back to Maddie with an accusing stare. "Everything okay in here?"

Maddie looked down at her hands. They were shaking. This wasn't how she'd expected today to go. At worst, she thought she might be confessing an inappropriate and hopeless crush. She'd figured she could brush off the humiliation, deal with a few gloating or pitying looks, and get back to work. But *this*... Hell. What had she done?

Elena was ashen, as she pinned her attention on her chief of staff. "Felicity, to your knowledge, has my husband ever touched you or any assistant inappropriately?"

Felicity's face lost all colour, and she shot Maddie a glower that said *shit, seriously*?

Maddie sighed. Felicity had the worst poker face, but her loyalty to Elena was complete. She had a terrible feeling about where this was going.

"Well?" The rage was coming off Elena in waves. Clearly, someone— or many someones—was about two seconds away from being fired, and by now everyone on the floor knew it.

"No, Elena, your husband has always been a perfect gentleman to everyone." Felicity did not meet Maddie's gaze. A small flush spidered its way up her neck.

It was a lie so blatant that at any other time Maddie would have laughed. Instead, her stomach dropped into her shoes.

Elena turned back to Maddie, rage etching her features. Her shaking voice was just above a whisper when she spoke: "You're fired. Pack your things. Get out of my sight."

"What? I'm fired?" Outrage flooded her. "So that brutal truth you claim to love? I get it now."

Instead of answering, Elena swivelled her chair to face the window, showing her back to Maddie.

Maddie squared her shoulders. "I see. Well, you're a fraud. I can't believe I thought you were..." She swallowed down the rest of the sentence.

"Oh, don't stop there," a low, harsh voice whispered from behind the chair. "No need to censor on my account."

"Someone worth admiring." Maddie couldn't stop the hint of sadness tinging her anger, as she ground the words out. "Someone worth..." She didn't say *wanting*. "You don't want the truth and never did. You just like to win. Or was it that you just wanted me to lose?"

"Felicity," Elena said, her voice a murmur. "Remove my former personal assistant from my office. Make the necessary arrangements with HR for a new one. We're done."

Those trademark words, normally delivered so casually, were vicious and cutting. The impact slammed into Maddie with the force of a pair of bullets.

Maddie turned to see Felicity's incredulous face. The chief of staff tilted her head pointedly to the door. Maddie left Elena's office, shutting the glass door behind her. Her last sight of the formidable media mogul, the woman who made her traitorous heart clench, was the back of her austere, black executive chair.

"Are you insane?" Felicity hissed the moment they were out of Elena's earshot. "What on earth possessed you to tell her that? Why would you do that to her? What were you thinking!"

"She demanded I tell her the truth, and I thought she meant it," Maddie snapped. She sat at her desk and systematically went through her drawers, wrenching them open, pulling out her possessions. "That's what I was thinking."

"Elena doesn't want the truth." Felicity looked at her as if she were a dense child. "She just thinks she does. So we all give her an edited version. What you did today was beyond stupid. How could you not know that?"

"And what *you* did today was lower than low. How could you lie like that?"

"Unlike you, *I* have a survival instinct," Felicity said. "Unlike you, I want to have a job at the end of the day."

"At what price?" Maddie tossed her contact book into her bag. "Did this job take your morals in exchange for being in the inner circle of the almighty Elena Bartell?"

"Don't you get all high and mighty on me! You didn't even know who Elena was a year ago. It's only since you've worked for her that you realise how brilliant she is. How remarkable. And how famous."

"Don't dodge the question." Maddie stopped packing to study her colleague in dismay. A colleague she'd been starting to think of as a friend. "How do you feel getting me fired by lying about her skeezy, handsy asshole of a husband? And don't think I didn't recognise your handwriting in the comments on the list. You know firsthand what he's like."

"You got *yourself* fired, thank you very much," Felicity said, not bothering to deny her charge.

Maddie saw the shadow of uncertainty in her eyes. "I hope that's a comfort when the next assistant complains about how she had to escape Gropey Richard."

"Please," Felicity said with an indignant sniff, "stop guilting me with those big, sad eyes and grow up. It's a scary world out there. We're all just trying to keep our head above water. I can't think of anyone who wouldn't have done what I did just now."

"Then I pity you."

"Oh-so judgmental. Let's see how moral you feel when you can't make your damned rent!"

"At least I'll still be able to look at myself in the mirror." Maddie hefted her bag to her shoulder. She looked around. She had everything she wanted. Her gaze went to the silent office adjacent. *Well, more or less.*

"In this city, you'd be lucky to even afford the mirror."

Maddie's attention snapped back to Felicity. They regarded each other for a long moment.

"What you did today, I'll never forget," Maddie said, steel edging her voice. She gentled her tone. "But I'll probably miss you, strange as it may seem."

Felicity bit her lip and looked down. "Yes, well. You always were the odd one." Her inflection lacked its customary bite. "And for God's sake, Maddie, it wasn't personal. At least believe that."

Maddie gave her head a rueful shake. "I know. I almost wish it was. At least then you'd have had the courage of your convictions."

Felicity's shoulders lost their trademark rigidness and slumped, as Maddie left Bartell Corporation forever. Along with Elena.

CHAPTER 15

Grey's Anatomy

Elena leaned back in her chair and stared out the window. Her office was in the garment district of Sydney, and her three-storey red-brick building was among those where the piecework operations for the rag trade had dominated in the mid-1800s. Grey, concrete alleys scribbled through the suburb, and old, leafy Moreton Bay figs punched the sky.

Today, the movements below didn't hold her eye. Elena's heart was in her throat. The one thing she'd vowed never to do at work had happened. She'd succumbed to a personal emotional display. She'd been weak after a lifetime of training herself to give nothing sensitive away.

Nothing had ever enraged her this much. Madeleine Grey had suggested her corporation was infested with harassers, and the long line of assistants in her employ had never been sure whether Elena had been turning a blind eye to it all along or simply hadn't known.

But that revolting thought paled next to the disgusting lie that each night she shared a bed with a man who groped women. Someone right under her nose.

She glared out the window. Richard wasn't perfect. She'd always known that. But he'd been so helpful to her career. He knew everyone. She'd had difficulty overcoming her natural reticence to engage the human race. He was charming, and people flocked to him, found warmth, and felt he was speaking directly to them. He could close deals and bring clients and rivals over in a way that had been thrilling to watch. The thought that he also...

Rage stirred in her belly. Madeleine Grey had ruined her image of the man she'd married with a single sentence. Elena glowered at the grey, inner-city streets, seeking answers. She turned the simple truth over of what she knew about her husband. Power was his turn-on.

Power. Was his turn-on.

She spun away from the window and stared at his photo on her desk. He was handsome, confident, and ruthless. Surely he wouldn't be...also *that*.

No.

He couldn't be.

How dare that woman hurl such a charge out there like this? What proof had she apart from hearsay from assistants long departed from the company? Anyone could put a name on a list.

But why would they? a little voice nagged at the back of her head. What benefit was it to them to do so? The list had never been made public. If it was part of some spiteful vendetta, the allegations would be all over the media. But no—this list had been tucked in the back of some handbook, passed from assistant to assistant to keep them safe.

Elena's stomach lurched again. It couldn't be true. She refused to believe it.

But if it was false, why would Madeleine tell her such a lie?

Her PA's accusation wrenched the rug out from under her. Had it been anyone else, she'd have known immediately their aim had been to hurt; that all this was about an ulterior motive. But Madeleine didn't seem to want to hurt her. She didn't have any motive. Indeed, Madeleine didn't seem to want to hurt anyone. She didn't have a malicious bone in her body. Elena frowned. This...cruelty was out of character for her former assistant.

But wasn't it true that everyone had a vicious streak when pushed? A darkness, when one was attacked, that led one to do and say things designed to injure. *Everyone.* Even an eternally smiling young woman who once presented her with exotic gifts while stuttering out speeches about how Elena was her inspiration.

She glared at the streets of Surry Hills and wondered at the strange disquiet she felt. That Madeleine had been the one to betray her with these allegations had caught her completely off guard. And that was what hurt most of all.

CHAPTER 16

Sweet Amour

Birds had the perfect life, Maddie mused, sitting on a park bench around the corner from her work (*ex work*). Pigeons swooped and strutted about, mooching for food. Humans complicated everything that should be simple. Like Maddie. She hadn't even managed just going into work, working, and going home. No, she had to get herself entangled in a silly bet that had gone thermonuclear.

She'd been sitting here for an hour, waiting for the sick dread to leave. Having Elena's rage directed at her for the first time was like being gouged and clawed. Her look of hurt and disbelief, though, was far worse.

Felicity's defeated expression, after she admitted selling her soul for her career, was burnt into Maddie's psyche, too. The woman wasn't entirely wrong, either. Maddie had no job, limited savings, and given she now lived alone, she could barely afford rent. Morals wouldn't keep her warm and fed.

Her phone rang. It was an unfamiliar number.

"Madeleine?"

Maddie's heart stuttered at the familiar pronunciation, then sank at the less familiar voice.

"Natalii?"

"Oui. Good. I need you. *Vite!*"

"What? How did you get my number?"

"Your Simon gave it to me. We are the Facebook friends."

"You've got a nerve." Maddie peered at a few kids playing on a slide on the other side of the park. "Your stupid stunt really pissed off my boss."

"Well, I have it worse than you! My Adèle, she saw the pictures on the internet. I am now *fini*!"

Maddie groaned. "So we're both *fini*."

"No, no, I do not accept this. You will come to my hotel now. I have the Skype; you will explain to Adèle that it was all just in fun. She knows I am crazy when I drink. Tell her it was our silly way to make your lady jealous."

"Why would Adèle believe me?"

"Ah *chérie*, if you could see the way your face alights when you describe your Elena! Adèle will see this too. I know it!"

Maddie snorted. "Well, there will be a lot less glowing now. Elena fired me an hour ago."

There was a startled intake of breath. "*Non!*"

"Oh *oui*. She shredded me, then tossed me out. So, yeah. I doubt Adèle will see much more than my anger."

"Was it because of the kiss? Oh Madeleine, I am sorry." At least she sounded genuinely remorseful.

Maddie sighed. "No. Okay, it's not like I'm doing anything productive here. I'll come and try."

"*Merci, merci, merci!*"

"Don't thank me yet. My bad mood is hard to hide."

"Madeleine, I will not forget this. So—I will see you soon?"

"Yeah, sure."

Adèle turned out to be a rather severe-looking punk rocker, with electric-blue streaks in her black hair and cheekbones so fine they could cut glass. She was striking and cool rather than beautiful, but Maddie could see why Natalii was so taken with her. Right now, though, she was glaring through Natalii's video link with blazing eyes.

"So you bring the *pute* to mock me?"

Maddie wasn't sure exactly what a *pute* was, but given it was said in the same biting tone as Véronique's "gutter wench" the previous night, she could guess.

"*Ma chérie, non.*" Natalii uttered a string of pleading French. After a few minutes, she turned to Maddie and gestured to the webcam, an expectant look on her face.

"Uh hi," Maddie said to the stony face watching from Paris.

"So," Adèle said in heavily accented English, "my Natalii claims all this was for fun. For small revenge to make your boss crazy by putting her assistant into the gossip papers. Because your boss sent so many of the flowers to Véronique."

"Revenge?" Maddie shot a look at Natalii, who looked shamefaced and guilty. "You... All this was *revenge*?"

"Just a little." Natalii did not meet her eye. "It was too tempting not to. But it was not the only reason—"

"*And* she claims she was drunk," Adèle continued, "and that you were innocent as a kitten, because you are feeling great love for your boss." She shot Maddie a sceptical look while misery etched Natalii's features. Adèle leaned forward and stared hard. "So, *Australian*, make me believe it. Tell me what is this Elena Bartell to you?"

Maddie closed her eyes, trying to rewind to before the horrors of the morning and thought about all the times Elena had studied her with interest and made her heart beat faster. *Before she cut it out and stomped on it and...shit, no...back to the day we met. Yeah.*

She opened her eyes. "The first time I met Elena, she insulted me. She implied that I was badly dressed. She even threatened to fire me over it. But she did it in such a way, it made me want to know more about her. I'm not sure how she did that. I spent weeks watching her. I discovered what she was really like. She's curious about things and people who intrigue her. And smart. She has a really dry sense of humour she doesn't share often. She likes to hide behind her scary persona and pretend she's a corporate machine. She's so much more."

Maddie paused as she thought about her, and a smile warmed her face. "And then one night we had this real conversation. She looked so interested. And...it meant a lot. After that, one chat became many chats, and it was all I could think about. I looked forward to it so much. Well, before...I came here. And now..."

She stopped again, as all the recent memories washed over her. "I know it's ridiculous. I mean, I know she's married and straight, but whenever she gave me glimpses of her real self, when we were alone and it was late, I felt special. Like she thought I was interesting enough to get to know. I started to believe that. But it was a mistake."

Maddie rubbed her eyes and gave a bitter laugh. "One day, she called me in and tore me apart. She made me doubt who I was. She told me I wasn't a journalist. I cared too much. Then she fired me and tossed me an assistant job instead. You'd think I would hate her for that. But no, even after everything, I still love to watch her at work. I love to watch *her*. I won't get that again, though. Hell." She choked on her words and stared at Adèle through tear-glazed eyes. "Did I mention Elena fired me today?"

Adèle peered back at her uncertainly.

Maddie shook her head. "I'm an idiot. She's fired me twice now, but still, I can't stop what I feel. I'll miss her so much. Which is totally messed up. I told the truth, and she fired me for it. But all I can focus on is that I won't see her ever again. What the hell is wrong with me? I must be a sadist or something. But you asked me what she is to me. Okay, when I think of her—Elena is beautiful and vicious and impressive and terrifying and charismatic and vindictive and a complete, utter hypocrite, and *still* even the thought of her drives me crazy." She paused, as a new thought hit her.

Oh God! Maybe she really did love her. Oh. Hell.

Don't let that be true.

Awareness mingled with surprise coursed through her, as she turned over that thought. There was a rapid-fire French conversation that seemed to go on forever, while Maddie sat in shock engrossed in her own fears. By the time tears were welling in Natalii's eyes and words of sweet *amour* were being exchanged, Maddie was jolted out of her reverie, her cheeks blushing at having understood way more French than she wanted to.

They stopped talking, and Adèle pinned Maddie with a contemplative look. "*Merci*, Madeleine. You have saved us when you did not have to.

You could have punished Natalii for hurting your life, but you did not. This is a noble act. And Natalii knows she will not be making so foolish a mistake again. I wish you well with your great *amour.*"

"I don't think she's that. After today, she hates me."

Adèle smirked. "Ah, Madeleine, you give up too easily. For shame." She waggled her finger, and her Skype screen closed down with a *blurp.*

Natalii looked at Maddie with profound relief. "You have done us a very great favour. So I will return it. I will give you something you want very much. *Maman* hates the media and would never grant you an interview. But I could ask her to give you the answer to one question. This I believe she would do. Okay?"

"Uh..." Maddie stared at her in astonishment.

"Just one," Natalii repeated. She gave a rueful smile. "*Maman* is a hard woman, driven, and always about the control. I think that even her own daughter she has difficulty finding pride in, so I do not have much sway. I do not think it wise to ask for more. So, one question. You will want this, even so?"

Maddie nodded quickly. One question with the world's most famous designer who had never, ever spoken to the media? Was there even any debate?

Her thoughts must have shown on her face because Natalii laughed and playfully slapped her arm. "As I thought. I will arrange this. Wait here. Think of a good one, though. Careers are made of less, *oui?*"

And with that she was gone.

CHAPTER 17

Of Cafards and Couture

Maddie's thoughts were chaotic and frantic. She mentally sifted through everything she'd ever read about Véronique Duchamp. She could ask about her influences, style, trends, what drew her to fashion. It all seemed too weak, too obvious. And she was no fashion journalist. She barely paid attention to what swirled around her at work. Her whole existence at *Style Sydney* had been focused on making sure Elena had everything she wanted. Predicting her needs.

She frowned and rubbed her forehead. Maybe that was the answer. What would Elena ask? Some question about the transcendence of seasonal trends incorporating all her lines for the last thirty years probably. In other words, a way to tie in an entire career into one article using a single quote. She could almost picture Elena instructing, in precise detail, her design team to lay out Véronique's fashions over the years to go with it. Because Elena lived and breathed fashion and revelled in seeing the big picture.

The problem was that Maddie didn't live and breathe fashion. And she couldn't see its big picture if her life depended on it. This was no good. She needed something else. Something different.

A profoundly daring idea hit her. She'd either crash and burn or...

Natalii returned, her usual wry smirk cemented on her face, indicating she'd just had another run-in with her mother.

"It wasn't easy, but she has agreed. Come, we do this now, as she wants it out of the way so she can have lunch."

Maddie followed the younger Duchamp into an adjoining room that was ludicrously opulent. She stared at the gold fittings and brocaded chairs and felt out of place in her plain pants and linen shirt. Véronique was arranged in one of those fine chairs, stiff and ramrod straight, looking regal in a green and charcoal dress that had bits of fluff affixed to it at random places.

"So? The little cafard who kisses my daughter. Sit!" Véronique ordered.

Maddie dragged one of the heavy "court" chairs over, as the imposing designer watched. It made an awful screeching noise. Maddie finally positioned it opposite the fashion icon and settled herself.

"I'll give you privacy to do this." Natalii turned to leave.

"No," Maddie said quickly. "Please stay."

Matching eyebrows arched, as mother and daughter swung to look at her.

Maddie gave a nervous grin. "Anyway, thanks for speaking to me, Madame Duchamp..."

"*Mademoiselle*," Véronique corrected. She waved her bejewelled fingers. "I am not some infernal *homme*'s property."

"Oh, sorry! The stories on you never said either way. There's nothing about your private life."

At the designer's indignant snort, Maddie rushed on, "Hi, anyway. I'm Maddie Gr..."

"I do not care. *Je vous accorde une* question. Proceed."

Maddie licked her lips and sent a prayer to any higher beings listening that her insane gamble would work. "You must love your daughter very much."

Véronique leaned forward, eyes flashing with outrage. "*This* is your question? What is this? You can ask me one question about anything, and you ask if I love my Natalii!"

"No, I already know you do," Maddie said, rushing in. "Very much. Or you wouldn't have let a *cafard* in here. So my question is, please could you explain, in detail, all the times and reasons over the years you have felt really proud of your daughter? A daughter who, I might add, you have done a wonderful job raising as an independent and strong woman with an excellent eye for design."

It was no lie—Maddie had seen Natalii's fashion sketches on Facebook, and she definitely had a gift.

Out of the corner of her eye, she saw Natalii pale and shoot Maddie a what-the-hell look.

After what seemed to be an eternity, Véronique gave a tiny upward twitch at the edges of her lips. "That would take a while."

Maddie grinned. "I have nowhere else to be." She placed her phone on her knee and hit record on the microphone app.

"Hmmph," Véronique said. "Well then, let us start at the beginning. My Natalii was always different. She didn't cry much as a *bébé*. She worked things out quite well by herself. She walked very young. And talked back to me always. I knew then that this one, she was special." Maternal pride lit her eyes, and the designer settled back with satisfaction, as she sifted through fond memories. "Very special."

Natalii blushed and didn't seem to know where to look.

Maddie nodded, trying to look encouraging. "I'll bet."

Véronique considered her squirming daughter, and mischief danced in her eye. "At age seven, I almost gave her the new name. Athena. Now why do you think that is? And not because I have any love for the Greeks." Her eyes became slits at the mere thought. "*Non*, Natalii was a heroine. Ah, it was a sight, barely in school, challenging two older bullies who had been hurting her friend. Her teacher said she had, what is it, the English words? A *mean left hook*."

"Oh, *non!*" came an appalled moan from beside Maddie.

Véronique laughed. It was an odd sound, a sort of huffing wheeze, but unmistakable.

"You had a junior boxer on your hands?" Maddie smiled. "I'm intrigued."

"Oh *oui*." Véronique slapped her hand on her knee. "She was that and much more. Let me tell you about the time I decided we should move out to the country and live off the land. It was not perhaps the best of my normally *géniales* ideas. Not good for either of us—we were both so used to the modern ways."

For the next hour, Maddie sat entranced as she learned all about the lives of the Duchamps—from their ill-fated attempt at milking cows, to the day Natalii decided she wanted to be a designer. Several times, the conversation dissolved into laughter, as mother and daughter were reminded of events long forgotten. By the time they got to the present day, the words were flowing freely.

"This so-called spat I had with Marcello and Donatella—never happened!" Véronique declared out of the blue. "*Cafards* bored with truth make up lies." She patted Maddie's hand. "Never become that, never ever. Truth always." She shook her finger at Maddie, who nodded with haste.

Véronique, Maddie discovered throughout their interview, was incredibly shy. She had such a fierce approach to protecting herself, her privacy, and her family that she'd been called a recluse. It was more a social anxiety, though—disliking strangers and unfamiliar settings. And it was one of the reasons she'd been so enraged with her daughter the previous night. Natalii had blown off an event she was supposed to attend with her mother and left her alone to fend for herself in a strange city.

"*Désolée,*" Natalii said, her tone filled with regret, apparently not realising the extent of her mother's fears. They shared a hug so awkward that it looked as if it had been years since the two had touched.

Maddie was wiping her own eyes by the time they were nattering away in French, soothing old hurts and misconceptions, which occasionally involved an explosive burst of words or a tearful regret.

"And I *do* like Adèle!" Véronique turned to Maddie. She huffed. "Do not let this one tell you otherwise," she added, pointing to her daughter. Her gaze shifted back to Natalii. "She has the passion of her punker music—which is an ear-exploding wail, it is true—but she is individual in a world of drab. People like your Adèle must be encouraged. I do not know why you ever thought I did not like her. Is it because she is a woman? Natalii Sabine Duchamp, tsk! I do not care about this! How could you ever think I would be so insubstantial?" She glared at her daughter, who rolled her eyes but looked pleased.

Maddie grinned. What a pair. She glanced at the clock and realised it was almost one.

Véronique caught the movement and gasped. "Oh! You have made us talk forever."

"Sorry," Maddie said. "I should go. I've kept you long enough."

"*Non!* We are not done yet. Lunch! And we haven't even talked about fashion."

Maddie blinked.

"Now then, *cafard*," Véronique said, and this time there was affection in the nickname, "what shall we order? Do you like the caviar? Too bad if you do not, for we are having caviar!" She disappeared to the next room, presumably to order room service.

Natalii, alone with Maddie at last, pointed an accusing finger at her. "You!" She shook her head. "*Merci.* I had no idea about so much of *Maman's* life. I thought, when I was young, she had punished me by taking us to that *merde* farm. I didn't know she was escaping a bad lover. Or that she was *that* afraid of strangers. I will never leave her alone at events again. Oh! And she likes Adèle! *Oui!*" Her face lit up. "You are most *incredible.*" She nudged Maddie with her elbow. "To think, an hour ago I was planning on murdering you!"

"Your *maman* is right," Maddie said in a dry voice, as she turned off her recording app. "You really are very violent."

Natalii burst into laughter. "As you will be when you see what *Maman* orders us for lunch. Her tastes of food—*fou.* Mad! She will have caviar and truffles and fries. Just wait and see."

Maddie laughed and waved her smartphone. "Then I think a photo or two will be in order. My *fou* lunch with the Duchamps!"

The three women shared more and more, as lunch turned into afternoon tea and then into dinner. It was like opening a faucet for Véronique.

The designer brought out some of the collection she was showcasing at Australian Fashion Week and asked Maddie to take photos of her testing the stunning gowns on her daughter. Natalii played an impromptu model, still wearing her motorcycle boots underneath.

The eye-catching photos were nothing the world had ever seen before. They were professional, yet intimate, and contained a sneak peek of new couture. Véronique had outdone herself with this season's line, and Maddie told her so. She knew just enough about fashion to know this would be an iconic collection.

The designer beamed with pride.

"My daughter has *très bon* taste in friends. You, *chérie,* are no *cafard.*"

It was well past ten by the time Maddie got home—dropped off by Véronique's driver at the designer's insistence. Maddie climbed out of the limousine, filled with elation over an incredible interview and just an all-round amazing day with two people she'd grown fond of in such a short time. She turned to go inside her apartment, just as a luxury silver car pulled up.

"Finally," came a drawled voice, as the tinted window rolled smoothly down. "I was starting to think you'd moved out. My driver was getting tired of circling the block."

"Elena?" Maddie stared at her, unable to believe her boss had somehow decided to sully herself by being seen in Maddie's neighbourhood. Actually, *again*, since she'd done this in New York, too. Was this a thing she did often? Car-stalk ex-employees?

"Get in." Elena's tone was a command that left little room for argument. "We need to talk."

Anger flared. She didn't work for the tiger shark anymore. Maddie tried to figure out which of fifty different ways to tell her where to insert her imperious demands. She was tossing up between a few tasty new French words she'd learned, too, when Elena said two things Maddie had never heard her utter before.

"Look, I was wrong, Madeleine. Now, get in. Please?"

CHAPTER 18

Driving

Elena studied her former assistant for a moment. She appeared irritated. Possibly angry. Well, that wasn't altogether unexpected. "Drive," she told the man in the front seat, not taking her eyes off Madeleine.

"Where are we going?" Madeleine asked. "Is this a kidnapping?"

Wasn't that a good question? "Nowhere. And don't be so dramatic."

Madeleine's gaze took in the folders and documents at Elena's side, scores of yellow Post-it notes sticking out of the pages. "What's going on? And before you answer, we're still under the rules of our bet."

"What is going on," Elena replied, "is that my soon-to-be ex-husband is packing as we speak. I had no desire to witness the ugly exit. He'll text me when he's gone. And I didn't want to be around people during this...transition period, but I needed to get work done, so..." She waved at the pile of work. "Here we are."

Madeleine's eyes widened. "Wait, you believe me now? Since when?"

Elena desperately wished to lie, but it was important not to in light of her recent poor behaviour. She sighed. "From the moment the words were out of your mouth. A part of me knew instantly."

"So, why fire me?"

Elena studied the street lights whirring by. They were almost pretty at this speed. "It was just one among many mistakes I've made in this sordid affair."

"What do you mean?"

Elena pressed the button raising the glass divider between her and the driver.

"Before I answer that, tell me one thing—did Richard ever...?" She hissed in a breath, as she met Madeleine's eyes. "With you?"

It had occurred to Elena after Madeleine left that she'd never said whether she knew about her husband's behaviour due to the list or whether her experience was first hand. The mere thought filled her with dread and white-hot anger.

"He tried once at a gala." Madeleine's jaw tightened. "He might be big, but I'm faster. So no."

The answer was a relief but still turned her stomach. She looked back out the window, unwilling for Madeleine to see her reaction. "No? Good," she said, grinding out the word.

If he'd laid a finger on Madeleine, she'd have wrung the bastard's neck. *How dare he even try?* Her breath fogged the window. A reminder of her mistakes in all this filled her head. She remembered one of the reasons she'd come here. Madeleine should know who she was.

"Three years ago, I fired a particularly insolent assistant," Elena said. "On her way out the door, she turned and screeched that I was 'as sick as him'. That I'd 'married my perfect match'. I was too stunned to ask what she meant. I just dismissed it as bitter ranting."

"That wouldn't have tipped you off," Madeleine said, apparently guessing where this was going. "You aren't a mind reader."

"No." Her fingers twisted, as she thought about how damning the rest was. "About a year ago, there was another one. A timid little mouse—quiet and efficient. One day, at home, I walked downstairs just as she was dropping off some paperwork. I heard my husband's footsteps retreating into the next room. The look on her face when she turned and I saw her eyes..." Elena slid her gaze back to Madeleine. "Fear. And do you know what I said? What I did next?"

Madeleine shook her head.

"Absolutely nothing." Her nostrils flared in disgust at herself. "She quit the next day. No explanation—and I didn't ask for one. I gave her a reference, something I almost never do. Yet I never stopped long enough to analyse why. There have been other moments—odd times when I have found Richard standing too close to a hotel maid or a waitress and stepping back quickly. I just dismissed these as my overactive imagination. Because I was...so taken with him." She sneered.

Elena would not say she loved him. It was hard to know what she felt anymore. All she knew for a fact, now, was that Richard Barclay had betrayed her, played her for a fool, and hurt countless women. She glanced over and caught Madeleine's expression. Distaste. *Oh.* It was to be expected, she supposed. She was confessing her sins after all. Still, the look stung.

"You're wondering how I didn't know his true nature," she said, tone flat. "Especially in light of these clues. I have spent the better part of two hours driving around tonight, considering my reactions and inaction to these...moments...to my intuition. And I do not like the conclusion."

"I can't believe it." Madeleine looked outraged. "All this time, and you *knew*. That's—God, that's..."

"No!" Elena said. She grabbed her hand and squeezed it urgently, needing her to understand. The warmth of it surprised her before she realised it was more likely that her own fingers were freezing. Elena dropped her hand. "No. There is a very large difference between a feeling, a hunch that something is wrong, and knowing. And do you really think, if I truly knew, I'd have let him anywhere near vulnerable young women?"

Her eyes bored into Madeleine's. "It might be obvious now, but it wasn't to me before. Because, as much as it pains me, it turns out you were right—I didn't really want the truth. Not on this. Especially not when two people laid it out before me so I couldn't hide from it anymore."

"*Two* people?"

"You and Felicity. Oh Felicity is cunning. She knew exactly what she was doing, telling me Richard was always a 'perfect gentleman'. He has become intoxicated at several events in front of us both— hardly a gentleman. She was aware I'd recognise the lie. So she was actually giving me the option to acknowledge it or not. How very... accommodating of her." Sarcasm dripped from her voice.

"Well, we are all well-trained."

"What? What on earth does that mean?"

"You know exactly what that means." Madeleine shot her a fearless look. "The Elena Bartell underling rules are clear: Number one is to protect the queen. I failed and you fired me for it. So now I have to ask—why am I here?"

"I thought that was apparent. I didn't circle your block for this long for no reason."

Madeleine waited, eyebrow cocked.

Finally, Elena forced out words that were foreign to her. "I'm here to apologise. I should never have taken out on you my anger and disgust at the shock of hearing the truth."

Madeleine studied her. "I think you forgot to roll your eyes, too."

"*Excuse* me?"

"Elena, you're acting as though you're doing me a favour. You're not the victim in my firing. Could you at least sound sorry?"

"I..." Elena paused and faded out. She *was* sorry, though. How dare Madeleine say... She stopped and shook her head. "I'm not good at this. Asking an assistant to return. It's, well, unprecedented."

"Why would I want to return?" Madeleine's tone sounded more curious than anything else. As though she didn't seem to care either way.

As Elena considered the implications, a coldness settled over her, along with fear. "You've already found a better offer?"

Maddie shrugged. "I didn't say that. But if you want me back, you'll have to do better than you're doing. Woo me properly," she said, eyes intense. "You know, tell me what a good assistant I am. Was. Just do something. Hell, anything's better than that half-hearted apology."

Elena smiled. She felt energised at having a mission she could get her head around, after a day of such overwhelming misery. "Woo you? Of all the... I had no idea you were this impertinent."

Madeleine laughed.

And it was the sweetest sound Elena had heard all day. The mood lightened.

Elena's phone lit up with a text message, and darkness mixed with relief as she saw the stark words. Her eyes flicked back up to

Madeleine's. "He's gone. It's done." She felt naked. This was just so galling.

"I really didn't *know*, Madeleine," Elena added. "I'm appalled and ashamed for what you and the other assistants went through. I'm disgusted I somehow allowed myself to be in denial about his true nature. I'm sorry that I hurt you today. You did not deserve it. You have been an exemplary assistant."

Madeleine gave her a long look. "Thank you."

"Just so you know, four of the five names on the list are ones I do have professional power over. I used it. I blacklisted them all—the photographers, the executive... They didn't even argue; they just wanted to know how I found out. I also dealt with...the board member. He..." She paused and her stomach twisted. Frank. Her most trusted adviser. The man who had been beside her from the first day she formed her new company. When Clarice died, he'd stepped in and become an invaluable mentor and friend. "I fired Frank. He protested his innocence and threatened to sue. I called his bluff. He backed down. He knows I don't say things I don't intend to do. He should; he trained me. So...I won't be seeing him again."

She pressed her lips into a grim line. The things Frank had called her. He'd said some things that could never be unheard. Suggesting she was a dried-up, frigid, closet job who'd probably fucked Clarice to get ahead. Where the hell had that drivel come from? His words clawed at her. Well, not the words so much as that it was Frank who'd been trying to hurt her. He'd acted as if she'd been the one to betray him.

"I'm glad you fired them all," Madeleine said. "That's...that's good."

"It's *necessary*. There is nothing good about the events that have transpired."

Madeleine gave her a thoughtful look. "So, it seems a few of your assistants would have lost their bet. I think your assistants mostly assumed that if you'd known, you'd never have punished your talented allies."

"And which side had you taken on this? What did you believe?"

"I bet on your humanity. Of course."

"As I said once before, that's not a safe bet—then or now, Madeleine."

"No. But I have seen it, no matter how hard you hide it."

"We'll have to iron out your belief in my human side if you expect to come back." Elena shot her an amused look.

"But..."

"Yes, yes, you must be 'wooed properly' first." Elena gave her a smirk. "Fine. I suppose it's the price I have to pay for luring back a not entirely useless assistant." She hid her mirth by leaning forward and pushing the button to lower the glass divider. "Home, driver."

"Not entirely useless, huh? High praise." Madeleine laughed.

Elena enjoyed the sound of it. She wished the woman had laughed more since they'd left New York. She'd missed those engaging green eyes teasing her.

"I would also notice your absence if you weren't by my side tomorrow," Elena said more seriously. "You are the least error-prone office employee I've ever had. And that includes Felicity. Some days, it's like you can read my mind."

Madeleine beamed.

"But don't let it go to your head."

Madeleine beamed even more.

"Oh God." Elena paused and eyed her former assistant with a small frown. "By the way, where were you tonight? Drowning your sorrows in some seedy dive?"

"Ha-ha. Is that how you see me? No—I was at Natalii's hotel."

Elena froze, as her thoughts went to dark places—Natalii comforting Madeleine, who had clearly been upset at being fired. The irritating woman, with that seductive French accent and trashy habit of latching her lips on to Madeleine's for the paparazzi, doing it again—possibly taking full advantage of her weakened state. Preying on her. Elena's eyes narrowed. A blacklisting was the least of what she could do to that predatory woman. It didn't matter who her mother was.

"Oh, it's not like that."

Elena paused in her vengeance plotting. "What *is* it like?"

"I was saving her relationship with her girlfriend. Adèle also saw the paparazzi photos."

"And how could *you* do that? Save this relationship?"

Madeleine reddened.

Elena frowned, wondering what she wasn't anxious to say. "I believe the bet still applies."

"I told her there was nothing going on between us."

"And she believed you? Just like that?"

"Yes."

"Why?"

"My earnest face?"

"I see. Now *you* evade the truth when it suits."

"I don't have any romantic interest in Natalii. And that's all I'm going to say."

"Why so late home, then?"

Madeleine's face brightened. "Well, I got caught up in a great story. I'd tell you all about it, but I'm not sure I want to give it to you. I mean the interview took place when I was no longer a Bartell Corp employee. So, really, I could take it anywhere. Make a bundle, too. Especially with the global distribution rights."

Elena went very, very still. Could she mean...? But how? No. It was impossible. But then again, Madeleine had been talking to her daughter today, so...it was possible.

"Madeleine, are you saying what I think you are? That you have an interview with..." She stared at her, raking her face for evidence of a lie. "You have..."

Madeleine reached into her pocket and pulled out her phone. She scrolled to a photo of Natalii Duchamp, sitting on the floor, legs straight out in front of her; black, chunky boots sticking up under a glorious, white tulle and taffeta dress. Her famous mother was leaning forward, adjusting the back of it, her half-moon spectacles perched on her nose and a row of pins sticking comically out of her mouth.

"Interview? Yes. Four hours' worth. And photos. Of the new line. Which I have approval to run in the magazine of my choice." Madeleine spun the phone all the way around to face Elena. She shot her a cheeky grin. "So, you'd better up your game on that professional wooing. Make it good."

Elena's hands had the faintest tremble, as she cradled the phone and stared at the photo. "Are there more?" Her voice was almost a croak.

Madeleine chuckled and swiped to the next one.

Here, Véronique was standing back, admiring another dress on her daughter, while Natalii looked right at the camera, all swagger and charm. It was intimate, yet breathtaking. There was vulnerability there, too. It was unexpected from one normally so guarded.

Elena allowed a faint gasp. "They definitely said you could use these?" She swiped to the next photo, and her eyes widened at what she saw.

"Yep," Madeleine said. "They loved them. They asked for prints after the story runs. Oh, that one there, that's Véronique's favourite."

The photo showed the designer adjusting the collar on a resplendent, satin women's pant suit, as her daughter glanced up at her, seeming impressed by the outfit and certainly unaware she was showing so much affection for her mother. It was a candid and powerful portrait.

"What resolution are these?" Elena asked almost fearfully. "What DPI?"

"I had my phone set on maximum. Here." She tapped a button, and the photo's properties appeared. "See? That's okay, right?"

Elena exhaled in relief at the numbers. "Inside, these shots will be fine as they are. As for the cover, it's right on the edge of acceptable. But have you ever heard the saying 'black and white hides all sins'?"

"No."

"Graphic designers have long known that if you turn a colour image to black and white, it looks artistic and interesting, even with flaws, instead of just low quality. Any of these would make a striking cover." She skipped past the next few shots and tapped the screen with her nail. "These are quite remarkable, Madeleine. Truly. You should be proud of yourself."

She lowered the phone carefully, her heart beating faster. For thirty years, no one had succeeded in getting this. And now? She slid her gaze over to Madeleine, filled with pride in her. A blinding thought struck, and Elena had to look away as she realised what it meant.

Madeleine, apparently now well used to her every twitch and expression, studied her in alarm. "What's wrong?"

Elena shook her head. "I just had a thought. But not now. Later. All right, I suppose you wish to write the story yourself?"

"Yes."

"Even though you have never written a feature article for any magazine in your life?"

"Yes." Madeleine's tone shifted to cautious.

"And you've certainly never written a fashion story."

"No."

"And yet you want to write this one, even though you will be on an exceedingly tight deadline?"

"I'm a fast writer."

"Hmm," Elena said in her most neutral tone. "You know I could put one of our top writers on it. You'd get full credit as the person Véronique spoke to and prominent photo credits. And you would not have to lift a finger, knowing your story would be in exceptional hands."

"No! No way. Give away the story of a lifetime? I can't believe you even asked."

Elena tried to hide her smile. "Well. To the finer points. You are aware of *Style Sydney*'s going rate? It's eighty cents per printed word for an unknown freelancer. I'm prepared to double it."

Madeleine stared. Incredulity washed over her face.

"Well?" Elena asked archly.

"Elena, I come up with the best fashion scoop in thirty years, which has international syndication potential and photos that even you call remarkable, and you offer me *that*? If you're trying to drive me to Emmanuelle Lecoq, this is a brilliant strategy."

Elena's jaw tightened at the mention of her arch rival. "Well, what do you suggest?"

Maddie gave her an impish look. "Why don't we skip the negotiations, and you just tell me what your best offer is—and please try and be brutally honest."

Elena stared, unable to believe the audacity. Then she smiled. It was her full smile, the one she rarely shared with anyone, and she felt a ridiculous amount of amusement at the confusion that flooded Madeleine's face.

"Good," Elena replied, "there's hope for you yet. Women must never be a pushover in negotiations. Too many devalue their own worth or, worse, try to be people pleasers. Excellent. Come along," she said as the car came to a stop outside her home. "I believe some professional wooing is in order."

At Maddie's still stunned expression and lack of movement, Elena smirked. "Well? Do you want a deal or not?"

CHAPTER 19

Reaching an Understanding

"Oh my *God*, you weren't kidding." Maddie sighed after her first mouthful of double-chocolate fudge cake. Her taste buds did a happy dance. They were in Elena's kitchen, perched on a pair of facing bar stools at the wide, central island. "When you woo a girl, you really do. This is gorgeous. How did you know I'd like it? God, how is it you even have food this decadent in your house?"

"Your mother told me, on your birthday, that chocolate is one of your favourites. We had a bit of a chat. Delightful woman. And Rosetta, my cook and housekeeper, is convinced I don't eat enough and that tempting me with such endorphin-inducing food will fix that. She usually leaves something fat laden in the fridge."

Maddie paused mid-bite, wondering if she was being pranked. "You think my mother's delightful." She waved her fork. "And you two just chatted? She sure left that bit out. Or are you just joking?"

Elena's eyes lit with amusement. "I do not make a habit of joking. Well, except, perhaps, about the amount I had planned to offer for your story."

"I see. By the way, this is a terrific opening gambit. Chocolate is my weakness."

"I would never have guessed." Elena eyed her licking the fork.

"Ha-ha. You've gotta admit this is glorious."

"I admit, I'm not immune to the wicked lure of chocolate. As a teenager, I craved it, but I refused to succumb." She looked at her untouched portion. Her fork wavered.

"It doesn't show," Maddie said, as she ran her gaze over Elena's trim figure.

"No," Elena agreed without a hint of modesty. "Although, I have a personal trainer, yoga instructor, and willpower to thank for that. So, now let's discuss what you really want."

"Do you even know?" Maddie gave her a challenging look, pulling her plate closer, her fork diving in again.

A mysterious smile greeted her. "Oh, I believe so. You are an open book."

"Let's hear it, then."

"If you insist." Elena examined Maddie's face. "I suspect, in order of desire, you require: love, approval, career success, and stability in all areas. The latter is probably why you were not in love with New York. You were too far out of your comfort zone. Possibly, you desire a pet. I'm thinking a cat—something cute and snooty."

Maddie loaded up her fork and shook her head. "No cats. Allergic. I also have an unfortunate habit of killing goldfish. And dogs need walking all the time, and one of us doesn't have a housekeeper to do that. So...no pets in my immediate future."

"And the rest?" Elena dug her fork in for a stab of the cake.

"I'd dispute the order of wants, perhaps, but it's pretty accurate—as it would be for everyone, even you. I mean, it's obvious you want success, so no contest there. And, come on, if you were dumped far enough out of your comfort zone, you'd crave stability, too. That's not just me. Of course, you also require love and approval. Who doesn't?"

"No," Elena said, voice firm, "I don't require approval. And love is highly overrated—as was proved today. Or whatever it was I had with Richard."

Whatever it was? Maddie would have loved to have gotten to the bottom of that comment. Instead she just chuckled at Elena's absolute certainty. "Come on, sure you want love. Who doesn't? Even approval—but I think you just pretend you don't better than most. Be honest."

Elena sighed. "Our word for the day. On that note." She pulled out her phone and pushed a button. After a beat she barked, "Felicity? Email me a J11 form immediately."

Maddie licked her fork, as her boss hung up and then dialled another number.

"Maxwell, Elena... Yes, I do know what time it is," she said, almost purring into the phone as she watched Maddie eat.

Maxwell had to mean Max Giles, Bartell Corp's chief financial officer. That was a very good sign that Maddie wasn't about to be offered peanuts again. She chewed slowly, listening.

"A very good reason," Elena continued. "It's about a large, unbudgeted editorial payment I wish to make. I'll text some numbers through to you so there are no mistakes. Call me back when you get it. And before you ask, yes, it's worth it." She ended the call, lowered her phone, and tapped out some figures.

Maddie caught a glimpse of the text just before Elena hit *Send*. She choked on her cake. There were six figures. *Six* figures. With zeroes. Many, many zeroes.

Tiny bits of chocolate cake sprayed across her plate, and Elena stalked behind her and slapped her back soundly, as her phone rang.

"Max? No, it's essential," Elena said without missing a beat, as though Maddie wasn't flailing about in front of her. "A story we cannot pass by. It's unprecedented."

Elena walked to the fridge and returned, placing a bottle of water in front Maddie. "No, that is not all," she said after a series of shocked verbal eruptions came from the phone.

Maddie cracked the bottle's seal.

Elena returned with a glass and placed it in front of Maddie, barely looking at her. "I want to redo the next issue of *Style* globally—yes, every issue in all five countries—and drop in a new twelve-page cover story in time for Australian Fashion Week."

Maddie choked again, this time in shock, and Elena's amused gaze drifted to hers. She gave her a slow, feline smile, revealing how much she was enjoying this.

"Yes, I'm aware of that, but we both know they don't actually *print* until midnight tomorrow, so you won't have pulping costs, just overtime. Mm. Correct. We will be able to recoup the costs from onselling the story to international publications in countries that don't sell *Style*. You will quadruple circulation for the next two issues; I stake my reputation on it. Just tell me you can do this. Tonight. Yes."

Her phone pinged with an incoming message. "I believe I have the freelancer release contract, so I hope to seal the deal shortly and will send it to you and Tom tonight. Give him a call and let him know it's coming, would you? All right. We'll talk soon."

Elena closed her phone. She opened the text message she'd sent to the CFO and showed Maddie the screen. "That is—honestly—my best offer. It includes global rights for your story and exclusive, first use of all your Duchamp photos. It's higher than we've ever gone before—for anyone."

Maddie stared at the sum, feeling numb. It beat anything she'd even remotely had in mind. That was a life-changing amount. She shot Elena a mischievous look. "Would Emmanuelle offer more?"

Elena's mouth twisted in distaste. The silence dragged out. "Yes," she said, as though someone was ripping her fingernails out. "I believe she would put an extra thirty thousand in. Possibly forty, if fiscal madness seized her. But she has a little more wiggle room on overheads than I do."

"I see," Maddie said. "Thanks for the honesty. So why would I go with *Style,* if it'll cost me forty grand?"

Elena returned to sitting beside her at the counter. She considered the question. "Well, you know us. You know that my team and I would never distort your words or images in the editing process. I would ensure that you'd have a final say on the last draft. I'll make sure that's in the contract. You know my commitment to quality. And you know my reputation—it *is* well deserved. I expect the best, because I produce the best."

"But you're not the best anymore, at least not in Australia," Maddie argued, playing devil's advocate. "*CQ* is the leading fashion magazine in this country, right now, and at least half the story is about *Australian Fashion Week.*"

Elena's jaw worked, as she seemed to digest that unsavoury statement. "Yes," she said tightly. "But *Style* is the leading fashion magazine in the world. You'd get more readers total, just fewer here."

"What if I didn't want to sell to a fashion magazine at all? I have quotes for a terrific profile. I'm sure *Vanity Fair, Rolling Stone, Time,* and many other general mags would buy my story. I'd reach an even wider audience."

"Yes. You likely would. But not a passionate audience. You would not reach people hanging off your every word, desperate to know more. You would not reach Véronique's ardent followers. But let's say you went with a mainstream magazine—do you know them? Trust them? Would you feel comfortable ringing up their editor and saying you hate what they've done with the layout and they have to drop the third photo on the eighth page, because you just don't like it?"

"Elena, I wouldn't feel comfortable saying that to you now."

"Hmm." Elena paused for a moment. "But you *would* say that to Perry, yes?"

Maddie nodded.

"So, that settles it. If you chose us, Perry would be your liaison. As art director, I'd want him involved anyway. His design eye is unmatched. And I'll have our best senior editor help you with our in-house writing style."

"Is all that worth forty-thousand dollars?" Maddie asked.

"*CQ*'s Australian Fashion Week issue went to the presses yesterday. Its next issue will be in a month. Your story would lack currency, if you had a series of photos about a fashion line that had already been photographed on the runway and seen on every blog and newspaper in the world. Your exclusive value would then only lie in the interview and the novelty of the photos, without their news value. You and *CQ* would look downright late to the party and silly. It would make you appear far less impressive. I wish you to be *spectacular.*" Elena smiled and reached for her hand, covering it. "Let's be spectacular together."

God. Maddie was having a hard time resisting that combination of words and smiles. And now touch? Elena's fingers squeezed Maddie's and released them. Maddie's heart thudded like the pathetic organ it was. She doubted her business brain could withstand the onslaught of Elena Bartell in full charm-offensive mode, either.

"I forsee a two-part series," Elena began with a flourish of the same hand that had briefly clasped Maddie's. "Twelve pages this issue, just on fashion week content to whet the readers' appetites. We'll tease them about the next issue, which will contain twenty pages on the life and times of Véronique. I assume that's all covered in your four-hour interview?"

"Yes. Everything—right down to her milking cows in the late eighties. Badly."

Elena ceased all movement. "What?"

"They lived on a farm for a bit. To escape Véronique's scary ex-lover. Philippe the rugby player. He once threw her sewing dummy off a motorway from his Ferrari."

"Dear God." Elena rubbed her temple.

"Are you okay?"

"That insane woman says nothing whatsoever to a soul about her private life for three decades, and you get all this out of her? How? What on earth did you do to her?"

Maddie shrugged. "I'm not sure. I was just, um, myself."

Elena stared at her. Finally she exhaled, nostrils flaring. "*That's* what we never tried. Sending a normal person in."

Maddie laughed. "You think I'm normal?"

"Madeleine, how do you take your coffee?"

"White with two sugars. Um, regular milk I mean. Not soy or skim or any of that stuff."

Elena gave her a pointed look.

"Oh. Right."

"Where was I? Oh yes, two issues. We'd promote them extensively in TV, print, and online. You will be famous, Madeleine."

"I didn't do it for that."

"Oh?"

"No. And before you ask, not the money, either. That's all just... extra."

Elena looked slightly alarmed. "Are you not sufficiently wooed, then? Are you still not convinced to go with us?"

"You make a good case." Maddie hesitated. "I was thinking more long-term. I did this interview to get ahead in my career. And, of course, yes, to prove to you I am a journalist. So, while your offer is great and all, it's just..." She faded out, not sure what she was asking for. Just something different. Less financial. More...

"Ah." Elena nodded, reached for a piece of paper and scribbled for a few minutes, then pushed it over to her. "The major events of the next twelve months that I will be attending. These will have a large VIP-publishing presence. Sell your story to us, and you will be my guest for the evening at any four of these you choose. I will ensure Bartell Corp flies you to and from them, should you select events not held in Australia."

Maddie's eyes slid down the page, widening as she examined the list. Peabody Awards lunch. Matrix Awards. Pulitzer Prize dinner. Time 100 gala. New York Times Fashion Week opening night. Met Gala. Sydney Magazine Publishers cocktail party. American Publishers black-and-white ball.

"As part of the deal," Elena said, "I would introduce you to the key movers and shakers there and explain all the ways I have found you to be acceptable. Further," she pulled the page back and wrote another line, "access to Perry's style expertise and his contacts should you need a dress or four. I can't have you looking like a sad garage-band reject while at my side." Elena's lips quirked the faintest bit.

"God forbid," Maddie murmured, amazed Elena had even thought of that. She studied the impressive list and slid her eyes back to Elena. "But you wouldn't mind? Having me as your... guest?"

Elena just looked at her as though she'd said the stupidest thing she'd ever heard.

"Right." Maddie's cheeks heated. "Can you give me a few minutes to think about it?"

"Of course," Elena said with an approving nod. "Take the time you need. I have to check on some things. And I'll print out the contract Felicity has emailed me, should you decide in *Style*'s favour."

She swept out of the room, and Maddie watched her sway of hips with a sudden sinking feeling. She tried to pinpoint why she felt deflated. This was an amazing deal. A career-changing one. Elena wasn't wrong—it was far and above anything *Style Sydney* normally paid. Maddie knew, because she'd filed plenty of contracts for her boss.

Elena was also putting a huge amount of faith in her. She hadn't even heard the Véronique interview. She hadn't seen Maddie's writing beyond the short news pieces that *Hudson Metro* had run. This would be a feature story—two of them, actually—and together they were almost a hundred times longer than anything she'd ever written before. Yet Elena hadn't questioned that. She'd just assumed Maddie could pull this off. Why?

Maddie slid off her chair and took her plate to the sink, washing it. A click, click noise caught her attention. She glanced down to find a pair of big, brown canine eyes staring up at her.

"So," she turned off the tap and crouched to greet the knee-high dog, "you must be Oscar." She allowed him to sniff her with his long muzzle, as she studied his lean features. Then she ruffled his red, pointed ears. Oscar's tail began to thump.

"You're beautiful," she told him, then leaned forward to whisper, "just like your owner. But don't tell her I said that. It might undermine my negotiating position. Okay? I gotta have some authority here. So mum's the word."

The animal snuffled, then licked her hand.

Maddie smiled, deciding she liked him. Oscar had a certain poise, too, which was down to the Cirneco dell'Etnas pedigree. She had looked up the breed the first time she'd had to book him into a vet. It was a rabbit-hunting dog from Sicily. Trust Elena to have an animal even more complicated than she was.

"Yep, you're all class and elegance, aren't you boy? Gorgeous." Maddie gave him another firm scratch, which made him arch his neck over more, seeking extra attention. "I bet you and your mistress look stunning out walking together."

Her heart clenched at the words, and a flash of sadness seared through her. She frowned.

What on earth was bumming her out?

Maddie returned to her bar stool and fished out her phone, thumbing her way through the photos of Véronique and Natalii. When she'd snapped them, she'd never thought her day would end like this. And then it hit her: *This was goodbye.* Elena had virtually said as much in every look and word since they'd entered her home. And the clause allowing her access to Perry? That would be unnecessary to include if Maddie still worked at *Style Sydney.*

She felt a warmth on her thigh and glanced down to find Oscar's handsome head resting there. Maddie ran her fingers through his fur, scratching behind his ear, and sighed. She was going to really miss Elena.

A noise broke her musing, and she looked up to see the woman at the heart of her thoughts leaning against the door frame, studying her.

"So," she said, "you've just worked it out, haven't you? I did earlier. In the car."

"Elena?"

"Tonight, I came to see you with one purpose—to get you back to my side, where I thought you belonged. And then I realised it was too late. You were gone the second you got the first quote out of the world's most reclusive designer."

Belonged? Elena thought Maddie belonged with her? Hope warred with regret. Elena didn't mean it like that, but still...

"I don't *have* to go." Maddie scrambled to ground her thoughts. "I mean, I have options now, yes. But, I mean, I could..."

"Madeleine," Elena said, tone stern, "we agreed to no lies. Why did you become my assistant in the first place? And don't tell me it was for my excellent company and superb people skills."

"I wanted to come home."

"Yes, I'm well aware. But why else? Because they do have flights rather often between New York and Sydney."

"It's like you said, it was a face-saving way to do it," Maddie admitted. "And it looks good on the résumé saying I'm your personal assistant."

"Madeleine." Elena's voice brooked no arguments...or lies.

"Okay." Maddie exhaled. "I also hoped you'd write me a nice reference. I know it was wishful thinking, since you rarely do, but... once upon a time we were almost friends. And I thought if you didn't entirely hate me when we parted ways, you might write me one."

"Of course," Elena said with a nod. "All my PAs have that vain hope. But why? Why did you want my reference?"

"To get a job anywhere in journalism I wanted. Your name has that power. A reference from you could open so many doors."

"Exactly." Elena gave her a triumphant look. "Congratulations, Madeleine. You are the first employee I have ever said this to—you don't need my recommendation, and you don't need me."

A denial coated Maddie's tongue, but she held it back as she thought about what Elena had said. Was she right? Well. Yes. Maddie had already "gone". *Who writes a world exclusive, then goes back to being an assistant?*

The realisation was sharp and awful. She'd wanted another journalism job, sure; that had always been the plan, but she hadn't even been looking. Because the thought of no longer seeing Elena filled her with pain. Whatever happened next, this would all soon be over.

"Yes," Elena said quietly. "Now you see."

Maddie didn't reply. It now felt so real. Leaving Elena. She ran her fingers through Oscar's fur, as she thought about that.

Elena's gaze tracked to below the kitchen island, to her dog which Maddie had somehow appropriated. "Well. I see I'm not the only one who appreciates your charms."

Maddie tried to smile, but her sadness was overwhelming. No more Elena.

Oscar lost interest, slid his head off her thigh, and padded out of the kitchen.

Placing some paperwork and a pen in front of Maddie, Elena said, "Feel free to get a lawyer to look those over. I advise you not to take too long. We have only twenty-four hours to redo twelve pages of *Style* magazines all around the world. The more time we have, the better. And I won't lie to you: it will be a brutal twenty-four hours."

Maddie looked at the paperwork. She'd seen it before. Quite often in her PA job. It was a standard two-page freelancer contract. Everyone signed them. They were fair, or so the writers would often tell her when she'd gotten to talking to them. Fairer than a lot of publications, they told her.

Maddie read the contract in detail and turned to the back page. There, in Elena's florid handwriting, were the words: *Madeleine Grey has final right of approval on the last draft of her story.*

Maddie picked up the pen.

"Are you sure?" Elena asked. Something about the way she said it made Maddie pause and really look at her. Excitement flashed in her eyes. Hunger. She'd seen that before in her boss. Every time she nailed down some big business deal, Elena glowed. But there was something else, too. A faint hint of...regret? Was it possible her demanding boss would also miss her a little?

Maddie remembered the odd frisson they sometimes had in New York. She'd sometimes catch a head tilt and a directed gaze that made Maddie's stomach feel so odd. She'd felt Elena's gaze on her in Sydney, too, more fleeting and guarded, not the way it had been. Not as it was right now. Right now, Elena's eyes seemed to bore into her—fascinated, alert, and encompassing. Waiting. Watching.

I'll miss you, too.

Maddie gave herself a mental shake. She was obviously imagining things. Of course she was. Why would Elena miss a lowly assistant? Especially one she'd fired fifteen hours ago while in complete bitch mode. Not to mention one she'd fired a few months before that. No, Elena Bartell would miss nothing but efficiently delivered chai lattes.

Non-fat milk, no sugar, extra hot, her brain supplied helpfully.

She almost laughed out loud, feeling slightly hysterical. Instead Maddie looked down, scanned the contract again. Nodded once.

And signed.

CHAPTER 20

Cheers

A celebration was in order. Elena cracked a rare and stunning bottle of claret, the likes of which had never danced across Maddie's palate before.

"God, this is delicious," Maddie said. "I think you may have put me off wine for life because it'll never be this good again."

Elena smiled. "Well then, I have done you a disservice. A good wine is like a good story—you have to be hoping for an even better one just around the corner. I'd hate for you to give up, now you've had a taste of it."

Maddie appreciated the conspiratorial purr to her tone. The intimacy of it reminded Maddie of their conversations back in New York. When Elena was relaxed, she would shoot her an interested look, as though she had all the time to discuss anything in the world. And right now, Elena seemed to want to discuss Maddie.

It was a heady feeling, being in the laser-like glare of Elena Bartell's focus. Part of Maddie wished they could stay frozen in this moment forever. Would this be their last real conversation? Maddie's only chance to connect with her, away from some party or event, before they never spoke again? Her heart gave a pained clench.

Maddie's voice was warm and low as she replied, "We're not still talking about wine, are we?"

"No." Elena smiled and swirled her wine around her glass. "I trust you'll keep striving to be a better journalist, despite starting your career with an international exclusive."

"Of course." Maddie grinned. "This is only the start."

"So, will you tell me how you did it? What did you ask to make her open up like that?"

"Truthfully?" Maddie gave her a small smile. "I'd only been allowed one question."

Elena stopped swirling her wine and stared at her. "You are joking. You got all of that with one question?"

"Well, most of it, but yeah."

"One question."

Maddie opened her mouth to tell her what it was, but Elena held up a silencing finger and looked thoughtful. After a minute she sighed. "No. I can't think of any single question that would elicit all that information from someone so private. So, I give up. What was the magical question?"

"I asked her to detail all the times and places she'd been proud of her daughter."

Elena frowned. "I don't follow. Why ask that?"

"Natalii told me her mother found it hard to admit when she was proud of her. So I saw it as an ice breaker, a way to keep the conversation going. If all else failed, at least Natalii and her mother could maybe break down some of the walls between them. It just seemed, well, right. Turns out, maternal pride can crack even the thickest walls."

Elena examined her for a few moments. "Well. You do have a knack for finding people's human spots, don't you?"

"Human spots?" Maddie turned that over uncertainly. "You think I exploited their weaknesses?"

"On the contrary—you picked up on something unsaid and worked with it. Something they needed to deal with and, more importantly, wanted to talk about but didn't know how. Understanding people is a skill. What makes them tick, what makes them talk. You have it." She shot Maddie a rueful look. "I don't."

"I don't know about that. You're talking to me. I'm talking back. You've always been able to talk to me. I'd say you've nailed the whole make-casual-conversation brief."

Elena didn't smile. "It's why I lost my promotion, you know. Years ago, at *CQ*. I was supposed to be the new editor. I was young and brash. I didn't read the mood of the room, the executives of the board.

Lecoq found my weaknesses—my age, arrogance, and lack of people skills—and hammered the *CQ* board with them. I always assumed my superior abilities would win the day. I said as much. I was destroyed. Lesson learned."

"Their loss. It's worked out better, though, right? You've proved them wrong now. And how."

Elena's eyes glittered for a moment. "Yes." Her expression turned cool. "They know they were wrong. Not that they'd ever admit it."

"Is that what you want? Them to say it?"

Reaching for the bottle of wine, Elena eyed the level and gave it a waggle. "I should get another."

Maddie waited for her to answer the previous question.

"Do you want a refill?" Elena asked instead.

So, she was avoiding it, then. Touchy subject. "I'm good. We have a big day tomorrow."

Excitement flared in Elena's eyes. "Of course. You have achieved a remarkable coup."

Her enthusiasm felt infectious. "Is this why you do it? For the rush? The thrill of signing the deal? Winning?"

"There's no greater high in life." Elena's expression dared her to disagree.

Laughing, Maddie shook her head. The beautiful wine made her feel so relaxed. "I don't know, I can think of one fun thing that's a bigger high." She gave her eyebrows a suggestive lift before she could stop herself.

Elena's hand froze on the bottle where she'd been about to top up her wine glass. Her gaze slid over to Maddie's. "Is that so?"

"Well, yeah. I mean come on!" Maddie started to laugh again. She petered out when Elena didn't join in. "Wait, you don't think so? You really don't, do you?"

"No." The word was as flat as her expression. She placed the wine bottle back on the table.

Maddie gave her a curious look. "But..." She stopped herself from saying something she couldn't take back. Like, how could someone as amazing as Elena not have found even one decent partner who appreciated her enough to give her great sex? Hell, Maddie would be more than happy to volunteer. She took a hurried swig of wine at that stray thought.

"What?" Elena studied her.

"Look, either I'm doing career wins badly, or you're doing sex wrong."

"And which do you think it is?" Elena's voice was low and smoky. "Specifically."

"Uh…" All coherent thoughts fled as Maddie pictured…specifically… Elena having sex. Her creamy, perfect neck tilted back. Maddie's throat constricted. "Well, to be fair, without trying both, I couldn't possibly answer that."

Her brain suddenly caught up to what she had inadvertently just proposed. Her cheeks flamed. "Oh! I didn't mean to offer to…with you… I meant it's like science." A high-pitched laugh came out. "You know? You have to try each scenario to reach a sound conclusion…um…"

Elena gave a slow smile that caused Maddie's toes to curl and her palms to sweat. This was so embarrassing. Propositioning, even accidentally, her straight, former boss?

"So," Elena said in an amused drawl, reaching for the wine bottle again, "thanks for clearing that up. You sure you don't want that top up?"

Maddie thrust out her glass instantly and nodded.

Maddie was trying to hide her growing exhaustion, but the day had been long and emotionally draining. It was just after midnight. She yawned for a third time.

"Stay," Elena said. "Here. For the night."

"What?" She was fairly sure her ears had just lied to her.

"I have a guest room. And there is no way I am about to risk the scoop of my lifetime and yours to a random taxi or train."

"Oh." Of course. Guest room. Bed. "That makes sense." She tried for a smile.

Elena nodded. "Good. I'll show you the way. And if you get peckish in the night, you can help yourself to anything in the kitchen."

"Thanks."

Elena's perfectly proportioned ass should be the subject of poetry, Maddie decided as she followed her up the stairs to the second level. It was so toned and undulated gloriously against her tight pants. Her brain went to a dreamy place.

"Here." Elena snapped on a light and gestured. "En suite is through there."

Maddie stared at a room that was like something in a five-star hotel. The wall facing the queen-sized bed contained a gleaming, integrated TV and stereo. Peaceful artworks, stylish fittings, and a lush carpet completed the luxurious picture. A person could stay in here for a week and never want to leave. She must have been making an odd face, because Elena paused.

"Is it not acceptable?" Her gaze took in the room. "Did you need something else? Extra blankets, pillows? The sheets are thousand-count Egyptian cotton, if that's an issue."

"No! It's not, it's... I mean, it's...*wow*. I think the room's bigger than half of my apartment."

Elena smiled, and Maddie was struck by the softness to her eyes.

"Good," Elena said. "Until the morning, then. Sleep well." She closed the door behind her.

They proved to be famous last words. It was like a curse. Despite the lateness of the hour, Maddie found it impossible to fall asleep. Her mind was still whirring about the evening. Elena's watchful, intense eyes. Maddie's story. How to structure it, what to put in. Elena's fingers, so long and supple as they grasped the stem of her glass. What to save for the next issue. Elena's smile. She'd smiled a lot tonight, sometimes teasing, sometimes amused. It was probably just the wine. But it was overwhelming seeing her with her guard down.

And then there was the six-figure elephant in the room, stampeding through her brain. She'd have so many opportunities now—she could freelance if she wanted to, not having to worry about meeting rent for a long while. Or put down a deposit on her own apartment. Or...

After two hours of tossing and turning, her stomach intervened and grumbled loudly. Véronique's bizarre preference for French fries and caviar hadn't exactly filled her up. Nor had Rosetta's chocolate cake. Maddie threw aside her bedding and padded downstairs to the kitchen, hoping to find a snack to tide her over. As she approached in the darkness, a noise made her freeze. She stilled and peered around the doorway.

There, in profile, Elena Bartell sat on a stool at her kitchen island, staring at an empty second bottle of wine, a half-filled glass in one hand, wiping her eyes with the back of the other. Wet trails on her cheek glistened in the low light filtering through the window from a street lamp. A second, empty glass was beside hers, which Maddie recognised as the one she'd been toasting her with only hours before. It looked as though Elena had made a move to clean up when Maddie had gone to bed, and then simply sat down and decided to drown her sorrows instead.

Maddie crept back upstairs, feeling guilty for intruding. She knew Elena would hate being seen like that. Devastated and lost, she was at odds to the powerful figure who swept the corridors of Bartell Corp. Underneath it all, she was still a woman who'd had the worst day of her life, tucked inside the best one, like some messed-up Russian nesting doll.

Somehow, in all the thrills of her big career-boosting scoop, Maddie had forgotten that today Elena had lost a husband she'd once cared for. Worse, she'd learned he was a disgusting bastard. No wonder Elena was numbing herself with twenty-year-old booze. But it was still a shocking sight. The ache in her expression was unforgettable.

Maddie tried to shut out the image of a tear-streaked Elena. Part of her wanted to just hug her until she lost that haunted look. Of course, that wouldn't be welcome.

Sliding back between the sheets, hunger forgotten, Maddie stared at the ceiling. Glossy paint had been matched to the exact shade of equally gorgeous drapes. The decor alone in this room would have cost a mint.

Money really wasn't everything, was it?

Dwelling on her big payday suddenly seemed tacky. One floor below sat a slumped, devastated woman, alone in her kitchen, crying into her expensive wine. It was Maddie's last thought before her eyelids drooped and shut.

Elena stared into her wine glass. The fine vintage tasted like ash. Her mind was a dulled blur of anger and hurt and something else. She pushed away the something else for now, as she focused on the start of her night. Richard's face. When she'd arrived home and first confronted him about Madeleine's allegations. She'd seen it, just for a split second. *Panic.*

He'd been caught, and he knew it.

Then came the bluster, attempted charm, and lies.

"Elena... honey...you know that's bull. Come on, love!"

But she'd seen it.

"You don't get to call me that ever again," Elena had said with a low hiss. "You groped women in my employ, vulnerable women who couldn't fight back. And then, to add to the depravity, you crawled into bed with me each night. You make me sick."

"It wasn't like that. Elly, please. Let's just sit down and talk. We've shared too much to throw it all away."

She'd given him a glare that could have bubbled the paint on the wall.

His expression fell, and his eyes became hard. Eyes she could well imagine sizing up prey. Hurting women. Getting off on the power. It was all there. It made her want to throw up.

Apparently, he didn't like her expression because his own morphed into a cruel parody of the face of the man she'd married.

"If you'd spread your legs a little more often, I might not have had to look farther afield," he said, a malicious gleam filling his eyes. "You always were a cold fish, Elena. Sometimes I wondered if you were thinking about your spreadsheets when we were doing it. If people only knew how often you 'have a headache', and how little you like to be touched. Actually, they already assume that, don't they? Well, I can confirm your ice queen chill goes right to the bone. I'm no saint, but you'd drive any man to seek his pleasure elsewhere."

Elena's lips thinned, and she gave him a look of such fury that he shrank back a little.

"All right," he ground out. "What do you want?"

"You gone. Tonight."

"Tonight! That's absurd! I can't just—"

"Tonight, or I'll make your life a living hell. That's a promise. I want no trace of you left in here by the time I return home. If there is, whatever you've left behind will be burnt. Text me when it's done."

She'd stalked away and never even glanced back.

Elena took another gulp of wine. The betrayal she felt was far worse than she could have imagined. It had only increased as she aimlessly rode around the streets of Sydney, trying to clear her head and waiting for the final text. That had been a hateful few hours picking over all the signs that should have alerted her to his true nature.

Then, finally, she'd remembered Madeleine. A woman she had kicked out of her office, out of her job, in a rage. Madeleine had not deserved that. A flash of her face, the burn of hurt in her eyes, had suddenly shocked Elena upright. So she'd instructed her driver to take her to Madeleine's apartment. She heard him, distantly, on the phone, getting the requested address from God knows where, and then doing a U-turn. As the car accelerated off again, she felt a surge of relief and calm, that *this* was right.

Besides, she told herself, the least she could do was offer the girl her job back.

Discovering Madeleine was out had simply turned her calm into a determination to wait her out. As the minutes ticked by, and the car circled the block over and over, she became even more perplexed by her own behaviour.

What was she doing, waiting on an assistant? A former assistant at that?

Just then, Madeleine had arrived home. A thrill had surged within Elena. The game was on.

Elena poured herself another glass, still unable to believe that Madeleine Grey, her teasing, blurting, intelligent, fashion illiterate, former assistant had scored the interview of a lifetime. She'd somehow swanned up and plucked the holy grail of interviews out from under the nose of far more seasoned writers, including herself, and then she'd placed it gently in Elena's lap.

This would make Madeleine's career. Everything would be different now. The woman had no idea what she was in for, but Elena knew.

How on earth had the young woman done it? *How?* Oh, she'd explained about her single question, but still. Had Elena asked the same question, she was quite sure the outcome would have been different. She frowned. What was it about Madeleine that made people warm to her and open up?

It had to be her charm. Madeleine had this way about her, a guilelessness that could get under anyone's skin. She'd gotten under Elena's often enough, despite her best efforts to repel her.

She'd originally tried to sever Madeleine from her when they were in New York. Nothing said "stay away" like "you're fired". Although, it had been a business decision. Well, mostly. That had lasted all of two days. Elena's resolve had crumbled, and she'd been forced to admit she'd missed her. So, Elena had allowed her back. Well, that's how she'd spun it in her head. In truth, she was at a loss as to what she'd have done if Madeleine had said no.

Swirling her wine, Elena stared into its crimson depths. What did all this mean? Her pride in Madeleine, her admiration for her scoop, was overwhelming. She'd rarely felt such an extreme response to anything. Her initial reaction washed over her again, and she shook her head. Elena had wanted to whisper in her ear how impressed she was and how pleased she felt for her.

She scowled. This anomalous response had been one of the things she'd been trying to avoid since basing herself in Australia. She'd come to the conclusion that she had a...well, a weakness regarding Madeleine. All those intimate blogs and late-night chats had somehow affected her.

But the preposterousness of actually going to Madeleine's home in New York and offering her another job, in person, simply because the woman had demanded it, was a sure sign she had a vulnerability.

Still, it was nothing she couldn't get past.

Elena had had it all worked out. She had allowed Madeleine at her side as a PA. That way, she could still have the woman in her orbit each day and enjoy the twitch of her lips in response to Elena's acerbic comments that usually sailed right over Felicity's head. Madeleine always got her faint half jokes.

Elena had thought they could still have a few tiny moments, but crucially, the PA role had been a fresh start. When she became Madeleine's direct superior, the lines became much more defined. It had seemed the wisest option all around, withdrawing from her. They had responded to each other in only the most professional way. Their intimate evenings of chats were over.

It had been for the best.

And now, Madeleine was gone. Elena had tried to get her back, only to fail. This time, Madeleine wasn't coming back, and Elena felt bereft.

In the space of less than a day, the swirl of hands around a clock face, her interesting and unexpectedly addictive assistant had outgrown her. She didn't need anything from Elena now and never would again.

A hint of regret stabbed at her. Was it wrong to be jealous of the whole world who owned Madeleine now? They would see her magnificence and never let her go. Who could blame them?

Her eyes fluttered closed. It *was* wrong. Still, she would miss her. Her smile could be quite cheeky. The line between her eyes, when she frowned over something unfathomable, was endearing. As was the way she looked at Elena, past her title and mask, as though what lay beneath was all that really mattered. She was unaccustomed to anyone caring that much for her.

Maddie's way of always neatly lining up her folders with a sharp tap before standing, slipping across to the filing cabinet, her impressive ass curving *just so,* as she leaned forward and dropped them in the out tray then headed off to lunch. Sometimes, she'd bring back something tasty for Elena, giving her an admonishing look for forgetting to eat, but saying nothing.

Elena appreciated that. She appreciated her eyes, too. That gaze followed her constantly, daring her to...what? She never could work out what Madeleine was thinking. It was usually unexpected.

Not to forget the fact she'd just won an international exclusive without seeming to break a sweat. The raw talent evidenced by her blogs alone was a revelation. She loved Maddie's talent most of all. It made her tingle with delight, like discovering a profound, scientific breakthrough. She loved Madeleine's unexpected, beautiful writing. She couldn't wait to see how she used it in her Duchamp story.

It was clear she appreciated Madeleine. On many levels. And soon, very soon, she would be gone.

At that depressing thought, she filled up her glass again.

CHAPTER 21
The Gates of Hell

Maddie woke to the gorgeous scent of coffee. She cracked an eyelid.

"Ah," said a voice that Maddie would recognise anywhere. "You're alive."

Maddie sat straight up and glanced around the room, feeling disoriented. Elena. She was in her guest room. And Elena was now standing over her, an impatient look on her face, offering her a coffee. Which she had yet to take.

"Thanks." Maddie scrambled to sit up and reached for the cup. How long had she had an audience, anyway?

"May as well enjoy it. That will be the last nice thing I do for you in the next fifteen hours."

Maddie took a sip. Her taste buds swooned. "You remembered the way I like it? White with two sugars!"

Elena seemed pleased by her enthusiasm but didn't reply.

Maddie glanced at the wall clock and started. "Oh my God!" It was almost eight! She made to fling off her sheets and rise.

"No. I wanted you to sleep in, so you were rested for writing today. Now drink, then go to the kitchen. Rosetta has prepared a breakfast for you. Then you will do nothing but sit and write. Victor is on his way here."

Maddie frowned. Victor had to mean Vic Salinger, the magazine's most skilled features copy editor. He was heading here? Why wasn't Maddie being bundled off to work?

"Why's he coming here?"

Elena perched on the edge of the bed. "Because this is where *Style Sydney* has gathered this morning. Again, and I will not stress this enough, nothing can come between me and this story. That includes traffic jams, car accidents, random hazards, bad weather, or anything else. So, today, downstairs, for all intents and purposes, is *Style* HQ."

Elena's phone rang, and she answered it.

"No." Her eyes narrowed. "Twelve *plus* the cover, not including. Why would we have an eleven-page story? Who in the history of publishing has an uneven-numbered spread? When was the last time you saw a feature article ending on a left-hand page?"

She glared at nothing in particular, gaze sweeping the room. Maddie sipped her coffee and watched her formidable boss, back to her old self. Well, her mask, at least, was welded back on to within an inch of its stubborn, proud life.

"Send over the other art designer, then." Elena snapped her fingers. "What's his name? Jonas? At least he knows how to lay out a feature." She huffed out a breath, as she ended the call. "I am dealing with idiots."

Maddie nodded and slid her now finished coffee onto the bedside chest of drawers, not willing to encourage a new diatribe. She scoured her room, suddenly aware she was only in her underwear under the sheet. "Where are my clothes?"

"You won't need them."

"I...what?"

"Comfort matters, Madeleine. I wouldn't want to write in yesterday's unclean clothes. It might impact performance. I have Rosetta laundering your clothing. Felicity should be downstairs with a new outfit I asked her to pick up on the way into work."

Maddie blinked. She knew Elena was a type-A personality with control-freak leanings, but this was absurd. "Poor Felicity."

"Yes, well, for some reason I find myself without an assistant." Elena gave her an intense look and tapped her foot impatiently.

"You know..." Maddie paused and stared at the tip of that percussive Manolo Blahnik that matched an equally blood-red skirt, swallowing a crisp white blouse, "I can't very well wander around your home in my underwear to find whatever clothes Felicity has brought for me."

Awareness crossed Elena's face, as though she finally understood the cause of the delay. She pushed a button on her phone. "Felicity? Bring those clothes I asked for upstairs. Second floor. Third door on the left." She ended the call without another word. "All right? And don't dawdle. We're down to eleven hours, twenty-five minutes."

With that, she was gone.

A minute later, the door burst open, and Felicity huffed in with her arms full of bags. "You!" She gave a dramatic gasp and dumped them on the bed. "I might have known!"

"Known what?" Maddie hauled the bags closer for an inspection and rummaged through them.

"That wherever there's chaos, you're somehow in the middle of it, making my life more difficult. It's been total mayhem since you left."

"Right. Everything's all about you." Maddie rolled her eyes. She found a pair of new designer jeans in one bag. *Ooh. Nice.*

"And what on earth are you doing in her guest room? She fired you yesterday!"

"It's a long story."

"Well, I don't have time to hear it. She's scrapped the Valentino cover story. Can you believe it? On deadline day! I have fifty things to do, all annoying, and for some reason we're doing it from here today. I am going insane! It took me ages to get all the contracts and releases to go with the spread to start with, and now, pfft, no reason at all, it's out at the eleventh hour."

Maddie pulled out a pretty Sass & Bide shirt and held it up. That'd work. "Underwear?" she asked hopefully.

Felicity tossed her a small bag. "Elle Macpherson Intimates range. God help me, if I'd known they were for you, I'd have picked up the Hanes Collection."

"Ha-ha." Maddie grabbed the clothes and padded over to the en suite, trying to ignore that she was wearing little more than her underwear in front of her bitchiest frenemy. Out of the corner of her eye, she caught Felicity's confused look.

"Seriously, Maddie, what are you doing here?" she asked. "And why is she being so nice to you all of a sudden, that I have to fetch you clothes? This is too weird—even for Elena."

Maddie gave her a mysterious grin. "You'll find out soon enough. Try not to mess up her walls, though."

"What do you mean?"

"When your head explodes." She closed the bathroom door with a snick and laughed hard.

Showered, dressed, and humming with nervous excitement, Maddie grabbed her phone and headed downstairs. She'd half expected Elena to have kidnapped that in the night too, but the editor had restrained herself.

Five minutes later, she was in the kitchen, munching on breakfast and chatting to Perry. The art director was fawning over her photos he'd copied over to his laptop and making awed gasping noises when Felicity tore in as if a bear were on her tail.

"You!" She pointed at her with a waggling finger as though exorcising a demon. "You got us a world exclusive with Véronique Duchamp? And photos? Of the new collection?"

"Surprise." Maddie shot her an amused look and took another sip of juice.

Perry snorted, swivelled his laptop around, and selected a photo. "Not just any photos. Check out our cover."

He enlarged the photo of Natalii on the floor, boots sticking out from under taffeta, and Véronique with pins in her mouth, as she adjusted her daughter's outfit. The faintest hint of smile dusted her lips, and her eyes glowed with warmth. Véronique Duchamp as no one had ever seen her.

There was a ragged intake of breath. Felicity's jaw dropped. "Oh my God," she whispered. "Are there more? Show me!"

Perry flicked through the photos, and Maddie laughed, as Felicity's eyes grew wider and wider.

"How?" She snapped her head around. "Hell, did you sleep with that Duchamp daughter for a story? Is that it? You cheeky, little slu…"

"Felicity!"

The sharp whip of fury short-circuited whatever crude suggestion Felicity was about to make, and all heads whirled to face Elena stalking into the room.

Maddie, who'd been seconds away from lashing Felicity for implying she'd slept with someone to get a story, couldn't have been more stunned at the anger on the media mogul's face.

"*Felicity*," Elena repeated, her voice low. "Do you know what is the only thing more foolish than deliberately insulting the writer who has an exclusive that the entire publishing world is desperate to run?"

Felicity shook her head mutely.

"Deliberately insulting the writer of an exclusive that *I* want to run," Elena snapped.

A red hue crept up Felicity's neck to her cheeks.

"You will apologise for your baseless, gutter insinuations," Elena said, tone icy. "*Now*."

"I'm very sorry," Felicity said, her words a contrite mumble. "I didn't mean it. Of course I don't think you… I mean…ah…I just got such a shock."

Elena gave a disbelieving sneer. "And every time someone gives you a shock, do you accuse them of prostituting themselves?"

Felicity turned scarlet.

"Why don't you take Oscar for a walk, while you contemplate how your future in my employ is linked to any further idiocy that might leave your mouth. About an hour should do it. He hasn't been properly walked since yesterday morning. And do dress him warmly."

Maddie, Perry, and Felicity all glanced at the windows. It was blowing a frigid gale.

"*Now*, Felicity."

Felicity scrambled up and left the room, shooting a mortified glance back at Maddie, as she went to track down the dog.

Mask back on, Elena turned to her, expression neutral once more. "I have a typist ready to begin transcribing your interview."

Maddie had a hard time following the sudden mood shift. "Sorry, what? Why? I can…"

"Unless you can type up a four-hour interview faster than 200 words a minute, it makes sense to outsource it to Sydney's fastest available typist," Elena said, tone brisk.

Perry pointed to his laptop and told Elena. "The interview's on there. On the desktop."

Elena nodded. "Good. Give it to Ingrid to type up. She's in the study. Then go over the cover work with Jonas, whenever our illustrious graphic designer deigns to show up."

Perry left, and Elena slid onto his vacated stool. She studied Maddie for a moment, then sighed. "They will say this about you, you know."

Maddie's brow creased in confusion.

"What Felicity suggested. Because of the gossip-column photo and now your world exclusive, that will be the first accusation you get. You will need to be prepared for it."

Maddie thought about that. *Damn. She's right.*

"And they will be even less kind than Felicity was. Trust me, I know what they're capable of. It's vile."

Maddie suddenly understood the source of Elena's anger. For years, when Elena had started out, gossip writers, under the safety of anonymity, had implied she'd slept with all sorts of investors and board members to make her way so far in the business world. They couldn't get their heads around the fact that a woman had come out of nowhere, without a rich family, a background in the business, or a sugar daddy, and become a self-made multi-millionaire. So, they'd made assumptions.

"It's the price successful and prominent women pay," Elena added with a sour look, "and what's worse is, you will find other women can be your worst enemies. We don't need fists to injure. Oh no, we are far more brutal than that."

Maddie digested her words. "I appreciate the warning. I also really don't think Felicity meant what she said."

"Then she should not say something if she didn't mean it." Elena paused. "I think this is where we came in," she added with a rueful look. "Was I not lamenting how hard it is for people to speak the truth, not so long ago?"

"True. God, so much has happened since we had that innocent little conversation before our bet."

Elena gave her a long look. Her lips twitched. "That conversation was many things, Madeleine, but innocent was not one of them. And I believe you know it."

Surprise rippled through Maddie. What was she saying? That she was well aware Maddie had a crush on her? Or worse than a crush? Fear and embarrassment wrestled inside her. Was she that obvious?

Maddie desperately sought the answers on Elena's face. There were none. The woman's smile merely widened.

Maddening.

"Now come on," Elena said, straightening. "I believe I promised you a day of hell."

CHAPTER 22

Filleting a Fish

Elena hadn't been kidding. The day was a wash of chaos and pressure, stress and anxiety. In the eye of the hurricane swirling all around her, Maddie wrote like a demon.

At times, people would appear at her side. Felicity, looking windblown after her excursion with Oscar, had slid a glazed doughnut onto the table beside her without saying a word. Her version of an apology, Maddie supposed. Being within the mere orbit of all those carbs was probably giving Felicity vapours.

Victor would appear whenever she had a question about magazine style. The man was like a walking bible of grammar and spelling.

Perry would breeze in and out, mutter something with the word "Maddie" in it, but after the first half-dozen interruptions, she'd just tuned him out as she focused.

Writing, writing, writing.

Her wrists were aching from typing, her shoulders groaned, and everything felt as if it was taking too damned long. The clock ticked on, food appeared and disappeared—she wasn't entirely sure whether it had come from Rosetta and whether she'd been the one to eat it—she never looked up. The words were starting to look ready, but now she had a flow problem. Her story jumped around too much, from subject to subject. If she could just concentrate long enough...to...there was a din from people talking just out of her zone of concentration...she had to think and...for God's sake, it was getting louder...

"Would you all please just shut up!" she cried out, as the hubbub near her working space rose to a dull roar.

She half expected a "sorry, Maddie," followed by Perry dashing off to bother someone else. Instead, she got eerie silence and a weird prickling sensation. She turned slowly to see Elena's astonished look, three feet away, a phone frozen in her hand, as someone on the speaker called from it, "Hello? Ms Bartell are you still there?" and Felicity's you-did-not-just-do-that wide-eyed expression.

Maddie gestured at her computer screen with a helpless look.

Elena's lips thinned. She turned. "Benjamin, I will call you back." She stabbed the phone off and stared at Maddie.

No one spoke. Maddie's pulse thudded like a jackhammer.

"Quite correct, Madeleine, we will steer clear of your working area." She turned to Felicity. "See that no one bothers her again." The steel was back in her voice, as Elena bowed out of the room.

With sweating hands, Maddie returned to her work. Her thoughts wandered, though.

Holy hell. That did not just happen.

For the first time in her life, Maddie understood what having power meant. Another thought struck her.

Is this what it's like all the time to be Elena?

Hours later, a sharp rap sounded, and Elena entered the room.

Blearily, Maddie lifted her head from her computer and realised it was almost five in the afternoon.

"Well?" Elena perched on a chair facing her, all elegance and regal coolness despite having endured just as intense a day as Maddie. "I trust I am not interrupting your tenuous concentration this time?" She slid up a challenging eyebrow.

Maddie caught a faint glint of humour in those blue eyes.

"First draft is done," she reported. "I emailed it to Victor forty minutes ago. I was just figuring out an approach for the second story, the life and times of Véronique. What do you think about starting it with the anecdote of her milking the cows? You know, setting the scene in the barn, and here's the world's top fashion designer perched on a rustic, old stool squeezing cow teats?"

Elena's mouth performed some amused contortions. "By all means, Madeleine, Véronique Duchamp and cow teats it is." This time the humour in her eyes was anything but faint.

Maddie grinned. She moved her laptop to one side and shook her wrists. "Less of a mad rush on the second story, right? I mean, that one runs next month."

Elena nodded. "Yes. But I will need it by next Wednesday. I don't wish to give the editorial teams worldwide two heart attacks over deadlines in back-to-back issues. Now, while Victor is editing your story, the pages have been laid out waiting for the words. The photos are chosen. Have a break and come take a look at what the artist has done."

Maddie stood. Every locked muscle in her body protested. "Ow."

Elena laughed as she exited the room.

The spread was incredible. Maddie ran her gaze across the pages, admiring the way the text drew the attention and flowed, begging you to stop and dive in. Long columns of copy were broken up with strategic, giant quotes from her story.

It was surreal to see the words that Véronique had spoken with a cavalier wave of her hand a day ago, now in bold, black Theano Didot font. The photos had been tweaked in some subtle way that Maddie couldn't quite work out. The greys had been softened in places, the contrast enhanced, and the balance of shades now popped from the pages.

"Oh my God," she whispered, her eyes tracing the design across the run of pages. Every picture told a story and each was chosen and positioned for maximum impact. Her photos looked gorgeous. She stared in awe. "Wow! You've made the pics look incredible."

Pride flickered across Elena's face. "You took the photos, Madeleine; we worked with what you gave us. But, yes, Jonas and Perry have done a fine job. I suppose, knowing the whole world would be studying their finished product provided some inducement for them to lift their game."

Maddie laughed at her joke. "Oh yeah, that must be it."

Elena scrolled back to the beginning. "I think you missed something on your first pass."

Maddie studied the first page. Her headshot was staring back. The words *World Exclusive—Maddie Grey* in huge letters sat underneath it.

She stared at the photo, unsure where it had come from. She finally recognised the hint of neckline visible. Some Sydney charity luncheon she'd had to attend with Elena. She'd been snapped standing beside her on the hotel steps and, thanks to a Perry Marks' intervention before the event, she was looking almost glamorous.

Her eye returned to her name. *Maddie Grey.* Somehow, Elena had resisted the urge to spell it out in full. It was nice that she'd respected Maddie's preference. "This is real," she said in wonder, looking at those two small words. "I mean, really real."

"It's real, Madeleine. You're in for one bumpy roller-coaster ride."

Maddie glanced up at her. "So are you. Right?"

"How so?"

"A Bartell Corporation publication is running this world exclusive."

"Ah." Elena smiled. "It's not my first, but it is my favourite. I would give rather a lot to see Emmanuelle's face when this comes out. She did so desperately want Véronique. Her pursuit of her has been an industry punchline for years. She tried far more often than even I did."

Maddie grinned. "Happy to help."

Elena gave her a curious look. "Did you actually seriously consider selling your story to her?"

Maddie hesitated. "I would be a fool not to consider all options. You taught me that, Elena."

Elena pursed her lips but didn't disagree.

"What would you have done if I had I sold it to her, though?"

Elena's eyes narrowed. "You should be glad you'll never find out."

"Are you serious?"

"Very."

"So you'd have blacklisted me? Just for taking a more competitive offer?" A surge of hurt and anger flooded her.

"Madeleine, I didn't say that." Elena shook her head. "This is business. I'm not nearly as petty as you clearly believe me to be. But I would have remembered where your loyalty lay, and that might sway my decisions at a later time. Do you understand?"

Maddie considered the vague threat of thwarted future opportunities. "I understand that you're a valuable ally to have."

"Then we understand each other perfectly." Elena gleamed with satisfaction.

"But," Maddie added, "that cuts both ways."

Surprise crossed Elena's face. "Oh?"

"At this hypothetical later date, I want you to remember who I chose to give this story to. I am also a valuable ally to have. Maybe not right at this moment, but we both know that's about to change."

A feline smile curled Elena's mouth. "Well now, look who's learned a few things."

Maddie's irritation rose. She was not some child to be mocked.

"No." Elena offered an aggrieved sigh. "Whatever insult you took from that was unintended. I agree, we might be useful to each other in the future. Now, shall we move on? Can we tell Jonas that you approve his layout? Or do you have changes you wish to make?"

"No changes," Maddie said, chastened. "It looks amazing."

"Good." Elena looked up. "I see Victor wants us to come over. Let's find out what his evil, red editor's pen has found in your copy. A word of warning about this process, thin skins are for fish only."

Maddie gulped.

Hours later, Maddie felt like a filleted and processed sea bass. Every line, every word had been scrutinised to within an inch of its existence. And Elena's insistence on fact-checking everything Véronique had said against what was known about her, to make sure dates and places lined up, was exhausting.

It turned out the fastidious designer was equally fastidious with her retelling, because there were no apparent errors or discrepancies. Nonetheless, come ten that evening, Maddie was worn out—an exhausted, sprawled lump of ex-assistant poured onto Elena's fancy, white sofa, while the media juggernaut powered on around her.

Maddie had learned the hard way that evening that the definition of a professional writer was nothing to do with being the best or most skilled wordsmith. It was the person who could take criticism on the chin, learn from it, and move on. Defensiveness and plaintive pleas to reconsider a change were greeted with an incredulous glance—and that was just from Victor. Elena would give her a cool look and tell her to stop being precious, that the writer's ego was irrelevant.

"You have to be willing to kill your babies," Victor said kindly, after Elena and her withering commentary left the room. "Those great snippets in a story that we writers think are genius? Sometimes, you must take a leap of faith that there's a reason why the expert is changing your words. You have to just be a pro and accept it. Let go."

So, Maddie let it go. She'd learned a lot. The experience was invaluable. But right now, she was thoroughly wrung out.

Her contribution to any part of the process had long finished. Copy editors in the next room were just checking for final typos now, while Elena was stalking the house, barking down the phone about overtime agreements for printing-plant workers at *Style*'s presses. She'd even threatened the plant manager with a lawsuit if he left early, buck's night or not.

Maddie suspected he was one best man who'd be missing his bachelor party, given the way Elena's eyes glowed with satisfaction when she ended the call.

Elena turned to Maddie in the lounge, where she lay flopped, semi-comatose, her brain nine-tenths mush, and her socked feet curled up under her.

"Honestly," Elena said with a smirk, "he made it sound like a night of ritualistic debauchery was somehow important. As though people don't get married all the time." Her eyes tightened, and the amusement fell away.

Maddie, so tired she could not see straight, let alone remember how to censor her words, said, "He never deserved you."

Elena froze. "Excuse me?"

Maddie stared up at her and saw veiled anger along with exhaustion. She felt immediate regret. Now was not the time. The media mogul had been up half the night drowning her sorrows, on top of handling the adrenaline of the exclusive. She'd have to be down to emotional vapours herself. Maddie shouldn't be going anywhere near her sore points right now.

"Sorry," she said with as much sincerity as she could muster and closed her eyes, hoping Elena would take the opportunity to end the conversation.

"So am I," Elena said. "About a lot of things. But that's what I have lawyers and certain other people of questionable standing to correct for me."

"Ah." Maddie flickered her drooping eyes back open. She wondered idly just how spectacularly Elena was going to screw over her slimy ex-to-be.

"Mm. By the way, it's done," Elena said.

"What is?"

"Your story. *Style*'s Australian Fashion Week issue. The first comprehensive Véronique Duchamp interview the world has ever seen. It was put to bed five minutes ago. It'll be on the presses within the hour."

As the reality of the words hit her, Maddie sat up.

Elena smiled. "Congratulations, Madeleine. You're about to be a legend in this town."

Maddie swallowed.

"And every other town."

"Thank you." Maddie injected every ounce of sincerity into her gaze.

Elena opened her mouth, as though about to ask what for. She closed it again. And nodded.

"Come Monday, this is all over." Sadness washed over Maddie as she said the words. "I'm not your assistant anymore."

"Well, I doubt you'll be short of work, somehow. And I still expect your second Véronique story by next Wednesday."

"Yes, Elena," Maddie replied in her best assistant voice. She grinned. "Not bad for someone who's not a journalist."

Elena studied her for a beat. "I stand by that. Madeleine, you are not a journalist."

"What? How can you still—"

Elena lifted her hand. "Don't be offended. I never meant it the way you took it. You are a *storyteller*. You translate and cut to the heart of what people are. You were born to write, but not news. These sort of insightful character pieces are what you were meant to do with your life. But the hunt of the journalist, uncovering the darkness, corruption, crime, kicking in heads to get to the truth, it's not you. Your emotions would prevent you thriving in that arena."

"A storyteller?" She tasted the word and wasn't sure what she thought of it. Being a news journalist was what she'd always wanted to do. There was no way she could throw away the dream. Not now, not when she was about to have so many opportunities. "I will adapt. I can adapt. They say journalists become more cynical the older they get. Right? I can too." She tried to smile, but it faded.

"Yes, they do. Is that what you want to be? A cynical hack?" Elena regarded her. "I suppose, if you work hard enough at it, you might stop connecting with people, feeling their pain, and you might even succeed at writing well the stories you don't care about or even hate. Would that be success to you, Madeleine? Is that what you really want?"

"I..." Maddie stopped. She hadn't thought about it like that.

"I know it's hard," Elena said not unkindly, "to give up a dream you've invested so much time and belief in. You probably had a fantasy of uncovering crime, bringing down a corrupt politician, and making a difference."

Shock coiled through Maddie at her accuracy.

"Every young reporter does. But is it really you? What if your future is, instead, in writing magazine profiles, as you did with Véronique? Or penning biographies? Basic news journalism is a waste of your skills. It's a mismatch. That's all I meant."

Maddie's heart sank. This wasn't how it was supposed to go. Elena was supposed to be telling her she'd had it all wrong. That Maddie was a kick-ass journalist. She rubbed her eyes to hide her hurt.

"See it as expanding your horizons, not retreating," Elena continued, and this time, there was a softness in her tone. "Learn to pivot. Find the thing that you are best at, not the thing you trained for."

They studied each other in silence for a moment. "You're talking about how you went from fashion to business," Maddie said.

"As I said, it's hard." Elena hesitated. "Giving up a dream is always hard."

"But you did. You became an entrepreneur. A really successful one."

"Exactly."

"And yet I've seen you at *Style*. You're so brilliant at it. You have more talent and passion for producing fashion magazines in your pinkie than everyone in Bartell Corp combined. Hell, your staff all freely acknowledge it. And yet, your job is axing dying papers and building skyscrapers like Hudson Shard and calling it art."

Elena's eyes narrowed, but Maddie pressed on. "So, from what I can see, you've pivoted *away* from where your heart is and what you're best at. I think you know that too, somewhere, deep down. It's why you can't let it go. Because any other owner would have just parachuted in a new editor-in-chief for *Style Sydney* and moved on. Not you. Elena, you're now unofficially editing this magazine, not overhauling it. Everyone knows it. You're doing what you've always wanted, and that's why you don't want to let it go."

Elena eyes cooled. "You feel free to say all this because you no longer work for me?"

"Someone has to say it," Maddie said. "And I'm saying it as a friend."

"Is that how you see us? Friends?"

Maddie's heart thudded hard. She looked away, unable to meet the eyes watching her so closely. "I thought, maybe, we could have been that in New York. Or almost were? Well until you showed me I was wrong. You thought I was just an employee."

Elena said nothing for a few moments. "You weren't wrong."

Maddie's head snapped back. "What?"

"But business came first," Elena said, looking uncomfortable. "The things I did were necessary. But it does not also follow that I enjoyed what needed to be done. It does not necessarily follow, either, that I wasn't appreciating your...company." She faded out.

"Is that why you asked me to be your assistant? You...missed me?" It sounded insane. And yet...

"That's…" Maddie could see the lie forming, but just then, Elena's intense gaze was back. "One reason. A major one. It will be odd, tomorrow, being at work without seeing you every day." Her tone became flat.

Maddie smiled.

"Stop that."

"What?" Maddie smiled harder.

"You know very well." Elena's eyebrow lifted. "It's that thing you do." She stood. "It's late. Feel free to use the guest room again. You've earned a decent sleep after the hours you put in today." Her voice was back to all business. She'd clearly used up her quota of sharing.

"Thanks, Elena. I appreciate that. Can't face the thought of the train right now, to be honest." She hesitated. It was now or never. "Um—by the way, you never said what *you* thought of my story. I mean the actual content, not the scoop itself."

Elena paused. "Oh. Well." She stopped again. "Don't let it go to your head, but it was…acceptable."

"Acceptable?" Maddie swallowed her disappointment. "Oh, okay. Great. Thanks for letting me know. I'll try and make the next one better." She uncurled from the sofa, intent on hauling her weary bones to bed.

"Madeleine?"

"Yes?" She reluctantly looked up.

"It was remarkable." Elena sighed and looked as though this was not something she ever wanted to discuss. "*You* are…quite remarkable. I've thought so ever since I read that blog of yours. To capture the loneliness of a soul in such a way? Well. I knew the moment you got the Duchamp interview that you would craft an exquisite story."

Maddie was stunned. "You read my blog? *Maddie as Hell*? You read that?"

"Without fail. I found it intriguing. I always looked forward to it. Your replacement is useless, by the way. That single father? No. He doesn't capture the beauty and sadness of the world the way you do. He is not an observer."

"Oh... uh...Why didn't you tell me?"

"And risk *Maddie as Hell* getting suddenly self-conscious? Or worse, quitting the blog altogether? I did not wish to risk that. Although you quit it anyway."

Maddie stared at her. "How long have you known? Wait, did you know the day we met in the elevator?"

"Of course not. Be grateful I discovered your identity shortly afterwards, however, as it did prevent your being fired for insulting me that day." Her eyes suddenly took on an amused spark.

"But I didn't! I mean, I didn't mean to insult you. You misunderstood. Come on, you know that, now!"

"You do have a habit of this, don't you?" Elena ignored her protestations. "Accidentally insulting me? That stunted shrub offering of yours comes to mind." Her smile was as wide and warm as it was unexpected.

"Oh. That was...awful." Maddie gave her a sheepish grin. Elena was actually teasing her. How much more surreal could this day get?

"The point is, you do have talent. It's all about directing it well." Elena reached out and softly slid her fingers across Maddie's cheek, leaving a scorching trail of heat where her fingers touched. She met Maddie's eyes with a dark look. "Don't waste your talent." She studied her, hand stilled on her skin.

Maddie held her breath, shocked into silence by the touch.

Elena's hand slowly fell back to her side. "I think that's more than enough truth for one night." She frowned, as though it was Maddie's fault she'd shared so much. Then, in a swirl of silk and intoxicating perfume, she gave her a tight nod and disappeared out of the room.

Staring after her, Maddie was unable to think of a single thing to say. Her fingers lifted to her cheek. That look. Even seconds after it had happened, her memory of the moment seemed faulty.

The idea Elena might like women the way Maddie did was wishful thinking. Obviously. She was straight. She'd had two husbands. And even if she touched and looked at a woman with lingering, appreciative gazes, as if she wished Maddie were hers, it didn't mean anything.

It didn't, she warned her hopeful, quivering heart.

Perry had even said it. Elena's first love was beauty. Right now that meant admiring the person who had gifted her a beautiful exclusive. Nothing more. Nothing less.

Maddie climbed the stairs to the guest room and tried not to think of all the ways that hurt.

The next morning, Maddie was by the front door, trying to figure out how to say goodbye to a woman who'd changed her life. She wasn't ready. Not by a long shot. This was so unfair, saying goodbye when all she really wanted to do was stay right here and see if she'd touch Maddie again the way she had last night. Her night had been tortured by dreams of those fingers brushing her skin.

Elena was half turned on the bottom of the stairs, her elegant fingers frozen on the sleek satin scarf she'd just slid around her neck.

Maddie's mouth was refusing to form words, not quite sure what to say.

Elena didn't berate her for being a door bollard or order her to move aside. They simply regarded each other.

"Well," Elena finally said, lowering her hands from her scarf. "Do you require a car?"

Maddie shook her head.

"Services of a mute translator, then?"

"Hilarious. But no. My tongue's not entirely useless."

"Glad to hear it." Elena's eyes twinkled, and she turned to pick up her house keys and shoulder her glossy, black handbag.

Maddie drank her in, knowing it would be her last look at Elena for some time. It was insane to be missing her so much already.

"The *Weekend Mirror*'s buyout paperwork was supposed to be ready yesterday," Elena said, tone brusque. "It hasn't arrived. I need you to..." She ground to a halt, glancing up at Maddie, surprise on her face that was quickly masked.

Had Elena actually forgotten she was no longer her PA? "I could make a few calls, if you'd like," Maddie said, brightening. "Get that paperwork moving? I'd be happy to." Not quite willing to let her go. Not yet.

Cool eyes appraised her. "No, Madeleine. It's time you left," Elena said with a softness that Maddie had never heard from her.

"I... Okay." Maddie tugged at the sleeve on her shirt. Her own, rewashed clothes had magically appeared on the guest bed when she'd come out of the shower that morning, and she'd donned them. "Thanks," she added. "For everything."

"I don't know why you're thanking me. I just made you unemployed. Yet again." Elena gave her an amused look.

"True," Maddie countered with a grin, "but not *unemployable*. Big difference."

"Indeed."

They looked at each other one last time, and then Elena strode past her and opened the front door. She held it open for Maddie. The first time she'd ever done such a thing. "Well?" Elena asked archly.

Maddie stepped forward, and they both headed out into the chill air.

The lightness faded from Elena the moment her car pulled away, leaving Madeleine behind. She had thought this would be easier than it was. What were they now? Former associates? Almost friends?

Elena didn't have many friends. Perry, yes. He was one. But trust didn't come easily to her. And Madeleine had dared her to trust her. She could see the look in Madeleine's eyes, even now. It was a look that said Maddie wanted more. She wanted to be let in. How much more, Elena couldn't be sure.

At times, like the day before the truth bet, she thought she knew. She thought she'd seen longing. It had been too tempting to find out if she'd been right. Too tempting to find out what Madeleine was thinking, given the young woman no longer shared her thoughts with her.

But that had all gone to hell. Everything since then had robbed her clarity of thought. Thanks to the Richard mess, it would likely be gone for some time. She tightened her coat around her, surprised Sydney could get this frigid. The ache in her chest this morning had to be just the cold.

"Is your assistant not coming with us?" her regular Sydney driver asked, glancing at Madeleine as they drove past her.

Elena tried to come up with a cool, sarcastic reply, but her head still hurt from the stress and adrenaline of the previous day. This driver had seen her with Madeleine every day for months. It was a reasonable question at any other time. But not today.

"Madeleine is no longer in my employ," she said testily. "She has moved on."

Elena turned to stare out the window, his question vexing her far more than it should. Madeleine was, indeed, no longer in her world at all. A handful of events ahead of them, and that would be that. No more.

The ache intensified. Elena briefly wondered whether she should check in with her doctor. This couldn't possibly be a normal reaction to losing one's assistant.

She's not just an assistant, though, is she?

Friend, then. Like it or not, fight it all she might, Madeleine had been a friend to her at times.

A friend?

Elena pushed away her irritating inner voice. She was one of the most formidable media moguls in the world. She did not have time for derailing thoughts like this.

"Can we go any faster?" she growled at the driver.

"Not without breaking a few traffic laws, ma'am."

"Then break them. I want to be far from here as soon as possible."

Far from the memory of Madeleine walking away.

"Sure thing. Oh and it's a shame about losing your assistant. She was about the nicest person you could ever meet. Don't think she contained an ounce of bullshit, if you'll pardon my French."

"Just drive." Elena closed her eyes.

CHAPTER 23
Fifteen Minutes of Fame

Maddie had always assumed the day she'd dreamt of as a little girl would dawn resplendent with sunshine, fluffy clouds, and an awesome inner soundtrack of angelic harp music. Instead, the moment after waking to the knowledge her world exclusive would be on the newsstands today, her thudding head made itself known.

She leaned over to check the time on her phone and discovered a missed call from Natalii. It had been left at five in the morning. Her stomach lurched.

Who calls at five unless they hate something?

Maddie sat up and called voicemail to hear the message Natalii had left.

"Madeleine! *Maman* is delighted by your story. And I also. But especially her. She says '*Vous nous avez fait justice. Un triomphe*'. Now then, today it is her big parade. At the Australian Fashion Week? You will join us, *oui*? Come backstage. She insists. You must not refuse! *Oui? Oui!* She has it all arranged. I have emailed all that you need to find us. *Au revoir!*"

Maddie grinned. Well, it sounded as if Véronique thought she'd "done her justice". And calling her story a triumph was an awesome start to the day. Her knotted stomach loosened a little, and she gave it a consoling pat. She rose, began her morning routine, and made breakfast.

When she returned to her bedroom an hour later, she found her phone now full of missed calls and texts. Maddie listened to them in astonishment. *Fashion Police* wanted to interview her about Australian Fashion Week. What did Maddie know about fashion? What a joke. *E! Online* left a breathless message as well, overusing the words incredible, awesome, and "Oh. My. God". The editor of *Elle* wanted to "seriously discuss" her future. *Vogue, CQ,* and *Vanity Fair* wanted her to call back at her earliest convenience. CNN wanted to talk about Véronique outside the designer's show in a live cross.

Um, live cross? Over Maddie's dead body. She'd probably stutter, blush, and forget her own name. How had any of the media even obtained her phone number? Was Felicity wreaking some divine revenge by handing it out to everyone? At that thought, she punched in the chief of staff's number.

"Ugh. You!" Maddie heard, by way of greeting.

"Hello, Felicity."

"What do you want? My life is utter, eyeball-bleeding chaos thanks to you! Again! That article appears, and now every two-bit blogger with a fashion bent thinks I can be buttered up to give them your details!"

"Uh, about that—I have a whole bunch of people who got my number. I was wondering if maybe..."

"What?" came the waspish reply.

"Um, maybe it's revenge for having to walk Oscar for an hour in a gale or whatever..."

An irate hiss sounded in her ear.

"You don't honestly think I walked that ridiculous excuse of a dog for an hour? That would be cruel and unusual punishment. For us both! I found a nice, warm cafe with a covered area for dogs and gave him a doggucino and caught up on my emails over a coffee. Are you completely deranged?"

"Oh. Sorry."

"Besides, if I wanted revenge, there are other, far more diabolical ways. Like, if you think the media having your phone number is terrible, imagine them camped out at your front door."

"You wouldn't!"

"Try me!"

"Felicity!" The panic leaked out of her voice.

"Oh, don't worry," Felicity said with a long-suffering sigh, "you're apparently a protected species. Elena has threatened to fire anyone who imparts your personal details to the media."

"She *what*? Why?"

"Of course I asked her at once. 'Please Elena, explain in detail your mysterious inner workings so that we may all understand'. Honestly."

"Oh, yeah. Right."

There was a pause. "It was good, by the way," Felicity said, her tone quiet.

"Huh?"

"Keep up. Your article. I read it this morning. It was... Well, it was far better than I expected."

Maddie laughed at how pained she sounded admitting that. "Thanks, Felicity."

She sniffed. "I hate you for it, but it was *exceptional*. Okay? Oh! Have you seen the ads yet?"

"Ads? Uh, no." Maddie's heart rate surged.

Felicity snorted. "Well, then, you'll be in for a surprise..." Murmuring interrupted her. "Damn. Elena needs the *Harborside Times* contract ready in ten minutes—"

"Felicity? What ads?"

The call was already ended. Maddie sighed and slapped the phone on her breakfast table. Immediately, it began to ring again. And again. Not recognising the incoming numbers, she let the calls go to voicemail. Her fifteen minutes of fame were going to take some getting used to.

After breakfast, she bought a copy of *Style Sydney* from her neighbourhood newsstand, then went home, curled up in bed and went over it again. She was awed at how beautiful her story looked in the glossy publication. As she turned each page and studied the attention to detail within those stunning layouts, it was clear Elena really was an artist who drew out the best from her team. What on earth she was doing wasting her talents on corporate takeovers was beyond Maddie. *This* was real art.

She sighed as a familiar surge of longing went through her. She was ridiculous. It had only been three days since she'd last seen her. With a huff of annoyance at herself, Maddie grabbed her phone and went through the rest of her new messages.

They ranged from some respectable magazines and newspapers to a few tawdry interview requests promising to pay her if she coughed up a scoop on her relationship with "the French chick you screwed to get that big interview". She ground her teeth.

Maddie spent about an hour returning the calls of the publications she'd heard of and looking up the ones she hadn't. Then she did some cleaning to clear her head, as she contemplated their offers. Did she really want to work for *Vogue, CQ,* or *Elle*? Writing more fashion? She barely liked it now. Nope, she was fairly sure she didn't want a job in an industry so shallow it guilted women into impossible ideals, while lacking its sole key benefit—working with Elena Bartell.

Her parents called by the time she was frantically vacuuming her curtains. Her *curtains*, for God's sake. Her mother sounded as if she were having an asthmatic attack, she was so excited. She declared they were going to send copies to everyone in the family. And given there were forty-five members in the extended Grey clan, Maddie wanted the ground to swallow her up. She tried to talk her out of it, to no avail.

"Really, honey," her mother said, "aren't you proud? I know we are. It turns out you were right about your career—you have a real talent for this. I'm sorry if you felt we pushed you into catering."

Well, she *was* proud, but still. Maybe she could write forty-five apology letters after her mother cleared out the shelves of *Style Sydney* in South Penrith?

She was steam cleaning the shower when Simon stuck his head in on his way to work. He dropped his own *Style Sydney* copy in front of her and solemnly asked her to sign it.

Maddie giggled like the kid she suddenly felt like.

He shook his head. "I mean it, Mads. Not kidding. This is, like, greatness right here. That story was bloody fantastic." He tapped the cover. "So, I'm keeping this for when you get super famous. Well, *more* super famous. If that's actually possible. Then I'll sell it online, make a shitload, and retire." He winked and passed her a pen.

She signed, trying to suppress more giggles.

He beamed, then hugged her, adjusted his corporate blue tie, and sailed out, waving the magazine.

She slumped back into a chair. Could her day get any weirder? Her knees jiggled impatiently. Maddie suddenly felt as though she wanted to escape her four walls. She was itching to do something, but what? Go where? She had no work and, due to her former all-encompassing job, no actual life. In fact, the closest thing to a life she'd had lately was when Natalii had forced her to go gay-bar hopping.

At the thought of the eccentric Frenchwoman, she opened up her email and re-read her directions for the Duchamp fashion show that evening. It contained a few cryptic promises of an extravaganza hidden somewhere within Hyde Park in the city, and a vague, hand-drawn map. Natalii mentioned in her instructions that they'd be crazy busy setting up throughout the day—so mad it would be like a zoo.

Now *that* sounded like something Maddie could help with. Who had more expertise at wrangling a zoo and its exotic creatures than an assistant who'd been based at a fashion magazine? Besides, it'd be better than staring at her phone, wondering why being an overnight success felt so unnerving.

After she got off the train at Town Hall station, Maddie jogged up the steps and decided she'd need a caffeine hit before deciphering Natalii's directions. She detoured towards the nearest coffee shop and was just about to head inside, when she made the mistake of glancing up.

She froze.

A man crashed into her back and barked, "Hey! Watch it!" before striding off.

She didn't even have the words to apologise. Her brain had been emptied of anything resembling English. Because there, on a high billboard above her, attached to a building site, was *Style*'s cover, trumpeting a world-exclusive interview with Véronique Duchamp. Her black-and-white photo of Natalii and her mother stared back at her. The words *On sale now* below it were in a cursive red swirl.

—

"Oh my God," she whispered. Maddie scrabbled for her phone, snapped a photo, and fired it off along with a message to Perry. She wasn't entirely sure what she wrote, but it was along the lines of *OMFG JESUS H CHRIST ARE U FUKNG KIDDING ME OH LORD!*

Caffeine cravings forgotten, Maddie sank to a nearby bus-stop seat and stared up at the sign. Her phone beeped after a minute, and she glanced down at the reply. And gasped.

CHAPTER 24
A Dish Best Served Cold

Elena placed her desk phone back in its receiver and spun her chair to face the window. So, that was that. She thought she'd feel more elated. She had the ammunition to destroy Richard now, to take him apart, limb from limb. Her supremely talented private investigator, Saul, had worked with Felicity and the list and tracked down every last woman they could identify who had ever been touched by *that* man. At Elena's urging, Saul had even gone as far back as Richard's college days.

How unsavoury that quest had been. Richard had a college nickname. Octopus. She'd shared her damn bed with a man dubbed *Octopus*.

Saul had now reported in with the grand total. Elena had fallen silent. She'd always thought the moment of having the proof to crush Richard would be as magnificent as crushing any business rival. Instead, she just felt sickened.

Elena's thoughts were racing. At least she'd had the Duchamp exclusive to take her mind off everything. But that story couldn't fill her long hours each night. After drinking more than she should, she'd acquired the habit of curling up in a ball in her bed and indulging a fury that felt bottomless. Then would come the tears. Then more fury. Occasionally, her thoughts turned to Madeleine, and her rage was replaced with loss. It was ridiculous to miss an assistant like this.

She'd already ordered a new bed. She wished she could pay someone to build a bonfire for her existing marital mattress so she could watch the flames scorch it.

Her focus shifted to the streets three storeys below. Ants hurried by. Sydneysiders in a screaming hurry. All, presumably, with their little secrets. A woman in last season's Stella McCartney sidestepped a young courier on his bike. Which one, she wondered idly, was more likely to have the darkest secret? And which one was the poor sap who should have known better than to trust their life partner?

All it would have taken was asking one question from any of them at the right time. The maid. The waitress. The mouse.

The sick lurch returned to her stomach. She scowled, hating Richard more with each passing second. That disgusting weasel.

"If you keep glaring like that, icicles will shoot up the glass."

Elena spun her chair around in a fury at having an interloper. "I wasn't aware we had a meeting." Perry had to have a death wish, interrupting her in the mood she was in—oldest friend or not.

He merely shrugged and slid into the chair opposite. "Then just say I'm early for the next one we do have scheduled." He folded a dapper, Tom Ford-attired knee neatly over his thigh, clasped it, and gave her a gentle look. "Felicity tells me Saul just called in. You got the final head count, then?"

She exhaled. "Forty-one." The number felt stuck in her throat.

Perry brushed lint off his knee, attempting to hide his shock, but Elena saw it.

"Hell," he eventually said. "I heard you're making him cough up donations to all those women's shelters. That's smart. Got him over a barrel, since he doesn't want anyone else knowing."

Regret reared up again and clawed at her. "Apparently, *now* I get smart."

He cocked his head. "Meaning?"

She glared at him again. He knew damned well what she was saying. Perry seemed determined to have her process this train wreck; he'd been trying for days. Elena debated throwing him out of her office so she wouldn't have to think about it. But it would just delay the inevitable.

"Well, obviously, you think I've been a fool not to have known. You all do. It is not pleasant being the last one to find out." Her voice cracked, and Elena almost did too. Hell. Her emotional disarray was not acceptable. Not even in front of Perry.

He gave her a soft look, rose, and came around to perch on the edge of her desk. "Hey, remember Christophe, my ex-boyfriend of, like, five years ago? The one with the rhinestone fetish and perfect hair?"

Elena peered at him, mystified. Who could forget Christophe? The man was walking performance art. She nodded.

"He has this sister, Lana. She's an MIT professor—a theoretical propulsion expert. When her husband left her out of the blue last year, she hired an investigator to find him. She regretted it. Turned out he had girlfriends coast to coast and a mistress shacked up two streets away. She'd been there for ten years. And here Lana was, literally a rocket scientist, and she didn't know. Not a clue." He gave her a pointed look.

"While all this is very fascinating, I fail to see— "

"So then, Lana's mother, who had been the one to set them up in the first place, I might add, suddenly announced to the family there'd always been something 'off' about him. And everyone acted like Lana must have known deep down and she'd turned a blind eye to it. The alternative explanation was that she had to have been an idiot not to see the signs, and they knew she wasn't an idiot, so she *had* to have known. Somehow. And do you know why they assumed this?"

Elena said nothing.

"It makes humans feel better," Perry said. "Safer. That it couldn't happen to us. They've done studies on it. People shift the blame onto the victims, finding ways to make the people who've been betrayed seem compromised in some way, just so they can sleep at night. It's easier to do that than admit *we* could be gullible or so easily tricked like that, too. But Elena, this stuff—it just happens. Even the smartest person in the room can't always spot it. So pin the blame and the crimes on the asshole who did it. And leave them there."

Elena glanced away, thinking again of her uncharacteristic move to give a reference to that fearful assistant. It had made no logical sense for her to do it. And yet she had. "I... There may have been signs.

Maybe…it's not wrong to be thinking I should have suspected. Or, subconsciously, maybe I did suspect." Her cheeks tinged with heat.

"Stop," Perry said, voice firm. "I mean it. You're not God. Much as you may wish it were so on occasion."

She shot him an evil look, and he smiled.

"Hindsight is all very well and good, but it's still useless," Perry continued. "Only one person knew, with certainty, what he was up to. And I understand that you are in the process of shredding his slimy gizzards. The end. We leave it there. Draw a line under it. So now what? What happens with the names?"

"I've given them to my lawyers. I'll leave it to them to sort out. There will be compensation. I even *generously* offered for any compensation to come from the money I would normally pay to Richard from our pending divorce settlement. Unfortunately, my lawyers say they can't swing that, because, officially, it would be better if I was not involved in any of this due to my company position. It could drop the share price if I look exposed to compensation claims or a scandal. A shame. I'd love it tattooed on his head what he's like. I will make him pay, though. He will suffer. But God, what a mess." Her tone hardened, as she thought of the headlines if this got out.

Perry regarded her for a moment. "Worried about what the media will do with it?"

"Another divorce and a grubby scandal as well. They'll dance on the tiger shark's shame."

A grin slowly curled around his lips. "You're forgetting one thing right now—today, you are golden. You have the exclusive of the decade. *Style* is selling out in stands all over the world. The media are too busy talking about Duchamp's crazy rugby player and her brilliant new collection to worry about your ex, even if it all came out today."

He grinned, and Elena tried to smile.

"I suppose." But she did feel better. He had a point. *Style* had been flying off shelves. The issue had already sold out in France.

Perry chuckled. "Hey, want me to tell you all the colours Emmanuelle's face changed when she saw our story? My brother-in-law knows the front security guard at *CQ,* and he says she stopped dead, hissed at the cover, then ..."

Elena's phone beeped, and she picked it up, listening to Perry with a half smile. Her mood was rapidly improving. She glanced at her phone screen. The name *Madeleine* greeted her. Tapping the text message, Elena stared at what appeared. She read with growing astonishment. And then it all became clear. She smirked.

"Who is putting such an evil smile on your face?" Perry paused mid dramatic anecdote and leaned forward, craning his neck to see the screen.

Elena spun the phone around to show him a picture of the mid-city, Pitt Street billboard and a text message below it. *OMFG JESUS H CHRIST ARE U FUKNG KIDDING ME OH LORD!*

"I believe my former assistant intended this for one of her earthier friends," Elena said with a drawl. "Quite possibly you, given her uncensored venting."

Perry snorted. "Ha! Yes, I think you're right." He wiggled his fingers. "Want me to reply?"

"No, no." She waved him away. "I'll take care of it. Now, make yourself useful and get me some of the proofs from the Morrison shoot that do not look like rainbows have exploded all over lime chiffon. I don't care what you say, rainbows are not the next big thing."

Perry grinned. "Sure, boss." He gave her a warm look, far warmer than she probably deserved, and left.

She watched him go, a fondness welling in her chest for her best friend.

Elena glanced back to that all-caps message. After a moment's delicious anticipation, she hit *Reply*, unable to contain her amusement.

CHAPTER 25

Monkey Business

The name *Elena* was staring back at Maddie. She was sure she'd sent that message to Perry. Well, sort of sure. Okay, not sure. They were next to each other in her Bartell Corp group contacts—Bartell, Marks, Simmons. She could have hit the wrong name.

With shaking fingers, Maddie clicked the text message.

I'm not quite sure why you are invoking deities or sending me profanities. Should world exclusives not be promoted? E

Oh crap! She stared at Elena's message. Actually, it was kind of weird to get it at all. Didn't Elena famously ignore everything she thought was beneath her? She wrote back.

Sorry. Just overwhelmed. Meant to Send that to Perry. Not expecting to see my happy snap 2 storeys high.

She debated whether to add a smiley emoticon before finally leaving it off. She held her breath.

Her phone beeped a few minutes later.

Only two? Well you mustn't have heard about the big one in Times Square. E

Maddie's mouth dropped open. *Holy mother of...* And, okay, this time she could definitely see Elena's smirk in that message. No doubt about it. She was amusing the hell out of her ex-boss.

She grinned as she typed back.

You know how to give a girl a heart attack, don't you? This might be all in a day's work for you, but I'm a puddle.

She hit send before she could rethink it. Her phone remained unlit just long enough for her to wonder if she'd been overfamiliar and maybe even angered her. Then it beeped.

Well it's a good thing I fired you then. Puddles are slip hazards. I can't have my employees injured. Will you be at the Véronique show this evening? E

Maddie blinked. Had Elena just cracked a joke *and* expressed an interest in seeing her tonight? She felt like doing cartwheels.

Yep. Want to meet her?

She typed that back, fingers a blur, before she'd engaged her brain. Seconds later, she mentally slapped herself. Wanting to be useful to Elena was obviously a habit that was proving difficult to break.

Sure, Véronique might have warmed up to *her*, but Maddie knew the shy designer hated strangers in general and flower-sending *cafards* named Elena Bartell in particular. She prayed Elena would mention another engagement she had to rush off to or maybe a sudden lack of interest in the world's most elusive designer.

Yeah right. God. Who am I kidding?

Seconds later, her phone lit up.

Certainly. Until tonight. E

Oh man. She bit her lip. Maybe she could throw herself on Véronique's mercy? No. Okay, maybe if she worked hard all afternoon, helping the Duchamp team set up for tonight, they'd take pity on her hormone-stunted intellect? Yeah, okay. Argh. Not likely. She sighed.

Maddie resumed trudging towards Hyde Park and looked up. The Véronique Duchamp tent was enormous. A zoo vehicle was parked beside it. Odd.

Maddie headed past it and found the front flap. A security guard checked her name on a clipboard and waved her through.

Maddie's eyes grew wide when she saw all the preparations underway. It looked like a circus tent. A really trippy, fashionable, highbrow circus tent.

"Madeleeeiiinnneee!" Natalii cried out the moment she saw her, causing the heads of carpenters, set designers, and a painter to snap around. The young Frenchwoman, dressed in splotched, torn jeans and a white T-shirt, rushed up and gave her a flying hug. "You came! And only seven hours early!" She kissed her on each cheek. "Good. *Maman* will want to see you at once. Come with me."

Natalii dragged her into a rear, private area, which had been adorned with a gorgeous array of red velvet chairs and had enormous sketches and illustrations stuck to all the makeshift walls. Maddie recognised them as being the designer's dresses for the show.

"*Non, non, non!*" Maddie heard as she entered. "The red gown must come *before* any white. Are you an imbecile? And where are the models with the breasts? Hm? Why is it you send me the skin and bone *children?*"

Véronique's arms were flung in the air, railing at the same man Maddie had seen in the airport footage pulling the designer's bags. He ignored her ranting as he jotted down notes. Véronique had an unlit cigarette hanging out of her mouth, stuck to her bright-red, glossy lips, and seemed to have forgotten it was there. Her arms were ringed by a riot of bangles, and she wore a silver jumpsuit studded with coloured glass, which flashed under the light as she moved. Véronique spun around at Maddie's arrival, and her face warmed.

"*Ma chérie!*" She raced over and attempted to kiss her on each cheek but became flummoxed by the cigarette in the way. She spat it out. "Filthy habit!" She smiled. "Madeleine, I loved this story you write. Already, I have so many compliments. From all over." She waved at the entrance, as if signifying the world.

Maddie relaxed at last. "Did Perry send you both a complete set of the photos? He said he would."

"*Oui.*" She stopped still and gave Maddie a thoughtful look. Her eyes narrowed. "Hmm."

She pointed to Maddie and glared at the implacable assistant. "See? It is not so impossible? Look! Skin and bones and flesh and so *joli*. Beautiful. Now go! Find me this. Exactly this." She gave Maddie's arm a light slap.

"So hard," Véronique said under her breath. "I try to design the dresses women want to wear. Women who want to look gorgeous. And we all have the breasts and the hips. These models? *Non.* Flat. Children who look like my ironing board. I need shape! Especially for dresses I have that need curves. I had the perfect model for these styles, and what has happened? Anastazie tripped on stairs on her way here. Now..." she snapped her fingers, "...like that, she is in the hospital. To get a replacement for her, you would think I ask Pascal for a field full of camels. Although *that* he probably could get." She scowled for a moment, then brightened. "Now then—you are here early? What occasion is this? You missed us?" She looked hopeful.

Maddie smiled at her enthusiasm. "Yep. And I thought maybe you need some help? I mean I'm sort of between jobs now, since Elena fired me, so..."

"The Bartell woman? Pfft." Véronique spat out the name like a curse. "Good riddance to be free of the insane one. Natalii, where are my cigarettes?"

"No!" Maddie said. "I mean, yes, she fired me, but she tried to re-hire me. Everything kind of went crazy before she could." Her chances of getting Elena an audience with Véronique were rapidly going south. "I mean, she published my story and was so great at mentoring me. But then she knew I had to move on, so she..." Maddie faded out, realising this was possibly the least flowery endorsement anyone had ever offered. "And, um, I like her. So..."

Okay, getting worse. Uggh.

Natalii found a packet of cigarettes and passed one over to her mother while shooting Maddie a knowing look.

"Mm." Véronique ran her finger along the cigarette and tapped it against her gold metal lighter. "And does she feel the same? Your boss that you like?"

Oh hell. Of all the questions, this was one that stumped Maddie most. She stared at the mercurial designer and wondered what to say. "God, I hope so?" Or "not like that". Or "she's the queen of mixed messages".

"I'm not exactly sure." Maddie looked down and blushed under Véronique's scrutiny. Christ. She could hire herself out as a heater at this rate.

Véronique lit her cigarette and drew in a deep breath. Then she gave Maddie a slow, teasing smile. "Oh, Madeleine, I think there may be a secret you keep from the flower lady." The tone was light, but her eyes were perceptive, curious.

Maddie groaned to herself. "She's married," she said in a whisper. "Well, was. It's complicated. She's not...I mean...not into women. Or me. I know it's all kinds of pathetic. Just ignore me."

Véronique appeared to consider that as she smoked, then shifted her gaze to her daughter, who looked more than a little interested in her mother's reaction.

"The only thing pathetic, *ma chérie*, is the soul incapable of *amour*." Véronique gave Maddie a stern look. "If she hurts you, though..." She jabbed her cigarette at the air in a vague threat.

"It's...nothing. I know it's silly. It'll pass." God, she was starting to tear up just thinking about it.

Véronique looked her square in the eye. "Madeleine, if the heart is involved, it is never silly. Although I do not recommend the French rugby *hommes*, as you know. Do not brush aside these feelings as nothing. They are real to you."

Maddie nodded and sucked in a deep breath. "Would it be okay if I brought her to meet you tonight? After the show?" she asked, her tone tentative. "I know you don't like meeting strangers, so it's okay if you say no. But I was just hoping..."

Véronique's expression became speculative. "This would make you happy, me meeting her? The Bartell woman?"

Maddie nodded.

"Why? Because it would make *her* happy?"

Maddie nodded again.

"Hmm." Véronique Slid her gaze around the room. It landed on a sketch on the far wall. She stalked over to it. "This is the centrepiece of my show." She traced the lines.

Maddie glanced at it, impressed at the beautiful flowing piece of couture. "It's stunning."

"*Oui*," Véronique said without a trace of modesty. "Especially here." She tapped the bodice. "And yet it accentuates a vital something *les modèles* lack."

She turned and studied Maddie. "I will do the deal with you. Wear my centrepiece for me tonight, show it as I intended when my thoughts gave it life, and I will grant your Bartell woman a meeting."

"W-what? Me?" Madeleine's throat closed over in panic. "I'm not a model! I've never modelled in my life."

Véronique gave a faint snort. "The model of this garment must do but *un* single pass of the runway. No more. Can you not walk only so far, pause, turn, and walk back? Are you capable of this much? Mm?"

Maddie gulped. "I don't know. Seriously. I mean I have two left feet. What if I fall over? What if...everyone laughs. And Elena will be there, too, watching. I can't! I'd die."

"Madeleine," Natalii said, "I will show you how. *Maman* taught me from a small girl. I know the way it is done."

"Excellent!" Véronique clapped her hands. "It is settled. Pascal! Cancel this call for the more bosomy models. It is done."

The assistant appeared, nodded, and disappeared again.

"Oh God." Maddie gasped, staring at both Duchamps in horror as they gave her matching wide smiles.

"Stop looking as if the world has ended." Natalii grinned and elbowed her. "You said you had no job, *oui*? Well then! We are, as you say, here to save the day!"

Maddie gave a faint, strangled moan.

CHAPTER 26

On with the Show

Elena settled herself into her reserved front-row seat at the Duchamp show. She looked around, taking in the colourful tent and an empty trapeze swinging from the rafters of the structure. The room was at capacity, as to be expected for the premier event of Australian Fashion Week.

She could not see Madeleine. Surely, being friends with the daughter of the designer, her former assistant could have scored herself a front-row seat? Although the seat to her right was empty, so perhaps she would be here soon. Anticipation shot through her, and she chose not to analyse it too hard. It was natural to miss a…friend.

Elena waited, her patience tested, as the rest of the crowd filled in. However, by the time the lights dimmed and the music started, there was no still sign of the world's suddenly famous fashion reporter.

Perry, at her left, inched forward in his seat, looking excited to see what lay in store. Véronique Duchamp always had some surprises up her sleeve in her exotic shows, so his enthusiasm was well placed. In a seat two rows behind her and just to her right, Felicity fanned herself with the program. Felicity, not being an official "someone", would never score a front-row seat at any fashion week, much to her irritation.

A shadow appeared to Elena's right, and she turned, a little more eagerly than she'd care to acknowledge. The word *finally* died on her lips. Instead of her former assistant, Emmanuelle Lecoq lowered herself into the seat.

Elena offered a glittery smile. "*Emma.* So lovely to see you again."

The *CQ* editor's lips gave a slight twist, offering a hint of a mockery. "*Elly.* I believe congratulations are in order. However did you get that story?"

Her words were almost lost as the music increased in volume.

"One of my enterprising employees," Elena replied.

A lime-green spotlight slashed a line up the stage and back. The *lime*light? Literally? How Véronique.

"You mean one of your *ex*-employees, surely? I was under the impression you fired her, almost a week ago, if industry gossip is to be believed."

Elena frowned into the darkness, wondering who the stool pigeon was. "Madeleine wished to seek new opportunities."

"Not quite how I heard it, dear." A bony hand lightly patted her wrist. "If she'd been one of mine, I'd never have let her go. In fact, I even offered her a job."

Anger surged. Elena snatched back her hand and folded it in her lap, well out of reach. The music drowned out any possibility of further talk. Elena had an irrational urge to rip the woman's large, pretentious Chanel sunglasses off her smug face. It was night, for heaven's sake. Instead, she gave an indifferent sniff and turned back to the catwalk, fixating on Emmanuelle's job offer. Had Madeleine taken it?

As the first model pranced out, she returned to wondering something else. Where on earth was she?

Véronique Duchamp really did know how to put on a show, Elena decided. The zoo theme was well executed, with models in sparkling, geometric animal heads lurking and prowling around fake bushes along the edges of the platform, as other models swished along the catwalk. Nature sounds and wildlife calls could be heard behind the stirring beats.

Towards the show's end, the purpose of the trapeze became clear when a svelte, leotard-dressed "monkey" swung down, snatched an exotic, floppy hat off one model, and, on the return trajectory, with perfect precision, plopped it on the head of the model following behind her. Neither model flinched at the aerial antics inches from their heads, while the crowd clapped its delight.

"Superb," Perry said in an awed whisper. "I think Véronique was a Broadway choreographer in another life."

Elena afforded him a small smile. The sweeping spotlights began to converge on one point, and a voice-over announced the *pièce de résistance*. Elena, Emmanuelle, and Perry all edged forward as the music built to a crescendo. Véronique always saved the best to last. She had never disappointed in three decades.

The spotlight captured and slid down a female form, revealing more and more. Her face was in darkness, but the dress was lit up ethereally. The gown was gorgeous—a swirl of wafting material so fine it seemed to flow over the body like liquid. The crowd broke into applause. All except for Elena, whose focus was on the model's form, not her couture.

There were no jutting collar bones, angular elbows, or sharp hips. This woman had a slightly fuller shape for a model, and an actual bust. That, in itself, was both unexpected and appealing. Elena appreciated soft, subtle curves like these a great deal. The model also accentuated the fluid dress as though she and its fine drapings were always meant to be as one. The woman's gait, however, was not precise or bold; her feet were not plucked up deliberately like a dressage horse and then drilled down. No, her walk was steady, almost leisurely, like someone strolling along the beach with a hat in one hand and not a care in the world.

Elena arched a brow. Did Véronique want the room to know: this model is you? *You* could wear this? Was that it? It would explain the body shape too. Elena marvelled at the cheekiness of Véronique in thumbing her nose at convention yet again.

As she watched the woman's feet, encased in slender, white heels (*Giuseppe Zanotti, perhaps?*), she saw the faintest wobble they made each time the model planted her heels. They weren't even that high. Elena stared in confusion. And then it hit her. This was *not* a model.

The spotlight began to rise up the woman's body. She felt Perry stiffen beside her, suck in a harsh breath, and whisper "Ah!"

Before Elena could ask him why, the woman reached the end of her saunter and looked straight at her, just as the spotlight fully lit up the model's features.

Elena froze at the sight of a face she had come to look forward to seeing every day. It took her a moment to process the impossible image. Why would Madeleine be on the catwalk? Was she imagining it? Before she could make sense of that, the model did the unthinkable. She smiled. It was not just any smile. But a wide smile that was as dazzling as it was out of place on any runway in the world. She seemed unaware she was even doing it.

Felicity's horrified squeak behind her was drowned out by the collective gasp of the room at the unexpected faux pas. To her left, Perry clapped his hand over his eyes and groaned softly. It was a smile so familiar to Elena that it made her heart clench to see it again. She could only stare back in astonishment at Madeleine Grey, her ungainly, awkward, constantly embarrassed former assistant, draped in a gown so exquisite she could pass as a goddess. She looked luminescent under the beautiful lighting, her eyes shining.

Elena swept her gaze over the stunning woman. That was what she was, she now realised. Hidden under all those ridiculous grunge clothes had been a woman of such beauty she now stole Elena's breath. She sat speechless, as she drank in the sight of her. Desire coiled inside her, sharp and dangerous, begging her for something she had never dared think about.

And she finally understood.

Madeleine was not her friend. Not like Perry. It wasn't normal to feel this way for a friend. It wasn't normal to want to dust your fingertips over a friend's body and map it the way she suddenly had a burning urge to do to Madeleine's. She savoured the sight of her. Her Madeleine. The woman she...felt deeply for.

This could never happen, a tiny voice of reason whispered to her. Of course it couldn't. For so many reasons.

She crushed the inner voice and drank in the sight of her, clapping hard now, along with the rest of the crowd. The cold, constant ache in her heart at missing this woman so much eased for the first time in a week.

How had she ever thought she could let her go? Not once, but twice?

The roar of the crowd and its drumming, loud applause faded out, and she could only feel the blood thundering in her ears at this most unexpected development. Her lips parted for a ragged in-pull of breath, then an equally uneven exhalation, as Madeleine did a jaunty hip swish when she turned.

Breathtaking.

Her heart thundered its approval. Elena heard one awed word, cutting through the background din.

"Oh."

It came from her own lips.

CHAPTER 27
Afterglow

Relief flooded Maddie. Under the spotlight, she paused, holding the pose as Natalii had shown her, her head straight, as the cameras flashed and shutters clicked. Even in the semi-darkness, she felt the presence of Elena, her gaze pinning her in place. Her former boss's lips were parted, and Maddie's pulse pounded even harder than it already was.

The music shifted—her cue to finish her walk. She pivoted and headed back up the runway. Maddie focused on keeping her toe straight and planted (*"It is all in the toes, oui?"*), leaning slightly back and sashaying her hips just a tiny bit. She'd love to have seen Elena's reaction to that bit of sass.

A whoosh from overhead announced the trapeze "monkey" was back, and she forced herself not to react as a solid weight dropped on her head. This dazzling, blue-jewelled crown was insured for $300,000, Natalii had informed her earlier, much to her dismay. She prayed it wouldn't slide off.

Seven more steps. Six. Five.

The crowd erupted, as Véronique stepped out from behind the curtain at the back of the runway and gave her an approving smile.

Two steps left. One.

Véronique passed Maddie, giving her a wink and...

That was it.

Safely behind the curtain, Maddie almost fell with relief into Natalii's arms.

Two leggy Amazonian models strutted out past her to flank the designer, who was taking her bows.

"Oh God!" Maddie exhaled and kicked off her heels. "I think I had a heart attack. Or maybe I'm still having it. Am I even conscious?" She looked enviously at a nearby chair but didn't want to risk the dress. Instead, she dropped the crown on it. A security guard rushed over to collect it.

"You were *magnifique*," Natalii said. "Come with me and I'll help you with your dress." She pulled her forward. "Tell me everything. Did you see Elena? She saw you? Was there skyfire?"

"Oh yeah." Maddie grinned, the vision of a shocked Elena floating in her mind.

Natalii led her to a now deserted backstage changing area that had been allocated to the missing star of the show, Anastazie. She pushed Maddie onto a stool before a well-lit mirror. Nimble fingers began undoing her corset, and Maddie's mind wandered back to Elena's reaction—until she met Natalii's knowing gaze in the glass.

"Uh-huh! I knew it." Natalii's eyes contained a triumphant gleam. "I am looking very much forward to this story."

Natalii pulled the ties through the eyelets which dotted down the back of her dress, as Maddie recounted what had happened. "I went through the curtain. I was thinking, eyes fixed on a spot at the end, heel, toe, lean back, not *too* far, just like you said, but a little way, nice and relaxed. I didn't fall; thank God for those low heels."

Natalii nodded as she worked.

"Then I reached the end. I saw her. Well, *felt* might be a better word." Maddie paused as she remembered the feeling. It was as if everything came down to the two of them. Elena's eyes had swept over her like a caress. Elation filled Maddie, as she remembered the admiring glance.

"And then?" Natalii asked.

"And then…" Maddie frowned. "It was weird. I heard Felicity groan like a distressed cow. I'd recognise her voice anywhere. I wasn't sure if it was seeing me or some stupid mistake she thought I'd made. It wasn't just her, though."

"Ah, *oui*, I heard the gasps. What did you do to provoke this, hmm?"

"Not a clue."

"Well, then, perhaps you should ask *her*." Natalii glanced to the left in the mirror. "Madame Bartell." She stepped back from the chair and gave Maddie a small, reassuring smile. "I will leave you to discuss things."

Maddie opened her mouth to reply, but she'd already turned and was headed for the door.

Elena stepped into view, her gaze ghosting across Maddie's bared back.

Maddie blushed, feeling as if she were naked.

"Sorry if I'm intruding," Elena said, not sounding remotely apologetic. Her eyes found Maddie's in the mirror.

"Did you enjoy the show?" Maddie asked, clasping her fidgeting fingers together.

"Very much," came Elena's soft, low reply. "Possibly Véronique's finest offering in many years. And her best show ever," Elena's voice became a purr, "for a variety of reasons."

"Really? Well, that's good." She tapered off, unsure what to say in the face of Elena's intense stare. "How's work?" she asked, before cursing herself for the lame small talk.

Elena cocked an eyebrow at the topic choice and took a step closer. "Incompetence surrounds me. So—it's much the same." Her fingers lifted to settle on the back of Maddie's neck. "This gown looked exquisite on you," she said, although she was only touching skin.

The fine hairs on Maddie's neck snapped to attention.

A trailing touch, faint as it was, drifted slightly lower, down the bumps of her spine and stopped between her shoulder blades. "The designer had the bodice so perfectly constructed and balanced that only someone with measurements like yours could have worn the garment and done it any justice."

The fingers at her back were placed exactly behind the bodice "measurements" at the front that Elena had just alluded to—a fact Maddie was only too well aware of. "Oh," she whispered.

"Mm, yes." Elena's fingers did a small, careless twirl. "So how is it you were selected for this task? I seem to remember you telling me more than once that you're a reporter and nothing else."

"Ah," Maddie said, relieved to have a safe topic to discuss. "Véronique couldn't find any model in Sydney as big as me with no notice." She glanced down and gave a self-deprecating laugh. "Even now, I'm not sure I've done this beautiful dress justice."

Elena's eyes bored into Maddie's in the mirror. "You're perfectly proportioned. Which is why you and this dress were meant to be. However, modelling and you..." Her lips twitched. "Well, let's just say you may have to work on that neutral face."

"My what?" Maddie lost her train of thought, as Elena's gaze, yet again, detoured across her bare back before darting back up to meet her own.

"You smiled. At the end of the runway, you struck your pose and then beamed like the headlights on my Lexus."

Maddie froze. She'd *what?* The memories flooded her of her walk and the heady rush of emotions and how great she'd felt and how she'd just... Oh. *Oh!* That's what the gasps had been about? She'd made a fool of herself. The entire room had been laughing at her. She gave a soft, pitiful moan.

"I did not say I disapproved."

Elena's tone was gentle, but Maddie couldn't meet her eyes. She'd had one damned job. And she couldn't even walk thirty feet, turn, and walk back without messing up.

"In fact it was refreshing," Elena continued. "I rather enjoyed the change from sour-faced, industry-standard models. I have no doubt Véronique is out there right now spinning it as some genius marketing ploy. Accessible fashion or some such thing."

That was definitely the kindest interpretation anyone could put on it. "Why are you being so nice to me?" Maddie asked, feeling dazed.

"Actually, I was being truthful. In case it's escaped your notice, this is the last day of my part of the truth bet."

It is? Maddie mentally flipped through her calendar. While she'd only had to be honest for a day, Elena had agreed to a full week. And she was right with her sums. "Okay." Maddie deflated again.

"You preferred the idea I was just being nice to you?" Elena regarded her with a curious expression.

"Maybe. I... Yes."

"Well, we both know how out of character that would be." She looked amused.

"I guess so. You'd never do nice, right?" Maddie left enough teasing in it so it would sound like a joke, but she wasn't so sure of anything anymore. Her ground seemed to keep shifting around this woman.

"I'm glad we agree." Elena tilted her head. "Look at you." The backs of her fingers lifted to Maddie's cheekbones. "The contours of your face have perfect symmetry. You could be an artist's model. A muse to inspire and study."

Maddie swallowed. "Is that what I am to you? Someone you like to study?"

"Yes." Elena's expression contained nothing but sincerity. "I do like to watch you."

"I like looking at you too," Maddie said, voice a whisper. "I've really missed you."

"It's only been a week." The words were light, but Elena's eyes were intense.

"A long one." Maddie glanced at Elena's sleek black dress. "You look stunning, by the way. I know that goes without saying—you always do. But I felt you watching me from the runway. You have this…presence."

"Then perhaps you should see me first thing in the morning. Not quite so impressive."

"I *have* seen you first thing in the morning," Maddie said with a small smile. "Also in the middle of the night. Even with the worst pressures and the tightest deadline for my story, you're always so focused. I've never met anyone like you. I think you're an amazing woman."

"Not everyone would share that view, I can assure you." Elena straightened. "Speaking of your story, the Australasian Legends of Publishing ball is the first on our list that you'd accompany me to. It's on the twentieth. See if you can find something to wear like this. The bodice really does suit your figure. I'll send Perry your way to help fit you."

Elena brushed the side of Maddie's dress, only barely dusting her ribs, just a little too close to her breasts for Maddie not to hold her breath. She glanced at Elena, uncertain, and was struck yet again by how naked her roving gaze was. How it felt like stroking fingers, the way her eyes lingered. Wait, was Elena holding her breath too?

"Ahh! My *remarquable, magnifique célébrité!*" A high French voice cut through the room, and Elena and Maddie started as Véronique swept in.

A rapid wash of cool air accompanied Elena stepping back.

Véronique rushed to Maddie and kissed her on both cheeks, then gave her left cheek a final fond squeeze. Turning, she faced Elena with a chillier expression. "Madame Bartell?" It almost sounded like an accusation.

"*Oui,*" Elena replied, before rattling off an entire greeting in the designer's native language. She sounded confident and fluent.

Maddie picked up something about the show being excellent. Or possibly something about monkeys?

Monkeys? Oh, the trapeze lady.

Véronique looked impressed in spite of herself. She responded in French, and Maddie let her thoughts drift, content to watch two powerhouse, fashion-focused women have a summit that was long overdue.

She fiddled with the hairpins on the counter in front of her. Read the brands of the hairsprays, marvelled at the vast array of make-up products. Her mind, though, was a dizzying blur. Her former boss had practically caressed her. Elena had slipped and skidded those long, sensual fingers all over Maddie's skin and set it on fire. And the look on her face, the burning of her deep eyes, was hypnotic. Maddie would have given every cent she owned to know what Elena had been thinking. Was it desire? Or teasing? What did she want from her?

She froze when she heard the word *amour*. Trying not to be obvious, she glanced back to the mirror to find Elena looking a little surprised. And then her cool gaze slid over to Maddie's.

Over Elena's shoulder, Véronique smirked.

Maddie started to panic. What had the bloody woman told Elena? She shot the designer a part mutinous, part terrified glare, which made her laugh heartily.

"I think a celebration is in order, *oui*? You will come to the afterparty? Both of you?" Véronique's gaze moved from Maddie to Elena and back again, and Maddie could see mischief brewing in those dancing eyes.

"Now, I will take this stunned silence as agreement, for who could say no to such an exclusive invitation? Mm?" Véronique asked. "An event the *cafards* have never before been invited to. So, of course, you are both thinking '*Oui*, Véronique! We will be there!' And now..." She threw her head back dramatically and roared, "Pascal!"

Her assistant scurried in.

"I need cigarettes. And champagne. Because tonight..." She clapped a firm hand on both women's shoulders, startling Elena so much Maddie felt her jump a little beside her. "We party!"

Pascal scuttled from the room in search of his boss's requests.

Véronique darted out after him, without another word, bellowing for Natalii.

"So, we're going to a party?" Maddie fiddled with the hair-colour canister.

"So it seems." Elena sounded distracted.

Maddie looked up to see those clear, blue eyes lingering, once more, on her bare back.

"I'll let you get changed," Elena continued, her voice huskier than usual. "See you at the...monkeys."

"The monkeys?" Maddie tried not to laugh. Because that was definitely not a thing she'd ever expected Elena to utter in her lifetime.

"Véronique informs me there will be monkeys at the afterparty. Didn't you know?"

"Oh." Well that explained the zoo van. "The monkeys it is."

CHAPTER 28
Just Business

The afterparty was in full swing, with a riot of jungle-themed decor in the adjacent tent. Four African drummers in traditional, colourful dress were setting an earthy rhythm, while the monitors ringing the area showed a video of monkeys at the zoo going about their day.

Maddie had been trying to get close to Véronique to find out what she had discussed with Elena. But the normally reclusive fashion star was the centre of attention among a throng of admiring, fellow designers, fawning fashionistas, and industry associates. Natalii was there, too, sticking to her side like the security blanket Maddie knew she was.

Scouring the crowd, Maddie tried to spot Elena. She'd caught glimpses of Perry's gleaming, bald head and knew that his boss wouldn't be far away. But so far, she was proving elusive.

"Well, look who it is. The star of the whole damn universe."

Maddie turned to find Felicity, hands on hips, shooting her a look that was nine parts jealousy, one part Felicity. Or was it the other way around? With Felicity it was hard to tell.

"Hey." Maddie wondered if this would be a long conversation about all her failings on the catwalk, or whether she'd get a chance to try those cute, melty, jungle cheese balls before they got cold.

"Don't even think about it!" Felicity followed her gaze to the passing platter of balls. "I've seen your eyes molesting those things, and they are pure fat. Don't do it."

"They look great." Maddie gave a wistful sigh.

"Don't they, though?" Felicity looked at them as if they were a new-line Versace handbag. She turned back from the parade of food trays and gave Maddie a slap on the arm. "And that's for before."

"Hey! What'd I do?"

"Everything!" Felicity scowled. "Nothing! I don't know—how is it you just waltz into the story of the decade, get the dress of the century to wear at the best show at fashion week, and then get invited to the world's most exclusive afterparty? An afterparty, I might add, that Perry and I couldn't get into until we said who we were friends with."

"Well, Elena's name does open every door."

"Not this tent flap," Felicity said with a disagreeable look. "Perry had to say we knew *you*. Sure enough the Duchamps had left some spare tickets under your name. I suppose your head is the size a bus right now." She snatched a passing flute of champagne. "Although, I know what you'll say."

"Really?" Maddie plucked a glass of orange juice off the tray. "What will I say?"

"Well, you'll look at me all doe-eyed with that aw-shucks Australian innocence and explain it all just happened, somehow. That you got lucky." She threw her hand up. "I worked my ass off to get a tenth as lucky as you in life. I swear, if I didn't somewhat like you and find you a damned good PA—although I will kill you if you tell a soul I just said that—I would poke your eyes out with a cheese knife. Well, I would, if cheese knives weren't so bloody close to the cheese platter."

Maddie shook her head. "Seriously? I have no idea, any more than you do, why any of this is turning out the way it is. But I know you'd sleep a hell of a lot better if you focused more on your own career than mine. Except you don't even like your own career, do you? Why are you a chief of staff anyway? You're a fashion worshipper." She thought about that and laughed. "My God, it's catching isn't it? You and Elena? Neither of you are doing what would make you happiest."

Felicity peered at her. "What would you know about what makes her happy? You've only known her for five minutes. I've known her *years*. She relies on me. *Me!*" She swayed a little, and Maddie realised the chief of staff had probably been indulging somewhat more than she should. That explained this more uncensored spray than usual.

"Felicity..." she began.

"No! You can't make this all right with your charms. That reminds me—did you have to smile like a hyena at the end of the catwalk? I almost threw myself under my seat in embarrassment."

A rising blush made Maddie grateful for the darkness.

Felicity took another huge gulp of champagne.

Was she deliberately getting sloshed?

"Elena liked my smile." Maddie hoped her blush wasn't obvious.

"Of course she damn well did. Everything you do now is somehow beatified. Hell, you even ruined her marriage, and you're still the second coming. If *I* ruined her marriage, she'd politely ask her driver to reverse over my still-twitching corpse a few times, and then she'd fire me posthumously."

"Richard ruined their marriage. We both know she deserves better than that sleazy bastard. I was just the one who told her about him."

"You are so..." Felicity shook her head and sounded defeated. "*Bah!* I need to get properly drunk and laid. And you—stay out of my sight until I can process how you keep scooping the lottery instead of getting shredded by shark teeth."

Maddie studied the confusion in her eyes. Felicity actually had a good point. Her luck had been insane of late. She was just superstitious enough to wonder when it would turn.

There was a screech as a microphone was turned on, and they both looked towards the stage to see a punkish, blue-haired woman wearing dark, ripped jeans and a green tank top.

Maddie squinted. If she didn't know any better, she'd swear the woman looked like Natalii's girlfriend, Adèle. The same one who had been squinting at her down a webcam only days ago, accusing her of sleeping with her lover. And now she was suddenly on one knee before the hushed room, speaking rapidly in French, offering a ring to Natalii.

Oh wow. A proposal?

She tried to make out the words, but they were speaking too fast. Then kissing. And hugging. And crying. And waving, as the crowd cheered.

"Well fuck," Felicity said, eyes narrowing, "that works out for you, too, doesn't it? Do you ever have any bad days that aren't wardrobe related?"

"What?" Maddie frowned. "How does their engagement have anything to do with me?"

"Well, now the press will stop implying you got your scoop by sleeping with her." Her finger jabbed in Natalii's direction.

"Honestly, Felicity, why do you even care if I get a few good breaks? I don't even work with you anymore."

"I *don't* care. But Elena does. And I just don't get it. She was in such a foul mood when she thought you were...dining out on French. Oh, that reminds me!" Her tone turned all officious. "The twentieth? That publishers ball you're going to with Elena? See Perry. Elena apparently has all these ideas for what you're wearing."

"She does?" Just an hour ago, Elena had expressed only a vague and passing interest in her outfit for the event. Where had "all these ideas" come from?

"A long list of ideas. Really long." Felicity's lips thinned. "Right after the catwalk show, she was having epiphanies all over the place. She was quite specific too. And don't bother asking me why she cares what you'll be dressed like. The mind of Elena is an enigma wrapped up in a Coco Chanel."

Coco Chanel! So *that's* what she was wearing. She looked gorgeous too.

"Can you just..." Felicity squinted at her. Then sighed. "I don't know, explain? You're the garage-band, dead-person crime girl. Why?"

"Why what?"

"Why *any* of this?"

And right then, Maddie saw it. Through all of Felicity's bluster and dramatics, a look of pain, devastation, and confusion. She looked as though there weren't enough jungle cheese balls and fancy booze in the world to make up for her feeling elbowed out of the way by some blow-in, clueless, fashionless upstart like Maddie.

Felicity had hero-worshipped Elena for years. Had been loyal for years. Maybe even loved her for years. And it was Maddie who got to go with Felicity's icon as a plus one to a VIP ball. Well, four of them to be exact. Felicity probably hadn't even been told about the other three events.

"Why?" Maddie said, her tone kind. "Because I negotiated a deal. It's good business. If Elena wanted Véronique and my exclusive, she got stuck helping me network at a few balls. Elena's a woman of her word. She agreed to help me meet some important publishing names. That means looking good, too. Hence her interest in what I will wear. That's all there is to it."

Relief seemed to swamp Felicity's features. It was almost palpable. "Okay," she said in a voice so prim it was as though sheer bravado alone could hide the jealousy she was leaking all over the place. "Yes, that sounds...of course."

She shot Maddie an unguarded, grateful look that told Maddie she was much shrewder than she pretended. Felicity didn't look all that convinced by her explanation, but it was palatable enough and she'd take it.

"It's business," Felicity repeated. "It makes sense," she said, as if trying the idea on for size. "Because Elena is a great businesswoman." She nodded.

"Yep." Maddie glanced around for the woman in question. She didn't see Elena, but she did spot the Duchamps, alone at last. Mother and daughter hugged for a moment. Maddie grinned, proud she'd had a tiny hand in bringing them closer together through her interview.

"I have to give my congrats to the Duchamps."

"Go." Felicity shooed her away, looking more like her old self. "It's not like I care. I mean *really*!"

Maddie laughed, shook her head, and pushed her way through the masses. As she neared them, Natalii rushed over, with her mother not far behind, and gave her a quick hug.

Brimming with enthusiasm, Natalii filled her in about Adèle's arrival. "She said she missed me too much." She was almost bouncing. "And she rushed on the first plane after her last show so that she could see me."

Maddie gave her a kiss on each cheek—which seemed to be the appropriate response to French exuberance—and grinned. "So pleased for you."

"I'll bet." Natalii laughed. "Now your sullied honour, it is restored!"

"Hey, that's not why! But, yeah, doesn't hurt. I'm just really happy you have found the one you're meant to be with."

Véronique, who had been quietly listening, leaned in. "On this topic, Madeleine, I think the one you wish you were with is not as without the interest as you like to believe," she said with a cryptic look. "I would say she is *captivée* by you."

Natalii seemed suddenly intrigued.

Maddie's gaze darted between the two women, seeing if they were joking. Neither laughed. "She's married, she's straight. Okay, she's kind of surprisingly tactile at times, but still, she's..."

"A woman," Véronique said. "And when I told her the emotion I had when I designed my signature dress was *amour—amour* for the beautiful female body, she looked right to you."

"That doesn't mean anything. Come on, eyes roam!"

Véronique laughed and gave her cheek an affectionate pat. "*Oui,* dear girl, they do. They roam all over you."

Maddie bit her lip, trying not to feel hopeful. She couldn't...wouldn't dare to hope. If she was wrong, it would be crushing. And maybe Elena just really liked the dress? She wasn't entirely sure what Elena was up to. The woman followed her own set of rules on everything.

Denial definitely seemed the safest course of action around a pair of far-too-curious, teasing Frenchwomen. Well, at least until Maddie figured the confusing woman out for herself.

As if on cue, she looked up to see Elena making a beeline for them. "Oh God," she whispered. She so wasn't ready for this.

Natalii and Véronique shared amused glances.

"Ladies," Elena intoned as she reached them.

Maddie swallowed. And right then, the sneaky, evil Duchamps made their excuses and exited. She glared after them.

"Madeleine," Elena said, drawing back her attention.

"Elena." Maddie gripped her orange juice glass hard and sucked through her straw for something to do. It hit an air pocket between ice cubes and a loud slurping sound erupted.

Elena snorted softly. "Thirsty?"

Maddie gave her a sheepish look. She glanced around. "Enjoying the monkeys?"

"I'm actually strongly opposed to keeping animals in captivity for humans' pleasure. I know some might enjoy this, but at what cost?"

"They do breeding programs, don't they? Zoos like this help keep them alive."

"Yes. But they can be kept alive outside zoos as well," Elena said with a firm voice. "How would you enjoy being kept in a cage? Even one where you can roam a little but never be free?"

Maddie didn't know how to answer that. She wanted to say she was as pro animal rights as the next liberal arts student and had been donating to the World Wildlife Foundation for years. *Pandas for the Win* had been her first bumper sticker on her beat-up, blue VW. Instead she said, "I wouldn't like it, no."

"I'm glad we agree." Elena touched Maddie's arm.

Maddie was so surprised, she twitched.

Elena withdrew her fingers. "What were you and the Duchamps discussing?" she asked after a beat.

"Natalii's engagement."

"Ah. Yes, a good thing for you."

"Why does everyone keep saying that?" Maddie's head shot up. "I am happy for them! That's all there is!"

"And you somehow don't feel you can be both relieved and happy?"

"I guess I can," Maddie said, hating how defensive she sounded.

"You're in a very odd mood, Madeleine. By the way, the first ball we're attending together, have you had any further thoughts on what you're going to wear?"

It sounded so casual, Maddie almost laughed. As if she hadn't given Perry a detailed list on how she wanted him to make her over. "I thought I'd see Perry."

"Excellent idea. He will be sure to have something acceptable." Her eyes gleamed at the prospect.

"Did *you* have any thoughts?" Maddie asked, feeling cheeky. "About what I should wear?"

Elena froze. Her gaze was long and assessing.

Maddie waited for the lie to come, the flippant brush off, and then remembered it wasn't going to come. Not tonight, not when this was the last night of their bet.

"Yes," Elena said, not looking pleased about the admission. "A surprisingly long list of things I'd enjoy seeing you in. There," she added, tossing her a small glare. "Is that what you wanted to hear?"

"Why do you care what I look like? It's just business, right?"

Elena seemed startled by the reminder. "That's good to remember." She placed her drink on a nearby table. "Don't you think?" She gave Maddie a long look, as though Maddie had somehow been at fault, forcing Elena into thinking unbusinessy thoughts.

Wait a minute... That meant Elena had been *having* unbusinessy thoughts. Her heart swelled briefly, until her irritation kicked in. Elena's comment was such a load of...

"Well, okay," Maddie said. "We agree, it will all be about business." She gave her a tiny smile and decided to press her luck. "But that won't take away from the fact you were staring at my back for ages tonight."

Elena's cheeks grew pink. Her eyes narrowed. "Well."

"Well?" Maddie supposed that was the equivalent of agreement in Elena's world. Or not. It was so frustrating.

"You couldn't resist asking about it, I suppose. Getting *that* out of me before the bet expired."

Getting what out of her? Was Elena saying she was not as indifferent to Maddie as she seemed? Back stroking notwithstanding, of course. Maddie still wasn't over that and probably never would be.

"So...you, ah, *like* me, then?" Maddie asked, desperate for some clarification. Because it was her last chance to ask, and Elena was confusing as hell with her cryptic answers.

"I could answer that, but then I would resent you for the temerity of the question. Do you really want me to resent you, Madeleine?" Elena's voice turned to honey, and Maddie had to admire what a clever little trap that question was.

"You don't play fair."

"No, I suppose not." She looked far too pleased with herself

Maddie sighed. There was a reason this woman ran a media empire, after all. She won at everything. On the other hand, a "no comment" about liking Maddie was way better than a denial.

They regarded each other.

"I suppose this is goodbye," Maddie said. "Until our media events together, I mean."

"Really, Madeleine."

Elena said it as though Maddie was making a huge deal out of something meaningless. Seriously? She was half tempted to re-ask the earlier question about liking her and risk the resentment rather than put up with such condescension. Her jaw tightened.

Elena seemed to sense her raging mutiny. "So irritated at me," she said with a knowing smile. "You don't hide much with those accusing eyes." Elena studied her for a few moments, and to Maddie's shock, she realised she was openly admiring her this time.

It was just like before, in front of the mirror, only more. So much more. A thrill skittered down Maddie's spine, as she felt the languid gaze shift and burn across her skin. She almost dropped her glass.

Elena leaned forward and whispered against the shell of her ear. "Madeleine, I have long admired beauty in all its forms. It comes with my job, running the world's premier fashion magazine. Your unblemished, creamy skin, the way it dips and flows and glows with vitality? What lover of beautiful things could resist looking at it? Especially one as excellent at her job as I am."

Elena gave her a rich, taunting smile that left Maddie rooted to the spot, as the high priestess of media straightened, turned, and headed towards the exit.

Maddie watched her leave and tried to swallow. She took in a shuddering breath and ran a trembling hand through her hair.

Elena had just called her beautiful. Oh, she'd dressed it up as business, but still.

Elena Bartell thought she was beautiful.

CHAPTER 29
Ivory

Maddie wasn't feeling too beautiful. Elena might have declared her so at their last meeting, and Maddie had been dining out on that ever since, but right now, five weeks later, she was feeling like a hot, hideous mess. June 20 had whizzed around far too fast, and before she knew it, she'd answered a call to go to *Style Sydney.* Now here she was, being poked and prodded by Perry and judged by model standards. And failing.

The art director yanked and tugged and pinned and flattened her into an assortment of dresses, each more gorgeous than the last. None, however, were suited to her average-woman proportions. The proportions Véronique had admired so much. She was clearly in a minority.

"God," Perry said, with a huff, "do you have to be so..." His hands made a curvy shape.

"We've known each other for long enough, so I don't get why you're so surprised about discovering my boobs now."

He ran a hand over his dark scalp. "True. They're just...inconvenient. Still, I am a genius. If all else fails—boob tape."

Maddie screwed up her face. "Perry, I am not getting strapped down for a publisher's ball. It's not the Oscars."

Perry glanced at his black Cartier watch. "We only have five more hours to Cinderella you, so you will be taped if I say you will."

"But..."

"No. And stop looking like I stomped on your kitten. By the time I've finished, you will be a feast for the eyes." Perry glanced around, snapping his fingers. "We need cleavage. Oh, what am I thinking? The Alberta Ferretti, of course. The things she does with chiffon and silk! Divine."

He strode off to several racks of dresses. "So," Perry called out from between the designer garments, "how is the life of the famous treating you?"

"Good. I get a lot more people wanting me to freelance for them. I'm doing a story for *Vanity Fair* next."

He gave a low whistle. "Ooh. Fabulous."

"Well, yeah." Maddie smiled to herself. "I was pretty excited when they—"

"Not that, *this* !"

He emerged like a proud father from *The Lion King*, holding aloft ivory, diaphanous material.

It appeared far too see-through to cover Maddie's dignity. "Uh-um... I don't think..."

"No objections, it's perfect." Perry gave the hanger a waggle. The dress seemed to float in the air instead of jiggle. "It was on her short list of dresses for you to consider for tonight."

Maddie cocked her head. "And just how long was Elena's short list?"

"Oh," he waved his hand, "thirty. She narrowed it down to a dozen. Give or take."

He held the dress up in front of Maddie's chest and nodded. "Right, underwear off." He tossed her a nude thong on a hanger. "This on. So you don't frighten the skittish horses."

"Perry! I'll get arrested!"

"Just try it...trust me. Now scoot." He pushed her inside the changing cubicle in front of them and closed the curtain. His footsteps retreated. "Heels," he muttered to himself. His voice got farther away. "Tall but not too tall, given you have the grace of a lumberjack."

"Hey! I modelled at Australian Fashion Week, I can't be too much of a disaster!" Maddie joked, as she shimmied out of her underwear. She slid on the thong. Ew. She shifted it about a little. Not much better. Thongs were devil spawn.

"One swallow doth not a summer make," Perry retorted. "Oh! Choos *pour vous*."

A minute later, a pair of sleek, Jimmy Choo heels appeared in the gap under the curtain, just as Maddie pulled on her dress. "Ooh!" The shoes were gorgeous. And, mercifully, not too high.

"I know," Perry said with far too much smugness from the other side. "You may now worship my greatness."

Maddie, however, was staring at her reflection. The dress redefined the word *risqué*. She stared some more.

"Come on, aren't you ready yet?"

Maddie stepped into the heels, and the complete effect was instant. She gasped.

In response, the curtain snapped open. "Oh my." Perry's gaze roamed her form. "Yes." He tugged the dress at the back of her neck, fiddling with the fastening. "Well, I've always said it—Elena has an eye for this. She knew it was made for you."

Maddie scrutinised her reflection, trying to see it the way Elena would. The front of the pale ankle-length dress was made up of crushed, sheer material, gathered in two, wide strips, forming a deep vee over her breasts, ancient Greek goddess style. Mercifully, the material's many layers hid her nipples. Tiny gold-threaded beading circled and cinched her waist like the finest of belts. The back was cut low to the waist. Only one layer of translucent gauze floated over her legs. This highlighted the length of her legs and created a filmy effect when she moved.

"I don't know, Perry." Doubt coursed through her. "I feel more uncovered than covered. I'm one stiff breeze away from badly oversharing."

Perry cocked an eyebrow. "Perhaps. But tell me you don't feel breathtaking even so."

Maddie's gaze slid back over her reflection. "It's not that. This isn't me. It's too...*too.*" *Glamorous. Otherworldly. Meant for a supermodel.* "I'm just a kid from outer Sydney."

"Are you, though? *Just* a kid from outer Sydney? Shall we review what you have accomplished of late? Tonight is your first outing among the who's who of publishing since your world exclusive. It's called the

Legends ball for a reason. Now, you could just find something average and hide against the wall, or you could stand up and be counted and *arrive*. You could look them all in the eye and make them remember who you are. Be unforgettable. This is your moment, Maddie; you don't get it twice. So knock 'em all over."

Maddie exhaled. *Well, when he puts it like that.*

Their eyes met in the mirror. He leaned forward and, eyes twinkling, whispered in her ear. "And she'll love it."

Maddie hadn't meant to be fashionably late. There'd been a mix-up with the cars, and then the new one had a flat. She'd already texted Elena to explain the delay and told her not to wait for her, in case she had thought it her duty to do so. The lack of reply just made her more anxious.

She stepped out of the car, adjusting herself as subtly as she could manage, and prayed every piece of pasty and double-sided tape kept doing its job. She did her best to sweep up the steps, remembering the lessons Natalii had taught her on how to walk in couture and heels.

The photographers waiting at the door went insane.

"Ooh!"
"Hey, love, look left!"
"Look this way!"
"One more, one more!"
"Here—Natalii's girl—look over here!"

She groaned inwardly, ignored them all, and headed inside.

The room was opulent. An orchestra played in one corner, a chandelier flowed from the ceiling, and the crowd mingled in fine suits and gowns. Maddie immediately recognised some of the big names in world publishing. These were people she'd followed for years. The head of an international magazine conglomerate wandered by, and Maddie's eyes grew wide. However, he wasn't the media boss she was most excited to see. It had been five long weeks after all.

"Oh. My. God," Felicity said, appearing at her side. "I didn't believe him."

Maddie turned to find Perry smirking and Felicity—looking elegant in a forest-green gown, her blonde hair elaborately piled high—eying her in shock.

"Believe what?" Maddie snatched a passing glass of juice off a tray.

"Nothing," Felicity said in a mumble. "Forget it."

Perry's eyes danced with mirth. "I gave her a heads-up about how you'd look."

Maddie gave an embarrassed laugh. "Ah, right. Thanks. I think."

A flash of slicked, jet-black hair and pale skin caught Maddie's eye, and all other thoughts emptied from her mind. "Oh." Her voice was a reverent whisper. She turned and took in the full effect. "Wow."

Elena was making her way towards them, nodding to various luminaries as she went, looking a vision in deep violet, her arms and shoulders bare, the dress caressing her every curve. *Lucky dress.*

It was only when Felicity nodded, seemingly without awareness she had, that Maddie realised she'd even made her breathy comment out loud.

Elena was twenty feet from them before she finally looked over and caught sight of Maddie. Her step slowed briefly before she continued. Cool, blue eyes raked her from hem to the top of her hair. Maddie felt as laid bare as she had the last time she'd seen her.

"Perry," Elena said, giving him an air kiss. She turned and nodded. "Felicity."

Her chief of staff nodded stiffly back.

Elena's eyes fixed on Maddie and darkened. She stepped closer. "And Madeleine," she said, tone pure socialite, "how nice to see you again". Elena leaned in for an air kiss. The faintest dusting of lips made contact before she pulled back.

Maddie shivered at the touch. "You too."

"How lovely you look in Alberta Ferretti."

"Thanks." Maddie tried not to get derailed as that all-seeing gaze studied her barely covered breasts, then slid higher, a small smile curling her lips.

"Perry." Elena turned. "You've outdone yourself. Felicity? Where's that new PA?"

"She's coming later. She had to—"

"I don't care." She waved off the excuse. "I need a wine. White. And find me a vintage older than you are. I am serious. Perry, Samuel from *The SMH's* Street Style page wanted to hear your views on the deconstruction of fashion minimalism or some such thing. Go and indulge him. Remind him that *Style*'s is the only view on any fashion topic that counts."

Surprise crossed his face at the dismissal, but he merely nodded. Felicity had already gone—not even bothering to argue that she was not a PA. Maybe that was the difference between Maddie and Felicity. Only one of them had ever said no to Elena.

Now alone with the woman, Maddie felt awkward and only too aware of the lack of space between them. "Hey."

Elena gave her an indifferent look, as though she hadn't just orchestrated their time alone. "Are you enjoying yourself, Madeleine?"

"I just got here. But it's been impressive so far." Her gaze shifted to Elena's dress. *Very impressive.*

"I see. And did you wear that just to get a rise out of everyone?" Elena's tone was taunting.

"Not everyone." *Just you.*

"Look at them." Elena lowered her mouth towards her ear. "The men can't keep their eyes off you, and the women are all green with envy. You're the talk of the room."

Her perfume was intoxicating. Maddie struggled to focus. "Even if that's true, and I highly doubt it, didn't *you* handpick this dress?"

Elena didn't deny the charge; she merely pressed her lips together and straightened. "So, who would you like to meet first?"

Maddie glanced at her, already missing her nearness. "Meet?"

"As per our arrangement. You wished to be introduced to the publishing world. Here are some of the best of the biggest names. Let's start with the obvious. Do you plan to remain in Australia for your career?"

"Yes."

"As I assumed. So, among these publishers, who would you most like to be talking to right now?" She waved her hand at the room.

"You." That just slipped out. Maddie wanted to groan.

Elena's eyes sparkled with amusement. "Well, that *is* flattering, Madeleine, but I cannot further your career in Australian publishing the way these people can. Not unless you plan to work in fashion. Follow me." She led the way. "I'll introduce you to the publisher for Beyond Magazines Consolidated. Maurice is a man with power, connections, and opportunities."

Maddie felt a hand at her elbow and glanced down. She was propelled towards a clutch of men in tuxedos.

They nodded politely as Elena and Maddie arrived.

"Ms Bartell." The oldest man stepped forward, clasped Elena's hands, and air-kissed her cheek. He turned. His gaze slunk its way all over Maddie. Twice.

"And who *is* this gorgeous delight?" he asked.

The hand at Maddie's arm tightened a little and Elena's smile became more fixed. "Madeleine Grey, author of the Duchamp world exclusive, meet Maurice Slater from BMC."

Slater's gaze leapt from Maddie's chest to her face. "Ah, I see," he said, respect tinging his voice. "Well, I'm honoured, Ms Grey." He pointed at a woman behind him. "My assistant will give you Colin Sattler's card in the features department. I hope you'll call us if you have any thoughts on other profiles. Especially if they're of the same standard as the Duchamp interview."

"Thanks, Mr Slater." Maddie accepted the card and slipped it into her clutch.

"You're most welcome." He shook her hand again and held it.

The grip on Maddie's arm just above her elbow became like iron. "Lovely seeing you again, Maurice. Now we really must circulate." Elena's voice was firm, as she quickly led Maddie away.

When they were out of Slater's line of sight, Elena's pace slowed and her smile slipped along with her grip. "Well," she said tightly, "brevity is a virtue with some in our industry."

Before Maddie could comment, Elena changed direction and propelled them to a different group.

As the night wore on, Maddie met anyone who was anyone in publishing and her purse filled with important business cards.

"How are you faring?" Elena asked, when Maddie's fixed grin slipped a little.

She tried to pull apart the threads of her emotions to answer that. "There's so much posturing, isn't there? A lot of ego. They're so ruthless, ambitious, and hungry. It's also a little disconcerting how much they want to talk to me. Last month they wouldn't have given me a second look."

"Well, that's publishing. Your story is all anyone's talking about. Many people in this room have tried to get that interview over the years. Yet here you are—an unknown who waltzed in and plucked the prize out from under all their noses. They want to size you up and see whether you're a flash in the pan or someone to headhunt."

"Interesting choice of words. Some of those editors made me feel like I was part of a game hunt in Africa."

"You do have quite the pelt." Elena smirked and dusted her fingertips along Maddie's forearm to demonstrate. She left a trail of goosebumps. Her intense gaze was back, too. The one that made Maddie desperate to know what she was thinking.

A harried Felicity reappeared, hair spilling out of her updo, and a large, bulging bag on her shoulder. She passed Elena a wine glass. Maddie recalled she'd requested, some time ago, a vintage older than Felicity. "Do *not* ask me where I got that from. It's best if you have plausible deniability." She gave her shoulder bag a waggle.

Elena took the glass without comment. She nodded to Felicity and tilted her head back as she took a sip, her elegant, pale neck on display.

Maddie was transfixed—until the intoxicating view was blocked by one of Elena's top newspaper executives. Jason Lucas stepped right inside her personal space and smiled at her.

"Well, hello again," he said in what Maddie knew was his suave voice.

She stepped back to restore her space. The man was harmless enough. He'd often stopped at her desk to chat while he waited for Elena to be free. He never seemed fazed by the fact the conversation was mainly one sided. But listening was not one of his strong suits.

"Mr Lucas," Maddie said.

Elena had stopped drinking, her gaze shifting between the two.

"Why so formal?" he asked. His eyes brightened as he took her in. "My, my, Madeleine, don't you look beautiful."

The way he said her name felt mangled without Elena's subtle French inflection. "Maddie. It's Maddie."

"Not according to my boss." He gave Elena a winning smile that was unreturned. He shifted back to Maddie, drawing her name out. "*Mad-a-lin.*"

Harmless or not, the man had all the comprehension skills of a toenail infection. She sighed.

"You promised me a dance," Jason said with a wink. "You can tell me all about why your name is on everyone's lips in here."

What promise? She hadn't promised anything. "No," Maddie said firmly, "I didn't—"

Elena's attention was now fixed on Maddie. "Don't let me keep you. If you have promised my *junior* executive a dance—"

Maddie gave an adamant head shake. "No! And, look, I'm here to network tonight—"

"*Mad-a-lay-na.*" Elena emphasised her own pronunciation. "One dance won't get in the way of that."

"See?" Jason looked delighted. "You even have permission from the boss. So let's..." His arm was around Maddie's waist before she could react, and he whisked her onto the dance floor.

Maddie, going with him by rote, was still trying to process what had just happened. Was *this* expected of her? Enforced dancing? Elena seemed to act as though it was. If this was networking, she hated it.

Jason swung her to face him, bringing her in line of sight of Elena.

Maddie stared at her former boss, trying to see some hint of whatever might explain what on earth Maddie was suddenly doing on the dance floor with Elena's junior executive. She saw only a picture of indifference. So the woman didn't even care Maddie had been press-ganged into this?

"Stop." Maddie exhaled. "Jason, come on, you know I didn't agree to this."

"Hey, it's just a dance. We're here now, so let's just go with it." He grinned and pulled her against him. "Come on, it'll be fun. One tiny, little dance. Where's the harm?"

Maddie stepped back and pushed away, her anger rising. "You can't seem to take a hint, so I'll say it with smaller words: Get stuffed!"

"What?" Jason's grin faltered. "Something I said?"

Christ.

Curious stares drilled into Maddie, and those dancing around her had stopped to watch. She shot them all dark looks and made her escape.

She exited the building, lifting her gown to allow her to navigate the stone steps in heels, suddenly irritated by all the admiring looks men shot her way as she hurried past them.

Part of her wondered what was wrong with her that she couldn't play the game the way everyone else could. They did it without any effort. Why was *she* so bad at this? Maddie just couldn't schmooze, couldn't fake it, couldn't fit in. She couldn't fit in New York, and now she felt like a fish out of water in this world, too. She was allergic to pretending to be something she was not. Like this bloody dress.

She threw up her arm to hail a cab, but none of those whizzing past stopped.

Great—now she couldn't get anyone's attention.

"Madeleine."

She jumped and turned to find Elena standing behind her. Not a hair was out of place, but a faint blush in her cheeks indicated that she'd moved fast to catch up to her.

"Oh. Elena." Could this get any more embarrassing? She turned to face the street. "Come to tell me what an idiot I am?"

"No. But please explain to me why you have run off."

"I won't be forced to dance with anyone."

"Forced?"

"I didn't want to dance with him. I know Jason Lucas is one of your rising-star executives and you thought I should network with him or whatever. But I didn't want him touching me. Why should I have to go along with it? Why do I have to make nice with someone who thought my eyes were at chest level? What's wrong with just not wanting to dance?"

Elena gave her an inscrutable look. "Nothing."

"But you virtually threw him at me."

"I did no such thing. I simply gave you permission, in case you felt obligated to remain at my side, networking."

She sounded so reasonable that Maddie felt foolish. Had she misread everything? She gazed at the streets that were shining from the street lamps. It had been raining earlier, and they looked almost pretty.

"All night," Maddie explained quietly, "I felt like a...thing, not a person. Everyone wanted a piece of me, professionally or...otherwise. And Lucas was the last straw. He didn't even ask, he just took what he wanted." She glanced down at herself. "I'm feeling too laid bare tonight." She looked back up at Elena. "I don't think I'm cut out to be displayed like a prime rib." She crossed her arms and shivered. "Maybe I'm not cut out for any of this."

"I thought you wanted to be with him," Elena murmured.

"Where would you get that idea from?" Maddie gave her an indignant look.

Elena regarded her evenly. "He said you'd promised him a dance."

"He lied."

"Ah." Uncertainty crossed Elena's features, and she glanced away. "I wasn't aware."

Wasn't that the nub of everything? Maddie rubbed her arms and thought about that. "Did you know that I could tell what you were thinking? When I worked for you. In ninety-nine out of a hundred times, I could predict what you would do or want from me next. It's what made me an effective assistant."

Elena eyed her, appearing mystified by this line of conversation. "You were an efficient PA," she said with a tiny nod.

"And what most annoyed me tonight was that..." Maddie faded out. She was being unreasonable. Elena was a busy woman with a multimillion-dollar company to run, on top of pretty much editing a global fashion magazine. She didn't have time to know things about Maddie. She might have a lapse every now and then, and touch her as if she meant something. But how often had Elena conveyed her indifference when Maddie worked for her? No personal questions or opinions asked or exchanged since they'd been in Sydney. Didn't that tell her everything she needed to know? She was being a fool, expecting this woman to truly know her. Or expecting her to want to.

"Nothing," Maddie said, feeling suddenly washed out. The adrenaline was seeping away and all she wanted to do was crawl into bed. "I'm sorry. I expected too much from you. I was wrong to. And I'm having a bad night."

Elena gave her a direct look. "Let me guess. It annoyed you tonight that although you feel you know me, I didn't know you well enough to deduce that you did not want Lucas's attentions foisted upon you. I was somehow expected to divine this telepathically. And you feel I more or less thrust you at him. Am I close?"

Maddie winced. "It's not your fault. I know it's absurd to expect..."

"*Absurd.* Yes. Because I'm Elena Bartell. And I'm oblivious in all things not related to business. I didn't even know what my husband was up to underneath my own nose. Correct?"

Maddie forced herself not to nod. But yes. Elena would never win awards for her interpersonal relationships. It wasn't her strength. Maddie knew it, and still she'd expected greater awareness from her. Because she'd thought they were closer than they were. That was on her, she supposed.

"I take silence as agreement," Elena said, her tone cool. "I had no idea that you felt one dance with that man was such a test case for where we stand with each other."

Maddie studied the watchful face in front of her. "And where is that? Where *do* we stand with each other?"

"Elena!" came a voice from behind.

They turned.

"Oh thank God." Felicity gasped. "I was afraid you'd left and..." Her gaze fell to Maddie. "Oh. Sorry. Am I interrupting another flounce-out?"

Maddie glared back at her. There was a limit to her patience.

Elena short-circuited her response by saying, with an impatient snap, "What is it?"

"Morgan Rosenfeld just made some preposterous declarations about *Style Sydney*'s future plans to a dozen media, and he was half drunk, and no one knows whether he was joking or not. Can you...?"

Elena gave a grim nod. "I will see to the media. Get Perry to divert our chairman away from the bar. I'll join you shortly."

Felicity hesitated, sliding her gaze over Maddie, then turned and clopped away on her heels.

"Madeleine," Elena said, voice soft, "where we stand is, I'm a married woman with a soon-to-be toxic, public divorce. The whole world will be watching me for cracks. I cannot afford mistakes. I can't start something with you now. Do you understand that there are things that are impossible in my position?"

Maddie felt the ground drop out beneath her at the truth of it being stated so starkly.

Impossible.

Elena leaned forward and whispered, "However, in future, I'll have Jason Lucas flayed alive if he touches you without permission." There was a pause, and warm breath danced against Maddie's earlobe. "And just in case you couldn't tell from the reaction you received, you looked beautiful tonight. Exquisite. But next time, for our ball in New York, why not dress the way you wish it, not the way you think someone else might appreciate? Although *appreciate* it, I most certainly did."

Elena straightened and shot her an amused look and said, "We're done." She turned and disappeared back up the stairs.

Maddie stared after her, tingles shooting through her.

CHAPTER 30
Green

The difference between writing for *Style Sydney* and *Vanity Fair* was as stark as day and night. Maddie spent every spare moment on her upcoming exposé piece. She was on her own this time, with no crack team to back her up, and she felt it.

Maddie had set out to prove to everyone she was not a one-hit wonder and, to one person in particular, that she could write hard news. She was a real journalist.

Her story was about whether the dreams of New York lived up to the experience of young hopefuls in the fashion field who had set out from all parts of the world. She focused on the fashion industry because that's where her contacts were, thanks to her first scoop. People knew who she was now. Her exclusive had opened fashion doors as if she were royalty. She had respect. And she had Perry, who hooked her up with some of his industry friends and contacts in New York.

The story had become a perfect distraction, so she didn't have to think about the word Elena had whispered in her ear. *Impossible.*

She'd come to hate that word. Maddie heard it over and over at night, and it never felt less painful. So she'd thrown herself into her work, pitched her story, won a green light, then caught a plane back to New York. She had to be here anyway, for the next ball in six weeks' time, so it worked out well.

For the lost-dreams aspects of her story, she'd found several young designers and models who'd been lured into drugs and prostitution by a sleazy magazine editor supposedly looking for the next big thing. Then there was the photographer with breathtaking talent, whose dreams had been realised at the cost of losing his family. Success mattered more—and he couldn't see a way to have both. Not in New

York. The worst part of it was, he knew he was losing them but couldn't see a way out of it. So he'd chosen. Every day he went to work, took astonishing photos, went home to an empty, swanky apartment, and drank to forget the addictive dream.

After much internal debate, Maddie decided to include the sexual harassment rife within the industry. She worked her way down the assistants' secret list. She'd made a copy of it the first day she'd found it, so she could take it home to read. Armed with the list, she'd tracked down and spoken to half a dozen of Elena's former assistants. The worst part was when she'd asked them about what it had been like when their boss's husband was among those making sexual demands on them.

Maddie used aliases for the assistants, but she knew Elena would be well aware of which company, which boss, and which husband these unidentified women were talking about. The wider world would be none the wiser, but the insiders—well, they'd definitely speculate.

It had been a difficult decision. Maddie had stayed up night after night, doubt crippling her and giving her butterflies. She wanted to shed a light on the issue, but she didn't want Elena to suffer for it. In the end, she decided the issue was too important not to be honest about. Besides, wasn't Elena famous for doing what was necessary, not what was easy?

Maddie hoped she would understand her decision. But if she didn't? Well... there was little she could do about that. Maddie was determined to give the victims their voices.

She found the solitude of the assignment strange. She'd never worked alone before and missed the human interactions. Even Felicity's dramatic huffs and acerbic commentary had made her feel part of a team. Working alone also gave Maddie dwelling time, and that was not good.

Her thoughts kept drifting back to that last ball together and Elena shutting down any suggestion of them for good. It had been confusing. Hadn't Elena been flirting with her? In the dressing room at Véronique's show in Sydney? Those fingers trailing across her back? Called her beautiful? What *was* all that?

As the days began to bleed together, she wondered if she'd just imagined it all. Or maybe it had happened, but it was just Elena's way of expressing her interest in beautiful things, be they newspapers or former assistants. Was Maddie little more than "art" to Elena? Or perhaps a game? Someone she pulled in to see if she could, and then pushed away?

Maddie sighed. No good would come of this line of thought. She flicked to her diary. She had two days before her *Vanity Fair* deadline and five days until she saw Elena again. The Foreign Correspondents' ball. She was looking forward to hearing the highly respected war correspondent Trent Dalton, who was the guest of honour. Maddie had been reading his work behind the lines of trouble spots in the Middle East. She appreciated that he often made the local people the story, not the military objectives.

Thoughts of the ball brought up her next problem: What to wear. She had rejected every suggestion Perry had emailed her. Her cheeks still burned in humiliation at Elena's softly worded suggestion. *Dress for yourself, not someone else.* That was rich, since Elena was the one who'd come up with the shortlist of dresses for her last time.

There was a sharp rap on her door. She frowned. Who would visit her? Only Simon and her parents knew the address of the Airbnb apartment she was staying at in Manhattan. Maddie scrambled to her feet and opened the door.

"Ah. Good, you are here." Natalii brushed past her in a rustle of packages. "Okay. I am ready. We must work with what we have, *oui*?"

"Um...what?" Maddie closed and locked the door behind her.

"It is no time to lose." Natalii wagged her finger. "Fear not! I have it right here!" She held up a garment bag.

Maddie stared at her. "Not that I'm unhappy to see you again, but when I emailed you for advice on what to wear for the ball, I didn't mean for you to turn up. And why aren't you back in Paris, making wedding plans?"

"I was already here for business. I have been on the Facebook talking with your Simon. He explained everything. Now my *mère* and I, we have the solution. *Oui?* A way for you to be unforgettable for your woman."

Maddie sank into her sofa. "My woman?" She shook her head. "Okay, I'm afraid you're going to have to back it up a bit. Can we go back to the beginning? What did Simon say?"

Natalii laid the garment bag across the kitchen bench and eyed her imperiously. "He informed me of this disaster of your Legends ball in Sydney."

"Disaster." Maddie's stomach plummeted at the reminder. "One word for it. So what *exactly* did he say?"

"He sent me the photos from the newspaper," Natalii said. "Of you in the *magnifique* dress. He said you were too, what is the word, *self-consciousness*, to enjoy yourself. And that your Elena did not care when an oaf in her employ forced you into dancing. And he says you think that she did not care for *you* at all. Your dress, it was the cause for this state of affairs, for you could not be you. Well!" Natalii waved towards the garment bag and then sat on a sofa cushion beside Maddie. "What is the use of knowing the greatest designer on the planet if you cannot use her? Mm? Do not worry, I asked *Maman* to help me a little, too!"

Natalii grinned at her own joke. "Anyway, this time, you will be *you*, and your lady will gasp and swoon." She nodded as though this was a certainty.

"Natalii." Maddie's mind was reeling. "It's really sweet you thought to do this, but it's useless. Elena made it clear she is not interested."

"Oh? And how did she do this?" Natalii gave her an arch look. "You forget I have seen you two together. The chemistry? It explodes!" Her hands flew apart like a bomb blast.

"She told me she was getting a divorce, being watched by the world for cracks, and couldn't afford to make mistakes. That it was impossible for someone in her position."

"And when did she say this? Before or after the dancing oaf?"

"After. I'd gone outside to leave, and she followed and said all that."

"Ahhh," Natalii said. "Let us review—your boss, the one who does not care, the one who has such indifference, runs after you to tell you these things. Your Elena, she does not do this often, am I right?"

Maddie was shocked the thought had never occurred to her. "I guess not."

"*Oui.*" Natalii nodded, satisfied. "And she told you she is to be divorced so mistakes cannot be made."

"Yeah."

"So if she is not interested, why tell you about this divorce? Hmm? Why not say, 'Go away! I do not like you that way and never will? Be gone!'"

"Um, because she didn't want to be mean?"

Natalii laughed and slapped Maddie's thigh. "Your Elena loves to be mean. I see her; it amuses her sometimes. It is a game. *Non.* That is not it. Divorces, they are temporary. She is telling you there must be patience. She says not now, not yet. She does not say *non.*"

"She said it was impossible."

"Because she is still married. *Oui?*"

"Um." Maddie was suddenly a lot less sure of what Elena's words had meant. But she knew, absolutely knew, she shouldn't dare to believe. Even so, the swell of hope in her chest was breathtaking. "Oh..." She exhaled again.

Natalii beamed. "So, here I am. Here to make you happy, the way you make me and *mon* Adèle blissful." She rose, unzipped the garment bag, and carefully lifted the outfit.

Maddie stared. "Holy...Oh!" She leapt up and rushed to the outfit and trailed her fingers over the material. Then she hugged Natalii, who laughed in her ear.

"I take this to mean *un succès?*"

"*Oui!*" Maddie was in awe. "Holy shit! Your mother could do a whole new line with this. You know that, right?"

"Oh, I do. But it is my design, and I am already doing a whole new line with it. This is the first piece in my own label, *Natalii.* You shall be my model for the evening. Make sure you tell them all who made it when the photographers go *snap, snap, snap.* Okay?"

"I will," Maddie said. "Oh my God. I think Elena's brain will explode when she sees this design."

Natalii frowned. "That is a good thing?"

"Oh yeah. Really good. A new Duchamp design? Except the twist is it's the daughter now? Wow, she'll...that is..." She faded out as a thought hit. "I mean if she's still speaking to me."

"Oh? Why would she not be?"

Maddie winced. "Just before the ball, a big magazine article I wrote will come out. It exposes a really touchy subject of hers. And it's a bit too close to home. Like, really close."

"It sounds an important thing, this subject?"

"Yeah."

"Then if your lady is worth anything at all, she will not mind. She will know you did not do this to hurt her. That it is worthy."

Maddie didn't say anything. She truly didn't know which way Elena would go on this. It was different when she had chosen her assistants over her husband. Everything had been out of the public eye. Punishments delivered in secret. Soon, though, people in Elena's industry, people she worked with every day, would figure out the truth. She would feel humiliated. Maddie's heart thudded painfully at the thought. She never wanted to hurt her, but she could see no way around it.

Vanity Fair splashed her story on its cover. It showed a picture of an artfully posed assistant-type woman with black gaffer tape over her mouth and a haunted look in her eyes. A broken camera, next to a pair of glittery heels, lay smashed on the floor. The headline read: *Fear and Clothing in New York: The Truth About Shattered Fashion Dreams.*

The story went viral the moment it hit the internet. Her article was linked to by every major fashion blog, and sparked conversation and debate about what fashion hopefuls went through to get ahead. Her phone went insane again, with congratulations from everyone. The only name that had not appeared was Elena's. Maddie didn't hear a single, curt syllable out of her.

Well, not until the day of the ball.

I'll be coming from the other side of town. You will have to make your own way there. E.

That text pinged six hours before they were due to meet and sounded way too pissy to be safe. Maddie immediately called Perry, who was based at *Style New York* again along with his mercurial boss.

"On a scale of minor meltdown to thermonuclear, how pissed off is Elena at me?" Maddie asked as soon as he answered.

He laughed. "Ah, Maddie, I wondered when you'd stick your head above the parapet and call. You have a mammoth set of ovaries, I'll give you that."

Maddie chewed her nail anxiously.

At her silence, Perry said, "Look, she's not talking about it at all. She went quiet and fired a few minions for incompetence, and that was it. She looks ready to explode, though, and everyone's keeping their distance. Felicity is threatening to throttle you on sight, yet again, for upsetting her goddess. So, you may wish to practice your duck and cover."

Maddie winced. "Did the fired minions deserve it at least?"

"Of course. I'm sure even you know the saying, 'Blue and green should never be seen, unless there's a colour in between'. Well, they didn't. They were walking eyesores at *Style's* accessories department and should know better. Speaking of, when are you coming in to pick out a dress? I've stashed a few from up-and-coming designers who want to be noticed. I can see you at...hmmm...two today. It's cutting it mighty fine, but still..."

"I'm not coming in. I've found my own outfit."

"Maddie! Are you cheating on me?"

She laughed at his shocked tone. "And how. Wait till you see."

"Please, tell me you're not cruising Target. I would have to disown you if you embraced the perils of polyblend. I have limits."

"No. A certain Duchamp lady has provided me with something. It's Natalii's new line. Reserve judgment until then."

"Natalii's?" Perry gave an intrigued half snort, which Maddie took as approval, and said goodbye.

The Plaza Hotel on Fifth Avenue was thumping with upbeat music and a crush of people when Maddie arrived. Her nerves were channelled into one thing, coping with the impending arrival of Elena. Would her former boss publicly flay her alive or take her into a side room for the inevitable?

"Here, over here! Miss?" A flashbulb went off, and she turned to see a few photographers snapping in her direction and several fashion bloggers holding microphones.

"Who are you wearing?" asked the closest one, standing next to a tripod-mounted camera. "I don't recognise it."

Maddie thought she knew her from a blog site, *Daring to Dazzle*? Dazzle-something anyway.

"Natalii. Two i's."

"Two i's? As in Duchamp? As in daughter of Véronique?"

"Yes. One and the same."

The woman's expression transformed. "Oh my God," she breathed, and hyperventilation seemed a real possibility. "Is this the world's first look at it?"

"Yes."

"When does the collection drop? Why you? What do the other pieces look like? How many are there? What do you know? I have so many questions!"

"All details are on her new website, nataliiduchamp.com." Maddie caught sight of an elegantly suited, dark-skinned man in the distance.

Perry stopped dead as he glanced towards Maddie. He pointed at her outfit, then fluttered his hand over his heart in approval. He pointed inside the building and then turned and disappeared into the crowd.

She smiled. "Sorry, I have to catch up with some people."

"Okay, sure. Any time. And thanks!"

As she moved off, out of the corner of her eye, Maddie saw the blogger tapping furiously on her phone, doubtlessly alerting the world of another Duchamp breaking into the fashion world. She threw back her shoulders and entered the ballroom with a confidence she truly felt this time.

"Maddie Grey, isn't it?" asked a woman approaching with a genial smile. She was blonde, attractive, with keen eyes and a slow, easy stride.

"That's me."

"Theresa Hunter from *Time Magazine*. I saw your piece on broken fashion dreams in New York. That was sensational stuff."

"Thanks." Maddie brightened.

"So who was the business executive? The one with the groping husband? We all want to know."

Maddie's enthusiasm faltered. "I'm not saying."

"It's all anyone's talking about. How about a hint?" Theresa grinned. "I'll take an initial. Can I buy a vowel?"

"No. If I told you the name, then that would help identify the victims."

"Good point. Well, if I can't buy a vowel, can I buy you a drink?" She threw in a cheeky smile, proving she meant it exactly the way it sounded.

"Drinks are free," Maddie said, unimpressed anyone in the media would suggest she put victims at risk. "Sorry. Right now I have some friends to catch up with."

"A shame. I was going to introduce you to mine. Trent Dalton and Alan Kadinsky. We've all just come back from the Middle East. I'm a war photographer." Her cocky smirk fell over the wrong side of the line on arrogant.

Maddie hesitated. She would really like to meet Dalton. "Maybe later. I want to talk to my friends first."

"Sure," Theresa said, and gave her arm a playful pat. "Later it is."

Maddie turned to find herself caught in the laser-sharp focus of Elena Bartell, watching from across the room. Her pulse leaped as she saw Elena's dress—a sleek, white gown, with a slit at the front up to her knees, the exact length of the plunge of her cleavage. Symmetry and style. Wow. She headed towards her.

As she closed in, a man stepped into her line of sight. "Maddie!" Perry gasped, grabbing both her arms and pulling them out wide. "Let me look at you! So this is it? Natalii's dramatic leap from the nest?"

He studied her closely, turning her. As he did so, Maddie felt a hole being burnt into her as Elena looked at them. She glanced down at her outfit, wondering what her former boss thought of it.

Black. Sheer. Feminine. A suit. Over the wide-legged palazzo pants lay the finest black mesh, filmy and floating, so from some angles it looked as if she was wearing a flowing, elegant skirt. Her jet-black jacket was formal, like a tux, with plunging lapels all the way down. The bottom of the jacket flared out at a forty-five-degree angle, which was matched by the parallel slash of cream-trimmed pockets at the hip and chest. Underneath, she wore an intricate, cream, brocaded waistcoat, like something out of the Palace of Versailles, with tiny gold-thread-embroidered buttons. A silk scarf, in matching cream and gold, was loosely knotted, giving her the effect of a rakish gentlewoman. There was no shirt underneath the vest, so Maddie's smooth, pale skin provided the final counterpoint. It was formal but daring; risqué yet covered everything.

"Superb." Perry nodded. "I don't often beg, but we need her for *Style*. You can't swan around with this on and not let us do a big write-up."

"I'll ask her."

"Good. Must be an exclusive, though. Oh," he turned, "Elena wanted a word. Meanwhile, I'll find out what's keeping Felicity with the drinks."

He headed off, and the distracted look on his face told Maddie he was mentally prepping shoots for a Natalii spread.

Maddie's eyes slid over to the woman studying her silently. "Hello."

Elena's gaze raked the outfit, and her eyebrow lifted. A hint of a smile dusted her lips. "Very chic. Elegant. Like mother, like daughter. I see she's not just a pretty face."

"No, she's not." Silence fell. Maddie fidgeted. "About the article—"

Elena's expression lost its lightness. "Did I anger you that much at the last ball? Or did you merely seek to advance your career through my suffering?"

Oh hell. Elena really *was* mad. "It wasn't about you. You were no factor in my decision to run it." Maddie begged her to see the truth in her eyes. "You were, almost, a factor in my decision not to. But in the end..." In the end she'd known she was right to do it. "In the end, I had to."

"Well." Elena took a sip of her drink.

"Well what?"

"Well done. It's important journalism. And a fine piece of writing."

"Wait, you're not mad at me?"

"You believed I would be so petty as to put my personal feelings ahead of the well-being of vulnerable people? I can't say I'm pleased to be at the centre of so tawdry a controversy tearing apart my industry, but your feature was honest, balanced, avoided clichés, and repeatedly pointed out who the true villains were."

"What about Richard?"

"Terrified. And frothing," Elena said with an evil smile. "So, there is that at least. He's suddenly being extra accommodating with the terms of our divorce. On that note, he had been encouraged to make several sizable donations to women's shelters around New York to avoid being named and shamed. But now your story's out, I'm informed he's shaking in his size-twelve boots that someone will put two and two together and reach Richard Barclay."

"I'm sorry by the way. About the divorce."

"I'm not." Elena regarded her for a moment. "Let's change the subject. What were you doing with Theresa Hunter? Give her a wide berth."

"Why?"

Elena's eyes narrowed. "Because I've suggested it. She's notorious."

"You do know I don't work for you anymore," Maddie said. Her indignation rose. "You know I don't have to run my friends or romantic interests past you either."

"Romantic interests? You must be joking. That snake?"

Maddie winced. This was getting derailed fast. "Right, stop. Look, can we...restart this conversation? I'm not interested in dating Theresa Hunter. We talked for a minute. Not even that. Okay? Could you please stop assuming I'm into everyone who shows an interest in me? First Lucas, now this woman?"

Elena said nothing, but her expression relaxed.

"Come on," Maddie said, more softly, "why do you do that? Is that what you think of me? That I'm just waiting for anyone to pay me the slightest bit of attention and I'm all into them now?"

Elena regarded her. "If you could see yourself as I do, you'd also expect everyone in the room to make an approach."

Maddie started at the unexpected words. "That's flattering, but for the record, I have no interest in some war photographer who asks me to dish the dirt on my sources and then uses her job title as a pick-up line."

"She truly is a snake." Elena's lips thinned. "I was not exaggerating."

"No, you weren't, but it's irrelevant." She sucked in a deep breath. "We've danced all around it, but you have to know by now that I only have eyes for one woman. And it's not her."

"Madeleine," Elena's tone was low and held a hint of warning. "We can't. I mean—"

"You told me, last time we met, there's no 'we'." Maddie studied her. "That there couldn't be. It's impossible. You say things like that, and yet you still act like you want more. And then you shut the whole conversation down, like now. Can you just tell me what you want? It's so confusing."

"I could say the same of you." Elena flicked some lint off Maddie's sleeve, with a careless sweep of her fingertips. "You say you can predict what I need and want, but on this you seem so unsure. I have explained why I cannot make promises or offer any hope."

"But you're no longer married."

"I'm not divorced yet, either, and I cannot ignore the fact that the paint's barely dry on my separation. I'm the owner of a company that has hundreds of thousands of employees, has a turnover of just under a billion dollars. If I make one wrong move, the share price plunges. If they sense weakness or scandal, investors flee. I cannot put a foot wrong. Tell me you can understand that."

"That sounds like hell."

"Hell?"

"Yeah. The worst."

Elena's eyes narrowed. "So now you minimise what I do? Do you even grasp how powerful I am? How important my position is? This is nothing to shrug at. It comes with enormous responsibility. You have no idea how—"

"You're not powerful enough to choose your own path. That's what I hear. You're actually less in control of your life than I am—and I am close to a nobody. Was *this* really your dream? You can't ever make mistakes. Can't put a foot wrong. Won't take a chance. I'm sorry, but to me it sounds terrible."

"You don't understand—"

"I understand that you're scared of making even one wrong move. It's sad. And a shame too. You know, there's a reason you loved my blog—it's because we see the world the same way. We're very different, but in all the important ways, we *get* each other. You feel it, too, or we wouldn't even be doing this...confusing dance. We think alike, appreciate determination, laugh at the same things, observe the world in a similar way, as outsiders. And I know you secretly like my Latvian folk music, so don't bother denying it," she added with a smile. "Do you know how rare and beautiful it is for two watchful, lonely souls like us to find each other?"

Elena said nothing, but it was all there in her eyes. Doubt. Fear. And something else that made Elena's jaw set hard.

Perry returned with Felicity in tow, bearing drinks, which they handed out.

Felicity blinked rapidly as she took in Maddie's outfit. "Good God. Perry wasn't wrong. Of course you get to wear that masterpiece. Because your winning streak isn't long enough."

Maddie opened her mouth, ready to suggest she stow the attitude, when Elena interrupted.

"Perry, please liaise with Madeleine about setting up Natalii Duchamp for a spread. The designer's concept outfit shows promise."

Perry's eyes flicked between the two women. "Of course. Um..."

"Now, if you'll excuse me, I have a headache. Felicity, get Amir to bring the car around. I need to leave."

Felicity scampered off to find a quieter spot to make the call. Perry turned away to nab a passing hors d'oeuvre.

"Please, don't go," Maddie said in a murmur the moment his back was turned. "Not over what I said. Come on, stay. It's been so long. I've missed you."

"Nothing has changed from earlier," Elena said in a low voice. "I have already explained my position."

"Please," Maddie tried again. "I think we…"

She petered out when she realised Perry's attention was back on them. His gaze darted between them, his mouth forming an O.

Elena saw the look, turned on heel, and stalked away.

Dismay filled Maddie as she watched her go.

"Why's she leaving?" Perry's brows knitted. "What's going on?"

"Nothing." Maddie sipped on her drink.

Perry gave her a sceptical look and sloshed the liquid around in his glass.

"What?" she asked him.

"Just promise me one thing." He gave her a stern look. "Don't start something you can't finish."

"Huh? I don't know what—"

"She's fragile right now. I know she doesn't look it, but I've seen this before, back when CQ threw her over for Emmanuelle. It gutted her. I know the look. She's hanging by a thread, thanks to that bastard of a husband. I swear, if you turn around and break her, I will be a most disagreeable human being."

"I don't know what the hell you're talking about, Perry."

"Sure you don't," he said, watching his boss's retreating form. He slugged a mouthful of booze and gave her a grim look. "Sure you don't."

CHAPTER 31

Red

When Maddie got home, she found Natalii sitting on her sofa. She'd told her to make herself at home earlier, when she'd come by to fit Maddie's designer suit, do her make-up, and make sure she was appropriately *magnifique* for the evening. She'd obviously stayed. A pizza box and red wine were on the coffee table, and the Frenchwoman was now busy shouting at the TV screen.

"*Non*! Not her. This is insanity." She glanced up as Maddie slumped onto the sofa beside her. "Look at her. She is one of the top models? Nonsense!"

Maddie peered at the screen to see an array of wannabes for *America's Next Top Model*.

"See her face? It is like the moon landing. Craters everywhere. Her eyes—they are crossed, you see? And what is that blind *homme* saying? She has an alien mystique? What is this? Alien mystique? Is she green? *Non!* This cannot be real."

Maddie gave her a wan smile. Her stomach grumbled, as she looked at what was left of a Mario's pizza. She hadn't eaten all evening because she'd been so stressed about seeing Elena again.

Natalii nudged the pizza box over. "There is more. I was having the, what is it you say? New York experience."

"Ah." Maddie reached for a slice and a serviette. "Say no more."

Natalii regarded her. "You did not have a *magnifique* night, then?" Disappointment edged her tone. "Your lady did not appreciate your..." She waved a hand over Maddie's outfit.

"She liked it very much." Maddie took a bite. Flavours exploded across her tongue. *God, just what I needed. A fatty, greasy hit to drown my sorrows.* She chewed and swallowed. "Everyone did. That reminds me—expect your design all over the blogosphere tonight. The fashion reporters loved it."

Natalii did not smile, although her eyes brightened with pleasure. "That is good, but I did not do this for them. What of you? What has happened?"

Maddie took another bite, feeling sharp eyes studying her closely. "Elena left early. We had a...um, like, a mini fight. Well, not even."

"A fight?" Natalii's eyes widened.

"Sort of." Maddie felt morose just saying it.

Without a word, Natalii took four steps into the adjacent, open-plan kitchen and fished out another wine glass. She returned, topped it up—high—with a red wine, and handed it to her. "Now, tell me. What it is you two found to argue about at a silly ball?"

Maddie sipped the wine and was astonished by how delicious it was. Her gaze flew to the label. Ah. French—of course.

"She objected to a woman she saw me with, who I didn't know and had no interest in knowing. She warned me off."

"And then?"

"I told her she wasn't my boss anymore and couldn't dictate my friends or..." Maddie paused. *Ouch.* "...um, romantic interests."

Okay, that sounded so bad in the retelling.

Natalii's eyebrows shot up.

Maddie gave her pizza a sheepish look. "We kind of backed away from that mess. But then she said she wasn't divorced yet, and she couldn't risk anything, she's the boss of half the fucking universe, and why can't I understand that?" That really had stung.

"Madeleine, why did you let her think this other woman might be of romantic interest if she was not? Ahh." Natalii snapped her fingers. "You wished her to be jealous. Green!" She smirked. "Well then, this game of *amour*, it is on!" She raised her glass and drank, as though she considered Maddie some sort of master tactician.

"I didn't want her jealous! And I'm really just mad at how she feels too afraid to take a chance. I wish she would."

"Did you forget the bit about how she says she is not divorced *yet*. She wishes to be considered. Later."

"Yet I asked her to talk to me more about this, and she just left. I'm tired of being the one who has to piece everything together. Why can't she just, for once in her life, stop being so cryptic? Can't she remember she's *The* Elena Bartell! This is hard for us mere mortals."

She gulped down the rest of her wine and stuck her glass out at Natalii, who refilled it.

"It appears that you are overthinking this thing," Natalii said. "What we need is to get you drunk so you do not. You need to relax more. You are far too uptight. And in my divine outfit no less? *Non,* I did not design this for you to be all so pent up."

Maddie glanced down at herself and was appalled to find she was sprawled all over the sofa in Natalii's designer outfit. "Oh! Oh God!" She sat up. "I should get changed. I'm so sorry."

Lifting a stilling hand, Natalii shook her head. "It is okay. It is yours to wear as you please. But get changed anyway, for I plan to make you merry enough to forget your woman."

Maddie stood. "Oh, that reminds me. Perry Marks? At *Style New York*? He wants to feature your line in a spread."

"Does he now?" Natalii's eyes sharpened. "And what did you tell him?"

"I said I'd ask you."

Natalii's face broke into slow smile that Maddie was sure did not bode well for someone. "Thank you for passing this detail to me. I will talk to your Perry myself tomorrow. Now go...find a garment that says 'drunk and carefree with my stylish friend Natalii'."

Maddie laughed and headed to her bedroom to change.

Maddie woke with a throbbing head, unable to believe she was still alive given the hangover she was experiencing. She rolled over and cracked an eyelid. A glass of water and an aspirin came into view with a note. She picked it up and tried to focus.

Thank you for the excellent night, dear Madeleine. I'm gone now. A
meeting, it is now set up with your Perry. Drink up, and call me later.
We will do dinner, oui? Natalii.

Maddie groaned. The thought of food was excruciating. Her gaze fell
to her cell phone beside her bed. God, the time! It was almost eleven.

There was a sharp rap at her door.

She struggled to her feet and made her way there on autopilot. She
was already opening the door when she realised she hadn't brushed
her hair or changed out of her sleeping shorts and tank top.

Elena Bartell stood there, face like thunder.

Maddie blinked at the furious woman, unsure whether she was
dreaming. No, she was fairly sure that if she was dreaming; Elena
would not be looking at her like this.

"Ele..." she began.

"What is *this*?" Elena said with a hiss, barging past her and
slamming the door behind her.

Maddie winced and held her head. "Not so loud. And please, come
in," she added sarcastically.

Elena waved a piece of paper at her as though it explained everything.

Maddie tried to read the words, but Elena was flapping it too hard. "I
thought I had made my position clear. And then you run off with *her*?"

"I...what! Who?" Maddie blinked.

Elena glanced around the room, pausing on the two wine glasses
and pizza boxes. "She loves greasy food, I take it? Hunter?"

"How the hell would I know? I didn't take anyone home, least of all
that arrogant woman."

Elena's nostrils flared. "Two glasses, Madeleine. Were you merely
drinking for two?"

"Natalii was here. She wanted to see how her outfit went."

That gave Elena pause. But then she straightened, and her
expression took on a whole new type of wrath. "Ah, yes. Natalii. Which
brings me to this."

She flapped the paper under Maddie's nose again. "Her conditions
for agreeing to be featured in a *Style* spread are that I must present

myself to you, alone, and talk for 'no less than one hour about matters that do not relate to work or fashion'. What nonsense is this? Why did you demand this? Well?"

"I didn't." Maddie sighed and rubbed her face. She was in no condition for this meeting. "I just woke up. This is the first I've heard of it. Natalii probably thinks she's being helpful."

Elena stopped and stared at her properly, her gaze raking Maddie's sleepwear and then settling on her hair. It was an odd expression.

Maddie reddened. "On that note, I should probably get some clothes on. Um...make yourself at home. Or leave. Whatever. I won't force you to stay. I'll tell Natalii you did what she demanded."

After shuffling into her bedroom, Maddie closed the door and slid on jeans and a white T-shirt. As she pulled on her socks, she wondered if Elena had gone, storming out in a state of high dudgeon. Probably while laughing at her for looking like a half-dead cat. She glanced at the mirror and groaned. Her hair looked as if it had been brushed with a balloon, it was sticking up so high. *Awesome.*

Maddie ran a brush through the bird's nest and put on a little make-up to hide the darkness under her eyes. She took one last look in the mirror. Okay, casual and relatively acceptable. For most people who weren't Elena Bartell. Curator of beauty.

Listening through the door, Maddie could hear no sign of movement. Elena had probably gone. Great. She'd have to kill Natalii later for her meddling. She stepped out of the bedroom to find Elena perched with her usual regal grace on a sofa that looked far neater than Maddie had left it. In fact the wine glasses and pizza boxes were also gone.

Had Elena actually cleaned up for her? She tried to picture the media boss stacking her dirty dishes. *Oh God, oh God.*

Maddie was working herself up to a full-on self-flagellation, when Elena cut her off at the pass.

"Don't," she said. "It needed doing, and I had nothing else to do." Elena fiddled with one of her rings. At least the enraged expression was gone.

"Thanks. Can I get you a coffee or something?"

"No." Elena glanced at her watch. "We have an hour. I'm an honourable woman, despite what the various gossip rags think of me. What would you like to discuss?"

Maddie stared at. "You're still going to do this thing? Talk to me for an hour?"

Elena gave the faintest of shrugs. "A deal's a deal. And I won't have Emmanuelle Lecoq getting a Natalii exclusive."

"Oh." Of course. This was business.

Elena cocked her head. "Well? You wish, perhaps, to explain to me why that Hunter creature thinks you two are an item? I was informed today that, after I left the event, she spread the word that you and she planned to do considerably more than look at her photo collection last night."

"She's full of crap. I didn't speak to her again for the rest of the night."

Elena studied her. Then nodded. "I see."

"It's a stupid lie. Why would I want to be with her when all I want is to be with you?" She couldn't go on like this, with so much left unspoken. It was time to lay their cards down. "But if you want that too, even if it's not now but later, I need you to say it, because I'm really not good at guessing. Not with this. Not with all the hints in the world. I need it spelt out."

"I thought you could read my mind," Elena said, eyes half-lidded. "Isn't that what you said?"

"On many things. Work things." Maddie folded her hands in her lap to hide their tremble. "On this, it's different. I need to know. Have I misunderstood? *Do* you want more from me?"

"I am getting a divorce," Elena said, her tone flat. "It will be messy. There will be press...and now, accusations levelled..." She faded out with a look of dissatisfaction. "I really don't want to muddy things."

"Oh." Maddie suddenly felt ridiculous. So Elena *had* just been flirting with her, nothing more. She was a little bit of fun to tease. And, occasionally, Elena got a little territorial, but she wasn't about to risk anything for Maddie. She wouldn't dare jeopardise her standing.

Actually, Maddie knew this already. In her heart, she *knew*. She'd been fooling herself. Nothing like hearing that out loud to punch a person in the gut.

"So," Maddie said, praying her voice would stay steady, "all of this was, what, a bit of fun for you? Do you even like women that way?" The trembling increased, and she balled her hands into tight fists.

Elena eyed her. "Aren't you bold?" She sighed.

Maddie wished she'd just put her out of her misery. A single bullet between the eyes would be better than this. Faster, too. She looked down. "Okay, well, I get it. Finally. Let's just forget that I ever said anything, and we can go our separate—"

"You are an intriguing woman, Madeleine."

Maddie's head snapped up.

"Smart, unique, and talented," Elena continued. "You create art with words and food. I told you once, I appreciate beauty..." Her gaze slid over Maddie's body. "In all its forms."

Maddie tensed, waiting for the "but".

"Anyone should be proud to date you."

She squeezed her eyes shut.

"Including me."

Maddie's eyes flashed open. "What?"

"But not now."

She stared at Elena, startled.

"I thought I was quite clear. At the Duchamp show? I was openly appreciative. I assure you I have never...done that with anyone before. But you are inspiring. You robbed my lungs of breath on that catwalk. You were a revelation. Honestly, can you truly not read my mind on this? How much I desire you?"

"I didn't want to be wrong." Maddie spread her hands. "You're *Elena Bartell!* And I'm just..." She glanced at herself. "I'm just the woman with a hangover, who thought she'd blown it."

"I do know the feeling." Elena gave her a rueful look. "On both counts."

Now that she said it, Maddie could see the tiredness around Elena's eyes that no amount of make-up could entirely hide.

Elena rose from the sofa, and Maddie scrambled to her feet.

"I know it hasn't been an hour, but I really am on deadline. Would you mind telling Natalii I have…*satisfied* you?" Her eyes crinkled with amusement.

"Only if you promise to actually do so later." Maddie grinned at her own audacity.

"Really, *Madeleine*." Elena tsked and took a step closer. "I believe you're flirting with me."

Maddie shot her a lopsided smile.

"It's a shame I'm still married and have no wish to risk losing the high moral ground during the divorce." Elena shot her an indignant look and swayed closer. "Or I'd kiss that smug smile right off your beautiful face."

Elena lifted her index finger and trailed the contours of Maddie's face, as though seriously considering it.

Maddie shivered and detected a tantalising hint of perfume. "I'd never tell," she said in a whisper. She edged forward. "No one would ever know."

"I'd know." Elena dropped her fingers and disappointment surged through Maddie. "I would think of nothing else if we…" Elena sighed and, shifted her hands to Maddie's shirt collar. She tugged her nearer and impatiently closed the gap.

It was an urgent kiss and Maddie met it with passion. Heat shot through her. Her knees weakened at the softness of her, the sweetness of their kiss. Their tongues met, and Maddie clung to Elena's waist as the arousing sensations threatened to undo her on the spot.

Elena gave a tiny, frustrated sigh and pulled away. Looking annoyed with herself, cheeks high with colour, she let out a ragged breath.

"That never happened," Elena said. With a rueful expression, she reached forward to wipe the lipstick off Maddie's mouth using her thumb. She did it slowly, as though hoping to also remove the kiss. She stopped and tapped Maddie's lip. "I wish…" She shook her head. "Many things. But until I'm divorced, we never did that."

"Did what?" Maddie asked with an air of innocence. "We were just talking."

Elena smiled and leaned her forehead against Maddie's. Her breath was warm against her lips. "I wish we could 'talk' longer, Madeleine, but I have to..."

She pulled back and glanced at her watch, her expression tightening. Her eyes met Maddie's, searching.

Maddie nodded. "It's fine. Go." She stepped back.

Elena paused, and then her lips gave a quirk as she shouldered her bag. "We're done," she said, injecting her trademark haughty steel into it, enough to make Maddie's breath catch as desire rippled through her again.

Elena's eyes, lit with a knowing amusement, held Maddie's. And then she was out the door.

No, Maddie told her thudding heart, they were definitely *not* done.

CHAPTER 32
Dear Foolish Girl

Elena sat at her desk, on the penthouse office floor of Bartell Corp, gazing over New York's skyline. The impressive view from her wide, curving windows held little sway. She should be celebrating. The official figures were in. The Duchamp issue had smashed every sales record and corrected *Style Sydney*'s circulation dive, bringing in new readers as well as most of the wavering ones who had dipped their toe in over at *CQ*.

Globally, *Style International* had never been stronger. So, she'd returned to her head office, ready for the next challenge. She was back where she belonged, she told Perry. The man had uttered a mangled half snort and given her a disbelieving look, which she chose not to acknowledge.

Of course she wasn't oblivious to his opinion. In fact, Madeleine and Perry seemed to share a certain viewpoint. But Elena hadn't built up one of the largest media corporations in the world just to throw it all away on following her teenage, fashion-editing dreams. Winning was not without sacrifice. And she did enjoy winning.

So...why didn't she feel better?

Elena was starting to wonder whether she was cursed. The Richard mess was bad enough. It had been unnerving, also, to discover that her inconvenient interest in Madeleine had not disappeared the moment she'd installed her as an assistant in Sydney and started treating her like one. Madeleine had taken her behaviour as a hint to withdraw from her, becoming a perfectly professional assistant. Just as she'd hoped.

Except it was a loss she'd felt more keenly than she'd ever imagined. If anything, her appreciation had grown the more she pushed Madeleine away. She'd started noticing the things she missed. Her beaming smile. Her laugh. Her wry commentary on life. The way she used to study Elena, her eyebrows knitted, as though amazed that someone like her actually existed in the world. The way her face brightened whenever Elena wore her vest outfit. She'd taken to wearing it more often, just to get a reaction.

Elena had been in denial. She could see that now. Looking back, it was so clear. With a single intrigued glance from Madeleine, Elena had felt more alive than she ever had before.

She'd assumed her confounding fascination with Madeleine would pass, eventually. The veil of denial was ripped from her at the Duchamp show. The sight of Madeleine on the catwalk made her hungry. Elena had been helpless to stop herself when she had the freedom and privilege to touch. Just for a moment. The memory of her fingertips trailing soft skin, leaving goosebumps in their wake, had distracted her at inopportune times for weeks. There was little doubt, after that night, what this was. This was not friendship or passing attraction. It was something alive. It burned hot and deep.

Elena wasn't just scared of losing it all. Or losing herself. If only it were just that. But it was all so impossible. There were so many reasons this was a terrible idea. She was fifteen years older. In charge of a global business empire. Separated. She had a reputation to uphold. She couldn't have some clichéd, midlife-crisis fling with the secretary. This was impossible.

It *was*.

And then along came *that* ball. It was, what, a month ago now? Elena had experienced such a vulgar stab of jealousy at the thought of Madeleine involved with that war photographer. Her reaction had been as unexpected as it was extreme. Elena generally avoided emotional extremes. But out of nowhere, this had smacked her between the eyes like a fist. Anger. Betrayal. Desire. And so much jealousy. The ugliness of the sensations crawled around her belly. It had been unnerving how biting the pain had felt at the idea of her Madeleine locked in a kiss with that woman. The chaos of the emotions was terrifying.

A month spent trying to understand what it meant had left an inescapable conclusion. Her heart had laid claim to the woman. Madeleine was *hers*. No wonder she hadn't recognised it at first. She had never felt this connection, this sensation, about anyone before.

The next day, Elena's mood had turned vile when she'd heard the nasty little rumour about what Hunter was saying about Madeleine. She had been murderous at the thought of that woman sliding her fingers over soft skin, kissing the freckles along the bridge of Madeleine's nose, burying herself in her hair, savouring her scent. Then the call came in from Perry revealing Natalii Duchamp's demand that she report to Madeleine.

Her rage had been magnificent by the time she'd arrived. To be summoned, like an underling, for a meeting after this humiliation? Was she to be the witness to the morning after? To have her nose rubbed in what she could not have?

And then...she'd seen. The confusion. The honest denial. The hurt. *That* shouldn't have been on Madeleine's face. To her shame, Elena knew she'd put it there. She'd immediately set about making it right.

And then...they'd kissed. Madeleine's lips had been a warm, sweet ambrosia that made her crave more.

Elena hadn't meant to allow that. She almost wished she didn't know how intoxicating Madeleine's kisses could be. She'd meant what she said—she wanted to look Richard in the eye, knowing her own conscience was clear, during the divorce. But after that? Would she dare then?

She could still barely process the thought. She'd never consciously considered a relationship with a woman, opting for the obligatory husband (or two), which had been more about protecting, or furthering, her one true love. Her business. Everything she'd done had been to ensure her success. And Richard hadn't been bad company. But she hadn't even understood the raw power of desire until the night she reached across the charged air and touched Madeleine's back. Never had she felt a thrill like that.

Subconsciously, had she always known? That her vaunted emotional control would be at risk with a woman? Was that why she'd never even considered anything beyond the safe norms? Was that why she'd never stopped to analyse her love for the beauty of the female form, which made her body hum in a way that never extended to the male form?

She shifted in her seat as a new thought rose.

Why her?

Elena often found women's forms pleasing but had never allowed her interest to cross over to intimate, unless you counted Jenny Copeland's artless but enthusiastic fumbles under the sleeping bag during school camp. But Madeleine was the first one to make her want to risk everything.

Why her? The thought hammered her brain.

The soft curve of Madeleine's ass or the straining tightness of a T-shirt had drawn her focus on many late nights in New York. Not to mention those curious eyes. And her even more curious mind. She was a riddle, a contradiction. Sad yet amusing. Isolated but keenly aware of her world. Her blog was another side of her again.

There was a reason Elena had started working later and later at that fishbowl of an office. She needed to know more. Her curiosity had to be fed.

Madeleine had a directness to her, a way of seeing beyond Elena's mask. She had no interest in Elena's fame. She asked nothing from her and remained as unintimidated by her title now as she had been the day they'd met. But what Elena most appreciated was the fearless way she put her passion into the things she cared about—words, food, or people. When Madeleine Grey cared for you, you felt it.

Elena *felt* it.

But now, little had gone right. She spun around to the computer to glare at the email she'd discovered. *Opportunity of a lifetime* was the subject header. Madeleine had apparently sent her résumé far and wide, seeking freelance work, and *Condé Nast Traveller* had replied. Maddie was thrilled with the job they'd offered her.

Vietnam! I'm going to Vietnam, all expenses paid by the Singaporean government. Okay, I know that sounds weird, but Vietnam is too poor to fly media in for travel stories, and they desperately need tourists for their economy. So, Singapore pays for their media junkets as part of a foreign aid deal and...oh, I'm rambling aren't I? Anyway, the brief from CNT was to go off the beaten track after I've done all of the usual tourist stuff the publicity team will send me to see, and whatever I do, make it interesting and different. They said if I could make a fashion designer's story fascinating, I can do anything. Three months! Can you believe it? So excited! I have some great ideas, and none of them involve the usual fluff. Sorry, I have to miss the next gala we were supposed to go to together, but I'll be back for the one after that.

Maddie.

On Elena's desk sat another not-parsley plant—both a reminder of the girl's absurd sense of humour and a partial apology. It had arrived not ten minutes ago.

"More exorcism plants?"

Elena glanced up to find Felicity glaring at it.

"Oh God! I'll get rid of it at once!"

"No." Elena brushed her hand away. "It stays."

Felicity backed out of the office with such a confused look on her face that Elena almost laughed.

Elena hadn't known how to reply to that email. She didn't have the words to explain that Madeleine would be greatly missed. So she didn't say a thing. She picked her up in her Lexus, put on that dubious Latvian folk band on her car music system, much to Madeleine's mirth, and drove the intrepid reporter to the airport herself.

She sat with her in the departure lounge, drinking terrible tea after terrible tea, for almost two hours. Madeleine chattered on, spreading out her Vietnam maps, and pointing out her plans. Elena trusted that she'd nodded in all the appropriate places.

When it was time to leave, Elena hesitated, then pulled her into a tight hug, savouring the smell and feel of her. She was all lumpy due to a padded jacket she'd filled with various supplies. Madeleine squeezed her back, dropping a tiny sigh against her ear.

Elena might not have spoken much at all that morning, but she hoped Madeleine understood what she was saying. Couldn't she read her mind, after all? Isn't that what she'd said? They stepped apart.

"I'll write as often as I can," Madeleine promised, swinging her backpack over her shoulders.

"See that you do." Elena was proud of how dry and imperious she sounded. Not at all like someone wishing they could ground a plane.

Madeleine laughed at her tone and waved, disappearing into the crowd.

Despite having a mountain of work backed up, Elena stayed and watched as the plane took off almost forty minutes later.

Three weeks crawled by after that. Deep down, Elena was beginning to fret. Okay, she was well beyond "beginning to". Vietnam was a stable and beautiful country, she reminded herself. It was rustic and, in rural areas, primitive by western standards. It was essentially all the things Elena recoiled from, because you could not control such variables. But Madeleine seemed undaunted. And yes, there were issues with poverty and crime, but Madeleine would be conscious of this. So all would be well.

Elena frowned and tapped her index finger on her desk.

On the other hand, Madeleine had delighted at the thought of going off the beaten track. That sounded risky, did it not? And what were these story ideas that didn't involve the "usual fluff"? Would she do anything dangerous? Besides, weren't parts of Vietnam malaria areas? Or cholera ridden? Elena was also fairly sure pirates still hid in Hạ Long Bay. She'd have to look that up.

Every time Elena asked herself these questions, a little voice in the back of her guilt-ridden mind whispered to her. *You told her she wasn't a real reporter. What if she wants to prove you wrong and do something foolish?*

Elena had made certain to spell out to Madeleine the necessity of not doing anything foolish in every email and during the rare phone calls Madeleine managed to make from whatever minor map smudge she'd moved to since they'd last communicated. Elena willed her to understand what she was really saying—*Be safe. You have nothing to prove.* But every night, Elena lay in bed fretting that if anything went wrong, this was entirely her fault.

After four weeks, she swallowed her pride and wrote Madeleine an email. She detailed, at length, how Madeleine was an exemplary journalist and, yes, that included a news journalist given her powerful *Vanity Fair* feature. Her stories were well received, and wasn't there something more interesting she could be doing closer to home?

There. That wasn't meddling, was it?

It hadn't worked. Madeleine had called her, voice burbling with excitement, telling her about more destinations in the middle of nowhere she'd learned of that she had to check out.

Another week went by, and this time a handwritten letter arrived. Madeleine expressed regret for missing their planned industry event.

I like to imagine what you were wearing. How your eyes followed me around the room. These are the things I think about in my lonely little tent. I miss you. Maddie.

Elena did not go to sleep picturing Madeleine looking beautiful at galas. All she saw was her green eyes on her. Caring and filled with desire, but always just that little bit too far away.

She frowned at the reference to a tent and searched online for *tropical diseases Vietnam*. Then, after a moment's pause, she also looked up *kidnappings Vietnam*.

Idly, Elena wondered how much Madeleine would resent her if she sent an armed security team over there to shadow her.

At one point, Madeleine had become quite good friends with some of the local women in a mountainous northern region of Vietnam, close to the border with China. Apparently, she'd discovered the secret to breaking the ice was cooking with the women. Sharing recipes. Of course, Madeleine would win them over. Her guileless, silly grin and food of the gods could win anyone over.

A few days and as many sleepless nights later, Elena considered putting the fear of God into the *Condé Nast Traveller*'s editor. His wasn't a Bartell Corp masthead, but surely the man would see reason and send his freelancer home if she "asked". Or bought him out.

Elation burst through her at that genius idea, before common sense prevailed. Her shoulders sagged. It would not be the most auspicious start to a relationship, ending Madeleine's budding career by buying the magazine just to get her sent home.

Five and a half weeks. The waiting was *not* acceptable. Elena mutilated a paperclip, as she glared at her to-do list. It was not getting any shorter, especially given the changes she had planned on implementing. They would send a rocket through her company. Madeleine's probing questions all those months ago had made her stop and really wonder about her life. Her work. Her happiness. Now, though, missing Madeleine had become an unexpected, engulfing distraction. Her mood was affecting her work. Her focus. Perry had begun side-eying her copy of *The Rough Guide To Vietnam* that she now kept within easy reach, and giving her puzzled looks.

Recently, he'd started with random trivia. One day, he waltzed in and declared, "I hear it's going to be a sizzler in Hanoi tomorrow. I'd sure want to slap on my sunscreen if I was anywhere near there and had a delicate complexion."

"Well, aren't you lucky you aren't and you don't?" Elena peered at his dark skin. "Besides, eighty-nine degrees isn't a sizzler in that part of the world. And Sapa is two hundred seventeen miles from Hanoi, so that's hardly relevant to anything, is it?"

He blinked. Then smirked. "How very specific. And right off the top of your head, too." And he swanned out again.

She'd gritted her teeth. Oh, she knew he was baiting her to trick her into talking about the thing they never discussed. He didn't *know*-know what was going on, but he had worked out something was up between them. Add to that, he also was aware that Madeleine was somewhere in Vietnam. (*Unsafe.*) Off the beaten track. (*Taking risks.*) So he'd joined a few dots.

Regardless, Madeleine was hers. Elena did not wish to share her with her nosy, well-intentioned best friend or anyone else. So, she kept her thoughts to herself and continued her regular stream of emails, hoping Madeleine would soon check back into a town big enough to have the internet.

Dear Foolish Girl... began all Elena's missives—she was nothing if not subtle, after all. She would fill Madeleine in on the minutiae, supplying her best unimpressed anecdotes about her life and employees, especially Felicity. God knows, Madeleine likely needed a laugh over there.

After her usual round up of office and personal insights, Elena would conclude her correspondence with a heartfelt signature. *Stay safe.—E.*

If she could have underlined this seventy times, she would have. She felt she was being clear just putting it into boldface.

Madeleine's replies, when they came, were always a thing to be treasured. Descriptive and perceptive. She was so observant of the surroundings, pulse, and temperaments of the places and people around her, a trait she had so ably demonstrated as her assistant.

As the weeks drew on, Madeleine's diplomacy and sweetness had, of late, apparently endeared her to a number of older local women in one remote village. They had formed the view she required fattening up and matrimony. A variety of sons had, therefore, been offered. Madeleine had felt it necessary to include a photo of the wiry young farmers in question with their hopeful grins.

Elena had an unpleasant lurch to her stomach and forced herself to calmness before replying.

Dear Foolish Girl,

How exotic the paramours you attract. I particularly admired the leering charms of suitor number six. Is his tongue supposed to be lolling out like that? His mother must be so proud.

Not long to go, Madeleine. The tenth. We have the next ball to attend in Sydney. Do not force me to take Felicity in your stead. It would end badly. Not only for her but for the editor of Condé Nast Traveller magazine, from whom I would demand to know why his publication is keeping its freelance Vietnam writer from urgent business in Australia.

She filled the remainder of her email with the usual industry insights that she knew Madeleine appreciated. After a moment's hesitation, she also added an extra paragraph.

Felicity will finally get the promotion to Deputy Chief Operations Officer she deserves. Her business sense is unmatched, although do not quote me, as she takes compliments like unexploded warheads. On a related note, Mark, Elizabeth, and Tony will be duly promoted to fulfil running the various day-to-day operations of Bartell Corp.

She finished with her usual line.

Stay safe—*especially from lecherous suitors. E.*

Madeleine's reply a few days later had been as perceptive as she'd anticipated.

Dear Elena,

Is there something you're not telling me? Either, one, you're dying; two, you're a pod person; three, you're retiring (in which case, see point two); or four, you're paring down your business workload because you've finally seen the light and are about to name yourself to Elizabeth's job as editor-in-chief of Style International. Which is it? And please know that if it's number one, I'll be on the next plane home. And also know that if you fake number one, I will be tempted to kill you myself. I'm really close to getting the recipe for a perfect cá kho tộ. So, just saying—do not get between me and traditional braised fish. I'll make you some when I get home. Assuming I can find a clay pot.

Maddie.

Elena had smiled as she wrote back.

Fine. It's not official yet and probably won't be for some time, but it's number four. I look forward to tasting your cá kho tộ. I will source a clay pot for you by the time you return.

Stay safe. *E.*

She sat back, greatly impressed. The woman really knew her far too well. Madeleine had been right when she said erecting soulless shard buildings would not make her happy. All it had given her was headaches and a mounting pile of contract issues she had little interest in. Hudson Shard would be iconic, of course, she'd see to that, but it did not hold her passion. No. Only two things thrilled her these days. And only one of them was the thought of finally, officially, editing a global fashion magazine.

Dear Elena,

I am so excited for you that you're finally doing what makes you happy—fashion editing is you. Never doubt that. You come alive at Style's offices. I really hope you had a well-placed spy to tell me what Emmanuelle Lecoq's response was to the news her old rival is back on her turf. I'm hoping she did a spit-take of expensive champagne somewhere public in front of twenty photographers.

How did Felicity take her promotion news? Or is she not sure what she'll do with herself without you flinging orders at her 24/7? I'll look into some Stockholm syndrome counsellors for her.

Where will you base yourself? With five Style publications, I suppose you have five cities to choose from. I'm hoping Sydney is on the short list, especially since you own a house there. If it's not, I'll be earning a lot of frequent flier points. You can't get rid of me that easily.

I know you're worried about me over here, which is kind of silly since Vietnam is such a lovely country. But you're not alone. You should read the emails from Simon and my parents. Simon's threatening to haul me back home by my hiking boots and hook me up with so much chocolate and alcohol that I'll never want to leave home again!

God, Elena, it's incredible being here. It's so different seeing the world from a non-western perspective, and the air is so fresh and clean outside of the cities, I may never want to leave.

But while I've been sent here to showcase the tourism possibilities of Vietnam, I haven't forgotten my news brain. And I have recently come across a story so heartbreaking that it made me cry every night for a week. Attached is the photo I took. I won't even say what it's about. You'll understand. People say they want the truth, don't they? The brutal truth? I know you thought you always did. So what will they say when they see this?

Maddie.

Dear Foolish Girl,

Your photo made my breath catch. The little girl lying on the ground, hugging the dirt drawing of a woman. Was that a sketch she'd created of her mother? She'd lost her mother? I stared at it for a good hour, fretting over what I was seeing. The pain and longing on the child's face. She looked barely six. This photo is everything I have said you are. You capture raw emotions.

After this, I trust you'll see that you have nothing left to prove. We may disagree about the "flavor" of writer I envision you to be, but that's not up to me, is it? I realise that it may have been slightly presumptuous to say otherwise once. But Madeleine, you do not have to be in some crime-ridden, accident-prone place to prove you can do anything. (Have you seen Ho Chi Minh City's vehicular manslaughter statistics? Eight hundred traffic police for ten million people. You do the math.)

Felicity took the news as I expected. I had an unsettling feeling she wanted to hug me, which would embarrass us both beyond belief. Mercifully, she kept her arms to herself. She has earned it. Not just for her business savvy, but I cannot tell you how long I have waited for her to protest being a pseudo PA. You objected, quite rightly, the second time we met, if I recall.

It has taken Felicity years to demand that she only does her chief of staff role. She finally did so in a spectacular outburst of anger and regret, with my favorite tea mug flung at the far wall of my office. I feel satisfied, at last, that she's ready and the promotion will be a good fit. And I like the new mug she got me.

Yes, Sydney is on the short list of two for where I will base myself. Style Sydney needs a much firmer hand, but Style New York is where my global offices are. We can discuss it when you're home.

Perry is all too smug about my career pivot, by the way. I have reminded him I still know how to fire even international art directors, and it would be no trouble at all. He took the hint.

I believe he wants to find you a dress for the next ball. He has met a new designer with something that would be perfect for you. Will you be back in time for a fitting? How tightly is your editor holding you to that three-month schedule?

Stay safe. *E.*

P.S. Happy birthday.

Dear Elena,

I couldn't believe my eyes when I got your present. It's beautiful, thank you. I'm paranoid about losing it out here or it being stolen, so I've taken to tucking it into my panties during the day. I'd like to return the favour. Oh, that came out wrong! Or right. Um, so when's your birthday?

Tell Perry no, I don't think I'll be back in time for a fitting. That's fine, I'm fairly sure I have something at home that should do. Why doesn't he dress you in his new designer's threads so we'll get to be amazed anyway?

And yes, that was a little orphan girl hugging a drawing of her dead mother. I've submitted it to a photo agency, with my editor's blessing. It will be sold and run as a standalone news story. Obviously, it doesn't fit Condé Nast's travel brief.

I really miss you.

Maddie.

———————⌒⌒———————

Dear Foolish Girl,

I'm glad you liked my birthday gift. I shall let Tiffany & Co. know their Blue Divine bracelet is safely carried in the underthings of Condé Nast Traveller's roaming Vietnam reporter. I'm sure they'll want to put that endorsement in all their advertising.

I saw L'Express picked up your orphan girl story, and your photo has gone viral since they put it on their website. It deserves to. People need to see this. How is it you keep surprising me?

My birthday is a state secret. But let's just say you identified the day once, why not twice?

Stay safe. *E.*

———————⌒⌒———————

Dear Elena,

Your birthday is the Ides of March? Wait a minute—that means you planned to celebrate your birthday last year by firing an entire newspaper's staff? Were you trying to live up to your reputation? Is this how a tiger shark parties?

I will not be able to write after this, as I'm heading out of internet range again.

Thanks for sending me the links to my photo online. You won't be too shocked to hear I'm setting up a crowd-funding campaign to get the little girl looked after and make sure she gets a good education. She has a foster family now too.

See you in Sydney soon. One week, one day in fact.

Thinking of you every day.

Maddie.

CHAPTER 33
Felicitations

Maddie crawled off the plane at Sydney Airport, looking like a rumpled blanket. Her backpack felt far too heavy. She turned to find the taxi ramp.

"Don't bother. I have transport," said a familiar voice beside her ear.

Maddie swung her head around. "Felicity?" It was nice to see a familiar face after being away, even one who only sometimes tolerated her.

"This way."

"Did Elena send you? I told her—repeatedly—not to send someone for me."

Felicity gave her an impatient look. "No, she did not send me. Now come on."

Oh. Well, so much for small talk.

Within minutes, they were in a high-end Uber, headed towards Sydney's CBD. All conversation had been forestalled by Felicity choosing to sit in the front seat.

Maddie shrugged and stretched out as much as she could, hoping for a brief bit of shut-eye after being cooped up in the air for the past half a day. She couldn't wait to see Elena again. After all their emails and a few calls, Maddie was beside herself with anticipation. She'd missed her so much.

Half an hour later, Maddie's eyes fluttered back open, and she glanced around. They were in the inner city. She squinted at the blur of signs. Paddington? *What the hell?*

"Felicity, this isn't the way to my apartment."

"Who said we were going there?"

"What? Jesus, Felicity, I only have two hours to get ready and get to the Oceania Media ball. I have to find my best dress and make sure it's at least ironed. I have to wash a layer of grime off from the airport, and I don't have time for detours!"

"Would you stop complaining? We're almost there."

"Almost where?"

Moments later the car pulled up in front of a row of terrace houses. They looked elegant, charming, and expensive.

"The blue one," Felicity told the driver. He stopped, and she paid. "Be back here in ninety minutes."

"What...?" Maddie looked around. Where the hell were they?

"We'll talk inside." Felicity didn't even glance back. She unlocked the terrace house's front door and held it open impatiently.

Maddie headed up the path, dropped her bag inside the door, and looked around. The place was decorated in pale hues, with tasteful art on the walls as placid and serene as everything else. None of it matched the tightly wound woman beside her. It was so conservative and safe. Surely Felicity didn't live here? How could she afford to? She had an apartment back in New York.

"Sit." Felicity pointed to a lounge room. "Drink?"

"Uh, water?"

Felicity disappeared behind an alcove, and Maddie sank onto a black leather couch and waited.

A clock ticked loudly, and Maddie fidgeted. This was too weird.

Felicity reappeared. "Here." She thrust a glass of chilled water into her hand and then slid onto the matching leather chair facing Maddie. Her fingers curled around the knees of her stylish navy designer pants. "I knew you'd be cutting it fine and wouldn't have had time to get a dress for the ball tonight." Felicity pointed at a hook on the wall near the door. From it hung a dress under clear plastic. "That's for you. Courtesy of Perry."

It was a simple dress, black, elegant, and classic. A V-neck and the sleeveless arms made it look like something Audrey Hepburn might skip around Rome in. A shoe box sat beneath it.

Maddie stared at her. "Did Elena...?"

"No, she did not. You told her not to, remember?"

"Yeah."

"Well, she listened." Felicity peered at her closely. "Don't pass out or anything, but this is my doing."

"Why?" Maddie was at a complete loss.

"Because you were right." Felicity stared at her fingers and played with a silver ring on her right hand. "At the Duchamp afterparty, when I got a bit sauced, you told me I should spend more time focused on my career than yours. And you were right. You were also right about telling her the truth about *him*, although the way you went about it was suicidal. But I was wrong not backing you up that day. And you were correct when you said I wasn't happy in my job. No, not because I'm a frustrated fashion junkie. Do you know I don't even care that much about fashion?"

"What?" Maddie blinked. "But you're at all the events with Elena."

"Yes. I am. I admire her a great deal. Sometimes I think too much. As a result, I've let her get away with things far too often." A frown knitted her pale brows.

"What do you mean?"

"I let her treat me like a glorified gofer when I'm a trained lawyer," Felicity said. "I am exceptional at the business side of my job. Do you know that? I am brilliant, damn it. My qualifications are impeccable... and yet I fetch her drinks. Because *she* asks. I worked out the reason Elena never cares how long an assistant lasts is because she knows I'll take over if she fires one. Well, I've thought about it and decided I'm worth more than that. I told her so. A little...er...more spectacularly than I had planned."

Elena's tea mug being hurled against the wall flashed into Maddie's mind.

"And do you know what happened? That ice queen of a woman who has terrified and impressed me and driven me crazy for years laughed her damned head off. She said 'About time'. And then she promoted me!" Felicity shook her head. "I'm to be the deputy COO, and she's training me to take over the running of Bartell Corp."

"That's awesome."

"Yes. Well. It *is* deserved." Felicity glared at her with suspicion over the praise.

"I agree." Maddie could see what Elena meant about her not taking compliments well.

"So, I wanted to thank you. And I have, I suppose, also come to terms with the fact you and she are more than former colleagues."

Maddie stiffened.

"Oh, don't look so shocked. You're secretly friends. I get it. I know she emails you all the time. Suddenly, she's taking calls from Hanoi or Kon Tum or wherever your ass has been. I *know*. And I'm...I can accept that." She gave Maddie a pained look, as though still convincing herself.

Wait. *Friends?* Felicity clearly wasn't as observant as she thought.

"So this is my way of thanking you for saying what I needed to hear." Felicity waved at the dress. "I organised an outfit for you that she'll love, and I have a bathroom for you to get ready here—we're actually only three blocks from the ball tonight. So you'll have more time. And I'll also..." she gave Maddie a disagreeable look, "stop fixating on all the ways you keep winning. Even if it is totally unfair."

Unfair?

"Well, I may still fixate just a little," Felicity amended with an earnest look before conceding a slight smile. "But you really are obnoxious, you have to admit."

"I admit nothing." Maddie laughed. "And I can't help a lucky streak. If you knew how crap I was at life in New York, how I barely coped with everything, you'd swallow your words. Besides, you're obnoxious too. You act like you're better than everyone else, and you talk like a repressed English nanny, but when you're upset, you leak your secret Midwest accent."

"That's just... That's... I do not." Felicity slumped and rolled her eyes. "You know, I paid a top British elocutions expert to get that beaten out of me. Mrs Allsop will be most unhappy."

"Well, I won't tell her." Maddie stood. "You know, there's nothing wrong with being from middle America. One day, I'd love to know how you went from there to the world's top media company, but I don't have much time. So, I'll just say thanks for doing all this and which way to the shower?"

Felicity pointed. "Second door on the left."

"I'll try and leave you some hot water. But I have a lot of sand and grit in unmentionable places."

"Don't worry about that. Take as long as you like. I'm not going tonight."

Maddie froze. "You're not?"

"No. It's part of a few promises I've made to myself. No attending events just because she'll be there. I'm only going to the essential ones in the future."

"Oh." Maddie couldn't even imagine Elena at a function without Felicity at her side.

"Besides," Felicity added, heat rising in her cheeks. She squirmed. "I have a date."

"A date? Anyone I know?"

"No. He's a lawyer I met at the Duchamp afterparty. You're actually in his terrace house, and he's kindly allowed you to get fixed up here tonight."

"He? Oh. Huh." Maddie paused.

"What?"

"I just thought maybe you liked women. Or Elena specifically. You know. Romantically."

"What?" Felicity's mouth fell open. "Why would you think that? And you *do* know she's straight, right? Oh, there've been a few assistants who've fallen for her now and then, but I've worked with that woman for years, and she's never shown even the slightest hint of—"

"Hey," Maddie cut her off urgently, "I'm sorry to have assumed, okay? I'm just really glad you've found someone."

Felicity huffed out a breath. "Yes, well." She folded her arms. "Phillip is a good man. He doesn't mind that I'm late for everything or work ridiculous hours, or..." Felicity lowered her voice to a dramatic, pained whisper, "that I'm from the *Midwest*."

Biting back a grin, Maddie said, "Great. I'd love to meet him sometime."

"Absolutely not! Do you think I'd let him anywhere near Miss Lucky Streak? No! Now go...make yourself presentable. The car will be back before you know it."

CHAPTER 34

The Last Dance

Elena had always assumed the unravelling of her second marriage would be as problematic as the first was easy. With Spencer, he'd just packed up and left. Not even an argument, let alone a whimper. With Richard, Elena had done some careful planning, preparing for any eventuality with her team of lawyers, from the moment she'd kicked him out.

It had therefore been astonishing to read how "much in love" he was with her in the gossip columns. Positioning himself to be the good guy when the word of their impending divorce leaked, no doubt. That was funny, given she'd since learned that he was now ensconced with Janice from the marketing department at his work—a woman with a reputation for appreciating men with money.

A week ago, Elena had called her acquaintance, Annalise Taylor, wife of the new VP at Richard's firm, and suggested a catch-up lunch. Annalise was the world's most indiscreet woman—which was easily her most useful asset.

And so, over a few cocktails, Elena happened to "let slip" about what Richard had really been up to for years. She had requested anonymity for her "lapse" in discretion, and Annalise had nodded so hard that her drop diamond earrings had bucked like a pair of broncos.

Annalise had lived up to her reputation. Richard had been suspended within the day while his superiors began a full investigation into whether he'd been inappropriate at their workplace, too.

The moment her cell phone had rung with his signature theme from *Ride of the Valkyries*, Elena knew her husband's wrath would be ferocious. She closed her office door and locked it before settling herself perfectly centre in her chair and exhaling. Then she answered her phone.

"Yes?"

"You bitch. It was you. Had to be. Who else knew?"

"And hello to you, too, Richard." Her tone was measured and hid the hate she now felt for him. Control was power.

"They might fire me, you vicious little cunt."

"For good reason, no doubt," Elena countered. "May the women at Better Health United USA all exhale in relief."

"Why'd you do it? We had a goddamn deal!"

"A deal?" she asked innocently.

"You know we did. Why'd you make me pay out all that compensation to those whiny slut assistants and make all those damn donations to women's shelters if you were just going to spread the story about me anyway? That's bullshit, Elena! Fuck you!"

She gave a grim smile and adjusted the position of her pot of pens on her desk. "It's hardly my fault if you somehow gained the impression I'd never tell anyone in exchange for your financial penance. I left all of that to my lawyers to sort out."

"It was *implied!*" he shouted. "You know it. One of those suited turds said we couldn't put it in writing, because I wanted nothing in writing, but that we had a deal. I trusted you. I trusted you and you betrayed me!"

"*I* betrayed *you*? Oh, poor dear. So tell me, how does that feel?"

Ragged breath was the only reply for a few minutes, as he digested her meaning. His tone went from heated to frosty cold. "I'll sue you, you fucking ice bitch."

"Dare you to try." She disconnected the call. He wouldn't sue her. The spineless bastard wanted his dirty laundry contained, not aired in open court.

It had only taken a week before Richard's company dug up enough dirt to turn his suspension into a termination, or so Annalise had told her over their next round of cocktails. His girlfriend had stuck by him, though, despite whatever rancid antics he'd been up to at work. How adorable.

Elena wondered how long Janice would stay besotted when she found out he'd been cleaned out of almost all his money. It didn't matter to her anymore. Her attention was on something far more gratifying. She was no longer linked to that man. Her divorce was final. And now everyone knew. This morning, Richard had announced the divorce along with his engagement to Janice.

It should have been humiliating for her, but it was unsettling to realise how little she cared.

And, disturbing as the past events had been, this was a new chapter for her. She was free. She could now focus on other things, better things. Such as the former assistant who would be meeting her soon for their third scheduled ball together.

She peered out at the city, as Sydney's streets flashed by. The night was still warm, but then it was summer in Sydney in December. Elena was glad she'd left the shoulder wrap behind. Besides, she'd been warm all day, just thinking about the evening ahead.

She was exiting her chauffeured car and adjusting her clutch, just as another vehicle pulled up behind her.

"Elena!"

She glanced up, her pulse picking up as she recognised the voice, and found her eyes settling on the most glorious sight she'd seen in months.

"Madeleine." She was surprised her voice sounded as steady as it did. It took everything she had not to step inside Madeleine's space and slide her lips across her jaw.

"Elena! Oh my God, you look gorgeous!" Madeleine's gaze was roving across her strapless, emerald Vera Wang gown as though she was ready to divest her of it on the spot.

Madeleine was adorned in a black, form-fitting sheath—a beautiful, classic cut. A rather familiar one at that. *Perry*. She'd know his fashion fingerprints anywhere. The effect was superb. She wore a magnificent bracelet—a Tiffany's birthday item she'd risked to global post. Madeleine was a vision.

Elena leaned forward to give her an air kiss, but she couldn't stop herself and her lips lingered. Finally, conscious that they were in public, she stepped back and studied her. Although tired around the eyes, Madeleine seemed to glow. The admiring way she looked at Elena vastly improved her mood.

"You are a sight. Divine bracelet." Elena tapped it approvingly, then let her finger pause on the wrist. "Such fine taste."

As Madeleine smiled, Elena's heart clenched at how much she'd missed that open, engaging expression.

Madeleine brushed her fingers over the bracelet. "I love it. God, it was the most impractical gift to have out there, and you were insane to send it, like, mad as a cut snake insane, but I adored having it. It was like a piece of you was with me at all times."

Elena warmed inside. "As it was intended." She glanced around. "Now, I should warn you—the media has, as of today, thrown up a new theory that Richard was one of the villains in your *Vanity Fair* piece. I may get grilled by a few vultures of the press on the way in tonight."

"Well, you could just tell them it was you who leaked his name." Madeleine gave her a knowing look.

Elena froze.

"Oh come on, Elena, of course it was you. I knew you wouldn't let him get away with it when you punished everyone else except him."

Elena shook her head faintly. "I do enjoy your vivid imagination. And I'm glad you're on my side."

Madeleine laughed. "You are hilarious. I don't think people get that about you, do they?"

Elena smiled, slid her hand down to Madeleine's, and gave it a quick squeeze. "Only the smart ones."

The evening had been acceptable. Elena had done her usual meet and greets among the Australian media world, finding it all the better for the company at her side. Her eye would sometimes be caught by the dazzle of a bracelet, the sweep of a supple neck, or the flash of cropped titian hair, accompanied by a genuine laugh. Sometimes, green eyes would connect with hers, and the promise burning within them made Elena forget her train of thought.

Madeleine reappeared beside her and said in a soft voice, "Your assistant says your neighbours are complaining the paparazzi are blocking your street out the front of your home tonight, looking for a comment on the Richard story. She thought I should warn you."

Elena pursed her lips. "The media are certainly persistent. I was trailed all over town today."

"Is this the reason you held off naming Richard for so long? You knew they'd hassle you too? If so, why put his name out there at all?"

"I held off because I wished to be divorced from him first. And once we were, I named him because I had the power, the means, and the ethical duty to do so."

"Then why keep your role in his outing a secret?"

"Haven't you heard? The tiger shark is fierce, ruthless, and vicious. She is *never* weak."

"And you can't be seen to show compassion," Madeleine said, comprehension dawning in her eyes. "Wow. That's awful."

"It was necessary. I have a reputation. It's useful at times."

"But now people might think you helped him cover it up. That you were complicit."

"They already do. The smart ones will work out the timing of the divorce and his shaming. But people always assume the worst. There's been speculation about my knowledge of his crimes that even my lawyers can't silence."

"So you're basically stuck being the villain?"

"It will only enhance the fear people have of me. People do enjoy a good villain. I accomplish more when people fear me."

"But I know the truth."

Elena regarded her. "The people I care about generally do."

Madeleine's face creased into a soft look.

"You have to stop looking at me like that. It's not good for my reputation at all."

"You're right." Madeleine straightened. She played with her bracelet, fingering its band, then twirling it left, then right. "So the big question is with Richard right out of the picture, does that mean you're available for...other opportunities?" She bit her lip.

Elena tilted her head. "You do ask good questions. I've always liked that about you." She smiled at the way Madeleine was trying and failing to hide her nervousness. "I am now divorced. There are no encumbrances that I can think of." Her heart thudded painfully, as she watched Madeleine's reaction. After all that time apart, Madeleine could have decided she didn't want a considerably older woman in her life with so much media attention and baggage.

"That's good to know." Delight lit Madeleine's eyes, and Elena felt a rush of relief. "You know, I'm feeling a bit jet-lagged. I've done the rounds now with this crowd. I think I should go."

"What?" Elena eyed her, worried. Had she offended her in some manner? Her mind raced back over her words.

"And since your home is barricaded, I think we should go to mine," Madeleine added.

We? Elena's breath stilled. "Are you really tired, Madeleine?"

"That depends." Madeleine's expression was playful. "Come home with me and let's assess me there. I might get a second wind."

Elena effected her most disagreeable expression. "Well, I can't have you collapsing here from exhaustion. As you're my guest for the evening, it would reflect poorly on me."

"Yes, yes, it would. We can't have that at all." Madeleine sounded earnest, but her eyes were dark.

Elena dragged her gaze away and pulled out her phone. "I'm ready to leave. Car. Now."

"Wise move." Madeleine placed her drink on a nearby table. "Looking after a former employee so well. I'm sure HR would approve."

"Oh." Heat rose in Elena's cheeks, as she conjured visions of their evening ahead. "I'm quite sure they wouldn't."

"Your new apartment is lovely." Elena's gaze trailed around Maddie's home.

Wondering if she could even remain standing, she was so nervous, Maddie swallowed. She glanced around the sleek lines, warm timber, and marble surfaces greeting her. It was a big step up from the last time Elena had visited her at a Manhattan rental.

"Yeah, well, thank *Style* for being generous with my first major pay cheque. Oh, and *Vanity Fair, Time, New Yorker, Rolling Stone,* and *Condé Nast Traveller* are no slouches either. I love the lock-up-and-leave aspect. It's also only one bedroom, which put it in my price range, so..."

Madeleine trailed off. Elena didn't need the real-estate spiel. She was just so damn nervous.

Elena took a step closer. And then another.

Her strapless green dress swirled as she moved, and Maddie was mesmerised by the daring bodice of taut, green silk held up by Elena's creamy breasts and little else. She imagined slipping her hands inside, cupping her breasts, and freeing them from their confines. She licked her lips. Judging by the half-lidded eyes watching her, Elena had probably guessed exactly where her thoughts had gone.

"Madeleine? What are you thinking about?"

As if she didn't know.

"Would you like a drink?" Maddie avoided answering by pivoting towards her fridge. "I have wine and water and not much else. Haven't had a chance to go shopping yet."

Elena trailed her fingers down her arm, short-circuiting the conversation.

Goosebumps broke out along Maddie's skin.

"Not thirsty, no," Elena said. "Hungry? Most definitely."

"Oh."

Elena slid her fingers to the back of her neck and pulled her in for a barely there kiss. She leaned back.

"Wow." Maddie's blood was roaring in her ears. Her lips tingled.

Elena's lips shifted to her ear. "Why are you keeping me waiting, Madeleine? Haven't I been patient? I believe you claimed this apartment came with a bedroom. I suggest you stop burying the lead and get to it." Her lips curled into a smile against the shell of Maddie's ear. Her tongue darted out.

Arousal shot through Maddie. She slid her fingers around Elena's and led her to her bedroom.

She looked back at Elena. Her lips were parted slightly, her eyes dark with desire. "You're so beautiful," Maddie said. "I felt you watching me from your office in New York. It felt like a caress. Like fingers on my skin, but so soft. I told myself I was imagining it. That someone like you would never be interested in someone like me."

"You were...a distracting temptation. You sorely tested my focus. But I was married."

"And now? Aren't I still a temptation? Or do you no longer lose focus?"

"Now, it's far worse." She smiled. "But I have come to appreciate the benefits of temptations, lack of focus be damned."

Elena's gaze slid to the queen-sized bed behind them. Her attention shifted to a solid-wood, white-painted dressing table with a mirror attached. Elena's lips curved into a dangerous smile. "Madeleine," she said, voice soft. "Come here."

Maddie stepped forward and Elena gently turned her to face the mirror.

"Look at you." Elena pressed in behind her and met her eyes in the mirror. "I see Perry has a sense of humour. Or a sense of the romantic. He knows how much I love Audrey Hepburn. The simplicity of her style was stunning. I recognise your dress. One of Perry's up-and-coming designers is going through a tribute phase. This dress is modelled on the one Hepburn wore in *Breakfast at Tiffany's*."

Elena plucked the black material at Maddie's shoulder and then trailed the backs of her fingers down Maddie's bare skin, leaving tiny hairs erect in their wake. Her eyes never left Maddie's as she touched her.

"Uh." Maddie gasped at the promise behind those teasing fingers.

"Mm," Elena murmured. "You are wearing an icon, and doing it superbly."

There was a faint *tik-tik-tik*, as the zip on Maddie's dress was lowered; Elena's fingers followed the zip in a fiery trail. Elena slid the short sleeves over Maddie's shoulders, then rolled the dress over her breasts before bunching it at her hips. Warm hands flattened across Maddie's back and smoothed across her skin.

"I admire the softness of women's skin greatly, and their backs in particular. Yours, in that stunning gown in Véronique's dressing room, very nearly got me into a great deal of trouble. I found myself in the shocking position of fighting my instincts to bend you over that make-up table and have my way with you right there. I would have enjoyed watching your eyes in the mirror as I made you mine. All while you wore the most exquisite dress I have ever seen in my life."

Maddie's throat went dry. Heat flooded her at the thought of that fantasy. A tug brought the dress down past her hips and to the carpeted floor. She stepped out of it.

"Of course, I can still do that to you," Elena said, voice soft and suggestive. "Can't I?"

"Ohh." Maddie whimpered. "Yes."

Elena's hands returned to her back, ghosting across her skin. "You can see it, can't you?" She playfully plucked at and then undid Maddie's bra. It fell to the floor. "My eyes on yours, the who's who of world fashion just outside. And when I lifted the white hem on that stunning gown, pushing it up past your hips, what would I find? Hmm? What undergarments were you wearing that night? Or were you bare?"

"Oh, I...th-thong. Lace thong."

"Mmm. Yes, I'd have enjoyed plucking that from you. Slipping it down your firm thighs. And doing much more."

Maddie gasped.

"You like that idea." Elena's gaze burned. "I do too. I think of it, quite a lot."

Elena's lips pressed into Maddie's shoulder, then the warm wetness of her tongue swept along it. She lifted her head, and her direct gaze examined Maddie's aching, erect nipples and the spreading flush across her chest. Her fingers curled around Maddie's rib cage and plucked at her nipples, rolling them between her thumb and forefinger. The sensation sent warmth between her legs.

"Your breasts are so distracting," Elena said. "Beautiful. But now I wish to stay focused. Where were we?"

They watched in the mirror, as Elena slid her hands to Maddie's waist while she nipped and kissed Maddie's shoulder. Her fingers slid into the top of Maddie's black panties and eased them down, baring Maddie's patch of dark curls. A telltale glistening on them caused Elena to smile.

"Oh yes," she breathed as Maddie reddened. "Very good. And what would I see in your eyes when I touched you, Madeleine? What would my fingers feel as they pushed inside you?"

Maddie groaned, as Elena's hand slid down her stomach to brush across her wet curls. She trembled. "Please," she whispered.

"Are you remembering how it felt that night when I couldn't have you, but oh how I wanted you? Did you want me too? Did you want me to push past your lace thong and touch you then, just as I am now? I would have slipped my fingers inside you. Watching you as I did it. Did you want that?"

"Yes," Maddie said. Her back arched into Elena's. "God yes, I did. I do."

Elena's fingers pressed down, against her swollen clit, causing it to pulse. "I knew that," she said against her ear. "That night, I felt your arousal as well as my own. Your face doesn't hide your secrets. I wanted you very much."

She rubbed her harder, causing Maddie to moan. Elena's fingers curled forward, sliding through heat and slippery folds, and entered her.

Maddie leaned forward, and her hands, now flat against the dresser, became slick. She gasped at the sensation between her legs and the flash of ecstasy across Elena's face.

Elena's lips parted, her eyes fierce and full of desire. Another groan reverberated, low, dirty, and raw, and it was Elena's.

"God," Elena said, her breathing harsh, "you're even hotter than I imagined."

She was rocking against Maddie, her fingers a blur as she worked them in and out, urging Maddie on. Her other hand slid up to Maddie's breast where it pinched and rolled her nipples.

Maddie was hypnotised by those eyes in the glass—burning, excited, and dark—and her control wavered. Slick noises filled the room, and her wetness gleamed on Elena's dancing fingers.

"So close." Maddie squeezed her eyes shut. God. It was exquisite.

"I know. I can feel you. You're almost pulsing. Look at me when you come. I want to see. Show me."

Maddie opened her eyes and locked on to Elena's naked gaze. The raw hunger she found in her eyes made Maddie crash over the edge. Her back arched, her centre clenched, and hot flares arced from her. Her hands trembled against the wood she leaned on.

"Oh, Madeleine, so beautiful." The words purred against her neck, as Elena withdrew her fingers and scribbled the wetness all across her stomach. She lifted them to her lips and tasted them. She smiled.

Maddie swallowed, her throat dry. She turned and kissed Elena. It was messy and hot and so damned arousing. Maddie kissed her like a woman deserved to be kissed. With every hint of passion she felt. With all the love she possessed.

She took a step back and slid her hands inside Elena's green bodice, lifting out her creamy breasts, and then studied her with satisfaction. "You're breathtaking."

Maddie's mouth closed over an aroused, deep-red nipple, her tongue sliding across it. Elena pressed herself into her more.

When Maddie finally pulled away, she whispered to Elena, "I've wanted to do that all night."

"Is that all you wanted to do to me?"

Elena's cocky smirk was back, and Maddie's heart lurched at the suggestiveness.

"No. Take off your dress. I want to see the rest of you."

Elena reached for a hidden zipper at her side, unzipped the dress, and lowered it to the ground. She stood before Maddie in nothing but a thin, white thong and thigh-high stockings. The thong was darker between her legs, revealing her arousal. Elena put her hands on her hips as if to say, *Well?*

Maddie's heart hammered at the intoxicating sight of Elena Bartell virtually naked. "Sit." She pointed to the dressing table.

Elena did as she was requested, leaning back on her hands, pushing her breasts out.

Maddie parted Elena's knees and lowered herself to the floor. She nudged aside Elena's thong and took in the sight of slick lips.

"You want me." Maddie's words were an incredulous whisper. She blew across her skin and marvelled at the tremble in response.

Elena widened her legs and arched back. "I want you."

Maddie's mouth covered her most intimate spot. As her tongue worked, she felt wetness growing on her chin. Elena's thighs began to quiver. Her hands had shifted to Maddie's hair, where they were clenching and unclenching. Elena tensed and gave a tight, strangled cry.

The sight of this magnificent, commanding woman coming undone, vulnerable, and gazing at her with such unmasked affection, was seared into Maddie's brain.

She wouldn't give this up, Maddie decided as she returned her mouth to her folds and slid her tongue all over her slippery flesh as she twitched and trembled. In response, Elena's whole body shook.

Maddie would keep Elena close and make love to her as often as she could. She could never give this up.

"Bed," Maddie croaked. "Bed before my knees give out. So we won't have to stop next time. Because we really have to do this again."

Elena slid from the dressing table to her feet, looking slightly dishevelled yet still regal and supremely satisfied. "By all means." Her voice was a purr. "Bed."

But as Maddie turned to head there, Elena grabbed her and pulled her close. "Wait," she whispered, her tone urgent. She kissed her, tightening her arms around Maddie as though afraid she might leave.

Her roaming tongue and soft lips made Maddie tremble all over again.

"Oh God," Maddie murmured, when they finally broke apart. "I had no idea you would be this amazing. Should have guessed, though. It *is* you. When do you fail at anything you set your mind to?"

Elena's smile was both brilliant and pleased.

No. Maddie absolutely would never give this up.

Elena was not a cuddler in her sleep. Nor did she spoon, Maddie discovered. Oh no. She conquered. When they had been too tired to do anything more beyond crawl under the sheets, Elena took up most of the bed, two-thirds of the pillows, half the blankets, and all of Maddie, like some sort of post-coital corporate takeover.

Maddie wondered if she'd need a prying bar to separate them in the morning, as she eyed the sensuous, nude body pinning her down, a leg claiming her hip.

She had never felt so desired, wanted, and completely taken. And by someone who was legendary for being stand-offish.

If only they knew.

Waking up, Maddie felt spent and dehydrated. Muscles she didn't know she possessed were complaining. She slid her gaze to the side to find Elena's soft eyes studying her. The woman wore a cat-got-the-cream, lazy smirk.

"H-hey," Maddie mumbled. Her voice was worse for wear.

"Well," Elena said as she stretched. "Awake at last. I thought millennials were supposed to have more stamina." The sheet fell down to her waist, giving Maddie a view of generous breasts. And given the look on Elena's face, Maddie guessed the intoxicating display was deliberate.

"God, how can you look so bright? Did you even get any sleep?"

"Sleep's overrated." Elena slid her arms behind her head, thrusting her chest out, and gave her an amused smile.

Maddie almost lost her train of thought. "Did you enjoy yourself, then?"

"I suppose you want to hear you were the best I've ever had?" Elena gave her a pointed look. Her face softened. "That would be more than accurate. It was exceptional. I believe I finally understand the appeal of sex. All those sonnets actually have a point."

Maddie preened.

"But don't let it go to your head."

"Too late. My head is already puffed up to capacity."

"It should be." Elena smiled then gave her a quizzical look. "Is this common? Three-hour sessions? Is this a thing women do together?"

Maddie's eyebrows shot up. "Was that your first time with a woman? Seriously?"

"I suppose I should be pleased you couldn't tell." Elena gave her a slow smile. "In practical terms, yes. But since I've met you, I've thought about it, in theory, far more than I'd care to admit. As I said, you've been terrible for my focus."

"I'm honoured." Maddie grinned. She let the sheet slide down her own breasts and gave Elena a cheeky look. "So this is distracting, then?" She lifted her hand to her nipple and squeezed. "Or this?"

A speculative gleam came into Elena's eye. "I'm not certain. Continue and I'll let you know."

Maddie ignored that and wriggled herself across Elena's body, pressing into her. "I'd rather do the hands-on experience. Besides, you should make the most of me since you've been waiting so patiently."

"Good point." Elena brought her hands up to Maddie's back. "I always knew you were smart."

"Yeah? Then how come every email you sent started *Dear Foolish Girl*?" Maddie tapped her in the ribs. "No more of that girl stuff, okay? I am a woman, Elena. *Your* woman. And I plan to show you how true that is over the next hour. Or days. Weeks. Months." She sucked in a deep breath and put it all out there. "Years."

Elena stared at her, unmoving.

"This isn't some fling for me. I hope you know that," Maddie said, swallowing. "I mean, this is... It means something. I don't...I don't play around with things like this. I don't like games." She wondered if Elena could hear her thundering heart.

Elena trailed her fingers down her cheekbone. "How can you not already know? I wouldn't be here otherwise. I have more to lose than you do. I don't do flings either. And certainly not with one I care for as much as you."

Maddie felt her stomach do a strange little swirl. Elena looked like she meant it. She sucked in a steadying breath. "I'm in love with you. I think I have been since New York."

Elena's look was soft and infused with warmth. "Oh Madeleine. And you said I shouldn't call you foolish. What do you see in an old, twice-divorced, workaholic shark like me? Even my dog finds me hard to live with."

"I see all the things you don't put on display. And, please, Oscar's more highly strung than Felicity. I wouldn't take your dog's opinion on what you're like to be around."

"Be that as it may, you don't know what I'm really like."

"Oh? I know you give secretly to organisations you think no one cares about. Trans bathroom rights, domestic violence shelters, Polish community centres. You were the one who gave Ramel his life back. That fancy lawyer you funded got all his charges thrown out."

Elena shot Maddie a surprised look at her awareness of Elena's secret donations but then shook her head. "Causes are not me. These are surface things, a place to give money that I believe in."

"All right, I also know you are a mess of stress over handing the Bartell Corp reins to your advisers, although you'd never admit it. You're afraid you might be making a terrible mistake. But you're just as excited to be back in fashion soon. You can't wait."

Elena blinked. "Well."

"And I know you drink far too much when you're sad. And you're sad far more often than you would ever admit to anyone."

At Elena's startled expression, Maddie added, "I was your assistant once. Who do you think paid the liquor bills you keep hidden from your housekeeper? I also know you followed my blog. I hate to admit it, but only sad people loved it and related to it."

Elena looked uncomfortable. "Yet you want to date me anyway?"

Maddie eyed her defensiveness and pressed physically closer. "You read my blog, Elena." She curled her fingers around Elena's ribs. "That sadness and loneliness goes both ways. You were drawn to me, because I felt it too. You had read about all my insecurities and flaws before we even met, and yet you liked me anyway. Isn't that what a relationship is? Knowing who someone is behind the mask and wanting to be with them in spite of it?"

Elena's fingers dusted Maddie's cheek. "What am I going to do with you?"

"You really have to ask?"

Elena raked her with an affectionate gaze. "Well, I trust your plans include staying closer to home now? That foolis...ill-conceived part of your career is now over? Or am I to be a travel writer's widow?"

"It's over. Because I found out while I was over there that my heart belongs here. And I don't want to be that far apart from you again. I'd miss you way too much."

"Well. There's a coincidence."

Maddie gave her a small smirk. "Hey, can I ask you something? Why the truth bet? I never understood why you did it. It seemed not like you at all."

"It was a reaction." Elena leaned up, her lips finding Maddie's neck. "I asked you to be my PA, because I found I missed you too much to not have you at my side. This was a difficult admission for me. So in Sydney, I hoped my interest in you would be lessened if I put some professional distance between us. In response, you stopped smiling, sharing, and challenging me. I missed it more than I can say. So I used the truth bet. It was an excuse, but I wanted to know you again. Of course, that backfired. I learned more about my life than yours."

"Funny thing is," Maddie said, "I thought you were just wanting me to admit I had an embarrassing crush on you."

"Oh I did," Elena said, sounding positively evil. "We were going to get to your longing looks. But events overtook us."

"Hey, that's so sneaky." Maddie gave a rueful laugh. "God, I did not want to have to fess up to loving my boss!"

"I would have enjoyed it, though," Elena said, her eyes taking on a faraway look. "It would have been only fair. After all, you've had me entranced for such a long time—before we even met I was taken by your words. So when I say I've been patiently waiting for you, don't think I'm exaggerating. In reality, I can't believe you made me wait this long for you. I mean really, Madeleine."

Maddie's burble of laughter at Elena's feigned high dudgeon filled the room.

Elena silenced it with a fierce kiss.

Then, as she melted beneath Elena's lips and fingers, Maddie felt sure she had never received a more beautiful declaration of love—even if it wasn't in words.

Who needed words anyway?

CHAPTER 35
Unspoken

Maddie's shoulder blades pressed against the front of her apartment door. She curled her hands up into sleek, black hair and moaned softly as soft lips covered hers. Saying goodbye after Elena stayed over was getting harder and harder.

She whimpered at the thought and enjoyed the answering tug of hands on her hips. Hands that began wandering. A thrill flooded her until her brain caught up. Oh no, they absolutely could not do this in the hall. And besides, Elena had work, and Maddie had beach plans.

"Mm," Elena murmured. She breathed against her ear. "Delicious."

Okay, so who needed work or sun anyway?

Maddie moaned.

A cough sounded.

Maddie almost jumped out of her skin. She opened her eyes, and Elena quickly stepped back.

Simon. With a look that was way too smug. Great. He'd tease her about this forever.

Maddie fixed her best polite face, annoyed at how warm her face felt. "Ah. Not quite how I'd hoped you'd first meet, but Simon Itani, meet Elena Bartell. Elena, Simon."

"Charmed." He waggled his eyebrows. Given his hands were full with a surfboard and towel bag, at least he didn't try and kiss her hand or something else desperately uncool. It was dodgy enough he was wearing a pair of floral board shorts, "Dad" sandals, and a faded *Big Bang Theory* T-shirt.

Elena took one long, supremely satisfied look at him and neatened her lipstick with her finger. "Well, hello." Her purred tone was so sultry it made Maddie's ovaries do a flip. "The audacious Simon at last."

"Me? Audacious?" He laughed.

"Your fashion choices gave you away." Her eyes sparkled, as though daring him to meet her challenge.

Simon grinned, looking completely unfazed. "So, the intimidating Elena Bartell. Although I gotta say, you're a lot less intimidating now I've seen your hand on my best friend's—"

"*Great!*" Maddie jumped in with a panicked cheerfulness. "Okay, um, so we will all catch up properly real soon. Good luck at work today, Elena. Simon, get your ass inside." She shot him a glare.

He laughed far too hard, as he pushed past her and disappeared into her apartment, closing the door behind him.

"Sorry about him," Maddie said. "Sometimes I forget he's all boy brain."

"Oh, but I can't disagree with him. I did have my hand on certain body parts that were far too tempting."

Maddie shook her head. "You're impossible. And I'm missing you already. Wish I could spend more time with you this weekend. We could, um, *talk* some more." She felt warm all over thinking about how that "conversation" would go.

Elena leaned forward and gave her a chaste peck on the cheek. "Have fun at the beach. Why not come over after you're done? Rosetta will doubtlessly love to see you again. I suspect she will stuff you full of more fudge cake. You could even do some work from my place if you like. Then we could extend our discussion more when I get home."

"That sounds great."

Elena left her with a look so smouldering that Maddie slumped heavily against the door. "Bye," she whispered to the now empty hall.

"Hey, Mads?" came the muffled voice through her door a few moments later.

"Yeah, Simon?"

"When you're done swooning, can we go to the beach?" His voice rose to a whine.

She rolled her eyes. "What makes you think I'm swooning?"

"Hello? I *have* met your girlfriend. And almost slipped in a puddle of her charisma."

Maddie smiled at the empty hall. Girlfriend. Elena Bartell was her girlfriend. Wow.

"You know, I'm starting to get sick of your attitude." Maddie, sprawled on the couch with a laptop on her chest, gave a petulant look. "Always so superior. You walk all over me, and I just put up with it."

Oscar ignored her pointed glare and resumed stalking up and down her thighs and stomach before finally shoving his long nose over the edge of her laptop.

"You wouldn't care if I was writing a Pulitzer Prize story," Maddie complained. "And you get away with it because you're cute."

Leaning forward, Oscar licked her cheek.

"Oh I get it. Think you can use your charm on me?"

Oscar batted the back of her laptop screen with his head, causing it to close over onto her hands.

"Fine! You win." Maddie shut her machine and placed it on the coffee table. She gave the dog a thorough scratch behind his red ears.

Oscar flopped onto her chest and closed his eyes.

"Lemme guess, you're going to fall asleep on me, and I won't be able to move for three hours? Because pet rules apply? What if I had a big deadline, did you ever think of that?"

Oscar blinked back at her. He showed no signs of budging.

"You're irresistible and you know it." Maddie sighed. Her fingers threaded Oscar's beautiful fur, and she smiled. "Just like your mistress."

"My ears are burning."

Maddie glanced up to find Elena leaning against the door, arms folded and an amused look on her face.

"Well, I see you've finally learned the house rules," Elena added. "It's Oscar's way or Oscar's way. You should be honoured. He doesn't like many people. Looks like he's well and truly claimed you."

"Maybe Oscar just has good taste."

"No argument from me." Elena walked over to her and gently pushed Maddie's feet along the couch, making way to sit beside her. "I was hoping you'd be here."

"Miss me?"

Elena gave a long-suffering sigh. "It turns out you're such a distracting influence that it was easier to just come home and get my work done here, than sit at work thinking about you on my Saturday."

A warmth suffused Maddie, and she found herself grinning stupidly. She loved it when Elena said things like that. She always looked so sincere. "That's my evil plan. To lure you to my side and love you to death. How's it working out so far?"

"I'd say it's the most cunning takeover bid I've ever seen. I'm impressed."

Maddie gave Oscar another rub behind his ears. "I wish I could be as brilliant in all other areas." She glared at her laptop.

"Ah. How's your latest story coming along? Need a second set of eyes to read it?"

"That'd be good. Later, though, when I'm not drowning in conflicting timelines. Right now I can't even work out what the agreed facts are."

"You'll figure it out. You're good at this."

"Good at storytelling?"

Elena regarded her. "Yes."

"But not news features."

"That too. You're an excellent journalist. As I explained in one of my emails to you in Vietnam. Did you not believe me?"

"I thought you were just trying to talk me into coming home."

"Oh, I was." Elena shot her a sheepish look, which she turned into an eye roll. "But still, I meant it. You're one of the best reporters I have ever seen. I'm not sure how I failed to notice your drive for excellence in New York."

"Well to be fair, you were right. I was inconsistent—on account of being miserably homesick." She studied Elena. "You seriously think I'm one of the best?"

"You surely don't need my approval anymore, do you? You have to know by now. From others. It's not just me saying it."

Maddie thought about that. She'd received a lot of accolades lately. "That's true, but it's just that your opinion means a lot to me. I think sometimes I really need to hear the words from you."

There was a silence as the unspoken question sat between them. What Maddie was really asking for. It had been months of flirting, dating, making love. She had no doubt she was madly in love. The mere thought of Elena drove her to distraction; she was like air, she needed her so much. But what did Elena feel?

Elena's fingers found the grey linen material of her own pants and brushed them down. "I appreciate beauty in the world more than anything else, Madeleine." She looked her in the eye. "And all I ever want to be is with you. Doesn't that tell you something?"

"It tells me you find me beautiful. And I love that, but..." *If she's not ready, she's not ready.* "Hey, never mind. It doesn't matter."

Except it did matter. Maddie looked down.

"I used to think I had all the answers," Elena said slowly. "Before I met you, I used to think I was so brutally honest. I wielded the truth like a weapon. Now I see that the truest thing I know is all the lies we tell ourselves. It's terrifying—like seeing tiny cracks in a glass window, everywhere I look. Now, I don't trust myself anymore. I've lost faith in my own perception. My world view is forever shattered."

"Because you didn't know about Richard."

"Because I still worry that I did know. I'm torturing myself with the thought that, somewhere deep inside, a part of me was aware, and I told myself lies to avoid facing it. So you see, I don't have faith any longer. My opinions on personal matters don't feel sound. But I know this: when I look at you, you're all I want to look at. I know that when we're together, I don't want to leave. But I don't know if I can trust what these feelings mean. Do you understand? It feels like...my foundations are cracked."

Maddie took in the uncharacteristic hesitation in her voice. "You need time. To believe again."

Elena nodded. "In the meantime, can't you see the truth, whatever that may be, when you look at me?"

"I can. I do see it." Maddie had often thought the warmth in Elena's eyes told her more than her words. "Thank you for explaining how you feel. And thanks for sharing your home with me today. I am pretty sure I get way more work done with Sydney Harbour to look out at. Do you know I have a snow dome of almost this exact view?"

She petered out when a strange look crossed Elena's face.

"What is it?" Maddie asked.

"It's nothing. I just realised how much I was looking forward to you being here. That's never happened before. I used to find having anyone around me at home stressful."

"I am pretty easygoing." Maddie smiled. "I'm just like Oscar but with better breath and no hang-ups about store-brand food."

Elena ran the backs of her fingers along Maddie's bare arm. "Well, I do appreciate your coat. And it's rather useful that you're house-trained." She scooped her dog from Maddie's lap and deposited him on the floor. Oscar protested with a half-hearted yip but then settled into a ball in front of them and went back to sleep. Elena stretched out beside Maddie then curled herself around her.

"Want to go out tonight?" she asked, closing her eyes. "I've been invited to opening night for a new play at Belvoir St Theatre."

Maddie studied her serene face, still amazed she was allowed to see her like this. She slipped her fingers through her dark hair. "No, thanks. Not when you're in my arms like this. Where's the incentive to let go?"

"Stay in, then? I have to make a few calls, tie up some loose ends, sign off on a deal, and bring back flares, but I'd appreciate some company later."

Maddie playfully slapped her arm. "Elena! You are not bringing back flares."

"Only over my dead body." She smiled, fluttered her eyes open, and gazed up into Maddie's face. "But the offer stands. Stay here? Unless you had plans?"

"I do have plans. A new vegetable slice recipe I want to try out on you that Mum gave me and says you'll love. How she assumes she knows your palate is a complete mystery."

"Well, we did bond that one time, discussing your birthday."

"Mmm. Well, we'll find out if she's right. I just have a few more quotes to type up. I can work on the rest of my story tomorrow."

"You could do your story from here tomorrow, too. Or longer if you wanted." Elena hesitated. "There's a spare study upstairs that's just gathering dust, so you wouldn't have to compete with Oscar on the sofa for real estate. And a guest room next to it if you just needed to have some time out. Or my room if you prefer. Stay as long as you like. Besides, I also have it from a reliable source that Sydney Harbour views are good for writing."

Maddie paused. *Did she just...?* She searched Elena's face, her heart starting to race. "Elena? I'm sorry if I'm reading this all wrong, but are you asking me to move in?"

"That depends."

"On?"

"Whether you'll say yes." Elena fiddled with her blouse sleeve. "I know you have your own life, and you probably don't want to give up your independence. I'm sure you like that Simon can just drop over whenever he wants now. I know he's important to you. Friends should be. But that wouldn't have to change. I think I'd very much like to share my life with someone I... Someone I respect, who challenges me, who I care about, appreciate, and who I can't seem to tolerate not being near. So, if you feel the same way..."

Maddie sat up straight. "Ask me, then. Because the inside scoop is I'll probably say yes."

Elena didn't ask. She was too busy kissing her.

Maddie had no complaints.

CHAPTER 36
What Goes Around

The Australasian Legends of Publishing ball was always the calendar highlight—and it had rolled around again. It was officially her and Elena's fourth and final event together under the terms of their contract. So much had happened—such as moving in with Elena four months ago—that it was hard to believe only a single year had passed since their first Legends ball together.

Their car rolled to a stop, and the bright, milling crowds, dressed in their finery, caught Maddie's eye.

The driver exited and opened Elena's door.

Maddie slid across the back seat and followed her out.

Within minutes they were inside the grand, heritage-listed hotel, in a long hall that ran around the edges of the main ballroom. Elena surreptitiously took her hand to lead her farther in, her warm fingers giving Maddie the boost of confidence she needed.

Elena paused in a shadowed corner and gave Maddie an intense look. "Relax. I've heard your speech. All eleven versions. And you will be superb. You will impress them. Just be yourself."

"This is nuts." Maddie ran a hand down her dress, wondering how any of this had happened—her career, her life in Sydney with Elena, being asked to give the Legends speech this year. "I mean, I know I'm filling in for Alan Kadinsky, but couldn't they find anyone else? It's a mistake. I'm not a legend. I—"

"Really, Madeleine, who was the youngest ever winner of the Coleman prize? Who had three major scoops in one year? One of them international?"

"This is not about winning things; it's about me." Maddie hesitated. "This is so *me*. All these doubts. That they've made a mistake. There's a lot of things I don't think I deserve. I worry it's all going to come crashing down."

Elena regarded her in silence. She leaned in. "I will never see you as a mistake, Madeleine."

"I didn't say that."

"Perhaps, but you may have thought it. Has it occurred to you I feel undeserving also? You are young and beautiful and smart, with the world at your feet. I'm a woman with a reputation for being cold and heartless. While it's gratifying that Bartell Corp is doing well, that's the only thing that makes me in any way impressive to the world."

Maddie started. "What? That's crazy! You're..." She squeezed Elena's hand. "Don't you get how I see you? You're amazing with or without your business. And this...us...isn't some passing thing for me. This is *it*. I'm in it for the rest of my life. I'm all in. Do you get that?"

Smiling tenderly, Elena shifted closer. "Madeleine, I plan to keep you in my life for as long as I am able. And then longer still." She curled her fingers around Maddie's cheek.

It was the closest Elena had ever come to telling Maddie she loved her. Still, the uncertainties about Elena's feelings danced around the edges.

"What about when the public finds out?" she whispered. "I mean the media isn't blind. They'll work it out eventually. Like at Natalii's wedding next month? What will you do if people call you a predator editor or me a gold digger?"

Elena stroked her hand with her thumb. "I have been called worse, and it was by a mentor. A man I trusted with my life. I got through it. So what do I care what strangers think? I will be fine. Will you?"

"Of *course*." She tried to breathe more evenly and shot Elena a smile. "Sorry, I think I'm going nuts because of this speech. It's just nerves."

"I can see that," Elena said. Her lips twitched into a smile. "It's a good thing you're successful and famous now, or there'd be no upside whatsoever to sharing my life with you."

Maddie started to laugh. "God, you're funny. I think I'll keep you around."

Elena smiled. "An excellent plan. Because finding someone who likes my dog and vice versa has been quite an ask. Oscar hated both my ex-husbands, which is somewhat amusing given he was a gift from my first husband."

"Oscar only likes me because you moved to Sydney for me, which comes with the warm weather he adores."

"Hm. Quite possibly. Yes, you're right. That's clearly all it is. But of course, it's not just Oscar who enjoys having you in their life."

Maddie grinned. "Ah, yes. Rosetta. Right?"

"Exactly. My cook I lured to Sydney who conspires with you often to keep me well fed."

"You do forget to eat."

"Allegedly. So, in sum, Oscar tolerates you. And Rosetta adores you."

"Yes. My two staunch allies."

"So, you can see that with your artful networking you would be quite impossible for me to replace. I'm stuck with you now."

Maddie laughed. "Thanks." She squeezed her hand. "For taking my mind off it. Making me laugh when I needed it. For being you."

Elena's eyes were bright, and her fingers curled tightly around Maddie's. "Of course."

Her smile was soft and unguarded.

It made Maddie's heart catch. Her lover always found a hundred different ways to tell her she loved her, without saying the words. She might not ever hear the words, but it was written all over her face, along with every soft touch and caress. Maddie leaned in and breathed a soft "thanks" into her ear.

Felicity and Perry rounded the corner in the distance, deep in conversation, and Maddie grinned with delight over Elena's shoulder. She'd missed them. Since both of her ex-colleagues were based in New York, she hadn't seen them in months. They looked good. Felicity, especially, looked so happy. It seemed that a lot of her uptight attitude had evaporated with her promotion.

Maddie stepped away from Elena to call out a greeting, their hands still clasped. "Hey! How are...?" she began, before fading at Felicity's startled expression. Maddie followed Felicity's gaze to where her fingers mingled with Elena's.

Oh. *That.* Seriously? Felicity really hadn't worked it out yet? Denial had to be her middle name.

Perry merely gave a smug snort and a friendly wave.

Elena ignored her employees and tugged Maddie's hand, pulling her back to her side. She caught Maddie's gaze. "Before you get engrossed in those two and I get swept up talking to the bland men in suits, I just want you to know something," she said, her voice pitched low. Elena leaned in, her lips against her ear. "You *will* be fantastic tonight. Your writing is entertaining, observant, and colourful, just like you. Believe me when I say you'll own that room. And I love you. With everything I am. Believe that too."

"Oh." Maddie exhaled. "Oh, I love hearing that." She hadn't expected it to feel this overwhelming. Her fingers tingled, itching to pull Elena into a tight hug. Tears pricked her eyes. "So does this mean you believe it now? You trust what you feel?"

"Very much so," Elena said, voice soft. "Something this deep, this beautiful? It can only be love. I've never experienced anything like it. It has to be the truth."

"It's pretty special to hear that." Maddie's lips curled into a tiny smile. "And I hope that wasn't just a one-off. I should warn you, it's all I'll want to hear in the future. You've spoilt me now."

"Is that so?"

"Mmm. And I must say I like your idea of truth."

Devilment danced in Elena's eyes. "As do I. After all, I may have mentioned once or twice that I prefer the truth in all matters."

Without warning, Elena pulled Maddie to her, kissed her thoroughly, and held her with a possessiveness that told anyone watching who Maddie belonged to. And whom Elena loved.

Warmth swamped Maddie, and she clung to her.

Out of the periphery, just before Maddie's eyes fluttered closed, she saw Perry beam and clasp his hands to his chest.

Felicity slumped against a pillar. Over the orchestral music in the distant background came the faintest words in a clipped voice, which at least sounded amused for once.

"Oh! Of bloody *course!* Longest winning streak ever!"

About Lee Winter

Lee Winter is an award-winning veteran newspaper journalist who has lived in almost every Australian state, covering courts, crime, news, features and humour writing. Now a full-time author and part-time editor, Lee is also a 2015 and 2016 Lambda Literary Award finalist and has won two Golden Crown Literary Awards. She lives in Western Australia with her long-time girlfriend, where she spends much time ruminating on her garden, US politics, and shiny, new gadgets.

CONNECT WITH LEE

Website: www.leewinterauthor.com

Other Books from Ylva Publishing

www.ylva-publishing.com

The Red Files

Lee Winter

ISBN: 978-3-95533-330-0

Length: 365 pages (103,000 words)

Ambitious journalist Lauren King is stuck reporting on the vapid LA social scene's gala events while sparring with her rival—icy ex-Washington correspondent Catherine Ayers. Then a curious story unfolds before their eyes, involving a business launch, thirty-four prostitutes, and a pallet of missing pink champagne. Can the warring pair join together to unravel an incredible story?

All the Little Moments

G Benson

ISBN: 978-3-95533-341-6

Length: 350 pages (139,000 words)

Anna is focused on her career as an anaesthetist. When a tragic accident leaves her responsible for her young niece and nephew, her life changes abruptly. Completely overwhelmed, Anna barely has time to brush her teeth in the morning let alone date a woman. But then she collides with a long-legged stranger...

Perfect Rhythm

Jae

ISBN: 978-3-95533-862-6

Length: 298 pages (107,000 words)

Pop star Leontyne Blake is over love and women falling for her image. When she heads home to be near her sick father, she meets small-town nurse Holly, an asexual woman who has no interest in dating, sex, or Leo's fame. Can their tentative friendship develop into something more despite their diverse expectations? A lesbian romance about finding the perfect rhythm between two very different people.

Party Wall

Cheyenne Blue

ISBN: 978-3-95533-886-2

Length: 223 pages (63,000 words)

The moment Freya looks at the new sex shop, she knows it will clash with her new-age store next door. She's right. Outgoing newcomer Lily begins to intrude on Freya's ordered life. The woman stands for everything Freya has lost—playfulness, spontaneity—even sex. But does Lily have more in common with Freya than the wall that divides them? A lesbian romance about crossing lines that hold us back.

Coming from Ylva Publishing

www.ylva-publishing.com

The Lily and the Crown

Roslyn Sinclair

Ariana "Ari" Geiker lives an isolated life on an imperial space station commanded by her father. The skilled, young botanist rarely leaves her living quarters, where she maintains an elaborate garden. When an imperious older woman is captured from a pirate ship and given to her as a slave, Ariana's perfectly ordered life is thrown into chaos. Her nameless slave is watchful, intelligent, dangerous, and sexy, and seems to know an awful lot about tactics, star charts, and the dread, marauding pirate queen, Mir. What happens when the slave also reveals an expertise in seduction to her innocent mistress?

The Lily and the Crown is a lesbian romance about daring to risk your heart with someone you shouldn't.

The Brutal Truth
© 2017 by Lee Winter

ISBN: 978-3-95533-898-5

Also available as e-book.

Published by Ylva Publishing, legal entity of Ylva Verlag, e.Kfr.

Ylva Verlag, e.Kfr.
Owner: Astrid Ohletz
Am Kirschgarten 2
65830 Kriftel
Germany

www.ylva-publishing.com

First edition: 2017

Credits
Edited by Sandra Gerth & CK King
Proofread by Paulette Callen
Cover Design by Adam Lloyd

Made in United States
Orlando, FL
18 April 2024

45919640R00221